PRIMAL PASSION

"I'm unlike other women in more ways than the one you mentioned."

Amaris could feel his heated gaze on her.

"Such as?"

She glanced at him from the corners of her eyes. "Such as I'm not afraid to go after what I want."

"Which is?"

Green oak boughs temporarily encompassed them in leaf-dappled shadows. The river's cooling breeze played the shorter tendrils of her hair that had escaped the clasp at her nape. She gathered her courage. "Right now, I want to know what it would be like to kiss you."

Also by Parris Afton Bonds

For All Time

Available from
HarperPaperbacks

Harper
Monogram

Dream Time

PARRIS AFTON BONDS

HarperPaperbacks
A Division of HarperCollinsPublishers

HarperPaperbacks   *A Division of* HarperCollins*Publishers*
10 East 53rd Street, New York, N.Y. 10022

Copyright © 1993 by Parris Afton Bonds
All rights reserved. No part of this book may be used or reproduced in any manner whatsoever without written permission of the publisher, except in the case of brief quotations embodied in critical articles and reviews. For information address HarperCollins*Publishers*,
10 East 53rd Street, New York, N.Y. 10022.

Cover illustration by Pino Daeni

First printing: June 1993

Printed in the United States of America

HarperPaperbacks, HarperMonogram, and colophon are trademarks of HarperCollins*Publishers*

❖ 10 9 8 7 6 5 4 3 2 1

This book is for Lucy Foulds,
A diamond in the sky

To where beneath the clustered stars,
The dreamy plains expand—
My home lies wide a thousand miles
In the Never-Never Land

To the skyline sweeps the waving grain,
Or whirls the scorching sand—
A phantom land, a mystic realm!
The Never-Never Land.

—Henry Lawson

NAN

1

For every woman born there is that ineluctable encounter with that one man. The woman's life is never the same, regardless of how many times she may fall in love afterward.

"Physical union between husband and wife maims the woman. A wife might as well bestow on her husband the legal identity of the tarantula, which gobbles its mate."

The twenty-three-year-old bluestocking believed what she said with a sincerity born of a passionate nature that she had channeled into her reading and writing. She was one of those intense people fully committed to living.

"Thus making the tarantula's mate, in a very literal manner, 'flesh of his flesh,'" a male voice interposed.

Nan lowered her long-stemmed glass to the dinner

table and stared over the gray head of Lady Albemarle. Standing behind the plump dowager, the gentleman who had spoken gazed at her with amusement curling the ends of his mouth. When a clean-shaven face was the mode, he wore a well-trimmed black mustache. That he was handsome, Nan could not deny. Nor her immediate attraction.

Her reaction infuriated her more than the man who dared challenge her. The fashionable world included her as a guest as much for her lively wit as for her minor success as a playwright. No one had ever maneuvered her into a verbal disadvantage. Not even her father, an articulate man in his own right.

She bought time, raising her glass once more. Her smile came as slowly. "Ahh, but in nature it is the female tarantula who is the cannibal. As nature goes, so goes man."

The nearby dinner guests were listening and watching the exchange with curiosity whetted by ennui. Most of the guests had come to the literary dinner for the express purpose of having their intellect stimulated.

The dark-eyed man grinned broadly. "And why not 'so goes woman'?"

Nan inclined her head in acknowledgment of his jab. "But then I am speaking of myths perpetrated by man. 'Women are illustrations of the inferior brain weight and subject to brain fever if educated'—or something along that line of reasoning, isn't it?"

"The same foolish line of reasoning that has led to Pitt's cannibalistic expansion of national debt to fight French liberty."

His retort elicited murmurs of conflicting opinions

among the dinner guests. Certain British factions said they would never support a war against liberty, while others were all for the witch hunts taking place in British villages for French agents.

Nan sensed that the direction of his remark had been purposeful. The gentleman had made his point and skillfully diverted attention to a subject most popular in London that first decade after the turn of the century: France and Napoleon.

Her challenger moved toward the end of the long table and dropped a kiss on the back of the hostess's hand. A flower-filled epergne partially obscured him but she could hear his smooth, modulated voice. "My apologies, Lady Albemarle. My master was in one of his workhorse moods. He is hell-bent on dictating letters that our ambassador to the Court of Two Sicilies never bothers to read anyway."

Lady Albemarle's mouth dimpled, and she made some remark in undertones to the young man. Nan forced her attention away from him and began speaking to the gentleman on her left, the impoverished romantic poet Sam Coleridge. He was untidy of dress but brilliant of mind.

Nan hardly knew what she was saying. She was accustomed to discoursing smoothly and easily while another part of her observed. And learned. Learning had got her from a stifling, well-ordered house in the not-so-fashionable district of Paddington Green all the way to the court of George III.

She listened intelligently, too: studying carefully the elegant people, absorbing their refined accents, taking full note of their almost casual manners.

Coleridge began discussing his friend Wordsworth's latest works. As a playwright who wanted desperately to succeed in a man's world, Nan normally would have been soaking in every word the poet uttered. Yet she was barely heeding his diatribe.

The rakish young man who had so boldly dueled words with her was watching her. She could feel it without even turning her gaze in his direction. She felt ridiculously giddy.

When Coleridge paused in his rambling, she asked, "Who is the brash young man who entered late?"

Coleridge looked askance, then peered at the far end of the table. "Randolph? Miles Randolph?"

"I suppose that is the ruffian." Privately she conceded she liked the careless way he wore his fashionable clothes.

Coleridge made an effort at straightening his cravat, which had worked its way askew. "Ruffian is hardly the correct term, my dear Miss Briscoll. Randolph is the undersecretary to Fox."

The bit of knowledge flattered her ego even more. Miles Randolph was a cohort of the secretary of state for foreign affairs and Prime Minister Pitt's political opposition. That lent stature to the man who had shown interest in her.

In her: Nan Briscoll, the rector's spinster daughter.

The remainder of the evening, she didn't glance once in Miles Randolph's direction and intentionally left before the women were excused for demitasse and the men retired to their brandies and smoking.

Nan took care in dressing for the royal reception. The young woman in the looking glass surely couldn't be Nan Briscoll. She peered at her reflection, scarcely believing the vibrant young woman who stared back. Gray eyes shimmered like quicksilver; a becoming pink flushed the cheeks. The brown hair, cropped short with the ends left loose and disheveled, a style known as à la Titus, shone with luster and seemed to curl with a will of its own.

From below, the pillar-and-scroll clock on the mantelpiece chimed out the half hour. Hurriedly, she tugged at her curls, rearranging them as artfully as possible about her narrow face. Then she pulled on her long white net gloves and donned her paisley shawl, a gratification her earnings barely afforded.

Before she went below, she took out one of the few possessions left her of her mother's, an ivory and pearl brooch. As a reminder, she pinned it on. She would not subjugate herself as her mother had done!

She hardly noticed her father's scowl as she bid him good evening. His bulky frame hunched over an opened, thumb-worn family Bible. He sat at his scratched and notched oval desk, preparing for Sunday's sermon. Through his thick spectacles, his pale eyes drilled into her. "'Tis perfume you are wearing, daughter."

"Aye. A Parisian scent." Another unbudgeted splurge of her earnings.

"To tempt man is the devil's work."

"I'm leaving, Father."

"Where are you going?" he asked without glancing up again from his Bible.

She almost lied and said she was going to a meeting of the underground Corresponding Society. King George's court was much more a sin than the repressed secret political societies. Excitement lent her defiance. "I'm on my way to a reception at Buckingham Palace."

This time, the Bible slammed shut. Her father sprang from his chair and shook a finger at her fashionable, but nearly transparent, white jaconet frock. "You are almost as naked as Mother Eve before the Fall!"

She refused to quail as she had all those years as a child. Then, her father's judgment had seemed as unimpeachable as King Solomon's. Even now, she might still be submitting to his authority had not her secretive attempts at playwrighting become lucrative enough to yield her a measure of independence. Her fingers fussed with the fuchsia ribbon girdling her ribs just below her breasts. "If I correctly recall, Mother Eve was innocent then, Father. So am I."

"You mock the Bible, Nan!"

"No. I simply don't find religion a consolation for human suffering and a defense against a wicked world, as you do."

She grabbed her cape from the peg and hurried out into the street. She found a hackney coach and instructed the coachman to take her to Buckingham Palace and King George III's court.

Spring's rains had deepened the potholes in the cobbled road, making the trip a jarring one. She cared not. Excitement, and November's crisp evening air, pinked her cheeks. Had she not gained entrée into a society that had been influenced by the luminaries of literature, Dr. Johnson and Boswell, Edward Gibbon, Horace Walpole, and others!

Upon arriving, she met disappointment. A liveried servant announced that the king was at Windsor suffering a slight indisposition. The reception was canceled.

"Indisposition?" George Romney said to her. The famed portrait artist arched a brow, almost dropping his quizzing glass. His reedy voice lowered to a whisper. "Indisposition is a rather euphemistic term for what ails Our Majesty, wouldn't you say?"

"Indisposition is a euphemism, my dear Romney, for what our illustrious king is really doing at this moment—languishing in a straitjacket."

Romney glanced around the green and gilded anteroom to check if any of the politicians, courtesans, and courtiers aimlessly milling about were within earshot. "Careful, dear girl."

As she had gathered courage around her, like a tattered shawl, to defy her father over the years, she now did so with public opinion. Hadn't the *Morning Chronicle* proclaimed her one of the independent and enlightened playwrights of the times?

Of course, the newspaper had added that odious phrase at the tail end, "for a woman."

"Must I be the one to tell the emperor he is naked?" she asked Romney.

"Only if you are sure what a state of nakedness is," a voice said behind her.

She turned. Miles Randolph was looking down at her, a smile tipping the ends of his raffish mustache. She knew now she had been hoping he would be here. She had chosen her clothes carefully, not for the royal occasion but for him. The knowledge frightened her. Such a concession to another was a weakness; it made her vulnerable. It made her dependent.

"There are many kinds of nakedness, sir. The truth, for one."

Romney chortled in that high-pitched voice peculiar to him. "Zounds! What about a jaybird? Naked as a jaybird, eh?"

Miles Randolph's attention was still focused on her. It was unnerving. At least a score of beautiful women could be found cooling their heels in the anteroom. Why was he singling out her? She was thin and nearly flat-chested when softly rounded figures and a vast bosom were the fashion. Her hair was sparse, her mouth narrow as the path of righteousness. Her too-round eyes were an unbecoming gray with the merest evidence of lashes to fringe them.

Behind the smile in Miles Randolph's dark blue eyes was pooled serious intent. "There is also a winter landscape—or one's defenses. Either can be naked."

Was she that transparent? The thin blood in her veins pumped erratically. "There is the touch of harlequin about this subject." Did her voice sound too arch? "Surely, there is some topic more timely to arouse the intellect."

"George Romney!" cried a fat matron whom Nan recognized as the wife of a chief magistrate. The muslin dress that clung to the matron's ample curves in the classical mode of the day was merciless to the middle-aged. "Dear man," she trilled, "I went by your Cavendish Square studio yesterday for a sitting only to find you were gone!"

With a smothered sigh, the artist turned away to greet his patron, and Nan was alone with Miles Randolph.

He stared down at her with a revelry dancing in his eye. "Perhaps a political issue would be more to your liking. That way we could circumvent any genuine exchange of information and feelings."

She blinked. She was stunned. No one spoke like that. With a flash of insight, she realized that she was the superficial one. She had derided the shallow topics of the drawing rooms—fortunes won and lost at Whitehead's, the prince's latest mistress, the gothic and barbarous trend toward natural waistlines. Her cleverness, her repartee, her wisdom, had been a hard veneer that was as superficial.

For the first time, she looked past the exterior of the handsome man. Yes, her objective gaze noted how he wore his brilliant green waistcoat and tight pantaloons with a negligent elegance that made a Bond Street gentleman look like a Bow Street footpad. A peripheral corner of her mind noted that he wore no makeup and his hair was brushed in the "Brutus" rumpled style. He wore York tan gloves and carried a knobby cane rather than a stylish tasseled one, a sign that he was among those few who flaunted and, by so doing, dictated fashions.

But that subjective part of her mind evaluated the keen intelligence behind the eyes, the determination in the set of the mouth.

Did he know who she was? Was it just possible he was attracted to her for those qualities that others did not notice immediately? Qualities like her yearning to love, to care for others; her soft heart that was afraid to love and care?

Here was a man to whom she might, just might, be able to relate, a man who just might need a woman like herself. A woman who was more than paint and powder. Could he actually see through her armor of trenchant words to the loveless child within her?

"I haven't had the experience of discussing such personal subjects with acquaintances before," she said and wished she sounded less stilted.

"For an acclaimed playwright, you haven't experienced life, Miss Briscoll."

So, he did know who she was. Pleasure warmed her skin. "One doesn't have to *experience* life to write about it, sir. To my knowledge, Sir Walter Scott didn't murder his father to experience the feelings in writing about—"

His smile was as white as his high stock. "I could debate the issue with you. I'd rather use this opportunity to point out that even now you are avoiding an honest, open exchange between us."

For once, she was bereft of words. Without the resource of speech, she was adrift, without bearings.

He looked down at her with interest glinting in his eyes. "I am patient, Miss Briscoll. We'll discuss politics, then. I understand you favor the Code Napoleon as a model for English law. At least, your article in the *Courier* indicated a leaning in that direction."

"Sections of it," she amended, pleased that he knew so much about her. "It grants liberties that Parliament overlooks here."

"You tremble. Do you fear what Pitt may do in retaliation for your article?"

"Hardly." Miles's nearness affected her. She shrugged, and her shawl, with its in-vogue Egyptian trimming, slipped from one shoulder. "Pitt has his hands full with your Fox."

Miles appeared pleased by her reply. His hand recovered her wayward shawl and drew it back up over her shoulder. "You have courage of the spirit." His fingers barely brushed her skin. "I wonder. Does that apply to courage of the heart, as well?"

She could debate with skill any subject but her own feelings. She floundered now for the right words. "My heart needs no courage."

One dark brow rose. "Because it has gone unchallenged?"

"I'm not certain I understand your question, sir," she said crisply.

She caught the gleam in his eyes. "I think you do."

A smile began at the corners of her tight lips. "Mayhap you are right." She was dismayed at her brazen behavior. Did she truly want to risk being shattered for the chance, maybe her only chance, at ever experiencing the passion of the heart?

Courage . . . yes, Miles was right. He knew her better than she knew herself. She had been living through her facade of writing, experiencing life secondhand.

She had harbored more than a little pride at her unconventional behavior. She spoke her mind in a deliberate attempt to inflame public opinion. She took up a profession that was largely male oriented. She disdained the shackles of marriage.

As if she had ever had the option.

Her behavior had made her a hostess's delight. Nan Briscoll's presence guaranteed an evening of stimulating entertainment. Men of distinction, invariably older ones, enjoyed her brilliance.

But she had no close friends. She was not loved. Men her age were usually intimidated by her quick mind and sharper tongue. Young women immediately picked up on her scorn for their coy deportment. Try as she might, she could not conceal that scorn.

Yet she had faith in her own strong will. She had successfully opposed her father's tyranny when her mother had died of nothing but sheer weariness of submission. Nan was sure she could win Miles Randolph's affection if she but put her mind to it.

2

Carriages and sedan chairs passed along Clarges Street. In the late afternoon shadows of fine old homes gone shabby, vendors selling homemade pies, hot roasted potatoes, and roasted chestnuts piped out their songs of sale.

Miles Randolph had requested that Nan meet him at 31 Clarges Street. Mercury's winged feet could not have arrived at that destination any faster. She was curious about the place he had picked for their tryst. Alighting from the hackney, she stared up at the modest two-story building, one of the many residences elbowing for space on the street. Although a certain air of neglect pervaded the facades, one could discern tracings of former stateliness in the solid construction.

Then she saw Miles descend from a splendid barouche coach drawn by six horses. His back was as straight as a guardsman's. A carnation was stuck in the buttonhole of his lapel, yet his cravat had been indolently knotted.

She watched him withdraw his gold watch and check the time. Then, as he tucked it back into his waistcoat, he caught sight of her and smiled. "I wondered if you had second thoughts about the propriety of my proposal."

In her flat heels, she was much shorter than he, although he was only of medium height. "I am not influenced by propriety or the opinion of others, Mr. Randolph."

"I had hoped you would take mine into consideration." Lightly, he grasped her elbow to guide her toward the house behind him. At his touch, her blood sang out. Human touch for the last ten years, since her mother's death, was foreign to her. Human touch was something she didn't know she had missed—no, needed, desperately needed—until this moment.

"And your opinion is?" she asked, the four words costing all her breath.

"My opinion is that you are one of the very few females I have met who have not bored me to distraction."

Her gaze flew to his face. She could scarcely believe that, at last, here was a man who appreciated her talents. In those dark marine-blue eyes she found no mockery. She was at a loss for a reply. Words that her lips were beginning to frame rang trite in her mind, and she swallowed them back.

Miles withdrew the key to the house, inserted it in the lock, opened the door, and stood aside for her to enter. Inside, the furniture was draped in dustcovers.

His expression solicitous, he detained her with a hand on her elbow. "There will be talk?"

That he should be concerned thrilled her. "The wagging tongues of neighbors would not bother me. My father, however, presents a problem. He's a rector."

"Ahh, and you depend upon him?"

With a grimace, she said, "My income as a playwright is valued in monetary terms of crowns not guineas. So I must keep house for him if I expect to have shelter from the storms."

Miles cocked his head. "There may be something we can do about that."

The remark puzzled her, but then he took her hand and gently tugged away the glove to press her palm against his lips.

"Your pulse thuds in your wrist. I frighten you?"

"You startled me, that's all." Her voice was calm, her manner poised, but surely he could hear her heart galloping; surely, he could see the fires of pure passion blazing in her eyes.

He grinned, and the hollows beneath cheekbones that were precipitous ridges softened. "From what I am told, you are fearless. You would have had to be to tackle Pitt for trebling the taxes on windows, carriages, and servants. Or your battle against the lord mayor. 'I fight not with sword but with pen for a revolutionary social and political issue, the reform of Newgate's inhumane treatment of its prisoners.' Isn't that what you wrote in the pamphlet *An Enquiry into Reform?*"

She was amazed. The article was an inconsequential piece dashed off several years before in a moment of anger, with limited distribution by the London Letters Club. "I am flattered you are aware of my works," she replied lamely. She wondered what had happened to her gift of eloquence.

He took hold of her shoulders and turned her

toward him. His voice was husky. "Let your heart and body be as courageous as your mind, Nan."

That she could excite him like this was in itself an aphrodisiac to her. He began kissing the inside of her elbow, her neck, and she tilted her head back, affording his scalding kisses the arch of her throat. When he lifted her in his arms and carried her to the sofa, she made no protest. Instead, her hand clasped the back of his neck and drew his head down.

Hungrily, her lips sought his. Exquisite little spasms traveled through her muscles, beginning with her legs and moving upward and outward. She caught her breath. Then her words tumbled out in a murmur. "I didn't know. I didn't know."

"There is more, I assure you, that you will find even more pleasurable." Faint amusement warmed his voice.

He was right. His hand slid up past her knee garter and pink stocking, which had made her leg appear to blush for total lack of petticoats. When his hand encountered the bare flesh of her inner thigh, she gasped.

Instinctively, her legs closed. "No," he whispered against her temple, "you are closing yourself off to the greatest glory of being a woman."

As his fingers pried further, she acquiesced to the splendor of the sensations churning upward from the apex of her thighs. Her breathing was as heavy and ragged as his.

Of their own volition, her fingers fumbled for the brass buttons of his tight pantaloons. Having never dressed, or undressed man or boy, she was unfamiliar with the process.

He guided her. He pressed her down onto the sofa. Its dustcover conspired to tug her dress above her hips, baring her lower torso. He rolled atop her. His weight! It felt so different—and so wonderful.

Then she felt his hard flesh rubbing against her abdomen. Excitement raced through her. A maelstrom of lust overrode all else. Her legs spread eagerly to accept him. She barely felt the tearing of her maidenhood, so explosive was his invasion of her, so filling. A rushing, full feeling. Silly, she thought, that she should see orange and purple images moving fluidly over the backs of her lids.

After that, not another thought came. Because she had left her body. Or, at least, she would later believe she must have done so. In that time span of his taking her, and her giving herself, there was only the thrust and the arching of their bodies in tempo.

A seizure rippled through her. A small cry erupted from deep in her throat. She heard, as if from afar, his deep groan. Then, moments later, he was gathering her against him. Dazed, she lay languidly in his arms for some time. The emptiness that had gnawed at her for years and years was, at last, assuaged.

"You see, my bluestocking," he said, nipping her earlobe, "there is more to life than the pursuit of knowledge."

Laughter enriched her words. "I thought that was what I was pursuing. Carnal knowledge, that is." The fact that she could joke amazed her. She had always considered herself humorless.

"This would be an excellent room to receive your literary friends, don't you think?"

Puzzled by the remark, she turned in his arms. "What do you mean?"

His mouth found hers and stilled it. Weakness that

she had belittled in other females eddied throughout her. She clung to his shoulders. Her maiden's inexperience was completely overwhelmed by the force of her newly discovered passions.

At last he released her. "This place is yours."

Feeling bliss from sheer delight of being in love, she glanced around and looked up at him again. "Whatever are you talking about, Miles?"

"I have a small income from a rental place in the Shires. Between that and your wages for writing political propaganda, we'll—"

Her brow furrowed. "I don't write political propaganda."

She knew a few who did. Political hacks. Their values and principles were liquid, to be molded by whomever was willing to buy their expertise with the written word. Their skill was in demand by a public that was limited but intensely and intelligently political.

"You do now." His pleased expression captured her heart. "I have made certain contacts and arranged for you to write for Fox himself."

She frowned. "I don't know, Miles. I've never—"

His light kisses stilled her lips. "Nan, Nan. It's the only thing I could come up with. It's only for a little while. If Fox should be elected in place of Pitt, then my financial circumstances will vastly improve. Then we can make more permanent plans. Here, at least, we can be together. I've already signed the papers on this house."

He took her by the shoulders and turned her to face the fireplace, with her back to him, his arms around her waist. "It is there we shall make love again. Within the week. No more hurried rendezvous like today."

All doubt was banished by his words—and his kisses dropped softly, tantalizingly, on her collarbone and upper chest.

He had to take his leave soon thereafter but made arrangements to meet her there on Friday. "You are certain your father will not stand in your way of moving here?"

She laughed shortly. "I am an embarrassment to him, Miles. For him, it will be good riddance."

He gave her some tracts of writing and kissed her good-bye. "This will give you an idea of what Fox is interested in. Mainly any issues that are in opposition to those of Pitt, but especially we want to champion the French reform measures."

She certainly felt there was some merit to the last and was deliriously happy that she could be sharing in a part of Miles's life.

Madness! Sheer madness, what she was about to do—to become the mistress of one of England's most prominent politicians and eligible bachelors!

When she packed her belongings in a portmanteau and left her father's house, he would not even tell her good-bye. He huddled over the remains of a fire, absently poking at the dying embers. In their flickering glow, he looked like a toothless old lion. Harmless. How had she imbued him with so much threatening power?

Sadly, she stared at the stooped shoulders he turned toward her. She crossed to him and dropped a kiss on the top of his head. There was little love between her and her father, but he was all she had.

No, that wasn't true. She had Miles. That very night she lay in his arms and stared up at the four-poster's draperies. Miles nuzzled her neck. "What are you thinking, my bluestocking?"

She turned in to his embrace. "How very, very happy I am."

"Then you don't regret this arrangement?"

"I wouldn't regret this for all the tea in the East India Company's warehouse."

Her boldness surprised even herself. The prudish, sexless Nan Briscoll was no more. For the first time, Nan Briscoll was wildly, deliriously, recklessly in love.

Miles Randolph neither drank excessively, nor used snuff or smoked tobacco from one of those obnoxiously long churchwarden pipes. Neither did he frequent the gambling tables. The only time Nan saw him wager was at the Newmarket horse races on a horse of Barb blood introduced by Godolphin more than a half century earlier.

Miles's innovative mind continually provided pastimes that would amuse her—a visit to a bowling green, which reminded her of a great billiard table; to a cockfight, where scandalous women bid as raucously as the men.

That she no longer received invitations to dinner parties and levees bothered her little. She was content in that charming old house on Clarges Street. Occasionally, when with Miles, she would run into an old friend—Coleridge, Lady Albemarle, or Romney. They were invariably cordial and circumspect, uttering nothing that would betray any censure of her new position as Miles's mistress. After all, wasn't Lady Hamilton well received?

When Nan wasn't with Miles, she wrote. He glanced over her pamphlets and newspaper articles, made a few suggestions, then submitted the articles to Fox. The thrusts of her articles grew more staunchly pro-French and Jacobinic as the weeks went by. That she was courting Pitt's displeasure bothered her little. Miles's love for her made her invincible.

Then one evening, Miles didn't come home. That night, as she paced and worried for his safety, she began to fear the worst. What if he had been set upon by footpads?

Restless, her stomach in knots, she would cross time and again to the window, peer out into the darkness, and retrace her steps across the inlaid mahogany floor.

That Miles might be dead was the most horrible thought she could envision.

Or so she thought.

A pale Romney knocked upon her door later that morning to bring her the news that Miles had fled England for France. "My dear," he said, twisting his cocked hat between his slender artist's hands, "I fear that Miles Randolph has been working as a French agent."

"What?" Her hand went to her chest, and she would have staggered had it not been for the support of the door.

"I'm afraid I bring far worse news than that."

What could be worse? She stared at him uncomprehendingly.

He took a deep breath and plunged on. "In letting your heart rule your head and rashly defending Jacobinism, you have been implicated with Miles. I come just ahead of the bailiff. You are to be charged with treason."

3

Newgate prison was a nightmare of surrealistic proportions. To think she had written an article denouncing the institution from an impersonal point of view!

Almost a hundred female prisoners were incarcerated in Newgate, and they were not separated from the male prisoners. For a woman of genteel birth to survive with all her faculties intact would be considered a minor miracle.

Between her physical pain and her emotional pain, Nan Briscoll easily distinguished the greater. Her body was resolute, but she was unprepared for the loss of love.

However wretched were the conditions in the prison, and they were incredibly wretched, her thin body was sustained by her inner resources and resilience.

She was imprisoned in the worst part of the prison—Commonside. It was so crowded with pickpockets, felons, ruffians, and murderers as to justify its title of Hell on Earth.

Coleridge was appalled. "My dear girl, when I heard about your circumstances, I came as soon as I could. Is there anything I can do to alleviate your . . . conditions here?"

Yes, she thought dully, kill me. Kill me so I no longer have to think, to feel. "No." Her reply was a mere whisper.

His bulbous nose wrinkled in response to the fetid smell. He glanced at the sordid women around him. His fingers polished the malachite handle of his cane. He cleared his throat. "Honestly, I think there is not much anyone can do about your legal situation, Nan. With a charge of treason being prepared against you, you will be lucky if you aren't sentenced to hang."

That she did not appear to be listening disconcerted him, and he started over. "I have some influence, very little actually, with certain Parliament members. Maybe a word here or there about obtaining a more favorable sentence—at the least, obtaining a grant of the Privilege of the Rules for you."

Those prisoners who had abundant financial resources could resort to the Privilege of the Rules. This meant paying for the right to reside in lodgings outside the prison walls but close enough to report back daily.

"Of course, we'll need to find some financial backing for this, but . . ." He paused.

She bestirred herself to reply. "No. No, I wish to be hanged, Coleridge. Hanged quickly. Do you understand?"

With the other women screeching like harpies, he

grew agitated. "You are distraught. You don't know what you are saying. I'll return as soon as I know more."

Within a few seconds, she could hear his buckled slippers tap-tapping down the cold stone corridor with a rapidity that did credit to a man of his girth and age.

She returned her mind to its own padded cell, where thought and feeling could not intrude. Little by little the slender shafts of sunlight from barred windows high overhead climbed the floor and walls to escape through the seams of the ceiling.

In the overcrowded prison, she found a space to stretch out for another night. Each prisoner was allocated floor space eighteen inches wide by six feet long. Those lucky enough slept in hammocks strung from one wall to a great oak pillar in the room's center.

The first night, she had worried about being molested by one of the male prisoners. Either they were as apathetic as she or they simply weren't interested in her. Not yet, anyway.

What she did not worry about was jail fever. The lack of ventilation and sanitation killed the prisoners off like flies. She could only hope she could be so fortunate as to catch the fever.

Sleep, of course, did not come. If the noise didn't keep her awake, the vermin did.

After nearly ten days of languishing in Newgate, Nan was taken to an antechamber to bathe in vinegar. By now, she had heard enough to know that this was a signal she was to be taken into court. The vinegar bath was a preliminary precaution against a prisoner's stench and transmission of jail fever to the judge, counsel, jury, and warders.

She was finally having a trial—but without even a barrister to represent her?

Along with several other prisoners, political ones from Fleet Street Prison, she was herded not into Old Bailey, the central criminal court of London, but into Westminster Hall. Alone, she was hauled before the Bar of the Court of King's Bench.

The enormous number of people who crowded the paneled room to watch was amazing. They stared at her in particular. She realized she appeared unkempt, haggard even. Her pride burned.

Then she understood why she was the source of attention. The white-wigged attorney general, appearing for the Crown, rose to give his opening remarks. "We have before us a woman who the Crown will prove is a support of the foolish doctrine of equality and who seeks to unleash terror like that instigated by the revolutionaries of France."

She was being tried for high treason by the supreme criminal court of the realm!

The spectators broke out in mutterings that sounded as if the room were filled with swarms of bees. Majority opinion in England was still opposed to reform. The bloodbath of horror attendant upon the French Revolution was enough to make a proper Englishman tremble in outrage.

A counselor had been appointed for her defense. There was little the white-wigged barrister could do to counteract the admission of blatant articles she had written.

"Jacobin!" spread throughout the courtroom. "The woman's a Jacobin!"

The spectators were becoming an angry mob.

Meanwhile a professional scribe recorded every damnable admission she made. When, after three days of being cross-examined, the trial was brought to a close, the jury never left the box. She stood before the chief justice to hear the verdict.

Her fate was only slightly better than hanging. "We find the prisoner, Nan Briscoll, guilty of high treason. The prisoner is to be forever banished from England. She will be remanded to transportation, to serve out the rest of her natural life in hard labor at the penal colony of Sydney Cove in New South Wales."

The will in that thin, frail body refused to be extinguished. Nan's hatred for Miles Randolph, her hatred for her own weakness that had resulted in her lapse of rational thinking, manufactured the sustenance her body needed to survive. Not just survive on her hate but thrive.

Along with 700 other convicts, of which only 169 were women, Nan slept and ate below the decks of the 98-foot bark the *Serendipity*. What little exercise the convicts were permitted was limited by intermittent gales that chased the bark on its six-month voyage across the seas. Some received no exercise, chained as they were in pairs to the bulkheads in the hold.

While others suffered the bloody flux and ague or vomited at the lack of ventilation and the maggot-infested food, Nan appeared to glow with good health. When others found sleep impossible on the narrow slats, she slept deeply and dreamlessly.

Scorched by humanity, she withdrew from its dregs there on the *Serendipity*. Most of them had been dependent upon crime for a living. The women, all forty or younger, appeared hags. The men looked a degree above brute creation. Hardly the image of God, the inheritors of his kingdom.

With two other women, she shared a bed of narrow slats. Lying there, she would stare at the slats above her and wonder if her disobedience to her father's god had brought all this down upon her.

Nan kept a vision of returning to England, somehow a grand lady to squelch London's high society with a frosty glance. A foolish dream of regaining respectability, perhaps, but it and her hatred of Miles Randolph sustained her during those long months.

But her dream of returning to England the grand lady was soon obliterated. She would never be going back, she knew. And Miles Randolph had left her a legacy. She was with child. If it were possible to abort, she would, but the mere lack of privacy prevented that. No, she was forced to carry the hated seed of the man who had exploited her weakness. During the voyage's last leg, Nan was preoccupied with only one activity: watching herself grow large with the child.

Her unvented rage grew as well. She knew she was strong. If she survived, it would be without leaving herself vulnerable to any man. A folly she would never commit again.

By the time the *Serendipity* neared the coast of New South Wales her initially healthy appearance had degenerated. Her complexion was a pasty yellow from the long months with only a modicum of sunlight, and the lack of proper food had sunken her cheeks and thinned her hair.

Waiting on deck with the other dazed prisoners,

she looked upon the awesome, lonely void of a trackless ocean. Along with the other prisoners, she fought to stand erect as the swells built to staggering heights, then descended into spumy troughs that paralyzed the brain with fear.

It was the first indication of a place that was upside down and backward from the familiarity of the Old World. A place where it snowed in July and where water went down the drain in the opposite direction.

At last, as the ship entered Sydney Cove, just north of Botany Bay, the waters quieted. January's endless blue sky and a balmy summer breeze riffling the palms greeted the prisoners. To Nan, everything was influenced by the harbor water and the fresh, intense marine light.

Drawing closer to the limestone cliffs, the impression of sheer beauty gave way to a pressing-down feeling of a tiny population clinging to a rock of an empty, barren, ghostly land. The bay took on an acid brillance.

Nan stared in disbelief at what was to be her home. Perched on that barren, sandstone rocky outcrop was Fort Phillip, over which the Union Jack stirred apathetically in the sea breeze. Fort Phillip was a six-sided citadel built on the western side of Sydney Cove. One side commanded a view of the harbor, another faced a pathetic excuse for a town, and still another looked out upon the dusty Parramatta Road.

The remnants of her decimated self-confidence withered. At that moment, she drew a curtain over her thoughts and numbed herself to what she rightly suspected was the ordeal that lay in wait for her upon disembarkation.

Because the British defeat in 1781 meant that the American colonies could no longer be used as a convenient dumping ground for criminals, Sydney Cove had become the repository.

Nan was only vaguely aware of being corralled in the palisaded Punishment Yard to stand with the women in one group while the men formed the larger group. The two groups were guarded by red-coated soldiers armed with flintlocks and a few antiquated blunderbusses.

The internment looked as if it would be an all-day event, yet no water was offered to ease the parched throats of the convicts. A single fern tree offered scant shade.

The stocks and gallows in the yard's center served as grisly reminders that His Majesty's retribution could extend even as far as twelve thousand miles.

Nan averted her gaze. Beyond the fort, she noticed what appeared to be a primitive settlement of wooden buildings with but a few interspersed ones of brick. Rising above them could be seen the single respectable and substantial building in the settlement, the Government House.

Only as she watched officers and soldiers and other men in simple brown perukes pause before her to assess her personage and that of the others did she realize the extent of what was happening.

The men were looking for not only workers but wives!

"H'its awaiting selection, we are," said an acne-scarred woman.

Instinct told Nan that in order to do more than merely survive she would need to escape the sentence of hard labor. But the one thing she prided herself on—her intellect—was certainly of no use here. Beauty or a strong back were a better commodity for life in New South Wales.

Not only was her lack of strength going against her but also her obvious pregnancy. In a primitive land where food was scarce, another mouth certainly was not needed.

Time after time, she was passed by.

From the corner of her eye, she watched a squat soldier amble up before a stout and coarse prisoner named Moll Cutpurse. Hands on her ample hips, Moll lustily eyed the bantam rooster of a sergeant as he circled her. Finally, he said, "I'll take ye to wife." The grin on both their faces said they were delighted with the bargain struck.

The sun continued on its path across the western expanse of sky. By the time it became a fiery globe hovering over the vast stretch of sea, the more appealing of women convicts had been taken from the Punishment Yard. Drained by the hours in the sun and her advanced pregnancy, Nan fought to stand upright among the two score or so of women left.

Humiliated beyond anything she had so far endured, she followed the line of shuffling prisoners, some of them still manacled in their irons. Burdened by the child she carried, her own gait was as awkward as the shackled convicts.

In the deepening dusk, their destination revealed itself as a collection of huts, which accommodated fourteen to eighteen women and were without the amenity of either bed or blankets. A woman in drab kersey ladled out a watery soup into bowls fashioned from the green wood of the country.

From the woman, the convicts learned what was to happen to them. Her empty eyes barely moved from the soup she ladled as she talked. "Be thankful that 'tis female yew are. The men work on the government farms or on the plots of the officers from five in the morning till sunset. The overseers' whips snap the livelong day. Us women, the ones that don't get selected as wives, are made 'utkeepers or set to work to make spirits or clothes. Only a few of yew will 'ave to pick in the fields."

Nan stared into her soup at the little white worms swimming there. She set aside her bowl. She was no longer hungry.

After what seemed a very short night of rest on bare planks, Nan was informed that, at least, she would not be required to pick in the fields. "Not 'til yewr term of delivery is over," the woman said.

Instead, along with several others, Nan was loaded into a two-wheel cart that rumbled from the quay through narrow dirt streets with names like Church Street and High Street. On Pitt Street, a pawnshop rubbed elbows with a milliner's and a wig shop, but most of the shanties housed cheap taverns, bawdy houses, warehouses, and grog shops.

As the cart rattled over a bridge and headed out a narrow road, Nan felt very lonely and afraid. Unaccustomed to direct sunlight for so long, her skin burned and her turbulent thoughts boiled.

She could not appreciate the raw beauty of the countryside. Wild grapevines and raspberries infringed on the road, and infinitely old and strange-looking trees formed a leafy canopy above. If she thought to escape, where would she run to in that wilderness?

The convicts were being sent to one of the government farms, someone said.

"Surry Hill Farm," clarified a woman whose head had been shaven for prostitution.

Nan could only hope that the conditions of the government farm were no worse than those she had left. She was learning to be thankful for the small crumbs of luck that life was allotting her.

At last, the woods receded to a clearing on the cart's left. With keen disappointment, Nan viewed the government farm. Primitive was the only word that came to mind. In the harsh sunlight, half-naked men toiled in fields of corn, beans, and squash. The forest had been pushed back to the fields' margins, and on a rise between the fields squatted a scattering of huts, sheds, and crude split-log buildings.

When the cart rolled to a halt before the largest of the buildings, dust flurried up to blind her. As it drifted away, she saw a burly soldier prodding the women ahead of her down from the cart and directing them to their workstations.

She almost stumbled but regained her balance in time to avoid a flicking jab from his whip handle. "You," he said, pointing the whip at her, "take yourself to the third hut yonder."

Wearily, she turned in the direction he indicated. The hated parasite within her belly weighed heavily, making each footstep across the grass-denuded grounds an enormous effort. Escape flitted through her mind and as quickly vanished. Escape from the only settlement on a continent said to be larger then Europe was in itself a death wish. Men had tried it. If any escaped and lived, they certainly hadn't talked

about it. The thought was not even worth the energy
of entertaining for a woman large with child.

Before she could reach the hut, a black woman of
maybe five and twenty came out with a basket of
folded laundry balanced on her bony hip. She was
built oddly, with a pouter pigeon breast and a tiny,
almost misshapen lower torso, which maybe
accounted for her limp. Nan thought her almost
ugly, with a broad black face framed by short hair,
and a band of tattoos spanning each cheekbone
beneath eyes deep sunken to protect them from the
sun.

As Nan moved to pass the aborigine, the woman
missed a step. Or maybe her ankle gave way, Nan
wasn't sure. Whichever, the woman stumbled and
fell, the basket rolling in front of Nan and the soldier
and strewing the laundry with it.

"Ye stupid, frigging slut," the soldier muttered in
irritation.

Almost as a matter of course, his whip lifted
and would have descended on the hapless woman
had Nan not grabbed hold of his sleeve. The
action was not so much a humanitarian one on her
part as it was purely reflex to keep her own bulky
body from tripping over the woman.

Regardless, the soldier jerked his arm away from
Nan's clutch. His expression was nigh comical.
Confusion and suspicion overcame his irritation. He
scowled at Nan. "Both you bloody bitches, pick up
the laundry afore I rip you a new arse."

The aborigine was already scrambling on her
knees, collecting the scattered items. Nan was slower,
and he jabbed the whip's haft in her ribs, more to
goad her than to injure her. Her breath whooshed

out at the pain. She went on all fours. The black woman's expression was a warning to keep silent. By now, Nan knew enough to heed it.

The soldier stomped away, leaving the two women to finish gathering the spilled laundry. The woman grinned, revealing perfect, small white teeth. "So, there be two of you to feed."

Comfort and compassion colored the aborigine's voice. For the first time since Romney had come to the house on Clarges Street to warn Nan of Miles's betrayal, she began to cry. Deep shuddering gasps were accompanied by a rain of tears.

"Sssh, baby," the black woman cooed. "Nutt' is as bad as all that. Trust Pulykara. Come, baby, and lie down. Them menfolks won't be comin' back till sundown. You can rest till then."

Strange, the aborigine woman calling her "baby," Nan thought, when she was no older than Nan herself. Then Nan forgot to think and fell at once into a heavy sleep. She awoke at the rumbling voices of convicts returning to the darkened hut. Her gaze darted over the large room, searching for the black woman. When she saw Pulykara's softly glowing eyes, Nan knew the woman was right. Nothing was as bad as all that—as long as one learned from the experience.

That was something else Nan knew—she would never be a foolishly romantic woman again.

4

All sorts of occupations were represented at the government farm—butchers, brass founders, hatters, grocers, needlemakers, hairdressers, curriers, and jockeys. Most of the trades cloaked professional thieves. Some of the men, however, had been sentenced to death for as little as stealing a fish and had escaped the gallows by the mercy of transportation.

If that was mercy.

One of the convicts not a professional thief was Jimmy Underwood. Only fifteen, he had worked in a shipyard for two years until the night watchman had caught him stealing lumber for firewood one bitterly cold winter. Or, at least, that was Jimmy's story.

Nan would have heeded him no more than she did the other men on the prison farm, except Jimmy somehow managed to get a knife and carve a bark cradle for her.

Her eyes had narrowed on the youth. "Why?"

His big ears had turned the color of his red-orange

hair. He had hunched his bony shoulders and stared at the sun-baked earth. "Ye remind me of me older sister, ye do. She was big with a babe like yerself." The bony shoulders shrugged. "But something went wrong. Lots of bleeding. The doctor wouldn't come . . . and she and the babe didn't make it."

Nan steeled herself against feeling pity. Soft hearts didn't make it. Ever. She had only to look at the convicts who occupied the hut that she and Pulykara kept. The men were like the walking dead. Their skins were burnt to a raw brown and stretched over their knobby bones. Like marbles, their eyes stared lifelessly from bony sockets. Welts from the overseer's whip tattooed their flesh.

Nan had to give thanks that her life was easier in comparison to that of Jimmy and the others. Her duty was to keep the hut clean and provide food for the men. When they returned each day, they were so weary that they never troubled her or Pulykara. They simply ate the broth and bread and fell asleep upon the floor, while she lay awake, feeling the thing stirring inside her, feeding off of her, draining her.

Sometimes she thought about escape, but Jimmy's terse tales of what waited in the forest deterred her. "The wood that I used to make the cradle, I found it near the outskirts of the millet field. Smithy, the arsehole overseer wasn't paying any attention, so I walked a little farther. Saw a large stand of sandalwood near an inky dark billabong."

Jimmy's light blue eyes glittered, and she realized he felt about woodcarving as she did about writing.

"Sandalwood is marvelous for carving jewelry boxes and canes, and I couldn't help meself. I crept closer to take me a look. Just then, *whomp!* Jaws missed me by the span of me finger!"

Jimmy's big ears twitched with just the thought. "You don't want to be food for a croc. They'll poke you beneath a log and let you rot, 'cause they can't chew too well. When you've ripened enough, they'll tear a chunk off. Crocs are the bloody nightmares of this Dream Time land."

Dream Time land. A name Nan was to hear often, especially from Pulykara. Something about the aborigine's explanation for the beginning of life and its continuation into the future.

"There is places called Dreaming sites, baby. Them places still have power and energy of the Dream Time."

Pulykara, Nan discovered, limped due to mistreatment by, not an overseer, but her husband. Because of her limp, she was spared work in the fields with the rest of the women convicts.

"For what were you found guilty?" Nan asked.

Pulykara gazed at her steadily. "For killing my husband. He was the master's dog man. While my husband slept, I drove a bamboo shoot through his ugly heart."

Nan's scalp tingled. The ferocity that glinted momentarily behind Pulykara's dark eyes reminded Nan how close the woman was to savagery.

Three times a week, an officer came to the government farm. His was a cursory duty: to inspect the supply room, the storage barns, and the prisoners and their living quarters.

In regard to Nan, his interest was more than cursory. That first time she sensed his stare, she had been washing convicts' clothing in a large kettle. Bending over it, she had felt a hitch in her back, prompted by her mounded stomach and her bulky body's uncomfortable position. She had paused to stretch—and caught him looking before he quickly turned away. She had thought nothing of it.

The next time, when she had fetched water pails, she had noticed him watching her from the veranda of the main building. The officer had stayed in the veranda's shadows, but she had felt him watching her, nonetheless.

He was there again today, observing her as she made her way to the kitchen larder. The clerk on duty, a beefy man, marked in a ledger supplies issued to each hut. So bedraggled was she, so unkempt and homely and large with child, that he never once looked at her. Not really looked at her.

The officer did. As he approached her on the veranda steps, she noted first his stripes. A captain, he was. She shifted the heavy burlap bag of potatoes to her other hip. Why would he be interested in her? Then she saw his eyes. Clearly saw the pity there.

"Can I help you?" His hand was on the railing, his arm blocking her descent.

Although he was a step below her, they were of the same height. She stared directly into his eyes. "Now why would you be wanting to help me, Captain?"

He blushed. She was surprised by this reaction, and her writer's curiosity got the better of her antipathy toward males. She studied him and realized he wasn't unattractive: tall, lanky, with ruddy cheeks and wayward brown hair. Hazel eyes fringed by stubby, curling lashes peered back at her.

"You don't seem like the others." Shyness made his voice rusty.

"Oh? Do I seem to possess more than the dumb intelligence of animals? That's how we're treated by the likes of you, you know. Like dumb animals. Beasts of burden."

His fingers rubbed the wooden railing. "You're felons. You committed crimes, and so you have to pay for—"

"Are you so sure each and every one of us *really* committed a crime?" With a boldness imprisonment had made her forget, she pushed past him and continued to her hut.

That night, lying on the floor with the men around her in the depths of fatigue-induced sleep, she was awake. She entertained thoughts of the captain. How old was he?

Twenty-five to thirty, she decided. A young man who was lonely for home and all that reminded him of it. She had judged him shy, but she sensed a certain courage he himself was most likely unaware of having.

The pity that had prompted his offer of help stung her pride. Yet, as she lay in the dark, her palms curving over the globe of her huge stomach, she decided that, yes, he could help her.

He could marry her.

The officer came again two days later. She was ready for him. She had deliberated over the man for the full two-day interval. What kind of man was he? Why would he want a wife? Some men wanted to be waited on, some constantly wanted to be reassured of their wonderful attributes, some merely wanted a son, some married for companionship.

So they wouldn't have to face living with their thoughts?

And this man?

This man, she decided, was one of those people who only felt good when he was helping. She had seen people like him at her father's parish church. Always helping, always trying to make things right, getting in the way, getting on one's nerves. These were the same people who fought revolutions in the trenches, while their leaders issued orders safely behind the line of fire.

In short, her captain was one of those foolhardy souls with the best intentions.

She watched him approach her as she carried water pails from the well behind the main house. Knowing the approximate time he arrived in the afternoons, she had dallied until she spotted the small plume of dust churned by his horse's hooves. The pails' handles cut into her palms. She set the pails down on the cracked earth and chafed the circulation back into her hands.

By that time, his bay was cantering toward her. He dismounted. Without looking at her, he said, "If you'll take the reins, I'll get the pails."

She waited until they began walking, then said, "I appreciate your help. And you need my help, Captain."

He looked at her askance.

She fixed her gaze on his profile, studying it as she talked. "The baby is coming soon. It will need a name—and a father. You need a wife to make a home for you in the wilderness outposts, wherever you are stationed. A wife who is clever, who can withstand hardships, who can help you get ahead in your career. I am that woman."

She was honest, if nothing else. She fully believed she could offer him something in return for his releasing her from a sentence of lifetime imprisonment.

He came up short. Water sloshed over the pails he carried. Behind them, his bay snorted and shifted its stance, as if also awaiting the outcome of this one-act play.

The officer's head swerved in her direction. Eyes wide, he stared back at her. "Good God, you are serious?"

She had nothing to lose if he turned her down. "Captain, I've danced in the same room as His Majesty King George."

"I looked at your record. You were transported for treason against His Majesty."

He was asking her to expound. She would explain herself when she was ready. At another time. First, the gaining of her objective. "I've supped with ambassadors and generals, including Nelson himself. What pretty lass with half a brain is going to follow you to the mountainous wilds of India"—she flung out a hand—"or to this strange, ungodly wilderness?"

He fumbled for words. She waited. "I had thought to . . . Mary had said she would wait . . . letters take so long getting here. . . ."

"Do you know when, if ever, you'll get back to England again?" she asked softly.

He shook his head.

They began walking again. She said nothing more. At the doorway to the hut, he passed her the pails. Without a word, he strode on to the main house.

The waiting that afternoon was long. She scrubbed and rescrubbed the rough-hewn table.

Soon Pulykara came in, toting a bag of peas she had been issued from the storage house. "We'd best shell these, if we gonna get them cooked in time."

"Not now, Pulykara," she said, her eye ever on the doorless opening, which gave full view of the veranda. Then she saw him. He had come out onto the veranda and halted at the steps. Indecision showed in his stance, the way his body was half-turned toward the hitching post and half toward her hut; the way his head was lowered, the way his hands rubbed against each other.

You need me. You need me.

As if her thoughts empowered his footsteps, he descended the steps and began walking in the hut's direction. His body blocked the sunlight that had heated the entrance. Pulykara turned toward him. "Yes, suh?"

"The lady. I would like to speak to her alone."

The ever-grateful, ever-protective Pulykara shot her a wondering glance, then rose from her squatting position before the mound of peas and limped past the captain.

Alone with Nan, he said nothing. She helped him. "The baby is due in a week or so. We should be married by a clergyman soon. I'll need a midwife. Pulykara will be worth your purchase, also."

She saw his dubious expression. "You won't be sorry, Captain. I'll be a good wife for you."

And she meant it.

She hadn't even known his name. Captain Tom Livingston. She gazed at him while he slept. The flickering light of the sperm candle lent him a little-boy look. Yet he had served in what was formerly the American colonies and against Napoleon's forces in India.

He had come to her twice this week. Using his rank, he had appropriated a small hut used by a night guard. The hut was filthy and the bedlinens stank, but at least she was sleeping on a mattress for the first time in almost a year. Within a few days, Tom assured her, a house on post would be vacated for them.

Tom had a gentle touch. Out of concern for her condition, he had not taken her. Out of respect for his condition, having gone so long without a woman, she brought him to a climax. Using her hand and mouth. Acts that would have appalled her a short year ago.

She drew the sheet up over his sprawled body. The gnats and mosquitoes were horrendous. Tomorrow, she would have Pulykara see about getting netting. Her gaze was almost tender, and she hoped she wasn't falling in love with him. Her foolish love for Miles Randolph had brought upon her humiliation and degradation that months of captivity had only intensified. She could never let herself be weakened by love again.

"Nan?" Tom stirred and flung out an arm across her chest.

"I'm here, Tom. I'll always be here for you."

He didn't hear her. He was snoring softly.

The following week, Nan began having contractions. Pain came unexpectedly, shooting up her belly as she bent over a large staved bucket to wash a pair of Tom's trousers. At her groan, Pulykara glanced back at her. Seeing Nan's face contorted by pain, the aborigine woman laid aside the damp clothing she had been hanging on the line of hemp stretched between two golden wattle trees.

"Your time upon you, baby?" she asked, crossing to Nan.

Nan grunted an assent and let the black woman lead her to the house. At that moment, she was more grateful than ever to Tom that he had put up little objection about buying Pulykara from bondage.

If Nan expected the relieving comfort of bed, Pulykara vanquished that idea. "The stool. Sit on it, baby, and whenever you feel the pushing, you move forward and squat."

While Pulykara sat on her haunches and observed, Nan went into quiet agony. The pain was ripping her apart. It radiated outward from the lower part of her abdomen, shooting through her veins and muscles ever upward, flicking like the overseer's whip that rent at flesh and blood. Her brain exploded with the pain.

Yet she bit back her screams. In silence she suffered, because she knew to be weak now would lose her Pulykara's respect. Nan needed that authority. Some sense of control of her life. She needed a friend, even if it was an aborigine woman.

"Talk to me, Pulykara. Distract me."

Pulykara talked of sandalwood trees with wood so heavy it would barely float and of great herds of seals, the whereabouts of which only her tribe knew, and of course of the Dreamtime. For her, it was a real place.

For Nan, it was an endless journey, this Dreamtime. An imaginary place where one might find oneself. Like the outback, Pulykara's Never-Never, this

Dreamtime must be a deep interior where the soul was free in an inner outback, a land beyond Disappointment and Good-bye and Alone.

Hours later, as Tom was returning from duty, she gave birth. Pulykara turned with the infant in her arms to Tom. He put away his scabbard and his shakar hat. With wonder, he stared down at the squalling mite of a human being.

From the bed, Nan said weakly, "'Tis a girl."

"Are you all right?" he asked, taking his gaze off the baby to fix on her. "You don't look well, Nan."

"I'm tired. That's all."

"What will you name her?"

Nan turned her head toward the palisaded wall. "I won't. I'm giving her away."

"You cannot be serious about this," he said. "The babe will die without your milk."

Nan's breasts ached with their heavy fullness, although scarcely six hours had passed since she had given birth. "No, the baby won't die. Pulykara says she knows of someone who has breast milk."

Tom stared at the aborigine, who was tearing strips of muslin to bind Nan's breasts. "Pulykara knows," Nan said. "I don't understand how news is passed along by these people with nary a written word, but some woman gave birth yesterday to a stillborn."

Tom asked, "You are certain the mother will want this child?"

She shrugged. "She's a mother who has lost a child. She'll want the—"

"But so are you." Perplexity puckered his thick brows. "I'm stupefied. I can't understand how you would so easily give away your own flesh and blood. It's unnatural."

"Come here, Tom." She stretched out her hand to take his and draw him down on the bed beside her. She had to convince him of the wisdom of her decision. Should he doubt her at the beginning of their marriage, she would never be able to steer their relationship through threatening waters that would undoubtedly besiege their marriage from time to time.

She rubbed his palm, feeling the calluses and comparing it to Miles's smooth one, the palm of a gentleman. Bemused, Tom watched her fingers. "Tom, dearest, the baby deserves the best possible upbringing." Her voice lowered, as did her lids. "I cannot help the pain I feel when I see her and remember . . . remember that the man"—she drew a ragged breath and went on—"the man who was responsible for fathering her was also responsible for my imprisonment."

"You have told me so little about what happened—"

"I was beguiled, Tom. Like a foolish woman who has never been courted, I let my heart overrule reason. I wrote pamphlets that infuriated his mentor's rival—Pitt."

"Not William Pitt!"

She was glad Tom momentarily forgot the issue of the child. "Aye. I was accused of being a Jacobin, and Pitt neatly arranged for me to be found guilty of treason. By loving a scoundrel of a man, I lost not only my freedom, but I was left to bear the child of a man who had used me only for political purposes. Should I keep"—she nodded toward the squalling infant—"the baby, I think I would always look upon it with resentment. For me, it represents the treachery of love and, worse, the demeaning of my soul and . . . well, another woman will love the baby far better than I."

He shook his head and rubbed his lantern-jawed

chin. "I don't understand you, Nan. This child is healthy and what's another mouth to—"

"Tom, think of the baby."

With a sigh, he rose. "I suppose you're right." He picked up his saber. "Tomorrow, I'll go and talk to my commander about placing the baby."

She knew Tom was hoping she would change her mind. After the door shut behind him, she allowed herself to turn her gaze on the baby. The child *was* healthy. And so tiny. A mite of a human being. Reluctance to give away the baby constricted the muscles in her throat. She found it difficult to speak but forced out the next words. "Pulykara, get your belongings together."

They were few enough. A blanket, a tin cup, a woven reed basket of trinkets, which she ascribed to as a source of power.

Nan watched the baby's tiny fists beat against empty space until Pulykara caught them in the folds of the blanket in which she wrapped the baby. "You want me to find a place for her now?" she asked.

The aborigine's eyes held no reproach, yet Nan felt guilty. She was feeling maternal pangs. No, her decision was the right one. The child would be better off growing up in a household where it was loved.

She turned her face to the other side of the pillow. "Pulykara, you are to stay with the baby. I helped you once, now you must help me. Guard the infant as your own for as long as the child lives." Tears dampened the pillow. "Promise me this."

Over the strips of tattoos, the luminous black eyes were sorrowful. "I promise, baby."

5

The Reverend William Wilmot watched his young wife suckle the infant in her arms. Her round face glowed. At that moment, she resembled a Botticelli Madonna. At seventeen, she was fully a woman.

When he had married her, she was a mere thirteen, a child. A child who had been sentenced to seven years for plucking cucumber plants from a private garden.

He had been thirty and sent out by the London Missionary Society with his wife. Clara had died en route, and he had ended up rescuing the elfin Rose from servitude through marriage to her.

His eyes fell on her breasts, engorged with milk from the stillborn she had lost two days earlier. He recalled how hard had been his struggle those first three years of marriage to restrain his growing passion for her. Then had come the night she had turned to him in bed and begun caressing him. All hope of restraint had vanished the moment her hand had found his manhood.

"I know 'tis shameful of me," she had whispered, "but I cannot be helping meself, husband."

He had taken her in lust and should doubtlessly spend the rest of his life repenting. But he wasn't yet, God help him.

Rose looked up at him. "Oh, Willy, h'aint' she lovely?"

"*Isn't,* dear. Isn't she lovely." His long, bony fingers ruffled Rose's deep red hair, then he gingerly touched the baby's pitch black, downy fuzz. "She is, indeed, beautiful. And nigh as bald as I. At least, I have teeth."

Rose chuckled. In the candlelight, her freckles glinted like half-pennies. "You say the drollest things, Willy."

"We must remember in our prayers the mother. One of the convict women, most likely. The Lord knows how they suffer so. Does the aborigine woman give you any clue about the mother's identity?"

"Nary a word. Like I told you, she just trotted out of the woods with the bundle like one of those dingoes."

William thought of the aborigine woman, squatting outside their timber-and-stone cottage. The cottage was on the edge of Sydney in a rural area known as Wooloomooloo for the mobs of gray kangaroo that inhabited the area. Dingoes that howled in the night, kangaroos that boxed like Welsh prize fighters, and aborigines that would have no qualms about slitting the throat of an Englishman who befriended them. That was Australia. A wild land with wild people. Still, this black woman was one of God's creatures.

"What shall we name 'er, Willy?"

"I suggest something biblical."

Rose's little nose wrinkled. "Bible names are so . . . so . . ."

"Unimaginative?" He mused a moment, then, leaning over the rocker to better study the precious gift, said, "What about Amaris. It means 'whom God hath promised.'"

"Amaris?" She rolled the name on her tongue. "I like it, Willy. I like it." Her short finger tickled the sleeping baby's dimpled chin. "Well, daughter, Amaris you are. Amaris Wilmot."

Within that first uneasy week of marriage Nan had discovered that her amiable and good-hearted husband had a serious flaw in his character: Tom was not ambitious.

Hers and Tom's military quarters were little better than the hut to which she had been assigned, only the single room with an attached kitchen shed. A lieutenant fared better, earning the privilege of two rooms. Nan smiled to herself. With her subtle guidance, Tom would earn a lieutenant's ranking.

Fort Phillip had been constructed of limestone quarried from nearby and built solely for defense against the savage aborigines. Cannons thrust outward from stone ramparts. Thatched barracks encircling a parade ground housed bachelor soldiers. Little thought had been spared for the few wives who had to live in a land on the other side of the world.

As she regained her strength, Nan began to realize just how bereft of intellectual stimulus Sydney Cove was. She longed to attend social outings like boating parties up and down the various inlets of the harbor or the gatherings for conversation, reading, and music at the colonel's house.

The elite of the officers and their wives clung to the refinements of Europe. Because Nan was an ex-convict, an Emancipist, she was held in disdain, as were the majority of the colony's population, still in chains and living in squalid conditions.

She and Tom were not on invitation lists issued by the Exclusionists, those handful of free settlers and army officers who saw themselves as Sydney's aristocracy.

This superior attitude galled Nan. Most of the officers' wives could barely decipher to the rule of three!

"'Tis not that important," Tom said as he poured a mug of ale brewed by a soldier's wife. "I couldn't care less about the opinion of Major Hannaby's wife—whether she approves or disapproves of what you were."

To better apply her rouge of rose-petal paste, Nan leaned closer to the mottled glass. Tom had purchased it from the shipment of goods off the brig that had put into port last week. At last, she and Tom were going somewhere—to the reception for the penal colony's new governor.

"You may not care, but I burn each time I am snubbed."

"They can't hold a candle to you, Nan. Your intelligence is far superior to that of the civil servants and common soldiers, not even mentioning the convicts and Emancipists."

She knew he didn't realize that her education most likely exceeded even that of the officers and their families. They were in control and clinging desperately to a modicum of civilized British living on the edge of an empty continent.

She turned and flashed him a dry smile. "You forget I am an Emancipist, a convict who has served my time—thanks to your taking me in marriage." Her tone softened. "Tom, you know I also appreciate your letting Pulykara leave of her own free will."

He wouldn't be sidetracked. "So why must you force others to acknowledge your worthiness? Isn't it enough that you know?"

Her fingertip dipped once more into the cosmetic pot. She was careful always to look her best. She took special pains with clothing and hair, so she would never be associated with the slatternly looking wretch who had arrived in Sydney Cove.

"Because we're stymied by that foul social order. Tom, this is a new world. I may have come here without beauty or birth, but I *can* create my own aristocracy here."

The one quality Nan prided herself on—her intellect—was of no use in the colony.

But her strong spirit would not be suppressed. Never again would she be a pariah. Somehow she had to achieve legitimacy and a sense of place there in Sydney, because she knew she could never return to England.

That need for recognition and acceptance became an obsession. That and her hatred for Miles Randolph.

The means to achieve recognition and acceptance came about quite accidentally. She had been trying to get a tea stain out of one of her few dresses. Ruminating over the lack of clothing, her mind tracked onward to the prohibitive price of purchasing anything imported.

If one had one's own vessel . . . An image of taking a single vessel and expanding it into a fleet took root. She knew that to become firmly entrenched with the Exclusionists it would take more than plying a single vessel for trading.

With that in mind, though, she began a campaign, a campaign that she acknowledged would take years even to implement. First, she and Tom needed land. At the present, the only land being granted to officers, other than those of age to retire, was to those members of the New South Wales Corps, known as the Rum Corps.

With money, land, and cheap labor at their disposal, the Rum Corps was making huge profits at the expense of the small businessmen. The officers were paying for labor and local products in rum and were buying whole shiploads of goods. Then they sold them at two and three times their original values. And all the while, the officers of the Rum Corps were getting richer and more arrogant.

For months, Nan pondered the situation. She could either wait for Tom to come of retirement age to begin her project—or she could finagle him a transfer into the New South Wales Corps.

Her decision against either was tipped by Miles Randolph.

The reception for the penal colony's new governor was being held at the Government House. Overlooking Sydney Cove, it was the largest and best built building in New South Wales. However, few windows ventilated the cavernous building, and in the summer crowded receptions could make the heat unbearable. The chandelier's hundred little flames heated the room even more.

Nan dressed carefully for that most propitious evening. Tom complimented her on the ostrich feather tucked into her hair, puffed with the aid of hair balls.

Little did her husband realize how discreetly she scavenged the settlement for clothing and food items to be had at bargained prices.

With a critical eye, she viewed her image in the looking glass. A slow smile eased the firm line of her lips. Somehow she was subtly changed from the spinster who had been shipped from England a convict. She was almost attractive.

The torrid tropical sun had given her face a healthy color. Her imaginative cooking, necessitated by the lack of staples, had filled out her sunken cheeks. Tom's amiable attention had made her feel feminine.

Lastly, she supposed, Miles had made his own contribution to her alteration, howbeit indirectly. The effects of childbearing had resulted in her wider hips and more pronounced bosom.

Strange that she should think of him when his image rarely crossed her mind these days.

Or maybe it wasn't so strange if she considered that her intuition, when she heeded it, was often close to presentiment. Especially, this evening, when upon entering the Government House, the first face she sighted was that of Miles.

There must have been more than fifty or sixty people mingling in the large, austere room. Yet her gaze locked instantly with his. It was as if two years had never passed. She experienced that same explosive excitement that made her weak.

Miles had proven to be a man who used people. For her, he could only mean heartache. He was dangerous and all wrong for her. That didn't stop her from wanting him. Inside, a reflexive wall of defense that insured emotional survival went up immediately.

With Tom at her side, she picked her way among the guests with a deliberate pace, drawing ever closer to Miles.

He wore a purple velvet dress coat, a white satin waistcoat, and silk gaiter pantaloons. At the moment, he was deep in conversation with the new governor. That a man who had been accused of treason should appear to be on the best of terms with an English representative of the Crown should have been amazing; but then Miles had popped up in a land on the opposite side of the world, a colony that often was forgotten and neglected by its English parent.

Few of the guests even noticed Nan and Tom, although the young and buxom Elizabeth Hannaby, the major's wife, offered a polite nod. She was as round as a wine vat and almost as large. The major, with his military carriage, had a strutting outthrust of the chest.

Nan had to slow her pace. To delay her progress, she paused often to comment to a bemused Tom. "Dear, isn't that a Romney above the sideboard?"

His gaze followed hers. "A what?"

She smiled indulgently. "Never mind, dearest."

Rum flowed freely, and the laughter and talk were loud, as if to drive away the massive silence that surrounded the tiny cluster of people clinging to the edge of the continent. Drinking was one of the few pleasures available and blotted out the terrible isolation lurking on the perimeters of each person's mind.

Ahead of her, one young couple appeared as ill at ease and out of place as she. While the female guests wore court dresses, though outdated in the hooped style, this woman had on a dingy, dull-brown dress, the folds of which her hands arranged and rearranged. Only her red hair saved her from fading into the wall.

Experience prompted Nan to classify the woman as a former convict. In the woman's countenance, Nan recognized the fear and anguish that awe of her surroundings did not conceal.

The husband appeared much older, and though not as uncomfortable with their surroundings as his diminutive wife, a faint compression of his lips suggested mild disapproval.

"Impressive gathering, isn't it?" she said to the couple.

They looked as startled as Tom, because these were people neither he nor she knew and certainly not Exclusionist aristocrats. "Oh, yes," the elfish-looking woman said, obvious pleasure brightening her freckled face. "H'it's ever so splendid."

Nan wasn't misled by the young woman's speech, which identified her as being from the Billingsgate fish market area. The lively intelligence in the woman's brown eyes elicited Nan's respect.

"The new governor should be suitably impressed," Tom commented.

"If only he can do something to remedy the mistreatment of the convicts," the man said. His guileless eyes scanned the assembled guests. "Prohibiting the devilish trading of rum would help the colonists, also. Their addiction to liquor promises trouble of the greatest magnitude."

"Prohibiting the sale of female convicts would make a difference," his wife added. "What we 'ave now is little more than outright prostitution."

Recalling the ignominy of standing before would-be purchasers, Nan might have agreed. She also remembered that had it not been for Tom's purchase of her, she would by now be slaving in the fields.

"My name is Rose Wilmot," the young woman said, her smile shy. "And this 'ere is my husband, William. The Reverend William Wilmot."

Nan thought she should have guessed the man's occupation. Yet the way his eyes crinkled suggested at least a modicum of compassion and humor that set him apart from her father.

She performed the introduction for her and Tom but was cut short when the colony's judge advocate rose. He was to administer the oath of office to the man who would become the captain-general and governor in chief of the colony of New South Wales.

Captain William Bligh was a short, stocky man. In his face could be read determination and courage. His florid complexion, however, betrayed either a drinker, Nan decided, or a rash man subject to fits of rage.

In a firm, unwavering voice, he repeated the oath, as all his predecessors had done before him. "I swear to preserve the Protestant succession, prevent dangers from popish recusants, and observe the laws relating to trade and plantations. I swear to display amity and kindness toward the aborigines, grant land, encourage religion, preserve subordination in society, and endeavor to educate the children of the convicts in religious as well as industrious habits."

Even as the governor spoke, Nan drew closer to the dais that had been erected. It was as if an undercurrent pulled her against her will. She left Tom in amiable conversation with the provincial couple.

With each step, Nan's heartbeat accelerated, because she was also drawing just that much closer to Miles. He appeared to be observing the swearing-in ceremony, but she knew he was very much aware of her. His gaze occasionally slid over the heads of the other guests to arrow in on her, then as abruptly to desert her.

She paused within a cloth bolt's length of him and stared at him with concentrated will. He had no recourse but to acknowledge her. Above those hollowed cheeks, his deep-black eyes locked with hers and held. In that prolonged gaze, she searched for fear of her, because certainly she was a threat due to what she knew about him. She saw no fear, no wariness, and was suddenly furious.

"You are bold to show up on English soil again, sir."

"I heard about your arrest, Nan. A calamity."

"A calamity?" He termed nearly a year out of her life in imprisonment and transportation to some God-forgotten land merely a calamity! She could hardly breathe, she was so filled with rage.

His mustache twitched. "But then, you seem to have landed on your feet like the proverbial cat."

How could he be so indifferent to what they had shared? He was a man of ice! While her fury battled with her desire, she managed a cool smile. "As you, too, seemed to have done."

He shrugged those broad shoulders. "I managed to avoid trial on a technical point raised by friends in high places. By the time a bailiff caught up with me here in Sydney, there was a question regarding whether London or Sydney was the correct location."

"Lucky you." She wanted to slap the indifferent smile from his lips. At the same time, she yearned to feel their kisses again. She numbed herself to his sexual power. "And pray tell what nefarious schemes are you currently undertaking?"

"Nefarious?" As if bored, he glanced around the room indolently then let his gaze return to hers. "I've only been here a month, but I am unaware of any import business that could be conducted nefariously."

"Of course not," she shot back, "because there are no laws regulating trade."

Almost insolently, he eyed her bosom. If he expected to disconcert her, she thwarted him. She stared back at him unwaveringly. "I take it you are a part of that most profitable business, the Rum Corps, Miles?"

"I have had dealings with them since my arrival last month." His lids narrowed to half mast, and his voice lowered to that intimate octave she remembered so well. "You know, bluestocking, I don't think you have forgotten any more than I those nights we spent together. The fact that you're married doesn't have to prohibit renewing the pleasure we once shared."

Even during her imprisonment, she had romantically fantasized about Miles. Only now could she admit that all the while she had wanted to believe there had been a logical reason behind his actions. She had wanted to believe that he would somehow return and rescue her. And even now a part of her was tempted to acquiesce to that addictive passion.

Foolish woman! She was a blind, foolish woman!

That weakness of sentimental and romantic daydreams had cost her dearly. All the painful feelings of the past engulfed her. For so long, she had suffered in her sorrow and cried at the injustice. Now anger blazed through her.

Her smile was brilliant, like cut diamonds. "Miles, the only pleasure I'll experience regarding you will be to watch you labor in chains on a convict farm or something worse. And before God I'll see that happen!"

"As I recall, you don't believe in God."

Before she could react, he took her gloved hand and bent low over it, as if to kiss its back. Instead, he squeezed her fingers, stopping just short of inflicting real pain. His smile when he straightened was dazzling. "Don't cross swords with me, Nan. You're not smart enough. Now, be a good little woman and go take care of that plodding husband of yours."

At that precise moment, she knew how the remainder of her life would be dedicated, and it wasn't to serving her father's god.

6

Occasionally, Nan was surprised by the realization she was coming to love Tom. Not with the wild abandon that she had felt for Miles but with a quiet, steadily growing affection that was as unbreakable a bond as fairy-tale love.

In that respect, Miles had shattered her dream. She meant to shatter his.

She shifted her focus from social climbing to shipping. A perplexed Tom listened as she explained her strategy. "I've even thought of the name of our enterprise—New South Wales Traders, Limited. What do you think?"

"Nan, we can't go up against the Rum Corps. There is no way we can break their monopoly. They control what boats are allowed to dock. They control the dockhands. The Rum Corps would never permit another boat to be loaded. And if you don't mind me asking, how the hell are we going to finance such a venture? We're living in a hovel, Nan. My lieutenant's salary barely stretches as it is."

"The Rum Corps won't last. The new governor will break them."

"They've outlasted several governors, so I don't—"

"This governor's different. Trust me. I've heard he faced a mutiny aboard his former ship, was put adrift in a dinghy, and sailed four-thousand miles across the Pacific to resume his career. He's tenacious. He won't fail."

"I won't even ask how you know this."

Listening, asking the right questions came naturally to her, something Tom couldn't comprehend. "The Rum Corps and Bligh will lock horns, Tom. Already, they're calling him Caligula. The day they rebel against him, I want you to resign your commission."

"What?"

He came halfway out of his chair, and she put a calming hand on his shoulder. "Listen to me. Not only will your bold act impress the colonists and the governor, but by that time—six months to a year at most—we'll be ready to begin our own trading venture."

"Nan, you're a female, you've never had experience in business. For that matter, neither have I. The only security we have is my commission, woman!"

She smiled serenely. "Trust me."

Food had never been bountiful in any of the Sydney Cove households. Even Tom, who rarely took an interest in what Nan prepared, noted that dinnertimes had become skimpy affairs.

"The johnnycakes taste like they've been baked on

a shovel. And yesterday's lamb stew was little more than broth."

Nan shrugged. "You know yourself the Rum Corps is controlling the price of what they import. We are paying dearly. With what you give me, I barely am able to buy food to last an entire pay period."

In actuality, most of the food was coming from what Nan bargained for when she visited the docks, outings of which Tom was unaware.

He was also unaware that at the dock she occasionally taught reading, writing, and ciphering to any soldier who was willing to part with a few hard-earned coins. Exclusionists rarely visited the docks. Her secret was safe.

He had quite forgotten her suggestion that they go into a mercantile business when nearly four months later, she said, "I've something to show you, Tom."

"The glint in your eye intrigues me if nothing else."

Evidently, he had thought she meant something close at hand. When she took up her parasol, his brows climbed in his high forehead. "Just where is it we're going?"

She smiled. "Be patient."

He followed her from their brick-thatched quarters and caught up with her as she approached the guard gate. Together, they descended the sloping streets leading to the wharves. Known as the Rocks, this derelict area of brothels and bars Nan had passed through in chains less than two years before.

She was understandably proud when she paused before a ramshackle board building that leaned precariously backward, as if unable to resist the might of the sea winds. Tom stared at it, then peered at her, his thick brows posed in question marks.

"The sign, Tom. Look above. The sign."

His gaze followed hers. His lips translated what his widening eyes scanned. "New South Wales Traders, Limited." His gaze slid to hers. "Nan, what shenanigans are you about now?"

"'Tis no joke, Tom. She looked at the signboard, poorly painted and barely legible. Pure pleasure, such as she had once found in Miles's arms, filled her. For an instant the memory of his skin texture and his scent hounded her. "I've leased the building for six months."

"You've what?"

"'Twill be slow going at first. I've my plans set on a stand of sandalwood a man named Jimmy Underwood knew about. The Chinese will pay highly for it. We can store it here, as well as seal hides."

"What?"

"Are you deaf, Tom? Pulykara had told me certain warriors of her tribe could provide as many seal hides as a person could pay for."

"I'm sure you will explain just how we will manage to pay for seal hides."

From inside, a secret smile threatened to make its way to her lips. Already she had her husband accepting her idea of New South Wales Traders, Limited as a done deed. "As we've managed to acquire the monies for the first three months' lease, by being frugal."

"Frugal, ye say? We can't get any more frugal. Your gowns are threadbare, our bedding is tattered, and our food supply would sour a convict."

She looked him straight in the eye. "No, it

wouldn't. Until you've eaten convict's dole, you don't know, Tom.

We'll survive quite well, just as we've been doing. Another six months, our warehouse will be filled."

"And then what?"

"When the Rum Corps' monopoly is broken, we'll be among the first to start trading openly. Sandalwood to the orient, sealskins to London. But only at first." Excitement grew in her as she talked. "We'll need a ship, but I've tracked down Jimmy Underwood. I told you about him. He worked on the prison farm and carved that bark cradle."

Wisely, she didn't remind him for whom the cradle had been carved. "Jimmy has the inestimably useful skill of knowing how to build sloops. We'll buy the remainder of his sentence—"

"Nan, you go too fast."

"Not fast enough. There's not enough time to do everything that needs to be done. And only you can do it, Tom. Why, with your knowledge of India and the United States, we can begin a trade with Calcutta and Madras and Philadelphia and Boston that will rival anything the Rum Corps even attempted."

Her gray eyes blazed with purpose, and watching her in that dying afternoon sunlight, Tom thought she was almost beautiful—and overpowering at the same time.

Nan's every thought was directed toward an enterprise that was based on two equally strong needs: the need to become firmly entrenched with Sydney's aristocracy and the need to break Miles Randolph.

Besides dealing in the rum trade, he had also undertaken staffing a workshop with convicts assigned to make consumer goods that were in erratic supply—candles, soap, boots, and leather hats. She had learned he was also constructing one of the largest private houses in the colony, with two stories and a basement.

Standing at the corner of High Street and watching the house go up, she swore her own would be of three stories, and with an elegant veranda and slender columns.

"Daydreaming, bluestocking?"

She didn't have to turn around to see who it was who addressed her. Her gaze still on a sweating, half-naked convict who toiled over mortar and sandstone, she said, "Only reminding myself, Miles."

"I don't have to remind myself about you," he said, his voice low and deep, reaching only her ears, though occasional passersby spared neither of them a glance. "I remember your passion. I have found that in other women but never combined with such sharp wit. And tongue," he added with his familiar dry humor.

Her head half turned, and she peered up from beneath the lace ruffle of her yellow parasol. "And you never will. You will rue the day, Miles Randolph, that you left me to face a courtroom of incensed Tories."

"You will live to see the day that you thank me for that, Nan Livingston. Shrewd and passionate, you were. But also naive and untested. You are a far stronger woman, I wager."

"As you will fully discover one day."

Mockery inflected his politician's rich voice. "Ahh, you plot to ruin me? I doubt you can even dream of climbing to the heights I intend. England might not want me but will have to recognize me as the leader of a country that will dwarf theirs."

At last, she turned to face him. Her heart was pounding with the fear of the weakness he engendered in her. Those blue-black eyes taunted her, and her weakness was burned away by her anger and pain. "We are both visionaries, Miles. But you set yourself too high and underestimate me, a woman though I might be. Good day, sir."

Returning to Fort Phillip, she admitted with the most reluctance and regret that she still wanted Miles. She also realized for the first time that it was those occasional encounters with him that energized her. She returned to her enterprise with renewed vigor.

However, her vigor soon ebbed as the months passed and Captain Bligh did not strike at the Rum Corps's officers as quickly as she had anticipated. Gradually, her warehouse became so packed it was impossible to move among the aisles.

Viewing her wares and stock one sultry afternoon, a part of her took great pride in all that she had accomplished. Another part of her worried. She was a month behind on the lease as it was. If she didn't find a legal outlet for her wares soon …

Then on a hot January night, the Rum Corps, unable to tolerate another tyrannical order from Bligh, staged a coup d'état. From the fort, Nan and Tom could hear the musketfire over at the Government House and glanced at one another. His expression was drawn, hers ebullient.

Early the next morning, word passed among the fort's inhabitants—a military junta had assumed power. John Macarthur, who had clashed with Bligh over the right to run sheep, was the instigator and apparent leader. One of the sub-rosa members, Nan knew, was Miles Randolph.

Retribution, however, did not appear to be forthcoming from Whitehall in London. As the months slid by, it became obvious that for this remarkable mutiny, none of the men involved would be hanged or even punished. Once again, Miles had flirted with danger and danced away.

Bligh returned to England, the junta continued to rule, and Nan's dreams of a shipping empire were fast fading.

To retain the warehouse, she sold off articles to a whaler at barely over her cost—and in secrecy. If the Rum Corps—or worse, Miles—should ever learn what she was doing, she would be clapped back in chains.

The danger of the enterprise was as stimulating as the danger of her relationship with Miles had been.

She repeated this clandestine operation time and again, cursing both the Rum Corps, Miles in particular, and herself most of all. Why had she formed no contingency plans?

Good-natured Tom did not bring up the calamity that would have occurred had he resigned his commission as she had urged. All events pointed to what seemed the obvious—that Nan had erred.

As if to further mock her, the whimsical gods struck next not at her intellectual pride but at her feminine ego. Miles hosted a party for the completion of his mansion that overlooked the harbor—and its slums.

All the Exclusionists as well as officers from every regiment were invited, which meant that Nan and

Tom presented themselves at the Randolph doorway. Nan glanced up at the elegant fanlight overhead and felt the sharp shaft of envy. Her good dress had been mended so often it was literally a patchwork. Everything she had managed to save had been put into the warehouse, all of which she was on the verge of losing.

The door was opened by a man in red livery. Nan's discerning eyes identified furniture by the master craftsman Chippendale. The floor of the large drawing room was of green, gray, and white marble, polished enough to satisfy even a Windsor. Hundreds of candles bedecked a crystal chandelier, heating the already overheated room.

"Nan," Tom said aside to her, "just what are we doing here?"

Her lips drew back in a tight smile. "Making contacts. Invaluable contacts."

Mingling with the guests was not the nightmare that Bligh's reception had been. The number of Emancipists slipping inside the fine weave of the Exclusionists' mosquito netting was increasing. A man named Simon Lord, transported for stealing several hundred yards of calico and muslin, had come up through the rum trade. Doubtless, Miles and the officers felt that by using such shady men as distributors, they were saved from demeaning contact with the penal colony's lower echelons.

While not exactly snubbing Nan, the majority of the guests found her bold manner irritating. She knew this and cared not. They would need her services one day—and pay dearly.

While Tom went to the refreshment table, flanked by vases of tall fronds, she scanned the guests for sight of Miles. In profile, he was talking to Macarthur and his wife and niece. Nan studied the young woman, who appeared maybe twenty at the most. She was one of those softly rounded women men loved to touch. At once, Nan's gaze returned to Miles's face and searched his attentive expression for other signs. She found only a formal politeness and sighed her relief.

As if he felt her eyes upon him, he turned, made his excuses to the three, and started in her direction. Occasionally, he paused to speak when someone detained him. He was so singularly handsome that every female eye followed him. She darted a glance at Tom, afraid he would return before she was able to speak to Miles alone. Tom was still enmeshed in the press of people at the refreshment table.

"Does it measure up to Windsor, Nan?"

She looked up at Miles. She hated that sardonic smirk. She hated even more her wanting of him. If Tom was more attentive in bed . . . "A touch of the nouveau riche, more gild than gold, but impressive all the same."

"And you still possess that same razor-edged tongue." His narrow-lidded gaze raked downward, past her throat, bare of adornment, to appraise her worn gown. His lips curled in private satisfaction.

Her pride rankled. "I am still in the game, Miles."

At that, his smile broke into a broad grin. "Your threat to see me labor in chains—a disappointment to realize that it was only a woman's temper tantrum. I had you pegged for better than that."

He turned his back on her. A calculated affront. Watching him walk away, she assuaged her fury by telling herself that he would always seek her out. If nothing else, he enjoyed the duel of wits she provided him.

Surprising her, he turned back to her, a risky action, considering that many would note that he talked to her twice. He leaned close, so close she could smell his cologne. A tingle of desire bubbled through her.

"Nan, dear," he whispered, "I know about the wharf warehouse. Your operations are your secret—as long as you don't step on my toes. The rum trade is my playground."

Stunned, she stared at his broad back as he made his way back to the Macarthurs and their niece.

What happened next sucked the air from her lungs. Tom had returned with a cup of pine punch for her when the portly John Macarthur stepped upon the dais and held up his palms for silence. The buzz of conversation ebbed.

"Fellow colonists, it gives me pleasure to announce that my niece Lucy Bentwater will not be returning to London. Instead, she will remain here to share a new life with her future husband and a partner of mine, the esteemed Miles Randolph."

Applause rippled across the room. Nan's hands refused to obey her brain's command to clap politely. She wanted to appear unaffected by the news, but that moment she could do little more than stand.

It wasn't as if she still hoped that Miles would come to love her. Yet all of her survival instincts had been grounded in that man-woman thing between them.

"Are you all right, Nan?" Tom asked.

She managed to nod. "Yes, just feeling a little queasy. The beef was stringy, didn't you think?"

Out of his element at the party, he seized the opportunity. "Let's go home, then."

Her father used to quote something about God closing one door and opening another. She didn't believe his god took an active part in the affairs of man and had told him so. Facetiously, she had said, "If I were omnipotent, I could do a much better job to alleviate suffering and pain."

The week following what she had come to think of as Miles's engagement party, she discovered that Miles's engagement might have closed one door for her, but another indeed opened in the least expected way.

"You are looking bonnier, lass."

Nan glanced up from the ledger. Josiah materialized out of the warehouse's gloom into her circle of candlelight. "Your ship's late by two weeks."

He peered down at her through narrowed lids. "Don't be telling me you missed me."

She bent her head and began tallying. "This is a business deal, Josiah. Purely business."

He sighed. "'Tis a cold heart you have, lass."

Something about the tone of his voice made her look up at him again. She respected him and was disturbed that he should so categorize her. "Not a cold heart. A numb heart."

"And I'm not the man to restore feeling, am I now?" He spread his giant hands. "Well, I'm not complaining. For the little you ask of me, I can enjoy a woman's body with a man's brain."

At that she had to smile. "I'm not certain if that is a compliment or not. Shall we do business?"

He thudded one of the crates with the flat of his hand. "Business—and then pleasure. Then I must be on me way. Randolph's cargo beckons me."

Her hand tightened on the quill. "What happens when the rum trade is squashed? It will be, you know. The Crown is losing too much money."

"I'll find other more profitable cargoes. It's not that diffi—"

"No, I mean to Miles Randolph, and the others involved in the rum trade?"

"The others—I don't know." Those bulky shoulders rose in a shrug. "As for Randolph, men of his ilk can smell trouble a'coming. He'll be heading for politics if I know anything."

"That wouldn't surprise me about Miles."

He took the quill and ledger from her and set it on one of the crates. "You aren't in love with the man, are you now?"

"Love? No. Not love. He's merely a competitor, a tough one." Something about Josiah's expression prompted her to ask, "Why?"

"Randolph is into, er, unnatural things. He buys convicted boys arriving at the docks on the transport ships. Randolph enjoys combining—" he paused, "—sex and sadism."

"You are sure about this?"

"I found a twelve-year-old, a Morton Freely, stowed away on my ship this morning. The lad appears to be badly beaten. Claims Randolph was responsible. The Freely lad escaped the Randolph mansion last night. Says Randolph would have his throat slit for revealing this."

"I'd like to see the boy before you sail."

"Later." He pinched out the candle, and its acrid smoke filled the darkness. His hands clamped on her shoulders and drew her against him. She liked the feeling of his solidity. Comfort. With Josiah, she felt comfort. With Tom, she had to be the stronger; with Miles, she had to be wary.

Josiah drew her down onto the sawdust floor.

"My dress," she murmured. "We're getting it dirty."

He kissed her neck just below her ear. "Forget the dress. I've brought one for you. Made by one of the best seamstresses in London."

She laughed against his beard. "You wouldn't be bedding that lass under the same business terms and conditions, would you, Josiah?"

With a chuckle, he loosed the strings of her bodice and palmed one small breast. "No complaining now, me lass. You were the one who specified this was to be a purely business relationship."

Her body responded to his rough touch with inner tremors. "Subtle whoring, you called it."

On his knees over her, he pushed up her skirts and parted her thighs. "With your mind and your passions, you would have made a marvelous and most successful madam."

"Alas, I want respectability more." She arched when he plunged into her, then began moving in unison with the big man.

Even though September's spring weather was balmy and cool, inside the warehouse a stagnant heat lay over the two pumping bodies. Sweat rolled off Josiah onto her. Normally fastidious, she reveled in this. That restrained part of her was temporarily free.

Tom would never have understood.

Miles always had.

Shafts of sunlight seeped between the warped door and its jamb. Gazing up at her business partner, she couldn't help but think what a gentle soul he was despite his rough-hewn ways.

When Josiah, at last, discharged his months of abstinence in a burst, he rolled from her. He stretched out on his side next to her.

Eyes closed, she lay silent, enjoying one of those few moments when her high energy wasn't in charge. She felt his broad palm splay over her stomach. Her lips curved in a faint smile. "Don't tell me you are ready to begin again, my lusty whaler."

"How long has it been since last you had your monthly?"

Her lids snapped open. She turned her head to stare at his ruddy face. "Whatever are you talking about?"

"I know your body well. You're with child, me lass, or me name isn't Josiah Wellesley."

"Well, then, it isn't!" She pushed up to a sitting position and began tucking in her wayward strands of hair and tugging down her skirts. "It's probably Smith or Jones."

His knuckles grazed her cheek. "You didn't answer me."

She stilled. After forcing herself to calculate, she replied, "Three months ago, I think."

He grunted. "Then the child isn't mine."

She wasn't sure if his expression was one of regret or relief. Without any inner searching, she knew exactly how she felt. Her future son was her ticket to the pinnacle of Sydney aristocracy.

"You must do it for the sake of our child. You must resign your commission and devote your energy and time to New South Wales Traders, Limited."

"Nan, the little you have socked away in that warehouse won't be enough to open our own business."

"Bah, leave that to me, Tom."

"Nothing daunts you, does it? You're impervious to despair. You survived the Rum Corps coup and maintained your neutrality. Wise, Nan. Wise."

She paused, the spoonful of gruel halfway to her mouth. She'd never admit it, but one thought did daunt her spirit: that of imprisonment. Losing her freedom again petrified her.

Yet she had risked her freedom to keep her enterprise solvent. Risked her marriage in her sexual business transactions with Josiah.

Did she dread poverty and its stigma even more? She still found it difficult to believe that after five years she was pregnant again. She had even selected the name for her son. Randolph.

And it would be a son.

From bitter experience, she knew that it was the men who had the opportunities in the world. Through a son, she could manipulate those opportunities to work toward her goal, a place in Sydney society.

She encouraged Tom to buy the papers of Jimmy Underwood. "He's skilled in boat building. We'll be needing our own ship, many ships, before another decade is out."

She didn't want to be dependent upon Josiah, and she knew she would have to expand if she expected her business to thrive.

Tom simply stared at her and shook his head.

"The profits from the last shipment Josiah is transporting will buy the finished lumber and materials needed."

Tom's protest that he knew nothing about navigation

elicited no respite for him. She stood firm. "Josiah has agreed to take you on his next voyage. We can always hire our own captain, but you need to learn the business."

When Tom returned, she intended to drain his brain dry of all he knew. She would never again allow herself to be put in a helpless situation. Wasn't knowledge power?

"What about you? Will you be all right here alone?"

She sighed. "Tom, I survived alone for six months under far worse conditions." She kissed his forehead, which was growing broader as his hair receded at his temples. "You just take care of yourself and come safely back to me and our son."

"I don't want to be away when the baby is born."

"You were there when I birthed the first one."

He eyed her steadily. "And you gave it away."

She flinched. "This one, I won't. I swear. The circumstances are different."

As Nan had predicted, Whitehall had enough of the Rum Corps governing the penal colony, and a new governor arrived. As a token gesture of suppressing the rum trading, Governor Macquarie sent Macarthur back to England as an exile.

This act allowed Nan to come out into the open—as far as she dared.

Conversely, Miles, having remained sub-rosa, was never implicated with the Rum Corps and escaped unscathed. Nan mentally shrugged. She had patience. One day . . . one day she would find the fitting retribution.

With Tom away, apprenticing under Josiah, she set up an office in her warehouse and hung out her shingle. There was no one with whom she could share her excitement, and so she stood alone in a cold, drizzling autumn rain and gazed up at the signboard proclaiming NEW SOUTH WALES TRADERS, LIMITED. April whipped her soggy skirts around her legs.

Pride filled her. "The first step," she murmured, then placed her hand on her stomach, as if in benediction. "And you will be the second."

As the weeks passed, two topics occupied the tongues of the Sydney citizens. The first topic, they placidly accepted—the leaders of the Rum Corps had not actually been ousted; they had merely transferred their operations to another sphere, Tasmania and Norfolk Island.

Miles invested his wife's money in establishing a newspaper. Considering that seven eighths of the colonists were illiterate, Nan found this amusing. But she knew there was a method to his madness. She sat back and watched.

The Sydneysiders sat back and watched her, because she was the second topic. Privately, she was acknowledged as the backbone of Tom Livingston's New South Wales Traders, Limited.

"Scandalous!" Major Hannaby's wife, Elizabeth, pronounced.

"A trifle unseemly for a lady," Lucy Bentwater said, her tone equivocal, as if Miles's fiancée followed the wind vane of public opinion.

Nan knew they talked. What they said didn't bother her. They would accept her sooner or later and eventually they would approve of her. She was breaking new turf as a woman, and it irritated her that she was having to operate in the background. She was a victim of her times, she lamented more than once. Had she been born in Greece a couple of millennia earlier, she would have had far greater latitude as a woman.

By her reckoning, she was a week or so past her due date, when she began to have labor pains. She was alone in the warehouse. Even in her pain, she pulled on her gloves and collected her parasol for the trip down to the bay, where Jimmy was working on her ship's wooden skeleton.

He looked up from the rib of lumber his adz shaped and wiped the sweat dripping from his face. Despite all the food she stuffed onto his plate, he still wore that emaciated look that would proclaim him a former convict for the rest of his days. "You all right, Mrs. Livingston?"

Apparently, her suffering showed.

"Jimmy, I want you to do something for me."

"Anything, Mrs. Livingston."

"Go to the Reverend Wilmot's house and ask for Pulykara. Tell her I need her. Tell her to come to my house as soon as possible."

Her breathing labored, she returned to the little hut on the post she and Tom called home, a far cry from Miles's handsome establishment in the Rocks.

Within the hour, Pulykara was at the door. "It's been a long time, baby," she said, her grin clumping the bands of tattoos on either side of her broad nose.

Nan managed a smile. "I've missed you, Pulykara." Then she groaned and grabbed her stomach. "'Tis my time."

At once, Pulykara went to work, stripping her former mistress of her clothing. Shivering and naked, Nan followed Pulykara's instruction about when to rise and squat with the labor contractions. Nan's lids squinched with the pain, and tears streamed from the corners of her eyes, but she did not scream out in those final moments of agony.

Then, the infant squeezed forth with a lusty howl that brought a smile of satisfaction from Nan. Collapsing against the side of the bed, she whispered, "Let me see my son."

Holding up the red mite of a human being, Pulykara laughed. "You've birthed yourself another girl, baby."

AMARIS

7

There is that secret yearning, that secret belief, in some women that they will find their soul mate, if not in this lifetime, then in another. Amaris Wilmot didn't know it, but she was one of those women. To dream is to acknowledge the possibility of fulfillment.

From her position outside the wrought-iron gate, the girl watched the birthday party for maybe as much as five minutes, a long time for twelve-year-old Amaris Wilmot to stand still.

Occasionally, Amaris's aborigine nanny, Pulykara, went in the place of Amaris's mother to collect unwanted clothing, goods, and foodstuffs donated to the church. And occasionally Amaris wangled her way into accompanying Pulykara.

When Amaris discovered there was to be a pickup at the Livingston household for a bag of cast-off clothing, she had begged her mother to let her go.

In the midst of making quince pie for an ailing parishioner, Rose had paused and smiled. "Just what is h'it that's so important at the Livingston place?"

"It's the Livingston woman."

"Aye?"

"She's the ship woman, Mother. The woman who does men's work."

"Well, not all men's work. But Nan Livingston is generous. Just don't pester her with your questions, Amaris. She might not be as willing to explain as your father."

As it was, Amaris never got as far as the front door with Pulykara. In passing an ivy-walled garden, Amaris heard the children's laughter. At the gate, her footsteps lagged. "I'll wait for you here, Pulykara."

The aborigine woman frowned. "Don't go getting ideas, Miss Priss."

Amaris's hands tightened on the bars and she peered between them. "I just want to look."

She didn't even hear Pulykara shuffle away. Several boys and girls were chasing a peacock through the manicured garden. Two girls swung on roped seats suspended from an old red ironbark tree. Three boys rolled a wagon wheel's metal hoop.

Amaris felt she was the outsider, always looking in, watching from behind a wall of bars or bricks.

At that moment, a girl who could have been no more than six or seven skipped down the carriage drive toward the gate. "My name's Celeste Anne. Would you like to come to my birthday party?"

Amaris stared at the apparition. Surely one of her mother's angels, made human. She was small, softly rounded, and blessed with creamy skin and pink cheeks and lips. Shiny light brown hair puffed like cotton fluffs around a face full of sweetness. Obviously, those rabbitlike brown eyes had never seen the rum-drunks of the Rocks.

But then, Amaris reflected, her mother had, on those occasions she helped her husband administer to "those lost souls." And Rose's eyes still held that same innocence. Amaris shook her head. "Birthdays are for children."

"You're not a child?" the little girl asked, her eyes large with wonder.

Amaris straightened her already too-tall frame. "Do I look like a child? I'm thirteen. Almost."

"I am seven years old today. Old enough Mother said to go down and see the Livingston ships."

Amaris tossed her head, and her long, black pigtails bounced against her shoulder blades. "I've seen them. They're all right, nothing special. Not when there's a whole forest of shipmasts in the harbor."

"You've been down to the Rocks?" The little girl drew closer to the gate's spiked bar. "What's it like? Horridly dangerous?"

Amaris paused and drew upon her few memories of her trips to the Rocks. "No. Sad. And exciting. Ships from China and South America and the United States of America dock there. And all sorts of queer people, not just pommies and paddies. They stroll the wharves and visit the pubs."

"You've been to a pub?" With awe enlivening its usually serene expression, the round face turned up to Amaris's.

"Wellll, yes." In the alley behind one, if that counted. It had been a Sunday afternoon, and her father had stopped on the way to the fort chapel to aid a body sprawled in drunken stupor.

"Sometime, could I go with you?"

Amaris thought quickly. "Of course not." She tapped the gate's ornamental bars. "You're in prison here. Convicts can't go wherever they want." The shadow that crossed the small, upturned face made Amaris immediately feel contrite.

"Mother says only riffraff go down to the dock." The eyes brightened and the voice lowered to a whisper. "I could sneak away. That would really be fun, wouldn't it? Can you come tomorrow?"

Amaris nodded at the gate. "How would you get out?"

"I don't know." The crestfallen countenance became animated again. "Could you help me?"

Something in the girl's appeal struck a chord in Amaris. "I'll think about it." Feeling very grown-up and omnipotent, she almost swaggered away from the gate.

A voice behind her brought her up short. "Don't you go and get that child into trouble, Miss Priss."

Amaris spun around to see Pulykara, toting the burlap bag of the Livingston's old clothes. The knotty little woman would scare a sailor, but to Amaris's way of thinking, Pulykara was a spritely old fairy left over from the Dream Time.

Dream Time was that time when the country being called Australia, the southern land, was a vast, featureless place. It was inhabited by giant spirit creatures that made epic journeys across the land, creating mountains, rivers, rocks, animals, and plants.

Pulykara told of Marrawuti, the sea eagle, who snatches away the spirit when a person dies; about Warramurungundjui, a female who came out of the sea to give birth to the people; and about Dreaming sites that contain power and energy of the Dream Time.

At least, that was how Pulykara related the legends. Amaris found her nanny's bedtime legends far more exciting than her mother's and father's obligatory prayers.

"She wants me to come see her tomorrow, Pulykara."

The old nanny's dark and scarred face darkened even further, if that was possible. "Amaris, you don't want to go mixing with them people."

She fell into stride with the aborigine woman, who was no taller than she. "Why not?"

Those rheumy eyes scanned Amaris's face with a love that was as powerful as a mother's, then shifted away from the girl's direct gaze. "Them people ain't like you."

"She's beautiful, isn't she? Celeste."

"Aye."

"And rich."

"Aye."

"I bet she never swears."

"Not at seven years old."

"I did."

Pulykara grunted and shifted her load to her other shoulder. "Your mama and papa, they don't know you do, lessen you go and forget yourself."

"They don't swear either."

"Their god will strike them with lightning."

Amaris's mouth screwed up. "I don't believe that."

"That's 'cause you're not like them either."

"Then who am I like?" she asked, her voice plaintive. She felt gauche and awkward, someone who belonged nowhere.

"You're a changeling, placed at the Wilmot household by the aborigines' gods."

"Bah. I used to believe you, Pulykara, did you know that? I really did."

"I don't lie. Wait and see. You're one of the Dream Time people."

Such was the intensity in the eyes and voice of the woman that Amaris was half-willing to believe her. Pulykara had certainly made the statement often enough for Amaris to give it credibility.

Not that Amaris was a silly, mindless girl. But at twelve, there was still enough of the child left, and a wise child knows *anything* is possible.

"You came!"

"Of course, I did." Amaris strolled closer to the garden gate. "I keep my word."

Celeste's light brown eyes reflected sunshine. "You'll take me to the wharf?"

The girl fascinated Amaris. She was everything Amaris wanted to be. Fleeting across her mind was a memory of the child's incredibly lovely dresses made of satin, faille, and zephyr, all tossed carelessly in the burlap sack. "Won't your mother miss you?"

"No, she's working in her office."

A *woman* with an office! "What about your nanny?"

"She sleeps when I play in the garden." A prankster's naughty smile curled her tiny bowed lips. "Only we made a pact that I don't tell my mother she takes naps. That way we both get to do what we want to. Where's your nanny?"

Amaris grinned. "Drinking Brazilian *aguardente*." Experimentally, she placed her foot on the gate's bottom railing and pressed her leg between the bars. "Here, step on my knee."

Biting her lower lip, Celeste gathered her courage, grasped the bars, and levered herself to a standing position on Amaris's knee. "Now what?"

"Why, grab hold of the top railing and pull yourself up."

"I'm too short and not strong enough." The little girl's tone was not whiny but apologetic.

Amaris thought for a moment. "All right. You can't get out, but I can get in. We'll work from that side of the fence."

Grabbing high on the railing, she easily hauled herself up, but the spiked bars caught on her long skirts. "Bugger the skirts," she mumbled beneath her breath. Two years before, her mother had made her start wearing long skirts because not only was she as tall as any woman but also she had already started filling out.

"You can curse?"

"Very well, as a matter of fact." Amaris dropped lightly to the other side and heard with a grimace the ripping sound. Looking behind her, she saw that her petticoats had snagged on a spike. With a shrug, she jerked hard, rending the cheap, coarse material even more, but at least the offending garment was loosed.

She turned back to Celeste, who barely came to her chest. "Ready?"

Celeste nodded enthusiastically.

"After I kneel, you climb onto my shoulders. When I stand up, you grab hold of the railing and perch there till you get your balance."

Celeste's eyes widened. "Then what do I do?"

Disgust curled her lips. "You drop to the other side, goose."

The young girl bit her lip, nodded, and taking a deep

breath, followed Amaris's instructions. When Amaris felt the slight weight lift from her shoulders, she glanced up to check on her protégé. Balanced precariously, Celeste was clutching the spikes in a death grip.

Disregarding propriety, Amaris lifted her skirt and, drawing her tattered petticoats between her legs, quickly tucked them into her skirt waistband like the women who cleaned fish at the docks. Then, with an economy of motion, she began to scale the gate. Beneath the weight of both girls, it swung slightly on its hinges. Celeste drew in a sharp breath. Her creamy skin paled.

Amaris pushed off and landed on the far side, purposely making the gate shift slightly. With approval, she noted that the frightened girl didn't cry out. She looked up at her. "Go ahead, jump. It's not that far down."

Eyes squinched shut, Celeste let go—and fell atop Amaris.

"Damn!" she said in a whoosh of breath. Amaris pushed the welter of limbs and crinoline off her. "Don't you know a bloody thing about climbing up and down things?"

Her lower lip trembling, Celeste shook her head. "Mama says a lady doesn't climb."

Amaris pulled the younger girl to her feet and started down the hill toward the cove. Celeste hurried to catch up. "Where did you learn to swear so wonderfully?"

"In brothels and pubs along the wharf." It sounded impressive, she thought; only the curse words came, for the most part, from the vagrants who let one slip occasionally when panhandling for food at her father's door. Only a few were acquired during her infrequent ventures down to Sydney's wharves.

Sydney was an unplanned straggle of shacks that perched on the rim of the shining, amethyst harbor. Discounting the Randolph mansion and a few other grand homes, the remainder of the buildings looked more like pigsties. There were no hospitals, and, like her father's church on the outskirts of Sydney, the few other churches were little more than huts.

The main road she and Celeste took to the wharves was a dusty track, and after a rain it was a creek bed. Celeste daintily lifted her skirts to sidestep the sewerage that ran down the center of the street. Amaris strode on, unheeding of the filth and stench.

The new governor, Macquarie, was zealously attempting to reconstruct Sydney into a Georgian city, financed with rum, by giving building contractors a trading monopoly on the spirits.

An ant string of convicts was working on a general hospital and the Hyde Park Barracks, designed to house all convicts employed by the government in Sydney.

Celeste's enthusiasm waned as they bypassed each gang of sweating, stinking, grunting men. With draught animals few in the colony, the human body served to move the quarried rock to its destination. The little girl's gaze fell on bloodied hands and tears rushed to her eyes. She turned on Amaris. "Why are they working so hard?"

Her wide mouth set in a grim line, Amaris nodded toward the end of the line, farther down the hill, where the overseer played out his lash on bare backs. "That's why, and you don't see them all teary-eyed. Tears don't get you anywhere, so stop your sniffling. I would never submit to being beaten."

In dismissal, she turned her back on the motley

waste of men dressed in coarse dingy-white woolen paramatta trousers.

"Would you fight that man with the whip?"

"Wouldn't need to. Escape is too easy here. Those convicts aren't chained, and the overseer is far at the other end."

"How would you escape?"

"You ask too many questions."

"But how would you?" Celeste persisted, fascinated by the knowledgeable older girl.

"Well, I'd wait until a whaling captain put in and stow away. The American whalers are always needing new crewmen."

Celeste wiped her eyes. "This isn't fun."

"Come on. We're not there yet."

The wharves excited Amaris's senses. The brilliant colors, smells, and sounds washed away the drabness of the town climbing the hill around the multilobed bay. Overhead, in an acid-blue sky, sea gulls shrieked. Corked nets draped fishing boats so they looked like clove-studded hams. In the turquoise water, dead fish bobbed alongside refuse. Salt-ladened air tingled her skin and tantalized her mind about the far places from which the wind had come. Caged cockatoos and rosellas plumed in gaudy reds and greens shrieked among the overflowing fruit stalls.

Determinedly she put away the sight of the silent caged men just off the convict ship and began to shoulder her way through the people of every color and race who thronged the wharves.

Then she realized Celeste wasn't with her. She spun around, her gaze darting from the water's edge to the ships and back to the stalls and shops. In front of the parrot cages stood Celeste, her little mouth open in awe. Amaris grabbed her hand. "Come on, we don't have long."

"It talks. The bird talks."

"No telling what all it says."

"Your legs are too long."

"I doubt it says that."

Celeste doubled her steps. "No, *your* legs are too long. I can't keep up."

She shortened her stride. "Don't you want to see the Rocks?"

Its name was well deserved as the rowdiest and most dangerous thieves' kitchen in the colony. The two girls strode through it with innocent impunity, oblivious to the stares.

Nantucket whalers, Chinese traders, Portuguese sailors, and the jetsam of Australia's five thousand souls vied for the charms of doxies. They dressed in remnants of British finery donned with disregard to color, pattern, or material. Frayed plumes, shabby satins, and battered chapeaus were flashed in enticing movements designed to catch the eye of prospective customers.

"Oh, they're beautiful," Celeste whispered.

"They're whores."

"What's that?"

She decided that Pulykara's explanation would not do for a seven-year-old. "Whores are women who take money to make men happy."

"Oh. Could we make money making people happy? I think that would be ever so nice."

"Not the way they do."

"How do they do it?"

"You ask too many questions, Celeste. There it is, what I wanted you to see."

Celeste halted alongside her and stared at the monkey and the street musician. An enthralled smile played across her cherubic face. "Oh, Amaris! A real capuchin."

"A what?"

"The monkey is a capuchin. My tutor has a drawing of one."

Amaris's education at William Wilmot's knee was less eclectic and more philosophically oriented. That a five-year-old should know more than she dampened her spirits. "Well, 'tis time we started back afore you're missed."

"What about you?"

"Pulykara thinks I am—"

The rest of her words never reached her tongue as she stumbled on her trailing strip of tattered petticoat and went sprawling. The wharf's wooden platform scraped her palms with splinters. Hands beneath her armpits hauled her to her feet. "Thank—" She looked up into eyes that were as blue—and empty—as a summer sky. Shivering, she staggered backward.

"A colleen who dresses like a wharf doxie should know how to walk like one," was the rough-voiced reply.

The straggly haired convict wore no shirt, and scars that were still fresh pink crisscrossed the taut and sallow skin of his prominent ribs and shoulders. He was skeletally thin. Chains shackled his ankles. His stench overwhelmed her, and she wrinkled her nose reflexively. "A man who is chained like a slave should know when to speak."

For a moment, the creature's eyes lost their eons-old look and flashed with that youthful resource, fury. Amaris stared back, snared by the power of the dark soul encased in the thin body.

The overseer's whip cracked, and his lash curled around the convict's left shoulder. Instantly, the glare in the convict's eyes was obliterated, replaced by pain. The glare, but not the inner power. His body jerked as the whip popped again in a backlash release.

"Get your bloody Irish carcass back in line, Tremayne."

"Oh, that horrid man!" Celeste said of the overseer. She turned to Amaris. "Do something, please!"

Amaris had to fight back displaying her surprise. Celeste clearly thought she could do anything. Her gaze returned to the convict. He shuffled back into line with the others, all who were fresh off the convict ship. A bloody stripe traced the path the lash had left. "Your mother and father hire convicts, Celeste. Talk to them."

By rights, Celeste Livingston should have been spoiled rotten. Her parents doted on her. But such a condition was impossible for her angelic temperament. She loved life and loved people and easily overlooked her mother's interfering ways that often put off some Sydneysiders.

Rose Wilmot stared from the neatly penned invitation to Amaris's bland expression. "Nan Livingston is inviting you to her daughter's tea party?"

Amaris shrugged. "I didn't know anything about it."

"Well, you must be on your best behavior, love. That wild streak in you that I adore, Nan Livingston just might abhor."

Amaris wanted to see the inside of a mansion; at the same time, she felt a little silly going to a seven-year-old's tea party.

Her curiosity won out, and she went to the tea party dressed in a made-over dress donated by none other than Nan Livingston herself. By the time Rose had plied her needle, the dress was indistinguishable from the one Nan had worn. True, it was a trifle small for Amaris, but as long as she didn't stretch or gambol about like a monkey, the seams wouldn't rip.

The Livingston house was a Georgian manor, imposing and out of place among the rural cottages and her father's rectory, skirting Sydney proper. As she waited for her knock to summon someone to the Livingstons' front door, she felt extremely uncomfortable and tugged on the hem of her bodice.

Behind her, Pulykara said, "Remember who you are—one of them Dream Time people. Don't be afraid of her."

"Celeste?"

"You know who, Miss Priss. You two are a lot alike."

Amaris almost hooted. "Me and Nan Livingston!"

A uniformed girl in black with a crisp white apron answered the door. Pug-nosed and freckled, the girl was not much older than she. Amaris gave her name and said, "I've come for Celeste Livingston's tea party."

Her fair hair straggling from beneath her mop cap, the girl curtseyed. "I'll tell the missus you're here."

So, she would finally get to meet the remarkable Mrs. Livingston. The woman had come to the shores a convict and was now a wealthy woman—and the formidable woman behind New South Wales Traders, Limited.

Amaris's curiosity was greater than any trepidation she had in meeting the imperious woman. Even though Amaris was well aware that she was at least as tall as Nan Livingston, judging by the cast-off clothing, Amaris hadn't expected the woman to appear so fragile.

She swept into the room with a rustle of puce crepe skirts. Her gaze flickered to Pulykara standing discreetly behind Amaris, then settled on Amaris to study her as intently as Amaris was her. Nan Livingston's brown hair was tugged back tightly into a netted chignon at her nape. Her thin face was heart shaped, her chin a mite too pointed.

The gray eyes scanned Amaris in return, doubtlessly finding fault in her wild black hair, and Amaris wished she hadn't unplatted it. Suddenly her feet and hands felt cloddish and clumsy, her dress inappropriate for her size and age. Worse, when every female in the colony strove for the fair skin that can only come from a sheltered life, her sun-browned skin was tantamount to evidence she was a former convict.

"It seems my daughter has taken a liking to you."

Amaris, copying Nan Livingston, folded her large hands calmly before her. Then, wincing at how unsightly they were, she quickly put them behind her. "It seems so."

"How did you two meet?"

"Celeste didn't tell you?"

"I'd like to hear it from you."

"We met at her birthday party."

"I don't recall you being on the guest list."

"I wasn't." Beneath the woman's basilisk gaze, Amaris felt compelled to elaborate but fought back the weakness.

At last, Nan Livingston said, "I see. Well, Celeste is out in the garden, awaiting your arrival. Molly will show you the way. If your aborigine woman will go to the kitchen, I'll see that she is given food and drink."

Amaris was too preoccupied noting the furnishings of the drawing room to pay any attention to the Livingston woman's and Pulykara's joint departure.

A marble bust stared out of vacant eyes at Amaris, and satyrs frolicked in a painting she was sure must be by some famous artist. She had too much pride to cross the parquet floor and read the signature.

The heavy red damask drapes and red floral-patterned carpet made the room seem too dark for her taste. She much preferred her bedroom's shuttered windows that were folded back each morning to let in the flood of endless sunlight and balmy air. Her parents' small house might be a building of irregular and crumbly bricks, fashioned by convicts, its walls not whitewashed clean, its roof only thatched. Yet, it possessed a personal warmth the stately mansion lacked.

"This way, miss," the uniformed girl said. "If you be needing anything, Molly Finn's me name." Her smile revealed bad teeth.

Amaris followed her along a corridor walled with more paintings interspersed with closed doors. After two right turns, the corridor ascended a short flight of stairs and emptied into the garden.

Sunlight temporarily blinded Amaris, then amidst the garden's lush greenery, Celeste was sprinting with arms thrown wide toward her. "Amaris!"

"So, are you going to serve tea?"

The little girl grasped her hand and drew her around an ell of the mansion to a grape arbor. "Look, Mama set it up. Come sit down, and I'll pour us a cup. Our cook prepared some crumpets. Mama never lets me have crumpets unless it's something special."

"Where are your other friends?" Amaris barely fit her Amazonian body into the painted-white wooden chair constructed for a child.

"You're the only one I wanted to invite. My friends are nice, but they're not all grown up like you—and brave. Me neither. Not yet anyway."

"Oh." She sat awkwardly as Celeste filled a porcelain cup.

Leafy shadows dappled the little round face. "The tea set is by Wedgwood." Celeste passed the cup to her. "Mama says she met the Wedgwood brothers."

She chattered on, and Amaris began to relax. Of the children her age, none were as educated as she, and at seven Celeste was a fountain of information that entertained her.

Celeste took a dainty sip, put down her cup and said, "Guess what? I persuaded Papa to hire that convict."

"What convict?"

"The one on the dock last week. Remember, he picked you up when you fell."

"An insolent man," she said, remembering with shame his mocking smirk.

"Sinclair Tremayne's his name. I made Papa promise not to use the whip on him, but then Papa never does on any of his workers at the shipyard."

"Your father's gentle, like you."

"Oh, yes, but it was Mama's idea. She said that a bottle of rum was more incentive to work than the lash."

"Your mother doesn't approve of me, I don't think."

"Oh, that's just Mama's way. She's really a nice woman."

Amaris didn't want to argue with the little girl, but

she could almost feel the woman's antagonism burning through her back.

Tom's skill in trade had brought affluence to the Livingston family, and Nan was knocking on the door of Sydney's upper society, although she chose to remain in the background. Eventually, the Exclusionists would trample each other to include her as one of them.

She trusted Tom's opinion. But not in this one matter. He didn't know all the facts. Pushing back the drapery, she peered out the window overlooking the grape arbor. "I'm against this girl coming here, Tom."

"Why? Celeste likes her well enough."

"There is something about her that needles me."

"It's because she is not from the right class, isn't it?"

"Partly. Partly because she acts too stubborn, too proud."

Sitting in the wingback chair, Tom laced his fingers over the slight paunch his stomach made. She often thought of Josiah and his rock-hard stomach. She missed him and occasionally regretted having sent him on his way. He knew too much. A mistake in judgment could lose her all she had worked for.

"Well, for once, Nan, I'm opposing you. You've picked all of Celeste's friends, and she and I both went along with you. But this time, you're going to let our daughter make a choice of her own."

8

Je voudrais un tas de—de—" Amaris abandoned her effort and threw up her hands. "I'll never use the French, Celeste. This is utterly—"

"*Non, non,*" Celeste's tutor remonstrated. The old convict, transported for book theft, wagged his finger beneath his bony nose and sniffed haughtily. "English is the language of shopkeepers, French the language of love. One day, if you ever become a lady, you will be grateful I insisted you practice.

"Now your turn, Mademoiselle Livingston."

"Oh, please, monsieur. Can we end the lessons for the day?"

The French tutor glanced at the mantel clock. "There are still ten minutes remaining, and your mother—"

The eleven-year-old girl broke in, saying, "Mama will not mind at all, I swear. And the dance master is waiting in the foyer."

"*Bon.* We resume next Friday."

When he had collected his hat and departed, Amaris sprawled on the settee, clasped her hands behind her head, and sighed. "I dislike the dancing master even more. His palms are sweaty and his breath smells of garlic."

Celeste settled at the sofa's other end. "He's only nervous. Mama makes him that way the days she comes in and watches."

Amaris felt the same way on those days. Well, not nervous, but she was certainly aware of the woman's obvious antagonism toward her. As for herself, she felt only a mild contempt for the materialistic woman.

Yet Amaris had to admit she was enjoying the fruits of this woman's labor: French and dancing lessons, family celebrations, outings to the new racetrack, the theater, and Hyde Park—all at Celeste's insistence that Amaris share her life and, of course, abetted by Celeste's father.

Regardless of the constraint between Nan Livingston and Amaris, the friendship between the two girls had only deepened over the last four years. It was impossible not to love Celeste, with her outpouring of love, but Amaris was also jealous at times.

At sixteen, she could justify the jealousy intellectually. After all, Celeste had everything—wealth, beauty, a doting family, friends, and the most enviable gift of all, her ability to see the best in everyone. Try though Amaris did, she couldn't explain away the dark torment inside herself.

The only real disagreement she and Celeste ever had was over Sinclair Tremayne, the Irish convict who had been working for the Livingstons for the past four years. Only the week before, Celeste had confessed to being infatuated with the convict from the first time she had seen him.

"I call him Sin, because there is something dangerously intriguing about him, don't you think?"

Amaris had stared at the precocious girl. "Dangerous maybe, but intriguing, no."

Her reply had been offhanded, when in fact she was disturbed by the convict. He was polite enough whenever their paths crossed, but his somber power threatened her where it reassured Celeste. "Besides, the convict is too old for you, Celeste."

"Not at all," she said in her grown-up tone. "Only twelve years. Papa is almost nine years older than Mama. Age doesn't make a difference."

At that moment, the new dancing master, turf hat in hand, entered the salon. As obsequious as the French tutor was pompous, Mr. Whitaker's claim to excelling in the art of dance was based solely on his mother's career as a dancer with the French opera.

"We begin early today, eh? In that case, shall we learn the steps to the quadrille?"

Celeste jumped to her feet. A smile of joy wreathed her mouth. "Then we will need a fourth!"

With that, she darted from the room before the startled dancing master could gainsay her. "Whatever can she be about?" he muttered. In distraction, the short, pudgy man fingered the brim of his hat, the shape of an inverted flowerpot.

"Most likely another homeless person or animal. She collects them and finds places for them." Amaris realized that Celeste had found a place for her, installing her as practically a member of the family.

Yawning, she rose and ambled over to the window. She drew back the curtains and let the sunlight nudge away the room's shadows. Open curtains annoyed Nan Livingston. The days she attended the girls' lessons, she would invariably cross the room and draw the curtains closed.

In the garden below, Amaris sighted Celeste with a reluctant Sin in tow. His large brown hand in hers, she tugged him toward the house. From his other hand dangled a hammer. He had been building a gazebo. "It appears our fourth will be Sinclair Tremayne," Amaris told the dancing master.

"Oh, my word, her mother will not like this."

"I think you are right." It suddenly occurred to Amaris that Celeste adored the convict because—like herself—he was so contrary to Celeste's sunny nature.

She burst into the salon, and even the sunlight seemed to pale beside her. "Now, we can practice properly!"

Behind her towered Sin. He wore homespun brown breeches and a coarsely woven kerseymere tunic. Little about the convict resembled the emaciated wretch Celeste had rescued from the chain gang on the wharf.

At twenty-three, his shoulders had broadened. Nourishing food had added pounds to his skeletal frame. Laboring in the sun had restored a healthy color to his flesh and a reddish sheen to his overly long, dark brown hair, clubbed with a leather thong at his nape.

The inner power of the man was still evident in a face that might have been termed homely. The cheekbones were flat, the nose too prominent and obviously broken sometime in the past, the thick brows sharply angled, the mouth long and the upper lip asymmetrical.

But, oh, the eyes. Fires burned there. The blue irises

burned as hot as the blue center of winter fires. Burning wild and powerful and threatening . . . and warming.

Celeste drew him forward. "We have partners now, Mr. Whitaker. Can we learn the quadrille steps, please?"

Mr. Whitaker bobbed his head. "Yes, of course, Miss Livingston."

"Sin, put the hammer down," the little girl told the convict.

Amusement curled one end of his mouth, but he laid the hammer on a secretary.

"If you will arrange yourselves opposite me and Miss Wilmot, we'll begin."

Amaris went to stand opposite her friend and the convict. Beside her, Mr. Whitaker was noticeably sweating. "Uh, if you'll place your hand in mine, Miss Wilmot, and if you'll take Miss Livingston's hand, uh, Mr. uh . . ." He clearly did not know how to address Sin.

His lips twitched derisively. "Tremayne. Mr. Sinclair Tremayne."

"Mr. Tremayne, yes. Well, on the count of four we step forward, forming an arch with our upraised hands. Think of it as a rose arbor, Miss Livingston."

Amaris stood opposite Sin. He was close enough for her to smell the odor of healthy sweat mixed with sunlight and fresh air. Without knowing why, she felt the urge to touch his neck, where the sunburnt skin was molded by muscled columns. His flesh would be warm, the pulse in his throat beating strongly with life. His mouth curled even higher at the one end. His thickly lashed eyes held a knowing look.

She swallowed hard. Her fingers fidgeted with the strings of her calico waist. Like Pulykara, he had some intuitive ability to read people's souls. Amaris resented his subtle divining of her less reputable thoughts. With a dismissive shrug, she turned her face away to focus her attention on whatever it was the dance master was instructing them to do.

". . . second count of eight, you will release your partner's hand, taking that of the person opposite you and march down the length of the room."

Reluctantly, she laid her hand in Sin's. His palm was rough with calluses. He was so big boned that, as tall as she was, she felt small for once. His maleness both tantalized and threatened her, and she was disgusted by both of her reactions. Her mouth flattened, her nose tilted, and she kept her distance—as far away as his grip would allow.

"Does me lack of eau de cologne bother you, mistress?" His voice was low and sardonic.

"Your lack of a bath does."

He clicked his tongue against his teeth. "Auk, a shame to subject a lady to such a distasteful and distressing situation. But then you are no lady. Not even a colleen. Only a coward."

She whirled on him, forgetting where she was. "A coward? You are an impertinent oaf who had best mind his manners!"

"Sin! Amaris!" Celeste pushed between them. Concern blighted her usually joyful smile. "Please don't fight. You two are my dearest friends."

The challenging mockery of his expression evaporated instantly to be replaced by gentle contrition. He bowed low before Celeste. "Me apologies for spoiling your day, little one."

Amaris could have exploded. The convict treated her with ill-mannered indifference and behaved toward Celeste as if the girl were a Mauri princess.

When he once again took Amaris's hand in his, a flush of fury heated her skin. She wanted to dig her nails into his broad palm, but her nails were too short and his palms too hard for her to render any pain. "Paddy!" she whispered, disgust lending the word the quality of an epithet.

In courtly steps that belied his rustic appearance, he returned her to the room's other end, where Nan stood watching from the doorway.

"I think that is enough practice for today," she said, her expression sealed as tightly as an Egyptian sarcophagus.

"But, Mama," Celeste said in bewilderment, "we're just getting started."

"Sinclair has the gazebo to finish building."

Sin inclined his head at Nan and, releasing Amaris's hand, strode from the room. He carried himself with the careless grace of an aristocrat, despite the mood of the savage that clung to him. The term Black Irish fit him well, Amaris thought.

She shifted her gaze back to Nan. The woman was no more pleased with him than she was with Amaris. Amaris's keen intuition perceived that for once Nan Livingston and she both had something in common. The Irish convict was a threat to both of them!

Yet Amaris at the inexperienced age of sixteen could not identify what kind of threat Sinclair Tremayne presented to either her or Nan.

". . . for my twelfth birthday. Come look!"

Amaris followed Celeste into the stables. Smelling of manure, they had been built by Sin that spring.

Since her clash with the convict last fall, she had not encountered him at the Livingston mansion. This was unusual because he worked more there than at the shipyard, if Celeste's random referral to the man was anything to judge by.

"He is absolutely the most beautiful animal in all of New South Wales!"

Amaris stared at the bare-chested man. He forked hay into a stall, and with each lift of the fork, his muscles rippled beneath the supple sun-toasted skin. Despite the white, puckered scars crisscrossing his back, he was a superb example of a magnificent animal. A mistreated animal.

She forced her attention back to Celeste, who stood in adoration before her birthday present from her parents, a chestnut mare of excellent confirmation. "Don't forget, Sin, you said you would teach me how to ride."

He paused in swinging the fork and looked over his shoulder. "I think your mother is intent on hiring a riding teacher, Celeste."

Celeste? So, the formal "Miss Celeste" had slipped now to the familiar "little one" and "Celeste." Amaris was piqued that the girl had not asked her to teach her how to ride. Of course, Amaris had learned on a nag of a horse rescued from the meat factory for use to pull the church collection cart. Nevertheless, must Celeste always defer to Sin?

"Can I take Misty for a walk?"

He speared the fork in the sawdust-layered earth and propped his forearm on the handle. "You'll have to ask your mother."

Overflowing with excitement, the girl sprinted out of the stables, forgetting both Amaris and Sin.

Without shifting his stance, he fixed Amaris with his hard blue eyes. They skimmed over her thin muslin bodice, and she was at once conscious of and mortified by her small breasts.

"I suppose your skill with horses comes from your days of horse thieving," she snapped.

His grin was slow in coming and as hard as his gaze. "I wasn't transported for horse thieving, but I will concede to a certain skill in horsemanship inbred in all true Irishmen. We are born in the saddle, you know." His voice possessed a deep quality and lyrical rhythm peculiar to street corner orators.

"What were you transported for?"

"Would it matter if I told you I was convicted of impersonating the king? Mad as a hatter, I am. No telling what I might do right now. It isn't safe being alone with me, you know."

She grew bolder, her words clipped by her sleeping anger. "I'm curious about something else, too. Last fall, you accused me of being a coward. I want to know what makes you think that?"

"You haven't forgotten that, eh?"

She stepped closer. Her hands clenched at her sides. The anger in her was fomenting. "What made you say that?"

"Well now, me curious student, either you're a female or a male. What's it going to be?"

She thumped her chest. "I am me."

"Which is?" he persisted.

"Me . . . me inside this body." With that realization, her confidence gained ground. "The outside trappings aren't important . . . not to me, anyway."

"Well spoken. But when you're as comfortable with the outside as you are the inside . . ." He paused, his eyes scanning her again. "When that happens, then you'll be a woman. A formidable woman."

She duplicated his dry smile. "I might place value on your comment, except I am told that, as a convict, you forget what sex you are and turn into mollies."

His hand tightened on the pitchfork. A muscle in his jaw ticked. "You'd best return to the house before I try to recreate the feeling of taking a woman beneath me."

His countenance was enough to make her chilled even on that hot and sultry December day. She managed an indifferent shrug and sauntered off. Her back could feel the sting of that fiery blue gaze.

Sinclair Tremayne had the Irish gift for nursing old wrongs. He had been a young Belfast law student whose ability as a speaker and a leader had led him to become involved with the United Irishmen. They fought for the same principles as the French revolutionaries had earlier.

Sin believed that no Irish Catholic could expect justice from English laws. Under the Popery Laws, no Catholic could sit in Parliament, vote, teach, or hold an army commission. The Catholics were disabled in property law, which was rewritten to break up Catholic estates and consolidate Protestant ones. Protestant estates could be left intact to eldest sons, but Catholic ones had to be split among all children. Thus Catholic landowning families degenerated into sharecropping ones within a generation or two.

Sin knew all about sharecropping. He was thirteen when his father had been forced to close their linen business because of the English overlords' trade embargoes on Irish linen export to America.

Sin's family had turned to planting. He and his four younger sisters and brothers knew nothing about growing potatoes. They learned. They learned about the dirt encrusted beneath their fingernails and the permanent stains on their hands, the needlelike pain along their spines from bending over twelve hours a day.

Potato rot Sin recognized instantly. The stench was something that to this day made his stomach muscles knot.

By being more frugal than any Scotsman could ever dream of being, Sin's parents managed to send him to college. By his second year, his family were no longer landowners. The bailiffs with their writs of eviction had installed new landlords in the ancestral home. Recalled to help the family sharecrop, Sin grew to hate the English landlords' bullying ways with their dogs and shillelaghs.

Those oaken cudgels struck him once too often. He rounded on the man, who was much larger and heavier. But Sin's anger generated inhuman power, and he pummeled the man with his own cudgel. If Sin's sister Lena hadn't stopped him, he would have killed the man.

As it was, Sin had to leave home and family. With another college student, he founded the Society of Irish Defenders. The Irish rebels made iron pikes on secret forges to attack English Tory soldiers and struck out at English informers by burning their homes.

In the end, musket was bound to prevail against pike. Sin was arrested and charged with treason. He was to be transported without trial. From the dock, Sin's mother and sister had wept as he was led aboard the transportation bark in chains. His public humiliation, his shame at leaving them defenseless, had burned his stomach raw.

The situation got no better. His ship had not carried the prisoners' records with it. So no one knew how long they had to serve in New South Wales or when they would be eligible for tickets-of-leave that were usually given after four years' good conduct.

He found his kind was unwelcome in the penal colony. The "specials," or educated Irish convicts "might contaminate the yeomanry with their seditious ideas," complained New South Wales's governor. The governor was most pleased to separate the specials, dispersing them to various outlying farms and stations.

Nearly flogged to death upon arrival in the penal colony for talking to Celeste and Amaris, Sin was sent to the mouth of the Hunter River, north of Sydney. There he'd hewn coal in a recently discovered seam. Guarded by starved, chained mastiffs, he subsisted on a diet scarcely above starvation itself.

He was already a skeleton, with flesh stretched across his bones so tightly it resembled parchment, when Tom Livingston located him. The amiable man had spent weeks searching for him, solely at the behest of his daughter.

If Sin could find it in his heart to love any English person, it would have to be that child. For him, Celeste Livingston was all that was good and kind in this world. She was radiant sunlight, an angel taking refuge in the spirit of a little girl.

His days working in the shipyard had been numbered, as more and more of his time had been diverted to service at the Livingston mansion. So much so that he had made himself indispensable. By the end of his fourth year in the Livingstons' service, he had actually been given a private cell of a room. It was wedged in the servants section of the house, that part that abutted the carriage house, Nan Livingston's newest vanity.

For this, he again had Celeste to thank. "It only makes sense," she had told her parents in that logical way of hers. "Anyone can drive a nail, but Sin can do so much more. He can be our handyman."

In the recessed shadows of the carriage house, he smiled wryly. A handyman! He didn't know a tinker's damn about the carriage trade, and here he was on his back under a landau, trying to figure out the best way to replace its broken axle.

"Mrs. Livingston wants you."

He slid out from beneath the carriage and sat up, his forearms propped on his knees, his grease-coated hands dangling between them. The Wilmot girl stood before him in the double doorway, as imperious as the Grand Dame Livingston herself. He hadn't seen Amaris in months. If it was possible, she had grown still taller. And had grown cabbages, as his mother had obliquely referred to his sister's breasts.

"How old are you?" he asked.

His question caught her off guard. She flushed, her betraying skin a dusky rose in the morning's early sunlight. She was almost pretty.

"Mrs. Livingston is waiting for you in her office."

Eighteen, he mentally tallied. And inexperienced. Her kind wouldn't know how to love a man. With her sharp tongue and rebellious nature, she should have been born Irish. She would be one of those women determined to have her own way, whatever price she and those with her had to pay.

He sighed, wiped his hands on the rag at his feet,

and rose to follow her. She walked with that free-swinging stride peculiar only to her. Her waist-length braids no longer bounced against her back but had been unplatted for her coal black hair to be gathered in a careless coil at her nape. Wayward strands coiled like moonvine tendrils along the long column of her neck.

Admittedly, her slender hips had a certain rhythmic sway that a man would find enticing. Except she was English. The colleens he occasionally bedded were usually Irish like Molly, who desperately wanted someone to take care of her. Amaris of the stormy gray eyes was one of those currency girls, second-generation Australian.

To put her in her place, he strode on past her and entered Nan Livingston's office without waiting to be announced. With Nan was a big lunker of a man with a ruddy complexion lined by the weather. He sat with one thigh perched on the edge of her desk. His face was vaguely familiar. He had the scent of salt and sea about him.

"I beg your pardon!" Nan snapped at Sin.

"You sent for me?"

She rose from behind her desk. Her sparse brows gathered like disturbed nesting wrens. "When I send for you, Sinclair, you will—"

"Josiah Wellesley," the big man said, sticking out his hand.

Sin stared at the large hand uncomprehendingly. Then, realizing the gesture for what it was, he made a short bow. "Sinclair Tremayne, sir, at your service."

"The Livingston family, as well as Jimmy Underwood, has been singing your praises."

Now Sin remembered him. The man had stopped

by occasionally to chat with Jimmy. The lad might be English, but he hated the English government almost as much as Sin did. Sin missed the camaraderie he had known in the shipyard. "Do they now? *All* of the Livingstons?"

Josiah grinned. "Well, most of them. Now, Nan, why don't you tell Sinclair why you sent for him so you and I can get back to business."

The middle-aged woman flashed the man a reproving glare. "Celeste has her heart set on riding over to Parramatta for the horse sale. She wants a horse for hunting. As some business has come up, I want you to accompany her and Amaris there and back. Macarthur will accept my word of payment as good as a draft, if Celeste settles on something suitable."

He inclined his head in acknowledgment, paused, then said what was on his mind. "I would like to request a firearm, mistress. There has been talk of bushrangers plying their trade along uninhabited stretches of the road."

Her hazel eyes drilled through him. "Convicts aren't allowed firearms."

"For Celeste's security, I would suggest you arm me."

She was silent, considering the consequences, and he said, "If I wanted to strike out for the Never-Never, the firearm would not be one of the more important factors."

She raised a sparse brow. "Really, now. What would?"

"The season for one. Road traffic. Whether the governor is in residence at his summer retreat. My own physical condition."

Then he leaned forward, his hand splayed on her desktop, an impertinent act. "I swear that regardless of how favorable the conditions may be for escape, I would never put your daughter's life at risk by deserting her."

"Perhaps you should assign him to Celeste on a permanent basis, Nan," Josiah said with a broad smile. "You would ensure the continued faithfulness of your servant."

Without taking her gaze off Sin, she said, "A servant's papers are easy enough to buy, Josiah . . . and sell, if one becomes impudent. You may saddle Mr. Livingston's bay for your use, Sinclair."

She paused deliberately, then added, "His pistol is in the holster on his bedroom armchair. Take it with you when you accompany Celeste and Amaris. And then return it."

He inclined his head. "Good day, Miss Livingston . . . Mr. Wellesley."

"Josiah, lad," the man corrected as Sin closed the door behind him.

Celeste was waiting outside for him. She grabbed his hand. "Did Mama say you could take us, Sin?"

Her enthusiasm drew a smile from him. "Go get ready. I'll meet you at the stables in half an hour."

By the time he had made full preparation for the day's outing, both girls were waiting, their horses saddled. Celeste's expression was full of exuberance. Amaris's was sullen, stating clearly that his presence spoiled the day for her.

His father had teasingly called him mule-headed, and he felt mule-headed enough at that moment to justify the girl's feelings. He clasped his hands for Celeste's booted foot and hoisted her into the saddle.

"Thank you, Sin." A cheerful smile accompanied her words.

He turned to saddle the bay, leaving Amaris to mount her horse, which to her was inconsequential. With her height and skill, she would give an Irish jockey a run for his money. Still, Sin's action was distinctly discourteous. He smiled to himself, thinking how much amusement thwarting the missionary's daughter afforded him.

The morning promised to turn into a beautiful day. Sunlight gilded the land. Some twenty kilometers from Sydney Harbor, Parramatta was almost a suburb. Only a few farms remained to remind newcomers that the stretch between Sydney and Parramatta had once been an agricultural area.

The feel of the sturdy animal beneath him, obeying his body's signals, the fresh air and open countryside tempted him sorely. He knew he could survive in that isolated region that was known as Never-Never. No one could ever find him out there beyond the Blue Mountains.

But first, he had to cross that formidable mountain barrier crouched ahead of them. The mountains got their name because of their blue haze, a result of the fine mist of oil given off by the eucalyptus trees.

In earlier days, the few escaped convicts and adventurers who had attempted to transverse those rugged mountains had ended up practicing cannibalism to survive. Sin shut a mental gate on that ever present desire for freedom and chatted with Celeste. She rode alongside him, with Amaris bringing up the rear.

"Is Ireland really as green as an emerald?"

"As green as moon cheese."

She laughed. "As green as Mama's pea soup?"

"As green as Amaris's eyes."

Really gray, her eyes only looked green in certain slants of sunlight. He was interested in what kind of response the Wilmot girl would make, and he wasn't disappointed.

From behind him came her cool voice. "Is it true the Irish are full of—of—"

"Blarney?" Celeste supplied.

"Earbashing." Amaris finished.

The bush was always interesting, never boring or monotonous. Here he was forced to look beyond the first impression to observe detail, to train his eye to pick out the subtlety. The rich beauty of Ireland was too brazen compared to this much older landscape.

The marvelous saltbush plains were dotted with gray and magnificent red kangaroo, some grazing by the side of the dusty road. They scratched themselves, watching, ears twitching.

Later, mobs of emus ran swiftly and stupidly with no sense of direction. Wedge-tailed eagles, two pairs, soared in the sky high above. Glorious flight so free.

So free.

Eventually the wastelands gave way to richer countryside and small farms owned by Emancipists. John Macarthur owned Elizabeth Farm, named after his wife. Their house was something of a Georgian/colonial mishmash but large enough to be impressive to the commoner.

Today, everyone had come to attend the horse sale, some from as far away as Cow Pastures and Camden. All the visitors had gathered around the main corral. Sin shouldered a path for Celeste and Amaris, so they could better watch the event, already in progress.

Celeste climbed on the bottom railing to watch the next horse paraded out by a little man in red livery. A mustachioed old man and plump little woman appeared to recognize Celeste and began discoursing. Protective and concerned, Sin positioned himself closer to Celeste.

Startled, the girl glanced up, then grinned. "Sin, this is Mr. Barnaby and his wife. Mr. Barnaby is our banker."

Noting the deplorable state of Sin's only jacket, a threadbare worsted item of clothing belonging to a former servant, the old man nodded condescendingly. The woman barely acknowledged him.

Their pompous attitude bothered him little. In fact, reflecting that it would be the banker who would eventually have to approve Celeste's selection for draft on his bank, he relaxed.

He concentrated on the horse being led around the ring. The mare was well formed, with a deep-barreled chest, straight legs, and a good slope to the shoulders.

"She's got a glossy coat, doesn't she?" Celeste said. "Can we get her?"

"'Tis up to you. Your mother said that you were to decide which . . ."

His words trailed away as he watched the horse move, too slow for such a young one. The mare walked as if her hooves were sore. "No, I don't think this one, Celeste. I'd wager someone has ridden the mare hard for a couple of days so it would be too tired to show its true nature. You don't want to be buying a 'throwing' horse."

Celeste's large brown eyes shadowed with disappointment, then just as quickly cleared to watch in absorption the next horse led into the corral.

An uneasiness assailed Sin. Amaris was missing.

He scanned the crowd. The girl was old enough to take care of herself. Servant gossip implied that Nan Livingston wouldn't be disappointed if Amaris never showed her face around the place again. Yet he felt responsible.

"Celeste, where did Amaris go?"

The girl looked up in amazement. "I didn't see her leave, Sin."

He let out an exasperated sigh. He hated to take Celeste away from the fun of the action. Hell! When he found Amaris . . .

"Mr. and Mrs. Barnaby, would you mind watching Miss Livingston for a moment?"

The gray mustache lifted in a perfunctory smile. "Not at all, Tremayne. I trust you won't be gone any longer than it would take to gain your freedom?"

He looked the man directly in the eye. "I don't think you need that reassurance. I'm here precisely because Mrs. Livingston trusts me not to escape."

Mr. Barnaby looked skeptical, and his wife interjected, "We'll watch Celeste."

After telling Celeste he had something to check on, he struck out in long, rapid strides for the picket area, where he had hitched their horses. Amaris was not there. Damn her! Where could she have wandered?

His boots thudded on the encircling veranda of the Macarthur house and he knocked on the door to inquire of the dowdy housekeeper if a young woman had entered.

"Not to me knowledge," the woman said, "but you might try the tent erected for repast after the auction."

Amaris wasn't there either, although the table

spread with kidney pie, mutton, and at least half a dozen different meat dishes tempted his hungry stomach. Concern drove him on past the tent toward the various outbuildings, sheds, and barns.

A quarter of an hour later he found Amaris behind the sheep barn. She knelt over a ragged-looking puppy that had the wild look of the dingo about it.

"What in the hell are you doing?" he demanded.

She sprung up and whirled around, her expression startled. When she saw that it was he, annoyance replaced her momentary dismay. Her almond-shaped eyes narrowed to slits. "Oh, 'tis just you."

Anger roiled through him. His hands gripped her upper arms. "Do not ever take for granted the saying that Irishmen are wild and lawless."

Nonplussed, she stared at him. Without thinking, he bent his head and kissed her open mouth. He felt her stiffen beneath his hands and realized instantly what folly he had committed. Where such desire had come from, he couldn't fathom, but he knew he didn't want to serve an additional fourteen years for forcing himself on an unwanting maiden.

He set her from him and watched her wipe his kiss from her mouth with the back of her hand.

His smile was grim. "I didn't think you were enough woman to appreciate that." He turned his back on her before she could retort with that sharp tongue of hers. Over his shoulder, he said, "Get back to the auction before I decide to take you in the hay here and now."

He strode on out into the sunlight with her curse of "Paddy!" tingling his ears.

9

"*Proper young women* don't go without petticoats, Amaris."

"Proper young women don't wear secondhand petticoats donated by the prostitutes of Brigsby Pub."

Rose Wilmot's face blanched, and Amaris was instantly contrite. "I'm sorry, Mama. I just don't want to—"

"Stand still, gal," Pulykara said. The wrinkles around her mouth undulated her once arrow-straight facial tattoos. With bare feet splayed, she squatted on her haunches before Amaris and stuck pins in the ruffled material to mark a long hem.

"Stand straight, luv," Rose said.

"—go to the Livingston dance," she continued, "because not only am I too tall, I am too old."

Rogue, the half-dingo stray she had insisted on carting back from Elizabeth Farm two years before, darted in and out beneath her ruffled hem.

Avoiding the playful dog, Rose stepped back to

observe the new hem length. The first hints of gray tinted the hair at her temples, and her once elfin frame was softened by middle-age weight. "Twenty isn't too old, and if a man loves you, he will ignore your height."

"Mother, I don't want a husband. Nan Livingston does. She's matchmaking for her daughter."

"Turn around," Pulykara grunted.

"Who does Nan have her eye on?"

Amaris turned and faced the open shutters. Across the street a drunk staggered from the George IV pub, the first grog shop to set up trade in what had been a largely rural district. Beyond, she could make out the Livingstons' red-bricked, turreted house on Darlinghurst Road. "Francis Marlborough."

Rose pushed back a lock that had fallen over her forehead. Hard work had etched her once-girlish face but not her champagne-fizzy personality. "An earl's son most likely."

"No, but the prime minister's nephew. Celeste says that although the law of entail has debarred him from inheritance, his prospects are excellent."

Not that his financial status was important to Celeste, or Nan Livingston for that matter. Nan had money. She wanted connections.

Francis Marlborough definitely had connections. Not only was he the prime minister's nephew, but his brother-in-law was Lord Hallock, vice admiral. Francis had made the grand tour of Europe the year before.

When Celeste, standing in the receiving line, offered him her hand, he made a leg and lowered his head to kiss her fingertips with all the grace of royalty.

Observing him from her vantage point slightly behind Celeste, Amaris found the man intriguing. Beneath the effete mannerism of the aristocrat ran a current of confident masculinity. For just a moment, his gaze brushed hers. The brown eyes twinkled. Then he moved on.

Curious about what made one a blueblood, Amaris continued to observe and listen to Francis. He engaged Sydney's prominent denizens one by one in what seemed to be fascinating conversation, because both male and female guests appeared disinclined to leave his presence. A suggestion of a smile invited the privileged recipient to partake of the man's warm and worldly charm. His manners were exquisitely and unfailingly courteous. He had a habit of tilting his head slightly to the side and forward, as if engrossed in his companion of the moment. His curling fair hair and lively walnut brown eyes only added to his appeal.

The women smiled coyly or giggled shyly. The men solicited his opinion about such a variety of subjects that Francis had to be a veritable Renaissance man to be so knowledgeable.

Soon the doors to the ballroom were thrown open and hired musicians began to play a minuet. Francis began his enchantment of one after another of the ladies, but Celeste Livingston in particular was singled out.

Amaris watched the dancing from the vantage point of a wallflower. At sixteen, Celeste had received at least half a dozen proposals, while at twenty Amaris had received only one. In the journal she kept, she made a notation that she suspected her outspoken manner and strong will had put off any would-be suitors.

A lusty sea trader with his tales of adventure mildly interested her for a while. His fumbled kiss that missed her mouth was the only romantic overtone in her life, unless she counted that bold kiss Sin had given her. But then at eighteen she had been inexperienced.

Her gaze moved over the resilient strong-willed women in old silks dancing beneath crystal chandeliers with tough and ambitious men. They signaled that Sydney society, though a child Europe had rejected, was nevertheless the best of Europe's offspring. Amaris felt a kinship with these visionary people, and yet felt an outsider.

At midnight, after the last minuet was played, the doors were thrown open to the dining room, and the guests paired off, with Celeste and the guest of honor leading the grand march. Francis Marlborough might be a charmer, certainly as irresistibly cocky as an Australian cockatoo, but his partner was clearly charming him at the moment. Her brown eyes sparkled, her cupid bow-shaped lips laughed.

Amaris melted farther back into the shadows of the staircase. She really had no desire to eat or make polite chatter. By the time Molly closed the dining-room doors, Amaris was already slipping out the garden door. She was to have spent the night at the Livingstons', but, as often happened, she felt the need to be alone.

Her parents' tiny, impoverished home beckoned, and she started along the moonlit, pebbled carriage drive. Careful to preserve the dress Pulykara and her mother had labored over, she picked up the ruffled hem of her blue satin skirt.

She was not at all afraid to walk the darkened

cobblestone street. The Wilmot family members, including Pulykara, wore an invisible shield of protection. This was due to the respect the clergyman's family had earned by its work among the jetsam of humanity crowded into the rabbit warrens down in the Rocks. No one would be foolish enough to lift a hand against a Wilmot.

No one but the lean-eyed ex-convict who lounged in tree-dappled shadows at the end of the drive. "Time for Cinderella to hurry home to her hearth?"

She stiffened. "Sin?"

"Certainly not Prince Charming."

"Certainly not. He's inside courting Celeste."

She moved close, lured by her insatiable curiosity. "Are you jealous?"

"Are you?"

She could smell rum on his breath. "You're drunk."

In the darkness, his smile gleamed white. "No. I'm drinking but not yet drunk." He held up a brown bottle. "Rum—the real currency and social anesthetic of New South Wales." Then, with a vicious whack he smashed the bottle against the tree trunk.

The following instant, she winced at the sharp sensation on her cheek. Her fingers flew to her face and came away scarlet-tipped.

"What is it?" Sin flung away the neck of the broken bottle to stride toward her.

"I'm cut." Surprised more than hurt, she stared at the blood.

His fingers cupped her cheek and tilted her head toward the moonlight.

"I'm all right."

"The cut needs attention. Come on."

He tugged her along behind him, but she soon caught up. "I can take care of myself."

He ignored her and strode on—toward his room, she soon discovered.

At the threshold, she yanked her hand away. "I can't go in there."

His laughter rent the deep serenity of the night. "Since when have you ever observed propriety?"

"Sin, stop this."

Inside, he released her. There came the sound of flint rasping against tinder. Soft candlelight spread a glow over the room, mellowing its harsh austerity. In two strides, he crossed the room's narrow confines and poured water from a pitcher into a chipped basin. From a peg, he removed a frayed towel to dip in the water. He turned to her. "Come here, Amaris."

She stared back at him. The candlelight muted his harsh features. Still, he looked every year his twenty-seven. Bitterness carved a hard line to his mouth. That mouth had possessed hers once, and recalling that kiss, she recoiled. That moment was the closest she had come in her brief span of twenty years to losing her sense of will. "No."

His smoky gaze held hers. "Don't be a child. You know I won't hurt you."

"No, I don't know that."

He canted his head. "Why not?"

"You kissed me once."

"And that hurt you?"

She paused. "You didn't ask my permission. That's as painful as a lash across your back—having no choice is."

His mouth lost the one-sided curve of its smile. His rugged visage took on what her mother called that Irish black look. "You be right," he said at last. "'Tis an apology I owe you."

Even as he talked, he moved toward her, like a stockman gentling a wild horse. "I know that feeling. Of having no choice. Ah, but that's a nasty cut now." He stopped only inches away and, without touching her otherwise, gingerly dabbed at the cut. "Of course, we fighting Irish have seen worse. Now hold still while I pluck out the glass sliver."

His thumb and forefinger cupped her chin and tilted her head. With someone standing so close, his face so near, it was impossible to focus properly. She closed her eyes, which made her vitally aware of his scent, his gentle touch, his warm, even breath. Then a tiny prick of pain made her twitch. Her eyes flew open. "Ohh!"

He grinned, and she was struck by the change in his looks. The fierce countenance was gone. His eyes danced with a vibrancy that was compelling. "I think an old Irish remedy will help." He crossed to a battered seaman's chest and took out a jar. "Axle grease, but it will lessen the scarring."

With slow, patient strokes that said he had all the time in eternity, he applied the unguent. She stood motionless, savoring the pleasant feeling of being cared for—and yet feeling uneasy.

His fingertip stopped its stroking. "I'm that terrifying."

She couldn't meet his eyes. "I don't know what you are talking about."

"Yes, you do. You're trembling. And it's not because you're cold."

"You make me nervous."

"I told you I wouldn't kiss you again. Unless you want me to."

She shrank back. "No!"

One angled brow soared. "So, 'tis not fear you feel but loathing. Tell me, do you loathe me because I am Irish or because I have not the handsome features of your Francis Marlborough?"

"He's not my Francis Marlborough. He's Celeste's."

He stared steadily into her eyes. "You did not answer me. Which is it?"

"Both," she blurted. She was anxious to be gone yet hated her cowardice at the same time.

That the gentle Celeste was unafraid of this man amazed her. She thought of all the barbarous men who frequented or lived in the Rocks. They were unconscionable in their treatment of women. She shuddered at the memories of how often she had seen the females—wives, mistresses, daughters even—battered by men. Like Celeste, Rose accepted these men, loving them despite their brutality.

"Well, you are at least honest. I can rest assured me ego will not inflate me head."

"Are you finished … tending my cut?"

"Tending your cut, aye. But not finished lecturing. You are a user, Amaris. You trade on Celeste's fondness for you so that you can ride the coattails of Sydney society. You'll never—"

"I do not! 'Tis Celeste who seeks me out!"

"—be accepted."

She stepped away and faced him, hands braced on her hips. "Why not? Nan Livingston is an ex-convict. And Sydney accepted her."

"They accepted her money."

"They'll accept me—and on my terms, Sinclair Tremayne."

His mouth twitched with a repressed smile that his fierce gaze belied. "I'll be watching over your shoulder. I don't want Celeste hurt."

When Amaris peered into a looking glass, the scar on her cheekbone, though paling with time, was visible enough to remind her of Sin's warning.

Perhaps that was why she stayed away from the Livingstons over the successive months. Celeste's time was being dominated by Francis, so the girl did not have the opportunity to miss her friend.

In turn, Amaris now had more time to devote to a project that was bringing her a great deal of satisfaction: writing. Once she had helped Rose collect and distribute clothing and food, the rest of the afternoon was hers. In that land of male dominance, Amaris's restless intellect drove her to champion her sex.

One afternoon, as she sat writing at the dining table, her father joined her to begin his own writing, his Sunday sermon. "Want a cup of tea, Papa?"

His eyes, surrounded by a netting of wrinkles, twinkled. "No, but I would like a peek at what you're writing."

She picked up the stack of papers lined with her neat penmanship and held them close against her chest. "Never," she laughed. "You would definitely not approve."

"Why not?"

She stared him straight in the eye. The subject was one they never discussed. "For one, I advocate less breeding."

A blush suffused his face and climbed upward to the line of his receding hair.

"See, you are shocked. But why, Papa? How can you turn a blind eye to what excessive childbearing does to the women who live in the Rocks? They are carrying a child on each hip and one in the belly and all the while the women's bodies are succumbing to all sorts of diseases from being weakened by childbearing."

He opened his mouth, as if to refute her, closed it, then said, "And there is more?" His hand gestured at her manuscript. "More such scandalous subjects?"

She smiled. "Yes. Remember Annie O'Malley? The washerwoman who left her husband?"

"A pathetic woman. She had been fetching until she turned to the bottle."

"Papa, she turned to the bottle because the judge gave her children to her husband! Don't you find it scandalous that a wife has no legal claim to her children? Yet a mistress's rights as mother are secure—because the *wife,* unlike the mistress, is the man's property."

He bowed his head, then peered up at her with a rueful smile. "'Tis a shame women aren't barristers, because you would have made a fine one, Amaris."

That was what she loved about her father, that he accepted her as she was and did not demand she conform to his religious idea of propriety.

"Yes, it *is* a shame that women aren't barristers," she said, her eyes alight with having made her point. "However, 'tis not a barrister I want to be. I want to be a writer. No London publisher will touch my material."

"London is staid and set in its ways. Why not try America? 'Tis as rebellious as you are."

"You truly think I am? Rebellious? Have I been that difficult for you?"

He smiled at her fondly and covered her hand with his veined one. "You've been a blessing. Although your adventures to the wharves occasionally made Rose and me feel like Job, unsure of God's intentions."

"So you know about them? I really didn't sneak out that often. Maybe half a dozen times."

He squeezed her hand. "Amaris, I'm not reproving you. About you sneaking out or your writing. I don't understand you or it, but I trust you. Do what you have to."

She did.

She reworked her manuscript and sent it to a publisher in Boston. Then she put her literary efforts from her mind. Yet, she was restless. She dallied with her poetry, grew bored, and realized she wanted a diversion that wasn't sedentary.

She found it that fall during one of her excursions to the wharves. By now, its riffraff, as Nan Livingston termed the wharves' denizens, knew Amaris on a familiar basis. So they weren't surprised the afternoon she walked into one of the seedier pubs, a black-timbered and bottle-glass-windowed bastion of sailors and quay hands. She slid into one of the booths close to a window, so she could watch the cove activity.

"A sherry, dearie?" the frowsy maidservant taunted, not unkindly.

Amaris smoothed her skirts with ladylike motions, glanced up and said, "No, I'll have a pint o'porter."

Her wide-brim hat lent her a certain privacy. Some of the customers, all male, of course, glanced at her and returned to their bawdy conversations. Others called a greeting. All politely left her alone. Had there been any drunk to bother her, he would have been summarily tossed over the edge of the quay.

Sipping her drink, she watched as a dozen females were discharged from a lighter, a small vessel used for transferring from ship to dock all manner of freight, including convicts. More lighters were going and coming from the convict transport ship anchored in the cove. She observed the drabs put ashore with guards. They looked starved and cowed and stunned by the sudden swarming of randy male colonists. Even the pub's clientele, accustomed to such events, emptied to watch what was in actuality a slave market.

The men ogled the women and waited impatiently for the military officers to get first pick. Some of the women stood apathetically but others posed and flirted, tossing a shoulder, winking an eye, as they waited for the rivets to be knocked out of their irons upon the anvil.

Those who played coy knew what the other women didn't: that their fate depended upon being selected by a man. The alternative could be the female factory at Parramatta. There their heads were shaved and they were forced to wear spiked iron collars and work a treadmill. Usually, the women sent here were ugly, old, mad, or pregnant.

Most of these girls and young women, Amaris knew, had not been convicted of any crime but had been swept off the streets of London and Dublin.

Then they were taken from workhouses and slums and orphanages for one reason—to satisfy the sexually starved male colonists of Australia. Many of these women would be forced to seek prostitution when a soldier or settler tired of them or threw them out.

The scene that unfolded several times a year on the wharves was a bizarre one. The women lined up in their coarse flannel dresses, some scowling and others primping hopefully. The bachelors, often elderly and tongue-tied and from the back country, made their way along the line. Once a woman was selected, that was the conclusion to the colonial mating ritual.

One man in particular stopped to watch the spectacle—and Amaris watched him. He was of medium height, dressed in the latest fashion of tight pantaloons, blue riding coat, and Wellington boots. His presence commanded attention. Yet with all attention centered on the poor females huddled on the quay, he stood unnoticed. Except by Amaris.

Finishing the last of her pint o'porter, she gathered her pad and pencils and slipped out the shanty door to join the aristocrat. "Planning on buying yourself a woman?"

Francis Marlborough's head jerked around, and at the sight of her he grinned. "If I were, I would select a better market. I'm told the quays of Calais offer the most beautiful women in the world."

"But, of course, you've never had that opportunity to establish the rumor as fact."

He held up his palms. "I surrender. I'm guilty of lusting in my heart after the female sex." Under finely drawn brows, his brown eyes twinkled. "Now, let's turn the tables and let me question you. Just what are you doing down in the most unsavory part of Sydney?"

"I don't recall you told me what you were doing down here?"

He inclined his head in that way that made him seem most attentive. "Shall we both agree to table this issue and move on to something more pleasant?"

His mischievous grin brought a slight smile to her own lips. She understood at once why the females were attracted to him. "Aha, then you *are* guilty of soliciting a woman!"

"My dear girl, I am guilty of soliciting *for* a woman. Mrs. Livingston."

"What?"

"Now I have your complete attention. Before, on the times our paths have crossed, you appeared somewhat disinterested in the affairs at hand."

She wanted to be away from the sorry spectacle of the female convicts and began walking in the opposite direction. Francis Marlborough fell into step with her. "You are not to be let off that easily," she told him. "Explain your remark about Nan Livingston."

He tapped his cane on each successive wharf piling. "Merely that the woman has suggested we might find a partnership profitable. With my connections, I could set up an import/export trade with London."

Nan Livingston, Amaris knew, had long considered the mother country as a potential source of revenue that she intended to one day tap. Francis Marlborough could prove useful but certainly not a necessity. "And what is in it for you?"

He glanced around at her with a stunned expression. "Don't you play the harp or something?"

She caught at her shepherdess hat as the sea wind bandied its ribbons. "No, I try to think for the most part."

He laughed. "Well, my dear, you should know that most men find women who try to think an annoyance."

"Does that include women like Nan Livingston?" she prodded.

"I've confessed my reason for being at the Rocks. Now what is yours?"

She nodded at the pad and pencil she carried. "Observation."

"Yes, I have noticed you tend to observe more than participate. What are you observing? Those woebegone women back there?"

"Yes."

She kept walking, her gaze on the sea gulls prancing along the dock and looking for edibles, while she analyzed Francis's statement: she had become an observer.

Somehow, over the past five years, she had stepped back from Celeste and watched the younger girl emerge from her parents' protective cocoon to become an inquisitive partaker in life's experiences. At the moment, the girl was enjoying the pleasure of being courted.

For her part, Amaris would have found the proprieties of courtship tedious and without spontaneity. But then, since she had never been courted, she had little on which to base her opinion, other than observation.

Which was exactly her problem, as Francis had unwittingly pointed out.

"You are a deucedly odd young woman," he said, peering at her through long black lashes that any maiden would have envied.

They had begun climbing the cobbled road leading upward and out of the Rocks. "Why?" she teased. "Because I think?"

"It's what you think. Miss Livingston adores you. She tells me you are the daughter of missionaries, that you want to be a writer."

"I *am* a writer."

"I envy that—that you know what you are."

His expression was wistful, and without the cocky attitude, she decided she liked him even better. "You have all that a person could want. Good birth, breeding, financial resources, appearances."

"Legacies of my predecessors. I want to make my own mark on the world."

"So that's why you came to Australia?"

"Here I can do it. Everything, everyone, is starting afresh." His eyes were alight with enthusiasm. His words were charged with excitement. "The increase of commerce between Australia and the rest of the world has resulted in the Sydney merchants' need of protection. With the income I have accumulated from several rental properties and farms, I would like to create an insurance company that one day would rival Lloyds."

Gazing at him, she wondered at the sudden attraction she felt for Francis Marlborough. In the next instant, she wondered why she would ever want to suffer the pangs of love, when she owed no one her time or thoughts. She laughed aloud, and Francis stared at her as if she were even odder than he had imagined.

Francis Marlborough wasn't the only one who found Amaris Wilmot odd. Those who had heard of the young woman who distributed clothes and food along the Rocks's seedy streets attributed her unconventional behavior to her aborigine nanny. Maybe, after all, she was a changeling, as the stories ran.

When Amaris Wilmot sold her first book that following year, the news elicited only mild surprise.

When she donated a portion of her advance to the Female Immigrants' Home project implemented by her father's church, the consensus was that she was singularly odd. Was indeed odd!

"Why would you do such a thing, Amaris?"

Celeste's horse danced beneath her as she waited for the older girl to mount up. The stirrup's leather strap had broken, and Amaris was removing the saddle herself. "Why should I depend on Sin, when I can do it myself?"

"No, I mean why are you plowing all your time and more into that home?"

Amaris wasn't really sure herself. To help correct injustices? Then why wasn't her writing and her attendant projects more fulfilling? She met every ship of immigrants that came in. Single girls needed protection against the consequences of being in short supply. "Aren't you helping by making dresses for the newly arrived convicts at the Female Immigrants' Home?"

Celeste's smile deepened the dimples in her pink cheeks. "That's nothing. You are diving headlong into this project as feverishly as you did your writing."

"Look, here comes your fiancé."

Celeste glanced through the stable doorway. "Oh, Amaris, don't say things like that. I truly like Francis. He's kind and charming and utterly handsome—"

"And all the females in Sydney are dying for a glance from him."

"Aye."

"And your parents have their hearts set on him for a son-in-law."

"Only Mama," she laughed. "Father doesn't care, as long as I marry a 'good man.' Francis would marry me now instead of waiting a year if I were willing."

Then she waved a hand in greeting. "Francis! You're keeping us waiting, you rogue."

He approached Celeste's mare, took Celeste's hand, and dropped a kiss on its back. "An unforgivable sin to keep two beautiful ladies waiting. Where do we ride today?"

"To the park. Amaris says the swan eggs have hatched."

Celeste and Francis cantered their horses down the pebbled drive, and Amaris let her gelding fall behind. She knew that one of the reasons Nan continued to welcome her presence was that she served as the perfect chaperon: young enough not to damper an outing but old enough to provide a restraint on any potentially developing intimacy.

Francis's restraint was not due to a lack of passion. At times, Amaris would catch his gaze upon Celeste, and in his eyes burned an ardent desire for the young maiden. And why not?

Celeste was not only the only heir to a business empire, but she was also a comely young lady, whose face was redolent of the soft-brush-stroked women Reubens painted. Never an unkind word about anyone passed Celeste's lips. She was loved, and in turn she loved people and life itself.

Amaris felt guilty about her own less-than-decorous thoughts. Despicable ones they were at times. Her contempt for Nan, her dislike of Sin, her attraction to Francis, her envy for all that Celeste was . . .

Sometimes, Amaris half expected to peer into a looking glass and see sheer ugliness reflected as a projection of her inner self.

She saw only plainness.

10

"You're looking peaked, Amaris."

"Just haven't been getting any fresh air, Father." She scribbled the last line of the paragraph and, putting aside her pen, looked up at her father. "You don't look too sprightly yourself," she teased.

The spindly rector pulled out a chair and sat down at the kitchen table. Rogue, the half-dingo/half-kelpie puppy she had rescued at Elizabeth Farm, stirred long enough to wag his scraggly tail and growl. "Old age does that to you. You don't have that excuse. You are running yourself ragged between the writing and working at the home."

Which was how she wanted it; that way she had little time left to expend on confused and frustrated longings for an answer to some secret, which she wasn't even quite sure existed. "You and Mother spend as much time at the home as I do."

"Aye, but you are young and should be being courted."

"Well, I'm late as it is. I told Mother that Pulykara and I would be at the home by the noon hour."

"Must you, in this weather?"

"As if you ever refused to go out to administer to a parishioner because of inclement weather!" She rose, kissed her father's bald head and, gathering her writing paraphernalia, hurried up to her loft bedroom to change clothing.

Her work at the Female Immigrants' Home consisted of finding employment for the girls and women who were recovering from malnutrition or abuse. Not that their employment there in Sydney guaranteed any better treatment. All Amaris could do was visually and mentally assess a situation when she inquired at either a place of business or a household about possible employment for a female.

For these occasions, Amaris dressed in a businesslike brown alpaca skirt, white blouse, and brown double-breasted morning coat. On that particularly blustery afternoon, she hurried toward the old tannery that now housed the female immigrants. August's cold wind whipped her coat about her. The winter had been a severe one, and she longed for January and summer.

The bay's gray water roiled and splashed over the wharves to lick at its rickety buildings and spray her with icy showers. Pinchgut Island wasn't even visible. Leaning into the wind, she held on to her hat. She hugged close to the shanties' walls, which turned out to be as perilous as being swept off the wharf.

A door swung open, hitting her. She staggered and clutched at a man's greatcoat to keep from falling.

"Amaris, what are you doing here?"

She looked up into Francis's handsome face. "I

might ask the same of you." The establishment he had just left was one of the more disreputable grog shops in the Rocks.

"Let's walk," he said, taking her elbow.

"I really can't, Francis. I have to—"

"I need a friend right now."

His color was high, probably from drinking, and she could smell the heavy odor of liquor on him. "All right then."

She fell into step with him. The wind whistled around them, enforcing a silence she did not attempt to break. When Francis wanted to talk, he would.

Eventually, he did, and it wasn't about Celeste, as Amaris had anticipated.

"I've lost my investment in High Seas Insurers."

"Oh, Francis! How?"

"This bloody bad weather. We lost four ships off the Cape and two more sustained heavy damage in the North Sea. Another floundered off the coral reef. My solicitor wrote that the company is virtually bankrupt."

"Will your personal finances sustain you?"

"Oh, sure. And the partnership with Nan Livingston is on solid ground." He whacked the tip of his cane against a mooring. "'Tis just that I am dogged by bad luck."

A high wave slammed against the wharf, sluicing them both. "You're a fool, Francis Marlborough, if you think that." Her mouth tightened. "Let me take you to the Female Immigrants' Home. Those women know bad luck."

He shot her a sideways glance. "You are a consoling person."

She laughed. "I am truthful. What better friend than a truthful one?"

He stopped to face her. Her woolen scarf whipped back and forth against the two of them. "I want more than the truth. I want you to plead my side to Celeste. I want her hand in marriage."

"I don't consider it necessary I plead your side. Mrs. Livingston favors you and that's enough."

He grimaced. "A pope's blessing could be no more beneficial. Mrs. Livingston is ready to publish the banns. Still, I would like to enlist you on my side."

"Celeste knows her own mind. I won't attempt to change it for her."

With a heavy sigh, he bid Amaris good day, and she continued on her way to the home. As it turned out, Celeste was waiting for her in the front office that was partitioned off from the tannery shop by a wall woven of bamboo. Candlelight from the single sconce fell on her face and cast shadows beneath eyes that obviously had had little sleep recently.

"Celeste," she said, crossing to the wobbly chair in which her friend sat, "what are you doing here alone?"

"Pulykara let me in." Celeste withdrew a small hand from the beaver muff. "Oh, Amaris, you must help me."

She almost laughed. "What am I today? An angel of mercy?" She struggled out of her wet jacket.

"Aye." Celeste's hand, clutching hers, was cold, despite having been nestled in the fur muff. "'Tis Mama."

"Isn't it always." From behind the bamboo wall came the cough of a sick woman and Pulykara's rough/soft voice bidding the woman to drink the medicine, undoubtedly some aborigine concoction. Amaris swore the potion's taste had often made her sicker than her malady.

"Mama won't delay any longer. She wants me to wed Francis this spring."

Amaris took a seat behind the desk, a renovated shipping crate. "What makes you think I can do anything?"

"You're the only one who doesn't quail before her. Please, Amaris." Celeste's eyes were large and imploring.

"Why not do as your mother wants? Francis is a good catch."

Celeste rose to her feet. For such a short person, she appeared as regal as Queen Victoria. From outside, the blustering of the wind almost drowned out her next words. "Because I'm in love with Sin, that's why."

"Celeste! You can't still be infatuated with him. I could understand that when you were a child, but you're nearing twenty."

"I'll be seventy and still loving him."

"He's twelve years older than you. He's a convict. He's Ir—"

"No, he's not." Her lips curved in a rapturous smile. "Sin's a free man."

"What?"

"He's served more than his ten-year term. Papa has arranged for him to be pardoned."

"Celeste . . . has Sin ever kissed you?"

Celeste blushed, glanced down at her muff, then said, "You might say so."

"Well? Yes or no?"

"I kissed him. At least, at first."

She couldn't help herself. "What was it like?"

Celeste's eyes closed. "Soft. Warm. Tender. Happiness so much I couldn't stand it."

Her stomach knotted. "Has Sin said he loves you?"

The girl's eyes opened. Her smile faded. She shook her head. "No."

She rubbed her forehead. Behind her, she could hear the immigrant woman's racking cough again. Lizzie Johnson and her daughter had been transported for theft of five potatoes. Her daughter had died the week before the ship had put into Sydney Bay. "You are under age, Celeste. Your mother can make you."

"I won't. I'll wait. If Sin won't marry me, I won't marry at all."

"Does your mother know how you feel about Sin? A foolish question, because little escapes her eye."

"Mama says that anyone who marries Sin is courting disaster. If she thinks to influence me, she's wrong. Well? Will you speak with Mama?"

"I have to agree with your mother. At least, on this point."

Celeste stared back at her with steady determination. "I'm not asking your opinion, Amaris. Only your help."

"All right." She held up her hands. "All right, I will, for all the good it will do. Your mother suffers my presence only because of you."

She intended to call on Nan Livingston the next day, but fate intervened. Pulykara awoke that following morning with a dreadful cough.

"You stay put for the day," Rose told her. "Amaris and I will take turns caring for you."

Pulykara didn't even respond. Her skin was dry

and feverish. To move her head seemed a monumental effort for her. Toward late afternoon, Amaris bent and kissed the old woman on her forehead. "I'll be back soon, Pulykara. I have to check on Lizzie Johnson."

The wind had abated, but the cold damp air seeped into Amaris's bones as she hurried toward the home. She wasn't too worried about Lizzie, since three other females still occupied the available beds and would be there should the ill woman need help. However, those three weren't in the best of health themselves.

When she entered the home, they were in various stages of grief—shocked numbness, hysteria, quiet weeping.

"Another one died," cried Margarite, at fifteen the youngest of the three. "Just like we all are going to! 'Tis the devil's grip."

Amaris shuddered. Usually the devil's grip ran its course in a week or so, but a virulent form brought in off the ships could claim lives. She glanced past the three women to the cot. The woman stretched out beneath the tattered covers didn't move. "How did Lizzie die?"

A wail from the one sitting on the end of Lizzie's cot was the only answer. Amaris crossed to the cot and took the woman's hand. It was marble cold. When she released the hand, it fell like an anchor onto rumpled sheets. "Let's prepare her for burial."

Night's blanket had already shrouded Sydney by the time Amaris began to climb the back streets of the Rocks and make her way to the outskirts of Sydney proper and home.

The woman's death had deposited an unsettled feeling inside Amaris. At one corner she stopped and turned to stare out over the bay. Boat lights twinkled below like fallen stars. She felt lonely. Lonelier than she had in years. And empty. What was it all about . . . this struggle through days that brought neither joy nor despair but only a slow and inevitable decaying of the life spark?

A fog crept in, snuffing the boat lights. Pulling her coat more tightly about her, she turned her footsteps back toward her home.

In Pulykara's tiny room, Rose slept upright in the cane-backed rocker. Gently, Amaris shook her mother's shoulder. Rose's eyes focused sleepily on her. "Go to bed, Mother. I'll spell you for the night."

Her mother smiled and touched her cheek. "You be a good colleen." She nodded toward the aborigine woman. "Her fever hasn't broken. I'm worried about her."

"Get some sleep. I'll wake you if I need you."

"Give her the honey and whiskey if her cough comes back, now."

"I will. I will. Now go on." When her mother was gone, Amaris pulled the rocking chair close to the bed and took the veined hand. Even though the flesh was hot, Amaris was relieved the cold of death hadn't set in.

Throughout the night, Pulykara coughed intermittently. Each time, Amaris would pour out a measure of the cough mixture, but the old woman would refuse it. Toward dawn, Amaris fell asleep with her cheek on the woman's hand.

When Amaris awoke, her cheek was damp from contact with Pulykara's hand. The aborigine woman was sweating profusely. Her eyes were open and glazed. "Amaris," she whispered.

"Yes? Yes, Pulykara?"

"I've been talking to them Dream Time people."

Oh, God, Pulykara was delirious with fever! Amaris forced herself to keep calm. "I'm going to bathe you in cold water, Pulykara. You'll feel like your old self in no time."

Her head barely shook. Her words were scarcely more than the breath of a breeze. "No. My old self is leaving."

"No! You'll get better. It's only a—"

Pulykara's hand squeezed her own with an amazing strength. The tatoos across her cheekbones furrowed. "No, Miss Priss. They say it is time."

"You can't believe cockamamy like that! You can't!"

Pulykara made no attempt to speak further and closed her eyes, as if dismissing Amaris.

Tom paced the floor of his office. In the front of the warehouse, the window looked out on Sydney Bay. This was his dominion. In the core of his heart, he knew that Nan made the more important decisions for New South Wales Traders from her workroom in their Georgian mansion. He didn't begrudge her assumption of authority. She was the backbone of the company, and he admired her astuteness and energy. However, her driving force wore on him, and he welcomed the occasional respite his company obligations afforded him.

Today wasn't to be one of those days of respite. For not the hundredth time, he wished he had Nan's gift of persuasion, although he suspected not even she would be able to change the mind of the man who stood, hands thrust in jacket pockets, as he gazed outward at Pinchgut Island.

"Is there no way I can convince you to stay, Sin?"

Without taking his eyes off the view, he said, "None."

"Even if I offered you a share in the company?" The convict—ex-convict—had become invaluable to both the Livingston company and the Livingston household. He probably knew as much or more about the ins and outs of the daily operations of New South Wales Traders. Nan had a grand overview of the company and instinctively and instantly knew the right decisions to make; but details she detested.

At this, Sin turned. His intelligent eyes searched Tom's face. "Have you spoken of this to Mrs. Livingston?"

Tom plopped down in the chair behind his desk and grunted. "No."

"I don't think she would agree to your proposal. And even if she did, I wouldn't."

Astounded, he stared at the former convict. "My God, man, do you realize what you are passing up?"

"I need to escape the loving bosom of humanity for a while," Sin said with that cynical grin Tom had come to know so well. "I have thirty acres due me as an Emancipist. I'm going to claim it somewhere far from places like that." He nodded toward Pinchgut. "Somewhere beyond the Blue Mountains, maybe—in the Never-Never."

Sin's entire possessions could fit into a saddle pack. He searched through what he had accumulated over thirteen years of service, deciding what he would take with him, what he would leave behind.

"You can't be going!"

He spun around. Celeste stood there, tears glimmering like diamonds in her eyes. "Aye. I am."

She shoved his door closed behind her and ran to him. Stretching on tiptoe, she wrapped her arms around his neck. "Sin, I love you! Don't leave without me!"

He tried to pull her arms away, and she clung even more tightly.

"I have no pride," she wept. "You are more important than pride or dignity."

He closed his eyes against the entreaty in hers. Like a lost soul he was drawn to her goodness and her sunny nature. "You are too fragile a flower for the Never-Never."

He felt her lips brushing his chest, where his tunic lacings were spread open. "A flower that will wither without your nourishing rain, Sin."

He gave a shuddering sigh. "Your mother is adamantly opposed to your marrying me. She has other plans for you, Celeste. Grand plans."

Celeste displayed an unexpected strength. "She can't control my life like she does New South Wales Traders. I'll make her change her mind, I swear. Oh, kiss me, Sin! Kiss me and let me know you need me and want me and love me."

He silenced her with a kiss that was full of all the sweetness and goodness he had buried where even his soul refused to tread.

"You have been raised to be a lady of first quality. Your father and I haven't struggled all these years to make a place in society for you to squander it on an ex-convict, for God's sake!"

Celeste's hands knotted into fists. "I might remind you that not only are you an ex-convict yourself, but you have several times professed your skepticism about a superior being, so please don't call upon his name, Mother."

Nan stopped brushing her hair, turned from her dressing table and stared at her daughter. "You are overwrought. It must be this muggy weather. I would suggest you go to your room and lie down a while."

"I am no longer a child."

"I know what's best for you. Trust me, Celeste. You think you love Sinclair. 'Tis because he's different, and so he's intriguing to—"

"He *is* different. He's not preoccupied with making money and acquiring things. Or acquiring people."

Nan laid aside her brush. "Just what does that mean?"

"That he wouldn't accept your offer of a share in the company."

"I didn't tender such an offer."

"Papa did."

"I see."

"Mother, I am going to marry Sinclair."

"If you love him, you won't. I am telling you truly, Celeste. Where he's going, the country is rough and unforgivable. You would be a liability to him. His kind needs a strong, hard wom—"

"Liability? Assets? Must you always think in monetary terms, Mama? What about personal terms like warmth, love, compassion, caring? Do you even know what those mean?"

Nan stiffened. Celeste saw the pain in her eyes and ran to drop down on her knees before her. "Oh, Mother, I know the sacrifices you have made out of your love for Papa and me, but it's my turn to make sacrifices for the ones I love. I really do love Sin. Ever since I was a child, I've loved him."

"Do you love me, Celeste?" her mother asked quietly.

She hugged her mother's waist. "Oh, you know I do!"

"Then do this one thing for me. Wait."

She opened her mouth to protest, and her mother said, "Hush, darling, hear me out. I'm not saying you can't marry Sin. But wait a year. Give him a chance to get settled on his land. At least, let him build some kind of home for you, not just the shelter of a canvas tent. Those bachelor halls are no way to start out a marriage. Then, if you still want to marry him after a year, you have your father's and my blessing."

What her mother was asking was so difficult: to watch Sin leave without her. "Mother, he might get out there and decide I'm better off here."

"If he does, then the two of us agree. I think what I'm asking is fair. Are you afraid to put your love to the test?"

She closed her eyes, hoping to find the strength needed to agree. Regrettably, she wasn't strong like her mother or Amaris. Whatever needed to be done, they did it. She was like her father. Passive, a pacifist, wanting only to please the ones they loved.

She sighed and opened her eyes. Her smile was tremulous. "All right, Mama. I love you and Sin both. If by waiting the year, I can still have both of your hearts, then it's worth the sacrifice."

Her mother squeezed her hand. "You'll see that I was right, that you made the right decision."

"Amaris! Amaris!"

Amaris's eyelids seemed as heavy as pressing irons. Surely it wasn't time to awaken already. It seemed as if she had just collapsed on her bed only minutes before. Her mother's pinched face, haloed by the light of the candle she carried, was a blur above her.

"Amaris, wake up."

The hand that joggled her shoulder was real. She struggled to an upright position. "What is it, Mother?" Then she saw her mother's expression. "Pulykara? 'Tis Pulykara?"

"She's taken a turn for the worse, luv. She's asking for you. Only you, no one else."

Amaris swung her long legs over the side of the bed, slid her feet into her slippers, and grabbed her chenille bed robe from the foot of the mattress. Knotting her robe around her, she tugged her braid loose from the back of the collar and hurried up the stairs. Her slippers thudded in time to the rapid beat of her heart.

For the first time, Pulykara looked ancient, her skin as wrinkled as wadded-up paper. A week of lingering in the devil's grip had taken its toll of the ailing and aged aborigine woman. Her eyes were closed, and Amaris wasn't certain she was even breathing.

Sitting gingerly on the bed, Amaris touched her leathered cheek with a loving reverence. "Pulykara?" Her voice was little more than a whisper.

Slowly, the old woman's lids fluttered open.

"Baby." The aborigine's eyes cleared. "Miss Priss. 'Tis time."

"No!" she cried. "Damn your Dream Time people and fairy rings and all that bloody mystic stuff. I won't listen to it!"

Like a child, she put her hands to her ears. Tears trickled down her face and dripped off. "Oh, please, Pulykara, don't die! Don't die, I need you. I need you!"

Pulykara's breath came in raspy gasps. "You must . . . listen to me."

Weeping audibly, Amaris obediently let her hands drop. Just as she had always been obedient to this cherished old woman.

"You are special . . . a gift from the Dream Time . . . people to . . . to Nan Livingston."

It was Amaris now who ceased to breathe. Then, "What? What do you mean?"

"Nan Livingston . . . not Rose Wilmot . . . gave birth . . . to you."

"How do you know this?"

"She saved . . . me from being beat. After that . . . I worked for her. When you were . . . born and she asked me to find a home . . . for you, I did . . . as she asked, anything she would have asked."

"Who is . . . my father?"

The old woman's eyes glazed over. "The Dream Time people. They . . . are your father. You are . . . one of the gods . . . a part of this land. Don't ever forget. . . ."

Amaris, weeping hot tears now, leaned over and kissed the wrinkled brow. "I love you, Pulykara," she whispered fiercely. "Don't *you* ever forget. Ever!"

* * *

Rose and William Wilmot gave Pulykara a Christian burial, although Amaris privately held to the conviction that the aborigine woman was somewhere scoffing at the ritual of such a newborn religion. After all, hers was hundreds of thousands of years old—a worship of the divine forces that created her beloved land.

A mist, blue and powerfully scented, hung over the graveyard that afternoon, as if the Dream Time people blessed her arrival among them with a supernatural gift.

Pragmatists would have said it was merely one of those weather phenomena that caused the mists of the mountain eucalypti to settle over the lower areas.

Rose wept as her husband read aloud from his Bible. Dry-eyed, Amaris paid no heed. She'd already said her farewell to the aborigine woman.

Pulykara deserved an aboriginal burial. She would want to be wrapped in a sheet of paperbark and placed on a platform high in a tree. A year or so later, her bones could be removed, painted with red ocher, and ceremonially placed in a small cave. Pulykara believed that these formalities had to be done correctly to liberate the person's spirit.

Someday, Amaris promised herself, she would return to the cemetery and carry out the burial ritual for Pulykara. First, there was something more important to be taken care of.

When the last word was spoken, she whirled from the grave site and, bypassing the waiting carriage, struck out for Wooloomooloo. Rose and William called after her, but there was no way she would have heard. Her head was filled with a deafening, incessant buzzing.

While Rose and William took the carriage to hunt for her along the roadside, she cut across fields overgrown with thorny brush that tore at her good black dress. Enraged, embittered, and heart-wounded, she entered the Livingston mansion, swept past the butler and the startled guests, to confront Nan Livingston, her mother.

11

The young woman was as out of place in that glittering gathering of Sydney's select as an aborigine strolling naked in Covent Gardens.

The low hum of polite party conversation diminished as one by one each guest in the ballroom of the Livingstons' Georgian mansion turned to stare at the creature in the doorway.

Towering almost six feet, the rather plain-looking young woman in black mourning crepe felt very fragile at that moment. She had known coming here was a risk she was running. Since no one could see that her insides had shattered into thousands of ice-cold slivers, she took one deep breath and let her gaze travel over the room of plumed and jewelry-bedecked guests—until it collided with that of the pale, middle-aged hostess.

Fury and heartbreak gnashed inside the young woman, then coalesced into courage she had momentarily lost. She bypassed silver and sideboards.

In three long easy strides, she crossed the intervening space to stand before the diminutive Mrs. Livingston. "You knew all along, didn't you. You knew and never said a word."

"We can discuss this in my office." Before the blast of barely contained rage, another might have quailed. Not Nan Livingston. Calmly, she turned and led the way to her office.

Once inside, she turned to face the younger woman. "Yes?"

"I am the daughter you so easily rid yourself of twenty-five years ago!"

If she had hoped her revelation would stun Nan Livingston, the young woman realized now she had miscalculated. Nan Livingston's controlled countenance showed boredom and not a whit more.

Her famous and terrible pride would never permit her to betray the shame and agony of this moment. Casually, carelessly almost, she replied, "I often wondered what you would do if you ever found out your origins."

It was a clash between two strong-willed females—and the younger vowed that she would leave the victor. "I'm sure you did. But not often enough. The other daughter you hold so dear—I swear I'll destroy your glorious plans for her. This I swear!"

With that, she strode from the office, past the influential guests, leaving them to believe that they might have seen an apparition.

12

For several minutes Nan stared into her
reflection in the mirror. Since she had been no
beauty, time did not have much to tamper with.

Indeed, she had weathered the years better than
other women her age. She was middle-aged and
looked it. No less, no more.

Beneath that structure of flesh and bones was the
essence of Nan Briscoll Livingston. All that she inher-
ited, all that she experienced had gone into her making. Her need for legitimacy and a sense of place had
been so important to her that she could not openly
acknowledge Amaris. And yet, at forty-eight, she sadly
recognized that the young woman who had boldly,
brashly, appeared in her drawing room this evening
was closer to her in spirit and soul than Celeste.

Tonight had been a clash of two strong-willed
women. Nan sensed that the confrontation was
just beginning. Could she—would she—destroy
her offspring?

Always there was her survival duel with Miles . . . now Amaris. Amaris would never understand . . . Amaris and Miles, these two people who made her the most vulnerable.

She dipped a finger into her rouge pot and marked with determined strokes two *X*'s onto her mirror.

"Miss Wilmot, what a surprise. I wasn't sure that was you riding toward me."

Amaris pulled on the bow beneath her chin and removed her broad-brimmed leghorn hat. "I suppose my old nag betrayed my identity?"

Francis laughed. "Well, aye." Frivolity, his black stallion, pranced smartly.

With her hat, she fanned her face. She missed riding bareheaded, but there was much to be said for a woman's hat besides the fact it was proper attire for a well-brought-up young woman and it kept that damaging sunlight off the face. A hat also added that allure of mystery. "I felt I couldn't write another stroke and had to get out of the house."

He stared at her as if seeing her for the first time. "You are an unusual woman, Miss Wilmot."

"You've said that about me before. Shall we ride a little while together?"

He looked uncertain. "I was supposed to ride over to the Livingstons'."

A fact Amaris knew well. Nan had taken to staging whist parties on Thursday afternoons. Mostly young people made up the tables of foursomes. Naturally, Amaris was not among the invited. Once, about two weeks earlier, right after Pulykara's burial, Celeste had come to the Female Immigrants' Home. "I don't understand it, Amaris. Mama absolutely refuses to invite you to the house, where before she was indifferent."

"Does that mean we won't be seeing each other anymore?" she asked Celeste. It was difficult for Amaris to look at her lovely friend and remind herself that Celeste was her half sister!

"Of course not! The house may be Mama's, but my life isn't. We'll simply meet elsewhere."

The hair at Amaris's nape prickled. Here she was, meeting Francis instead. Fear suddenly struck at her. Was the darkness inside her the mirror of her mother? The mirror of Nan Livingston? Would she, like Nan, become a calculating, domineering old woman?

"Well, then Francis, I'll ride a ways with you. I am taking some sweetcakes to the miller's wife for Mother."

Not waiting for an answer, she pulled on her reins and trotted her mare up beside his stallion. "How is the shipping business?"

His finely drawn brows met over the bridge of his nose, and she was reminded how very handsome the man was. "It couldn't be better."

"Ahh," she teased, "but you don't discuss business with women?"

"No, that's not it. It's—my part in New South Wales Traders is limited. Nan is in control and has her finger on its pulse."

"And you don't feel needed. That's it, isn't it?"

He inclined his head toward her. Uncertainty passed over his face. "You're a perceptive woman." He paused. "But it's more than that. I sometimes wonder if there isn't some fatal flaw in my character."

He looked relieved at his admission. "What makes

you say that?" she asked.

"Every attempt I make to establish something of my own is thwarted. Accidents, poor timing, bad weather. Nothing that I can say is absolutely my fault, but too many adverse events to be mere coincidence." He shrugged. "Mayhap I'm just one of those fellows dogged by ill luck. Or, at least, it seems that way for as long as I can remember."

"Ill luck? How can the rich have ill luck?"

He tossed her a withering glance. "When I was small, I had a high fever. Money can't buy back the hearing in my right ear."

So that was why he tilted his head toward the person speaking. In silence, she rode on with him. She set aside her compassion and concentrated on steering the subject to her purpose. "Francis, your problem might be the area of your business pursuits."

He stared at her with a puzzled look. "What do you mean?"

"Maybe you don't belong in the office. You're a man who enjoys the physical challenge—riding to the foxes, pheasant hunting, boxing. I imagine you would find the detail work of an office tedious."

"I do." His scowl ebbed. "Say, why don't you ride all the way to the Livingstons' with me? Whist can get bloody boring if your partner doesn't—come to think of it, why haven't I seen you at the Livingstons' recently?"

So, gossip of that confrontation with Nan had not reached him.

Amaris let a wistful smile touch her lips. "You'll have to ask Nan about that."

"You are being mysterious. Then you won't come?"

She drew back on her reins and began repinning her hat. "No. But I'm sure our paths will cross again."

"I hope they do, Miss Wilmot. I enjoy talking to you. When I'm with you, 'tis not merely drawing-room chitchat."

She peered up at him from beneath her upraised arm, a definitely seductive glance. "I feel the same way." Her hat secure, she smiled and said, "Until next time." Then she tugged her mount in the opposite direction.

"Next time" wasn't that long in coming. Celeste came to the rectory the next morning. "Mother is abed with one of those awful headaches," Amaris said, inviting her in.

As Celeste's gaze took in the shabby furnishings, Amaris realized again the disparity between her life and that of her half sister's.

The thought crossed Amaris's mind that perhaps she should tell Celeste of their relationship, but Amaris knew it would serve no beneficial purpose. Only bring pain to Celeste.

Celeste took off her bonnet, hugged her, and stepped back. "I miss you. We're going boating on the Hawkesbury. Won't you come along?"

"Who's we?"

"Francis. Thomas Rugsby from Wales. He's visiting Major Hannaby. Their daughter Eileen is taken with him. And Lieutenant O'Reilly, you remember him. He was courting Becky Randolph. Most of the regular whist players. Do say you'll come, Amaris."

Guilt pricked her conscience. More than even

being with her friend, she wanted to take advantage of Francis's presence at the boating party. "All right. How are you getting to the landing?"

Celeste dimpled. "Sin. He brought me here. Our new carriage driver ran off with Molly Finn. Mother had to ask Sin—most diplomatically—if he would drive the carriage. I suppose she thinks that since he is leaving in just two weeks with the wagon train, I won't have time to recant my—"

"A wagon train is leaving for the outback?" It had been almost a year since the last one, made up of graziers and squatters, had attempted the perilous passage through the Blue Mountains.

"Aye, Sin said he would be traveling with it. At least, initially." Suddenly she covered her face with her hands. "Oh, Amaris, he almost seemed relieved when I told him I had promised Mama to wait a year!"

"What did he say?"

With the back of her hand, Celeste wiped away a tear. "That he agreed with Mother, that it would be better if he had a place prepared for me." She managed a small, rueful smile. "But you know that distance doesn't make the heart grow fonder, it only makes the heart go yonder."

"If there were no reason for your mother to hold you to that promise, would you go with Sin into the Never-Never?"

Her eyes brightened. "I'd go with Sin to hell." She glanced apprehensively around the room. "I suppose my blasphemy would shock your father."

She laughed. "I imagine he's heard plenty of blasphemy working with the derelicts of the Rocks. It'll only take me a minute to change clothing."

After she had slipped into a white dimity dress and her straw shepherd's hat, she went to her mother's room. Leaning down to kiss her cheek, she said, "I'm spending the day with Celeste, boating on the Hawkesbury."

Her mother squeezed her hand. "Good, you have spent too much of your time on work and not enough on pleasure."

"Mother, what do you know about Nan Livingston?"

The question took Rose by surprise. "Why, I imagine no more or less than anyone else in Sydney. I do know that Nan Livingston, despite the stories of ruthlessness, has much to be admired—her indomitable spirit, her love and devotion to this land, her kindnesses to those less fortunate. Just look how generous she's been to you over the years."

"Yes," she said, barely able to restrain the bitterness from her voice, "Just look."

The drive to the Hawkesbury River was a pleasant one, made even more so by the morning's spring sunshine that gilded the landscape. Sitting on the coachman's seat, Sin said little. To her, his broad back was no less menacing than his devil-black scowl.

She knew he was aware of every word she and Celeste exchanged. In his presence, Celeste seemed as golden as the countryside. Every so often, she would lean forward, touch his shoulder, and make a comment or ask a question. Her need to have contact with him was a tangible thing. With her, he was so patient. There was no getting around it, Celeste brought out the best in everyone.

By the time they arrived at the landing, the rest of the boating party was already there. Sin helped both Celeste and Amaris from the carriage, but Amaris noticed Celeste's hand lingered in his. Then Francis strode toward them, and Celeste relinquished his hold.

Watching Francis make a leg, then straighten to smile down at Celeste, Amaris couldn't help but be envious. Celeste's joyous disposition and gentle beauty attracted all men.

That morning, Francis stood out as usual. He wore a superfine black frock coat over Petersham trousers that were drawn into his boots in a cossack fashion.

When he turned to Amaris, she affected a lighthearted smile. "Our paths crossed sooner than you thought."

"And I'm glad." His manner held an attentiveness that had been lacking in their earlier relationship.

Celeste might have noticed this, but her whole being was focused on Sin. "I'll return this evening for you two, so don't stray off should I be late," he was saying, his critical gaze running over the assembled people, as if he thought one among them might want to harm the delicate woman who stood silently adoring him.

When everyone had boarded, the sloop set off along the river's sluggish current. A canvas cover had been erected for the outing, and the young women were already spreading a lavish array of food beneath it.

Nan had had her cook prepare an assortment of cheeses, cold cuts garnished with savory herbs, freshly baked bread that was still warm, and a couple of bottles of French wine.

Here and there a pillow was tossed on the deck, and Eileen Hannaby, who had her mother's pouter pigeon form, was already flirting with Thomas, a short, wiry man reclining across from her. At first, everyone was busy exchanging bits of news, joking, and pointing out the brilliant-plumaged birds or exotic plants along the banks.

Despite the measure of respect Amaris had earned as a writer and a champion of the downtrodden, she was still considered, even after all these years, an outsider. One of the drone class, as Becky Randolph had termed it. Did Becky realize that her own mother was supporting her father with funds to run a newspaper?

If Amaris felt an outsider, she took advantage of that position to stand at the wooden railing and listen, to observe, to glean insight into personalities she might use in her writing.

Becky, for example, was talking faster than an emu could run. That she was more nervous today than usual was obvious.

Concentrating solely on Becky, Amaris gradually noticed an almost imperceptible but continual movement of Becky's gabardine skirts, too heavy to be rustled by the river's light breeze. At last, Amaris perceived that Lieutenant O'Reilly, who lay braced on one elbow next to Becky and slightly behind her, had one hand hidden from view.

When Amaris fully realized the implications, that Becky's nervous patter was the result of O'Reilly's fondling fingers, she couldn't contain an outburst of laughter that she abruptly choked off with a cough.

"I see you have taken note of the animal world's peripheral activities," Francis said with a chuckle from behind her. He was standing close enough that the river breeze entwined her skirts about his legs.

She was partly embarrassed and partly curious about this intimate aspect of courtship. She forced herself to turn and share a conspirator's smile with him. She knew she had to capitalize on what she had seen in Francis's dark brown eyes. Her voice was lowered to an intimate level. "I think the animals know something we don't."

His pupils dilated. She was smitten by the look in his eyes. Staring into them, she knew what he was thinking—that she was no coy maiden.

One of their party called out that the sloop was docking, and Celeste's approach interrupted whatever reply he might have made. "Come on," she chided with a smile, "you two are slower than tortoises today."

"Go on and I'll catch up with you later," she told Celeste, including Francis in her glance. "I wanted to take a look at the female factory."

Celeste stared at her. "I admire you, Amaris. When I help out at your females' home, I don't feel good or anything but sorrow for those poor women."

Amaris was ashamed. She never felt good on those occasions either. Sometimes, in fact, she was repelled by the women. For whatever reason some of her anger dissipated the hours she worked there. It was as if she was letting authorities and people in high places know there was one less outsider looking in.

"I won't stay long. I'll join you at the Government House Park."

What she hoped for happened. While Celeste and the others deboarded to stretch their legs under a brilliant midday sun, Francis tarried to chat with the captain of the vessel.

She took her time raising her parasol, a foolish thing to carry. She was already tanned by the sun from the many occasions she had either neglected or flatly refused to wear a hat or carry a parasol.

Just as it looked unseemly for her to dally a

moment longer, Francis ended the conversation and hailed her. She looked over her shoulder and flung him what she hoped was an inviting smile. "Don't tell me, you were negotiating with the captain to carry New South Wales Trading cargo."

He laughed. "No, I was stalling until I could catch you alone."

Her hopes brightened. She continued walking. "Any particular reason?"

He groaned. "Miss Wilmot, you have yet to learn the tricks of the female, which is perhaps why I enjoy talking to you."

"The tricks being . . . ?"

"You don't ask why a man wants to talk to you, you say, 'I'm so pleased.'"

"I thought about that and decided it wouldn't work on a man with a reputation for being a heartbreaker. Especially, one who knows he is."

A flush suffused his face, then a smile began at the corners of his mouth and finally took hold. With a broad grin, he spread his hands in a gesture of helplessness. "Knowledge is power, to thine own self be true, and all the rest."

They turned their footsteps, as if in mutual accord, along the river walk, deserted at the noon hour. Her voice took on a deliberate husky quality. "And I know myself. I'm unlike other women in more ways than the one you mentioned."

She could feel his heated gaze on her. "Such as?"

She glanced at him from the corners of her eyes. His head inclined toward hers, titillation flaring in his own eyes. They both knew the preliminaries of word play had to be adhered to. "Such as I'm not afraid to go after what I want."

"Which is?"

Green oak boughs temporarily encompassed them in leaf-dappled shadows. The river's cooling breeze played the shorter tendrils of her hair that had escaped the clasp at her nape. She gathered her courage. "Right now, I want to know what it would be like to kiss you."

His breath inhaled sharply. Then he grabbed her shoulders and pulled her against him. His mouth took hers in a hungry kiss.

She had expected this of Sin but not of Francis. Her body surprised her by responding in a sudden heat. An aching knot formed low in her stomach. Yet it was as if another part of her stepped outside her body to observe and dissect the gamut of emotions that obliterated her usual rational thought processes.

He slipped his hands from her shoulders to the back of her waist and pressed her into him. She could feel the hardness of him—and that even harder part wedged against the apex of her legs.

Excitement rushed through her. Her hands clung to his shoulders to keep herself from sagging. The spectator side of her was fascinated by the intensity of her reaction.

Her next reaction fascinated her even more. His tongue pushed between her lips, and, moaning, she boldly joined her tongue with his. Her parasol dipped to the ground. Her hand clasped the back of his head, her fingers curling in his sun-gilt hair.

His hands strayed from her waist to cup her hips and pull her into him. Suddenly, both she and Francis were panting heavily.

"Over here," he said, pulling her deeper into the seclusion of the oaks, where afternoon strollers wouldn't espy them. He pressed her against an oak's trunk. Its rough bark abraded her skin through the thin dimity material of her waist.

His cheek nuzzled hers, then his lips found her ear, below it, and just above the collar of her waist. "Your scent," he said. "It intoxicates. I'm dying to know what you smell like elsewhere."

She laughed. She felt lightheaded herself. "You don't have to die to find out, Francis."

"You are real, aren't you?"

She heard the wonder in his voice. "If admitting that I want what you want makes me real, then I very much am." What amazed her was that she was putting on no act; she really wanted Francis.

He reached around her, and his hands began loosening the fastenings of her waist while his mouth made forays across the planes and angles of her face. Her blouse fell to her waist. A low, rusty sound came from his throat. Then his hands cupped her breasts and began to knead them. Her eyes closed, and she shuddered at the wave of pleasure that washed through her.

Even as he kissed her breasts, he pulled her downward with him, until they both lay side by side in the sparse grass growing at the base of the oak.

Somehow, she wasn't exactly sure in the rush of passion, he divested himself of his clothing and hers. Maybe she helped him. She did know that when he at last thrust into her, she felt no pain at losing her maidenhead, only an excitement that was unequalled by anything she had ever felt before. Whenever he plunged, she arched in return.

Her fingers dug into his back, and she gasped out the word, "More!"

"Aye," he said hoarsely. "This is not enough. Not yet!"

The power of her senses escalated, so that the sound of their breathing, the slap of the river against the bank, the salty taste of his skin, the feel of his muscles contracting beneath her hands, the scent of the damp earth, the vegetation, the dank river, and he and she commingled, overrode all external reality.

In an instant, within her body a multitude of sensation points burst in an overflow. She cried out, her surprise and intense pleasure were strangled sighs, crashing one upon the other like waves slamming against the beach.

He held her tightly against him. Then, with a mighty shudder, he collapsed on top of her.

For what seemed a long time, they lay together, unstirring. She could hear his heavy breath in her ear. Her own had already evened out. And, as she lay there, she wondered if she had been the ultimate of fools.

Had she given away freely that from which she might have wrung a price?

Yet something very certain, very strong, very female, whispered in the recesses of her mind that what she wanted from a man like Francis, she wouldn't have gotten in barter for sex.

No, what she had that most women did not was the use of her brain. Or rather, no fear to use her brain to achieve her will.

Her hands captured either side of Francis's face, and she kissed him with abandon. She could tell she had caught him off guard by his fleeting expression of amazement. He had undoubtedly expected her to bemoan the loss of her virginity.

With a husky laugh, he returned her ardent kiss. Gasping, he released her lips to whisper raggedly, "I cannot let you wander far from me, my Amazonian maiden."

Nor you from me, she silently promised both herself and her nemesis, Nan Livingston.

13

"*You haven't changed your mind* about refusing to marry Francis, have you, Celeste?"

"Of course not." The young woman walked the length of Amaris's bedroom, tiny enough to fit in the Livingston pantry. Celeste's hands rubbed together. For once, her eyes weren't lustrous. Her teeth chewed nervously on her lower lip. "Sin leaves for the outback in two days, Amaris. With a wagon train Major Hannaby has put together. I can't give Sin up."

Amaris sat back on her bed in a most unladylike fashion, with her knees drawn up. She clasped her hands behind her head and leaned against the wall. "I have a suggestion."

Celeste paused in her pacing. Hope shone in her eyes. "What?"

"I'll marry Francis. Cheated of her prospective son-in-law, your mother will have to give her blessing to your marriage with Sin."

Celeste's wing-tipped brows knitted in perplexion. "Francis wants to marry you?"

"He will. With your help."

"And you want to marry him? You love Francis?"

"No, I don't love him, but I could come to love him. And, yes, I want to marry him. We could make a good life together by starting out somewhere new."

The light went from Celeste's face, and she sighed. "Even if Francis were to marry you, I don't think Mother would permit me to marry Sin. Not now, anyway. You see, I gave my word to wait a year."

"She would agree to a marriage, if she thought you were carrying his child."

Shock at the implications behind the suggestion played across Celeste's lovely face. Then she said quietly, "You know I couldn't lie to my mother."

"You will if you ever want to see Sin again."

Celeste's expression revealed the inner battle being waged. "All right," she said at last. "What do I need to do?"

"First, manage to talk with Francis when he calls on your mother tomorrow. What is it—around elevenish they do business? Tell Francis to meet me at the Brigsby Pub tomorrow night at eight."

"You can't be serious!"

"I am. Talk to your mother—and, Celeste, don't let her talk you out of what you want to do."

Celeste stopped before her. Determination steeled that usually gentle expression. "I shall be Sin's one way or another." She smiled brightly. "I feel like we're conspirators. It's terribly exciting, don't you think? I'll take care of Mama, you take care of Francis."

Amaris deliberated all that night about what to say to Francis and how to say it. In the end, he made it very easy for her to lead into what she wanted to say.

He was already waiting for her, sitting at the same table where she had watched the fracas among the newly arrived female prisoners that rainy afternoon. His tankard was nigh empty. Pipe smoke hazed the air, lending their tryst a further air of mystery.

"I've been thinking about you," he said. "About last Sunday afternoon at Paramatta."

His eyes held the same heat she had purposely ignited on the sloop. She delayed a moment, sipping from her pint o'porter. "I would have thought you would have more important matters, like business for instance, to occupy your thoughts."

He chug-a-lugged the last of his ale. "Business matters are exactly what I don't want to think about."

"That gloomy, eh?"

He sighed, set the tankard down, and stared at its tarnished pewter. "One gets tired of being a puppet."

"With Nan Livingston pulling the strings? You don't have to continue to be the puppet, you know."

He raised his gaze to meet hers. His mouth twisted wryly. "I do. I happen to enjoy living in the style of luxury in which I was raised and would like to continue doing so."

She leaned forward and stared into the depths of those brown eyes, hoping to touch a chord somewhere inside. "You can do that, and never have to have a puppet master again."

He laughed dryly. "Were you drinking earlier, before coming here, because there is no bloody way I could ever—"

"Francis, a great wealth awaits the stout of heart who aren't afraid to brave the Never-Never."

He made an exasperated sound. "A pipe dream, my girl."

"A pipe dream?" she scoffed in turn. "Not when one can get hundreds of acres for merely applying for a grant from the governor. Or you can do what Sin and others are doing. Simply become a squatter. With your connections, I would imagine thousands of acres would be more applicable. Think of it, Francis! With a sheep station, you could create your own empire."

"Sheep station? What do I know of sheep?"

"I know enough to make a start."

Those weeks of preparation would now be tested. She had made it a point to talk to anyone who knew anything about sheep: a former convict who had herded sheep in Ireland; an old woman who had worked in a carpet shop, weaving wool; a retired soldier who was running a few imported Merino sheep on land granted him by the governor.

She had even ridden to Elizabeth Farm to talk to Macarthur's wife, who ran the place in his absence in England. Elizabeth had told her that sheep were more important than cattle. Sheep had two advantages over cattle. One, they needed less water and did less damage to the edge of the creek; the other was that sheep produced income from wool without having to be slaughtered.

Amaris leaned forward. "Francis, there are vast open areas in the Never-Never with potential grazing land belonging to no one. All you have to do is apply! Most of the sheep stations have been started by people who knew very little. I'm not afraid to try. I'm not afraid to take risks. I can learn. Most important, I have saved enough from my writing to buy a small flock."

"You've already given this a lot of thought, haven't you?"

"Francis, a wagon train leaves for the outback in a week. You weren't afraid to take risks as an insurer of ships and cargo. Can this be any more risky?"

"What about Celeste?"

She looked straight into his eyes. "She'll never marry you. I think she would kill herself first."

He looked at her in amazement. "Am I to understand that I am that repulsive?"

"She is a woman in love—and you're not the man."

He raised his tankard to finish off its contents, and she placed the flat of her hand over the tankard's rim. "Francis, I am the woman you need."

For a second, the expression in his eyes was bleak. "But am I the man you need?"

"You suit my purposes perfectly."

"Which are?"

"A home, someday children. The usual things a woman wants."

"I have the distinct feeling, Amaris, that you are not the usual woman."

With a slightly bewildered expression, William Wilmot intoned the words for the early morning marriage ceremony. Clearly, the hasty double wedding wasn't quite proper, even though it was understandable with the wagon train leaving within a mere matter of hours.

The two brides wore hastily sewn gowns of blond lace over white satin and blond lace veils held in place by wreaths of orange blossoms. Francis

Marlborough had donned the traditional black coat and pantaloons and gold-trimmed chestnut-colored cashmere waistcoat. Sin Tremayne was dressed more conservatively in a double-breasted blue coat and drab-colored breeches.

William's gaze passed over Celeste Livingston's radiant face to settle on that of his daughter. Radiant, no, but a calm, serene expression transformed that wistful, defiant look that he often caught in her eyes when she didn't know he was watching her. His daughter was doing what she wanted, what she needed to do, and that was enough for him.

The two grooms each wore dispassionate expressions. This troubled the rector. What was going on in their minds? Why did they take no joy in the occasion? He peered at Amaris again, and his heart overflowed. She had brought such joy to his household.

The little changeling was so different from him and Rose. Headstrong and determined she was. But where his wife's mercurial emotions bubbled to the surface for all to view and his own ran like a quiet, shallow creek, Amaris channeled her emotions into a subsurface stream. He was never quite certain what his beloved daughter was feeling.

More than that, he wondered every so often what her natural parents were like. Convicts of the lowest class, most likely. But from somewhere in their ancestral lines had come that challenging intelligence inherent in Amaris.

Amaris rolled off her garters and carefully peeled down her white silk stockings. Meanwhile, Celeste unfastened the heirloom pearl necklace her mother had bestowed on her as one of many wedding gifts, few of which would fit into the bullock dray Sin had purchased for the trip.

Amaris had asked her parents only for her mother's cane rocker and several of her father's books. In the outback, where diversion and socializing were limited, one could easily go through a hundred books in one year.

The two young women hastily changed. The wagon train was leaving Sydney in less than two hours. Celeste held the necklace in her palm, as if weighing its worth. "I'm putting all this behind me, Amaris."

Amaris sat on a low, three-legged stool, with Rogue lying patiently at her feet. "I know you love Sin, Celeste, but I don't think you realize just how much you will be giving up."

"Whatever it is, it is worth the sacrifice. I'm not blind with love. I'm stronger than anyone realizes, even you. Sin needs me to temper his wild streak. And you need Francis, whether you know it or not."

She laughed. "Do I? I would say he needs my strength."

Celeste's mouth set in serious lines, so unlike her usually mild expression. "You need to discover that soft, nurturing part of yourself, Amaris. Francis will force you to face yourself."

Dumbfounded, she stared at the girl. Then she smiled. "Am I really five years older than you?"

Celeste stopped to hug her fiercely. "Oh, Amaris, I can't believe our good luck! Married on the same day, going on the grandest adventure of our lives toge—"

"Hmmm." Behind them, Nan cleared her throat.

"Mama!" Celeste said happily. "Wasn't the wedding wonderful!"

Nan entered the tiny bedroom, and Rogue gave a low growl before Amaris hushed him. He lay back down again beside the stool.

"Aye," Nan said, her voice terse. "That it was."

Amaris often wondered how such a small woman could intimidate others. Money was power, of course. But Nan had knowledge, knowledge of people, their inner desires and fears, and she used that knowledge effectively.

"Celeste, I also have a wedding gift for Amaris, and I'd like to be with her alone for a moment."

The girl looked puzzled. "All right, Mama. But we have to hurry."

Nan glanced at Amaris. "This won't take long."

When Celeste was gone, Nan faced Amaris and took a small package from her reticule and passed it to her with a shrug. "A gold and ivory brooch. Hardly useful where you're going."

"How kind of you," Amaris mocked.

"You fight hard."

"So do you."

They spoke in hushed whispers. "I fight fairly. Until now. I want you to know that twenty-five years ago, I did what was best for everyone all around. I did not intentionally hurt anyone."

Amaris's hands clenched. "You thought only of yourself."

"And you are not doing so now? You haven't given a thought to the possibility that your revenge will hurt others besides just me. You have ruined my dreams for Celeste. Even more, you have taken her from—"

JOIN THE
TIMELESS ROMANCE READER SERVICE AND GET FOUR OF TODAY'S MOST EXCITING HISTORICAL ROMANCES FREE, WITHOUT OBLIGATION!

Imagine getting today's very best historical romances sent directly to your home — at a total savings of at least $2.00 a month. Now you can be among the first to be swept away by the latest from Candace Camp, Constance O'Banyon, Patricia Hagan, Parris Afton Bonds or Susan Wiggs. You get all that — and that's just the beginning.

PREVIEW AT HOME WITHOUT OBLIGATION AND SAVE.

Each month, you'll receive four new romances to preview without obligation for 10 days. You'll pay the low subscriber price of just $4.00 per title — a total savings of at least $2.00 a month!

*Postage and handling is absolutely **free** and there is no minimum number of books you must buy. You may cancel your subscription at any time with no obligation.*

GET YOUR FOUR FREE BOOKS TODAY ($20.49 VALUE)

FILL IN THE ORDER FORM BELOW NOW!

YES! *I want to join the Timeless Romance Reader Service. Please send me my 4 FREE HarperMonogram historical romances. Then each month send me 4 new historical romances to preview without obligation for 10 days. I'll pay the low subscription price of $4.00 for every book I choose to keep – a total savings of at least $2.00 each month – and home delivery is free! I understand that I may return any title within 10 days without obligation and I may cancel this subscription at any time without obligation. There is no minimum number of books to purchase.*

NAME_____

ADDRESS _____

CITY_____STATE_____ZIP_____

TELEPHONE_____

SIGNATURE _____

(If under 18 parent or guardian must sign. Program, price, terms, and conditions subject to cancellation and change. Orders subject to acceptance by HarperMonogram.)

GET
4
FREE
BOOKS
(A $20.49
VALUE)

"To go to the outback with Sin was her own choice."

"She would have had second thoughts had you not encouraged her by going yourself."

Amaris shot to her feet. "You can't control people's lives, Nan Livingston!"

Fury blazed in the older woman's pale eyes. "I have and I will. Beginning with yours. I shall never forgive you for this. Someday, I'll destroy your dreams, as you have mine."

Amaris was all too eager to put the Blue Mountains between herself and Nan. Traveling by covered wagon, she and Francis, along with Sin and Celeste, began their honeymoon in the company of ten other families—graziers and squatters. Some of them, like Francis, were graduates of Oxford or Cambridge.

A dozen or so people walked or rode pack animals. Among those walking was Jimmy Underwood, whom Sin had hired away from New South Wales Traders. Thomas Rugsby, a friend of the family, traveled with Major Hannaby, his wife Elizabeth, and their daughter Eileen.

Molly Finn had petitioned Amaris to take her with her. "Ye will need an extra hand, ye will. I'll work cheap." Nan's carriage driver had forsaken Molly, and the girl was desolate.

Apparently, half of the females in Sydney Cove were desolate at the loss of such a wonderful candidate for a husband. That Francis Marlborough had chosen to marry a mere rector's daughter, a plain spinster at that, astounded the Exclusionists.

With her own money, Amaris purchased a hundred

sheep, merinos brought in from the Cape of Good Hope. Rogue kept a mother hen's eye on them, herding them in the trail of the wagons, along with two milk cows.

For his part, Sin had decided to wait until he was settled on a run before he bought sheep. "In addition," he had said, "I want to diversify. I don't like being completely dependent on sheep. Maybe start a horse farm."

By the end of that first day of traveling, dust had mixed with sweat to form a gritty paste that the sunlight baked on Amaris's face.

In the brief hour that she had spelled Francis at the reins, her gloved hands ached from controlling the plodding bullocks with whip and reins. Her hips hurt from sitting on the wagon's board seat. No cushion alleviated the continual jouncing. She rubbed the area at either side of the back of her waist. The hard monotony of miles was also mentally strenuous.

Riding on his sleek black steed, Francis asked, "Spine ache?"

She managed a smile that she envisioned as more resembling a grimace. Even Molly had grown tired of riding and had elected to walk awhile. "*Every*thing aches. How about you?" She didn't need to ask. Since leaving Sydney, he had been in high spirits.

"You were right." The man she had considered a London dandy cast her what was almost a shy smile. With one slender hand dangling his mount's reins, he flung the other out to indicate the vast vista of prairie and mountain. "Out here, Amaris, I am my own man. I am being judged not on my background or my financial portfolio but on me. On me alone!"

This was something they both shared: Their marriage

union was symbolic of their joint commitment to create a place for themselves in the Never-Never. Some of Celeste's joy that came from being caught up in the "great adventure," as she had termed it, was apparently rubbing off on Amaris.

"Why don't you let me take back the reins now," Francis said. "Frivolity has had his exercise for the day."

She readily acquiesced. While Francis tied Frivolity's reins to the rear of their wagon, she turned back and searched along the string of wagons. Dust hazed the air, but she was able to find Sin's wagon two back of their own. Celeste's face was upturned to his, and they appeared to be engaged in deep conversation.

Evidently, this trek was liberating in more than just the physical sense of the word. Today, Sin's scowl was noticeably absent. This morning, when he had assisted Celeste in boarding the wagon, she had thanked him with a smile, her hand briefly touching his chest. The gesture could have meant little, but Amaris had seen the intimate glance that had passed between the two.

Around late afternoon covies of partridges began to scatter before the thudding of the wagon wheels. Francis quickly pulled his flintlock from the floorboard, loaded a ball in the muzzle, and took aim. The thunder of the shot was deafening, but his aim was true.

"Partridge for dinner tonight," he said with a smile and handed the reins to her.

She watched him alight and retrieve a bird some yards away. Pleasure that her husband would be a good provider filled her. She had made a good choice. She recalled her mother's concern, expressed only an hour before the wedding. "Ye forceful nature, luv, may have compelled Francis to marry you. Mayhap it would have been best to let nature take its course."

If nature had taken its course, she might have been an unwed mother. As it was, she had had her anxiously awaited monthly.

At the front of the wagon train, Major Hannaby was waving his upraised arm in a signal for the wagons to encircle and make camp. The dreaded ascent of the steep Blue Mountains would be postponed until after dawn of the morrow.

After a full day of working the reins, Francis was becoming remarkably proficient as a teamster. "Ha ya!" he shouted at the two plodding bulls. Steam rose off their flea-coated flanks, and the smell traveled with the dust.

Francis's slender hands snapped the reins and whip with a strength that surprised her. The bullocks fell into place in a circle rapidly forming near a line of pink eucalyptus that marked a creek. At the creaking sounds the wagons made, a screaming cloud of white cockatoos exploded out of the trees.

When Amaris climbed down from her wagon, encircled with the others, pain shot through her hips. Francis had bounded from the wagon to help her step down, but she noticed he moved with as little agility as she.

"Do you hurt as much as I do?" she asked with a small laugh that was close to a groan.

The groan turned to an audible sigh at the thought that the most difficult portion of their journey was only hours away. Once through the pass, the weeks of travel to the confluence of the Darling and Murray rivers would be less arduous but certainly more hazardous. Or so the stories went from the few stouthearted pioneers who had started farms and ranches in the outback of the past decade.

In the dusk, camp fires took spark like lightning bugs within the contained encampment. The fires then erupted into blazes that lit the tired faces of the men and women as they began to fish pots and pans from their traveling chests.

There was little enough within the wagons: the most important items—a rifle and an ax, a few pots and pans, a little extra clothing, several blankets, perhaps a spinning wheel, and such prized possessions as a clock or a family Bible.

While Molly gathered firewood, Amaris lugged out a kettle, and Francis took it from her with a gallant flourish. "You should not be carrying heavy things like that."

She had to laugh. "Francis, I have lifted a lot heavier things than this at the Female Immigrants' Home. If you'll start the fire, I'll begin to peel—"

"Start a fire?" He looked at her blankly.

It was her turn to look blank. "You don't know how to start a fire?"

In the half light, his face was visibly red. "Of course, I do. In a fireplace. But what about containment and—"

"You have never camped out on your pheasant or partridge hunts or whatever it is you shoot?"

"That's what servants are for, Amaris. That's why we hired Molly."

She ignored his caustic tone. "Why don't you amble over and talk with Sin."

Relief and gratitude crossed her husband's face. She observed him as, spurs tinkling, he strolled over to the Tremayne wagon. He knelt with Jimmy over the fire they were building.

Molly returned, her arms laden with twigs and branches from the wattles that lined the nearby creek. She set to building a fire with the twigs and smaller branches. Every so often, she would glance toward Sin's wagon.

Amaris thought Molly might be watching Francis or Sin. That Molly liked men, any man, was the general assumption. Then she surprised Amaris. "Jimmy Underwood, does he have a wife waiting somewhere, missus?"

Amaris hid a smile. So forty-year-old Jimmy Underwood and not Francis had been the object of Molly's intentions all along. "Not that I know of." She set aside the kettle of plucked birds Francis had shot. "I'm going for more water."

Close by, Celeste was stirring a broth while the three men chatted. Amaris was about to join her friend, when she saw Sin quickly rise from his camp stool to lift the heavy kettle from the fire. Celeste thanked him with a smile, her hand briefly touching his arm. His glance lingered on her hand. There was a world of gentleness in his gaze. Celeste had tamed the beast.

Amaris wisely left the couple alone and walked on down to the creek. It was a wide and shallow meandering stream. In the rainy season, so she had heard, it would overflow its boundaries and carry away any sheep and cattle grazing nearby.

When she returned, Molly already had the birds skewered on a makeshift spit. Dripping juice sizzled in the fire. Amaris's mouth watered. She was tired, and her appetite voracious.

At last, dinner was ready, and she and Francis and Molly filled their plates and joined the others. Talk of the next day's haul up the mountain, of the latest trouble with the aborigines and what kind of grazing land could be found in the Never-Never, that unknown interior, was bantered around by the pioneers.

Afterward, when the dishes had been cleaned and the men got together to smoke a pipe, Amaris and Celeste walked down to the creek. Several other women were already there, delighting in the fresh water that soothed away their aches and cleansed the dust off their skin.

"Ah, Celeste," called Elizabeth Hannaby. Her husband, after soldiering for thirty years, had sold his commission for acreage in the outback. Like most, they aspired to become landed gentry. "'Tis a grand evening, isn't it."

Her smile even included Amaris, who was now the wife of a nobleman, no less. Amaris took the change of attitude in good stride. These people would be neighbors, and it was best to be on good terms with neighbors who could mean the difference between life and death.

"Lovely," Celeste said, "but I miss the sunrises against the ocean horizon."

"I imagine, dearie, we'll see sights quite as beautiful. So 'tis brides you two are."

Her patronizing tone went over Celeste's head. The moon's light betrayed her blushing face.

Amaris had put from her mind later tonight, when she would go to bed with Francis. That one time, when he had taken her virginity there on the Paramatta River, she had been overwhelmed by all the discoveries and revelations that had only been whispered about by both women who had husbands and those at the home who had already been "deflowered."

Only Pulykara had addressed her question of how a man and woman make a baby. "Watch the dogs and cats and sheep and horses. No different, Miss Priss."

Pulykara had been right. After all the impassioned words, the act itself was little more.

After Elizabeth left, Amaris knelt where the creek pooled over a bowl of shale and scrubbed her arms and face. The water smelled stale.

By the time she finished, Celeste was already rebuttoning her sleeves. She reached out and touched Amaris on the shoulder. "You're happy aren't you, Amaris?"

She stared down at the young bride. In the moonlight, she was like a pale blossoming flower. "I'm tired," she told the younger woman. "Let's go on back."

But returning to the wagon wasn't exactly something to which she was looking forward. Honesty compelled her to admit that she had bartered herself for the opportunity not only to seek retribution against Nan but also to escape the mundane life: her writing was mediocre; her social work was less than fulfilling. She feared she had Nan's grandness of vision.

A sheep station! How grandiose of her to think she and Francis could create an empire out of unseen, infinite stretches of the Never-Never.

Francis had trusted her wisdom. Had married her. She knew she owed Francis devotion. Any more than that she did not know if she was capable of giving.

When she returned to the camp, he was kneeling to spread out their bedrolls beneath their wagon, where it was cool. Molly was already inside, seeking sleep as a relief from her hard day.

Amaris glanced back over her shoulder. Strange, to be looking to Celeste for reassurance. The girl stood, her hand in Sin's, peering at whatever it was he pointed out on the dark-fringed horizon.

Resolutely, Amaris switched her gaze back to Francis. When she knelt beside him, he said, "Tired?"

She saw the desire in his eyes. Her smile was forced. "No."

In the deep darkness beneath the wagon, she peeled down to her petticoat and chemise. The nightgown she tugged overhead was voluminous—and hot. As she divested herself of the remaining underclothes, she couldn't help but think how wonderful it would be to sleep naked on the prairie, at one with nature, as Pulykara had once told her she had always done until being sold off to the white man's lumber camp.

Far in the distance a dingo howled. Looking out at the night sky, she felt pulled upward into that shimmering immensity. She experienced a certain affinity for its stars. She felt a reassurance seeing the Southern Cross tilting on its side, its points ever northward. She had a personal position on infinity.

Francis gathered her against him. "The others," she protested.

"There were others nearby that day on the river," he said, kissing her neck, "and that made it all the more exciting."

She steeled herself. His kisses were no less hungry. If anything, he seemed more ravenous for her. She was amazed to find herself responding.

Quickly, it was over. Afterward, she lay beside him as he slept. She stared at the wagon bottom's knotted pine boards and wondered at the mild distaste she felt for the intimacies of marriage with Francis.

She felt as if she had somehow given away something precious of herself but was at a loss to explain what.

14

If Amaris thought her journey the day before had been dusty, she felt buried in dust today. On that second day, the Marlborough wagon was last in line—all because Francis had insisted on shaving at the creek that morning.

She slid a sideways glance at her husband. She supposed she should feel pride at his fastidiousness, when the rest of the men were looking unkempt in their dirty dungarees and matted, scraggly beards.

Even Sin, who wore no facial hair, sported a shadowed jaw this morning. Thinking about her run-in with him at dawn, she shuddered.

She had risen in the dark, when only two or three others were stirring in their bedrolls, quietly dressed, and walked down to the creek. Cool, fresh water had been the one vision in her mind, and she had not detected any movement in the brush until she was caught fast from behind and her mouth silenced by a hand.

She struggled, kicking at her captor's shins and elbowing him in the ribs, but she was held fast. Her screams came out mere groans.

"Amaris!" Sin spit the name as if he had tasted something rotten.

In that lax moment, she sprang free of his grasp, but not far enough. Instantly, his hand latched onto her wrist. "Stop!"

The harshly whispered word had its effect. Like a snared rabbit, she went still.

He pointed just beyond her feet. Her gaze followed the direction of his finger. Tracks of bare feet cut the damp earth. "Aborigines," he said in a hushed voice.

She stared at the prints, then looked up at him. "So?"

"You are accustomed only to Pulykara. The bush aborigine is something different."

She resented his superior tone. He hadn't grown up in Australia. He didn't understand and love the land as she did. "How would *you* know?"

With that uncanny ability to read her mind, he said, "I may not have been born here, but 'tis many things I have seen that you can't even begin to imagine."

"Such as?" Why did she dally here with this man she didn't even respect?

"A coal mine camp ... the aborigines ran in packs of a hundred odd, so that their numbers compensated for their primitive weapons. They surrounded the huts. Then with blood-curdling yells and the growling of their kangaroo dogs, they clubbed some of the workers' heads to jelly. Most of us were lucky enough to hide in the bush until they left—and then the overseers' mastiffs caught up with us."

She shrugged. "Savages, all of you."

His hand tightened on her wrist. "A savage, Amaris? Aye, I suppose I have become one. And yourself?" He studied her in the gray light that preceded sunrise. "A scavenger, methinks. Aye, a savage and a scavenger. What a disgusting pair we are! Now, go on back to camp, while I track down these prints."

She jerked her wrist from his grip. "I don't know what Celeste sees in you."

She could have sworn he smiled. "I don't know what you see in Francis."

"Francis? Francis is a gentleman, but then you wouldn't understand the meaning of that term."

"I can't risk acting like a gentleman. Gentlemen don't survive out here."

A superior smile had tugged at her mouth. "Oh, I don't know. Francis managed to provide fresh meat for our supper last night."

The bridge of his nose had creased in a frown. "His hunting spree also managed to call down a pack of aborigines on us and endanger everyone in the wagon train."

Frustrated, she had shouldered past him. Heading back to the wagons, she had run into Major Hannaby, who had looked as startled as she. Why hadn't his ability as a leader been questioned? If the wagon train had to depend on an Irish ex-convict for information, then the pioneers were indeed in trouble.

She asked Francis, "Did Major Hannaby give you an idea of how long it would take to reach the Darling and Murray rivers?"

"Maybe six weeks—if we make it over *that.*"

She stared at what was causing his dour expression. The wagons and drays in front had already prepared for the steep ascent of the passage through the Blue Mountains. Long chains were linked between a wagon, and pullies built into the rocks. Celeste and Sin's wagon was even now being drawn up the almost sheer incline.

As Amaris watched, one chain popped loose. A tremendous whirring sound echoed between the foothills. The wagon began rolling back. She heard Celeste scream. At the same moment, Sin leaped from the wagon.

Bloody coward! Amaris's mind cried out even as she jumped down from her wagon and sprinted up the hill toward the runaway wagon. What in God's name did she think she could do? Another sixty seconds and the wagon would smash her flatter than a johnnycake, then smash itself and Celeste to oblivion on the rocks below.

All at once, Sin was flinging himself at the second pulley station. A grinding screech of the chains reverberated throughout the pass. The wagon, as if running up against a rock wall, stopped immediately, then jerked forward with the backlash of momentum before coming to a halt. Two wheels spun off in opposite directions. The wagon lurched drunkenly to one side.

Before Amaris could reach the wagon, Celeste jumped down and started running up the hill toward the second pulley station and Sin. He pushed himself off the pulley and straightened. At her shout, "Sin!" he turned toward her. Blood covered his arm and shirt. He took a step, staggered, and fainted.

Celeste pushed her way through the men who rushed to his side. "Oh, my God!"

Amaris, just behind her, saw the reason for her

outcry. Sin's left hand was mangled. Blood pumped furiously from finger joints that were nothing more than bare bone and shredded flesh. Amaris's breath sucked in. Her stomach knotted.

"Move aside," Major Hannaby said, crowding his bulk past the others. "I've dealt with things like this on the battlefield. Hands shattered by rifle fire."

He stooped over the inert Irishman. The old man made noises that sounded to her like a bumblebee droning. He glanced up at the blanched faces above. "No doubt about it, gentlemen. At least two of the fingers will have to be amputated."

"No!" Celeste cried.

Amaris put her arm around her friend's waist. "Come away. 'Tis best to let them do what they can."

"But he hasn't come to yet! What's wrong, Amaris?"

She tried to sound convincing and patted her friend's shoulder because she didn't know what else to do. "His body has simply received a shock to its system. He'll come around soon."

Four men shouldered the limp body and carried Sin away from the dusty, rutted path to a small, grassy clearing bounded by boulders. "Start a fire," the major said as he began rolling up his shirt sleeves to reveal bony arms sprinkled with gray hair.

Amaris followed Celeste to the clearing, where she sat down beside her unconscious husband. Seeing Sin like that, his face in repose, Amaris thought he was not nearly as fierce.

Celeste stroked his dust-coated hair back from his face. "It will be all right, my Sin." Tears rolled from her cheeks to clear paths through the dirt caked on his beard-stubbled face.

His eyes fluttered open. The pain must have struck immediately, because he winced, then groaned. At once, his eyes glazed over.

"Any water?" Amaris heard a man call out behind her. It was Jimmy Underwood. "We'll need water."

"Rum'll do just fine," Thomas Rugsby said. The Welshman's baby face was starting to grow peachfuzz.

"The things we'll need to watch for," the major was saying as he knelt between her and Celeste, "are infection, shock, and hemorrhage."

"Amaris," Francis said, shouldering through the onlookers to her side. "Is Sin all right?"

The major looked up from the knife he was holding over the flame. "He will be if he survives the operation." His expression was bleak.

"Give the Irishman a liberal dose of the stuff," said a bean pole of a man called Sykes. He was an ex-convict who had worked as a stockman and now wanted his own run.

So many people were crowding around that Amaris found the lack of fresh air nauseating. Or maybe it was the spectators she found nauseating. They were treating this like it was a circus.

Francis surprised her by squatting beside her. In his hand he held a bottle of rum. "Here you go, friend," he said, lifting Sin's head to pour a stream between his slack lips. "A round of drinks on me."

Then Francis tilted the bottle to his own mouth, took a deep draught, and returned the bottle to Sin's. The amber liquor spilled over the man's lips and ran down his neck and under his sweat-stained collar.

"Let me through," the major said. The knife he held rapidly parted the onlookers.

Amaris stared up at the red-hot blade.

A strangled, "No!" escaped Celeste's pale lips. Her face was as white as the dust on Sin's.

A chubby young squatter named Lemuel followed the major. Benny, a clubfooted man, carried a torch. Realizing the awful act that was about to come, Amaris swallowed hard. "Come with me, Celeste, and let the major take care of Sin."

"Let me up," Sin mumbled behind them.

Celeste pulled away from her. "No, Sin needs me."

The major whispered, "Lemuel, strap a tourniquet on his arm. Mrs. Tremayne, talk to him, distract him."

She knelt beside Sin and propped his head on her lap. "Darling, how are you feeling?"

His brow was sheened with sweat, and pain whitened his lips. "Like hell."

He glanced down at his mangled hand, lying on his stomach. Blood gushed into a pool around the splayed fingers—or what was left of them. The ghastly sight made even Amaris want to wretch. The major bent over him, and he asked, "Me hand? It has to come off?"

"Only a couple of fingers. Nothing to fret about."

"In that case, let's have ourselves a party," he rasped with a wry smile.

As deftly as a sailor, the cherubic Lemuel knotted a leather cord from a bedroll around Sin's forearm, then, with a grunt of satisfaction, stood back to watch.

"Marlborough," Sin said, his voice ragged with pain, "give me another couple draughts of that nectar."

"Here, Francis," Celeste interposed, "I'll give my husband a drink."

As if she were serving tea, she took the brown bottle and, supporting Sin's head, daintily tilted the bottle to his dry lips. "There, my darling, you'll feel better in no time." With a tremulous smile, she returned the bottle to Francis, who made way for the major.

Sin swallowed, then said, "Get on with the party, Major."

The old man glanced at Amaris, kneeling opposite him. She also had the misfortune to be closest to the major. "Push back his sleeve, Mrs. Marlborough, and hold his hand steady for me."

Her heart missed a beat. She had thought one of the men, maybe Jimmy or Sykes, would assist the major. In front of her behind the line of kneeling men, Eileen Hannaby, Molly, and Elizabeth watched with worried faces.

Swallowing back her queasiness, she half tore, half pushed the frayed sleeve up Sin's forearm as far as the tourniquet would allow. The muscles in the forearm stood out like pulley chains.

"Tremayne," the old man said, "the last two fingers are coming off. You ready?"

Sin nodded.

Celeste cradled his head in her lap. She was smiling brilliantly at him. The tears in her eyes were hard diamonds. "Did I ever tell you what a handsome rake you are?"

Thinking Celeste had picked a poor moment to make a tasteless joke, Amaris rolled her eyes. Then, seeing her friend's adoring expression, she realized Celeste really meant what she was saying.

Sin's laugh was brittle. "The fairies have been whispering nonsense to you while you sleep, Celeste."

At that instant, a harsh breath came from deep in his throat. His arm shook. His eyes closed. "God . . . damn!"

A vibration traveled from his wrist into her fingers. Against her will, she glanced down. The major was sawing into the base of the shattered finger bones. He worked with concentrated intent.

The noonday sun seemed unmercifully hot. Boiling hot. She closed her eyes, and Sin said, "Don't you dare go"—he winced at the renewed shaft of pain, then finished—"weak on me, Amaris!"

"Not Amaris," Celeste defended, her voice a light humming in Amaris's ears. "Amaris is the strongest of us all. Why, she nursed the convict women at the home through the cholera epidemic. Do you remember, Sin, when Amaris stood up to the port official because—"

Whatever it was Celeste was recalling, Amaris didn't hear. There was a terribly loud droning in her ears now. She forced herself to think about the run she and Francis would be claiming. With luck, it would have a good flowing creek. Was Rogue staying with the sheep below?

"Take another drink," the major was saying. "You're going to need it, man."

Francis bent near and passed the bottle to Celeste, who once again tipped it to her husband's mouth. At that same moment, the major laid his knife onto the torch Benny held ready, until the blade glowed once more with a pulsating red.

Sin had no more swallowed than the major laid the knife over the two bloodied stubs. She heard a hiss, then smelled the stench of burning flesh. What would have been a shriek issued from Sin in a muffled groan, and then he fainted again.

Sin Tremayne lost the next day due to the amputation. Amaris handled the Tremayne wagon reins, while Sin rested fitfully. Elizabeth's home concoction might not have made him sleep as promised but it did keep down his fever.

Celeste counted that a blessing. Sitting in the back of the wagon, she smoothed back his hair from his face as he dozed that next evening. "We're both so lucky, Amaris. It could have been so much worse. I—I might have lost him."

Amaris, standing outside the wagon, leaned against its drop-down door and peered through the dark at her friend. "Did it ever occur to you that you might have died in that accident?"

"Better me than Sin. He's strong. He could go on without me. I wouldn't want to live without him."

Amaris couldn't understand this sort of rationale. "Look, why don't you get out and stretch your legs. Wash off the day's dust. You'll feel better."

"I can't leave—"

"Yes, you can leave Sin. I'll spell you."

Celeste paused, then said, "All right. But come get me if he—"

"I will, I will, I swear." She had to smile. "Now go on."

After Celeste left, she climbed inside the wagon. The canvas top was folded back to catch the evening breeze, and by sitting just so she could watch the twinkle of the clear stars that made up the Southern Cross.

"We can't see the crux in Ireland, you know."

His voice startled her. She glanced over at him. In the darkness his blue eyes glowed as bright as the stars.

"Then the Irish are missing something beautiful."

"Oh, I don't know. You currency people have never seen the true color of emerald."

There was such longing in his voice that she overlooked his reference to her as a currency child, a first-generation Australian. "Tell me, Sin, will you ever go back to Ireland?"

He didn't answer, and she wasn't sure he had heard her. "No," he said at last, "me life is here. For some reason, fate has brought me here to Australia. Somewhere out there in the Never-Never, I will find out why."

She could have chided him about his Irish penchant for fatalism, but his philosophical mood intrigued her. "You don't believe in mere coincidence?"

"No more than you do. Fate is taking you into the Never-Never, also."

"No, not fate. I control my destiny. I make my choices."

His eyes drilled into hers. "Wait and see, Amaris," he said in a low voice that made her shiver. She wasn't certain if her reaction was elicited by the prophecy of the voice or its deep mellifluous tone that stirred as yet unawakened longings.

Australia was a man's land, rough and raw. This was land much older than Europe, worn down by time, passive and long-suffering, enduring the severest droughts, extreme heat, heaviest floods, and devastating winds. Its vegetation bent, distorted, adapted—and survived.

Yet this was also Arcady: the land rich, the climate beneficent. Sheep and cattle thrived. Enterprise was open to all.

At least that was the image Amaris strived to keep before her. In the meanwhile, she made biscuits with weeviled flour, brewed post-and-rail tea in which ticks floated to the top, went weeks without a bath due to the scarcity of waterholes, and endured Francis's increasing frustration with the disillusionment of his dream.

She guessed that he had expected, despite all warnings, the green, rolling meadows of his homeland. To his credit, he was stubborn, and she knew he would see this venture through to its realization.

No one complained if the wagon train crossed over another's land, for no roads existed. Apart from small yards of rough timber close to huts, no sign was seen of settlement as they approached the fringe of that great tract of emptiness known as the Never-Never.

Eventually, the area of land grants was reached: a vast, grassy plain. Relief flooded Amaris. Her dreams had not been dashed. Each squatter selected the acreage that would make up his run and made a note of its natural boundaries, such as a creek or a hill, and cut notches in a line of trees or ran a single furrow with a plow to mark the edge.

By now, Amaris knew that rich, green grass country was synonymous with bad sheep country. The reason for this was stock disease. In high rainfall areas, standing water led to a high incidence of disease. The result was the wethers barely had enough time to fatten before they died of the disease.

She and Francis selected a run dotted in places with saltbush and blue bush and desiccated acacia trees. Another plus was the wide, shallow creek, trickling through a swath of the run. The creek was called Yagga Yagga, aborigine for Quiet Quiet. Which was what it was. Softly came an oboelike birdsong, infinitely lovely. "A curlew," Sin said.

Standing on the ridge beneath a silver ghost gum, she surveyed the green meadows where young kangaroos grazed and the timbered stretches beyond. The place had a spirit. At least, she thought so after chancing on aboriginal rock art one day when riding boundary. The area was a Dreaming Site, a place that still contained the power and energy of the Dream Time. It was mystical. It was hers. Pulykara would commend her for being a Dream Keeper.

Later, she and Francis lay side by side in their swags that first evening. A little apart, Molly slept soundly, tiredly. Amaris was too excited to sleep. "When we have time we can build a dam. Besides, Francis, this is the dry season. If we don't build on that hillock, our house will be flooded when the rains come."

Build they did, as did all the other squatters over the next several days—if what was little more than a roof on supports could be considered a house. All the squatters assisted in erecting each house.

The first job was to cut split posts to make a rough pen for livestock. She and Francis had only the sheep and their two horses to pen.

The hut she and Francis shared was put together with sheets of bark stretched out and tied by strings of bullock hide to a framework composed of saplings, also bound with strings of hide. Not a nail was used in the entire building. Abutting that shed were a primitive kitchen and a nook that served as temporary sleeping quarters for Molly. Amaris foresaw more permanent cottages for all the workers she would one day employ.

Inside, bunks and a table were likewise constructed of sapling. Their fireplace was chinked together from stones gathered by the women.

Throughout the day, the men looked to Sin for advice. For a man who wasn't one of the currency lads, he seemed to be respected for his knowledge. When noon brought a respite, the women were ready with fresh water and pot-roasted beef.

Amaris stood and watched the sweaty men eat their fill. A dread filled her. These people had been her daily companions through all sorts of hardships for six weeks. Once temporary homes were erected on each of the runs, she did not know when or how often she would see them. Tens of miles would separate nearest neighbors.

As though her thoughts had been voiced, Celeste came up behind her and whispered, "We'll miss seeing you as often as we used to."

Amaris turned to her. "We?"

"Aye, Sin, too. You know how he feels about you."

She floundered for words. "Well, I would say he doesn't exactly approve of your associating with me."

Amazement deepened the brown in Celeste's eyes. "I don't know whatever made you think that, because he says your strength is what will make Australia."

Eyes narrowing suspiciously, she looked at the men, lounging in various positions beneath the bark shed, to find Sin's sun-weathered face. Propped on one arm, he was sinking those white teeth into a hunk of the stringy kangaroo meat while he listened to a point the major seemed to be making.

"What made Sin say that?" she asked. Had he been mocking her queasiness that day she had steadied his hand for amputation?

"Why, Sin has felt that way for as long as I can remember."

Astonished, Amaris returned her gaze to Sin. Had she been wrong about him all this time?

15

Noah couldn't have witnessed this much rain, Amaris thought as she stood beneath the porch awning and surveyed the overflow of the creek's turbulent water. It inched threateningly closer to their newly built home. The roof Sin and Francis had labored on the past four months was still unfinished. Rainwater dribbled into a bucket in the rooms upstairs. The house lacked many amenities of even the houses in the Rocks. A real criterion of destitution. Yet she had never lived in anything so nice or so large. The house had its own parlor, office, and four bedrooms, as well as a cottage for Molly.

How many sheep was she going to lose to the rains? Francis and Rogue could only work so many sheep. Both her husband and her dog were looking ragged those days. Nine months of isolation and deprivation in the outback was taking its toll. She, Francis, and even Molly, who did all the cooking and cleaning while Amaris helped Francis work the sheep, suffered from fatigue, lack of sleep, and perhaps most of all a monotonous routine that was interrupted only occasionally by some holiday gathering.

With a sigh, she turned and went back inside.

She strode into the downstairs bedroom, where Francis slept. His hair was still damp, and mud glistened on his forearms. He was determined to make a working ranch out of their sheep station, Dream Time. Gently, she shook his shoulder. "I'm going to check on the sheep." Rogue couldn't gauge water rising.

Francis's eyes opened. He tried to focus, gave up, and closed them again with a mumbled, "All right."

Pity softened her gaze. Francis's life had been one of lightheartedness and luxury. He had had no experience with hard labor. He blundered often in his decisions, but she could understand that because he didn't know and love the land yet.

Nevertheless, he was determined to make the station a success, and for this she respected him. In truth, the station was gradually prospering. Six lambs had been added to the flock out of lambing season.

She swung away and took her rubber slicker from a peg along with her wide-brimmed bush hat, under which she tucked her braid. A wry smile tugged at the ends of her mouth when she recalled the adage that the brim of a station owner's bush hat was in inverse proportion to the size of his station.

His station? Descending the veranda's wooden

steps, she glanced down at her long legs, clothed in men's riding trousers. She supposed that, wearing those and the bush hat, she did look like a man.

The wind had picked up. She tightened her hat's drawstrings and braced herself against the wind's brunt. Renegade stood placidly in the shed, tail-end to the wind. Wearily, she saddled the gelding, mounted, and set off in a direction that paralleled the creek.

Driving rain slashed at her face. Rain, wind, dust, the glaring sun—she had made them her companions. Them and a loneliness that Francis's and Molly's presence did not alleviate.

Suddenly a thought from out of nowhere leaped into her mind: On those occasions when Sin and Celeste rode over for a dinner party or when she and Francis went to Sin's to celebrate a holiday, she wasn't lonely. More specifically, the time flew during those few times she spent talking to Sin about sheep breeding or the price of wool in London or shipping charges.

She shook her head. No, it was only the subject, not Sin, that made the time pass so quickly, so pleasurably.

Dream Time was becoming her passion, her dream to replace the emptiness her writing and her charity work had not done. She would somehow make Dream Time Sheep Station an empire in Australia, though just how she didn't know. Not when there was so much land, so little money, so few hands to do the work.

She rode on in the afternoon's sullen half-light. The wind keened in her ears like one of Sin's banshees. Some minutes passed before she realized that not only the wind was keening. She sat more alert in the saddle and strained to differentiate between the timbres.

Her ears detected a human quality!

Her hand dropped to the saddlebags to search for the reassuring bulge of her pistol.

It wasn't there. Suddenly, all the horror stories she had ever heard about the savage aborigines of the outback and the even more ruthless bushrangers, those escaped convicts and robbers who terrorized the outback, shot through her mind.

Then a quality in the keening mitigated her panic. Instinct prompted her to turn her horse in the direction of the sound, which was coming from the creek. The ground grew more sodden. Renegade, picking his way down a muddy incline, avoided debris of bush and weeds left by the storm's rising and receding waters.

The green line of trees below and the amplification of the rushing water indicated she was coming upon the creek. Little more than the tops of trees were visible above the cascading water. A bloated sheep bobbed past. One of hers?

The power of the raging creek was overwhelming. Just the thundering sound made her dizzy. She scanned the area, looking for the source of the strange wailing she had heard. Finding nothing, she was in the act of wheeling her horse around when her eye was caught by the flash of red among green.

She rode closer. Perched precariously on a swaying limb was a near-naked aborigine, wearing a red bandanna knotted around his neck, a leather breechcloth, and boots. The man was so small, she at first mistook him for a child. Fright was etched in the whites of the wide eyes. The lips were taut with pain.

Then she saw why: A long gash laid open his leg to the bare bone, beginning just below his breechcloth all the way to his knobby knee. That explained the keening—he had sensed imminent death.

She called to him. He didn't move. She rode closer—as close as safety would permit—and yelled again. Only his gaze shifted toward her. The rest of his dark body was like petrified wood, almost undetectable from the eucalyptus to which he clung.

She gauged the distance of safe ground that separated her from him. Not enough. She glanced at the swirling waters. A flirt with death should she try to reach the man.

She saw the fear color the man's eyes a yellow glaze. He knew she knew that certain death awaited him. He nodded, he understood and was resigned. When one lived in the Never-Never, each day one awakened was one more day than had been expected.

Not wanting to witness the man's death, she turned her horse around to trot up the rain-washed knoll. She got no farther than a couple of yards, then tugged so hard on her reins that Renegade reared on his back legs and neighed his displeasure.

Taking her rope from the saddle ring, she knotted it through the ring in the surcingle. Then she led old Renegade down the incline toward the tree where the aborigine was perched. Each step she carefully tested against mud slide.

When water swished over the toes of her riding

boots, she stopped. The man in the tree stared at her uncomprehendingly.

She held up the looped rope.

A glimmer of hope brightened his eyes.

She twirled a loop of the rope and tossed it toward the man.

He had sat in one position for so long that his reaction time was slow, and he missed the rope by a hand's length.

She hauled the rope in. Even in the lapse of those few seconds, the water seemed to have risen to her ankles. Or else she was standing on mushy earth that was sinking. She tried again and lost her footing. She splashed into the muddy water. It stole her hat, then swished into her mouth, opened in outrage.

Sputtering, she came quickly to her feet, grabbed at the floating rope, and calmed a now spooked Renegade. The whites of his eyes and his whinny proclaimed his nervousness. He was accustomed to a wagon—and to her. And more recently, the nuisance of sheep.

The horse tried to shy back, but even the distance of a handspan would be too far at that point for the rope to reach. Restraining the horse by its bit, she tossed the rope a third time.

This time the aborigine caught it. Did he speak English? "Tie it around your waist," she called.

He stared at her blankly.

She went through the imaginary motion of knotting her end of the rope around her own waist.

He nodded and awkwardly mimicked her action.

She could only hope he had tied it tightly enough.

When that was done, she yelled, "Now, climb down out of the tree." Elaborately, she pantomimed her instructions. Despite the dire situation, she grinned at how absurd she must look.

She was absolutely startled when the man grinned back at her. Then she started laughing—and he started laughing. At that, she laughed harder, making silly wheezing sounds that made her laugh even more. The little man laughed so hard that tears glinted in his eyes like prisms of sunlight.

At last, both she and the aborigine stopped and stared across the expanse of white-capped water. He would have to avoid the wood and bush and other jetsam bobbing past. She would have to nudge her nervous old nag into a slow but steady ascent of the knoll.

With the pressure of her knees to clue him, Renegade performed admirably in hauling the man through the water. The current kept tugging at him, and he went under the water's surface several times. She was afraid he would drown.

When finally he gained footing, staggered ashore, and collapsed half in, half out of the water, she halted Renegade and, dismounting, ran to the man.

He looked like a gnome, all shriveled, making it difficult to tell his age. He could have been fifteen or fifty. She guessed somewhere in between, maybe thirty. His long hair was a scruffy mop.

His eyes opened. Dark brown irises stared back at her. Then he grinned. She realized three of his front teeth were missing.

"Your leg." She pointed. "We need to take care of it." She knew she didn't ever again want to take part in an amputation. "Let's get you back to the house."

That part was harder than rescuing him from an island tree. He was very reluctant to mount Renegade. When she finally persuaded him to do so, she found pushing the man into the saddle was like hefting deadweight.

Riding tandem with him, she turned Renegade back in the direction of the house. The man sitting in front of her, and no taller than Nan Livingston, stank something awful. She finally identified the smell as that of emu oil.

She tried not to look at the canyon of a gash running the length of his thigh. The rain started pouring down in wind-driven sheets. She didn't know whether to feel grateful that the smell was obliterated or feel miserable in her soggy state.

Renegade's steps picked up as he sensed the proximity of the stable. At last, the vague outlines of the house appeared. Supporting the man with his arm across her shoulder, she stumbled toward the shelter of the veranda. They got no farther than just inside the door and, panting, collapsed on the floor.

A bewildered Francis staggered through their bedroom door. Seeing her entangled with the aborigine, her husband rushed toward them.

"No!" She held up a staying hand. "It's not what you think."

He stopped short and peered down at her. "What the devil . . . !"

"He's been hurt, Francis."

"We'll be hurt if any of the squatters discover we're harboring an aborigine savage. You know better than to do something like this."

She ignored him. Getting to her feet again, she

slipped her arm underneath the aborigine's and dragged him toward the spare bedroom. As yet, it had no bed, but she well remembered Pulykara's preference for the floor.

A pallet compiled of old blankets was quickly made for the man. His eyes watched her as she moved around the room.

She left to prepare hot water for cleansing the gaping leg wound. Francis was pacing the floor. "I was going to check on the sheep in the back pasture, but I never got a chance," she told him. "You'd better see what you can do."

He glowered at her. "I don't have to be told like a child."

She was too tired to apologize. Wearily, she returned to the other bedroom and the wounded man. When she entered, his eyes brightened. The gash had been soaked in the dirty river water for so long that red streaks radiated upward from it. She felt the man's forehead. It was feverish all right.

She finished cleansing the wound and wrapped it in clean cotton strips. "You need something in your stomach," she told him and felt foolish since he probably didn't speak English. He gazed at her uncomprehendingly, but that might be credited to his condition. God knew how long he might have been perched in that tree.

She prepared an herbal tea and a bowl of corn mush, but either he was so weak he couldn't eat or he detested the white man's food. With the advent of evening, darkness turned the room as dark as the Styx. By the light of her candle, the aborigine's eyes appeared quite glazed, and he was making a low, raspy moaning sound.

Within the hour, she would need to decide whether to stitch the gash or take off the leg. Medication was nil in the outback. Should she chance only stitching . . .

She was worried, too, about Francis. He should have been back by now. When the door opened, she spun around, arms outstretched in a relieved welcome—only to fling herself into Sin's arms. He was as startled as she. In automatic response, he held her against him. Only a second, but an eternal second.

Confused, she stepped back, out of his embrace.

He removed his bush hat and slapped it against his thigh, showering water droplets everywhere. His forelocks were plastered against his temples. His gaze, usually forceful and direct, was troubled, preoccupied.

"What is it?" she asked. "Francis? Is it Francis? Something's happened to him?"

His puzzled expression told her she should have realized that he would not have known Francis was late returning home. "No. It's Celeste. She's . . . bleeding . . . too much, too soon."

"Miscarrying?!" Amaris hadn't known Celeste was with child. Only last month, Amaris had seen Celeste, and the girl had looked as slender as ever.

The occasion had been a dinner at the Tremayne house in honor of Sin's birthday. The major and Elizabeth had traveled even farther than she and Francis, almost twenty miles, for the party. Sykes and his new wife Betty, a middle-aged woman who had come to Australia as a governess, had been late, having ridden more than twenty-five. Distance didn't matter when the opportunities to get together were all too rare in the outback.

Tom, who was courting Eileen, especially welcomed these opportunities. So did Molly and Jimmy, who had spent a great deal of the evening in each other's company. Amaris and Francis had gotten home at four that next morning.

"How far along is Celeste?"

He tunneled his fingers through his thick, damp hair. "Four, maybe five months. Can you come help?"

Strange, how self-sufficient, how competent, the Irishman was—until it came to something like this. She rubbed her temples. "Oh, Sin, you know I will. Meanwhile, though, everything around here is going to hell in a handbasket. In the next room, I have an aborigine whose leg is badly hurt. I don't know where Francis is. He was going to the back pasture, and he should have been back before now."

"Let me take a quick look at the aborigine. Then, I'll search for Francis."

His decisiveness took some of the weight of worry from her shoulders. "Thank you. I'll ride on over to your—"

"You're not going alone."

She stared at him. She stood so close she could see the silver matrix of his blue irises. "Well, pray tell, whom would I ride with? If you stay here—"

"We'll take care of the problem here, then I'll escort you—"

"Sin! You're not thinking. Celeste could bleed to—"

"You listen to me, Amaris. I don't need *two* women to anguish over."

She stared at him, wondering if he realized what he had just said. Or was she putting more emphasis on the word *anguish* than he had meant?

"Let me see this guest of yours," he was saying. "One problem at a time, me girl."

The aborigine didn't seem surprised to see Sin enter with her. Sin hunkered on one knee beside the little man. Outside, the whistling wind and monsoonlike rain were so strong that the rafters overhead seemed to vibrate.

"Hold the candle closer, Amaris." He prodded the reddened area around the wound, apparently observing the reaction of both the surrounding flesh and the little man as well. The aborigine never winced.

"Well?" she asked kneeling beside Sin. Her gaze lingered on his left hand. Strong and brown, its mutilation of the last two fingers was almost unnoticeable, at least to her anyway. Maybe it was because she rarely looked at hands, since her own were so large. "Will he be able to keep the leg?"

Though Sin looked tired and worried, he managed a grin. "I'd wager my last two fingers on it. A few dozen stitches ought to do it."

Her concern for the man ebbed with her sigh. "Good." There were still Francis and Celeste to worry about.

"I'll ride back, after I know Celeste is all right, and show you how to rig a traction for his leg until it mends."

"I'll manage on my own."

Sin rose to his feet beside her. "Ever the stubborn, independent woman. Which way did Francis head out?"

"Toward the back—"

The front door blew open with a bang. She hurried from the bedroom to close the door before the rain soaked the carpet. Francis stood just inside, trying to remove his rain-drenched slicker. "Where have you been?" she asked. "I was so worried."

A silly smile curled his lips. "Decided to wait out the downpour at the shepherd's hut." He peeled the slicker's sleeve from his arm. "'Cept the downpour never stopped. When I was as wet inside that leaky hut as I would have been outside, I started on back."

Her fingers rubbed against her thumbs while she tried to control her agitation. Francis had been drinking again. She supposed he felt drink alleviated his boredom. "I'm nothing but a bloody shepherd," he often complained.

She couldn't blame him for despising the daily routine of taking the flock to an area to graze, making sure it didn't wander off, plodding along behind the sheep as they grazed at their own leisurely pace, then herding them back to the outstation by a different route in the evening. The work was repetitive and, aye, boring.

Yet she derived a certain pleasure from riding the land, observing nature—the animals, the plants, and the weather. There was so much to absorb and conclude from nature's activities.

The day before she had seen a pair of white-breasted eagles at their nest on a ledge thirty feet up a riverbed's limestone wall, a huge crocodile catching fish in a billabong, flocks of hundreds of thousands of geese feeding in a marsh, and flying foxes squabbling noisily in their daytime roost.

"Sin's here. Celeste is miscarrying."

Francis didn't evidence any surprise that Celeste was with child. But his mind wasn't that sharp at the moment.

"I'm going to ride back with him. I shouldn't be gone more than a couple of days or so. Will you have Molly check on the aborigine while I'm away? See that he has food and water and doesn't try to move that leg."

"Most certainly," Francis said, making an exaggerated bow.

His slicker fell onto the floor. She collected it and hung it on a peg. "Go on to bed, Francis, and get some sleep. I know you must be tired."

She turned back to the spare bedroom. Sin stood in the doorway, watching. So now he knew. He had a comrade with whom he could share his drinking bouts.

Except that Sin didn't seem to drink that much anymore. At his birthday bash, he had drunk only moderately.

His eyes studied her so intently that she felt compelled to shrug off the incident with Francis. A defensive gesture, she realized, but it was necessary. Sin must never guess her worries, which were also her weaknesses. She couldn't afford to be vulnerable. Not out here. If she wanted to be taken seriously as a station owner, she couldn't be weak. In fact, she knew she had to be stronger than any of the men. Stronger even than Sin. "Ready to help me sew the leg?"

He nodded.

"Sin!" Francis said, only just taking note of the Irishman's presence.

"Mind if Amaris accompanies me back to me station when we finish tending the aborigine?"

Francis's hand waved in a generous gesture. "Not at all, my friend."

She watched her husband weave his way toward their bedroom. She recalled a time when he had donned his fox-hunting costume and then had proceeded to get quite drunk as he rode Frivolity in circles around the yard.

She didn't even want to look in Sin's direction, to see whatever expression mirrored his thoughts—pity, contempt, condemnation.

She went on in back to the bedroom where the wounded black man lay. By now she had collected an assortment of rudimentary medical supplies. Sin helped hold the gashed flesh closed while she deftly wielded her needle and thread. Never once did the aborigine wince with pain.

She smiled across at Sin. "All of my mother's lessons in needlework were worth the tedious hours I suppose."

Beneath the angled brows, the blue eyes held hers. "You wield a needle as well as you do a stockman's whip. You are an accomplished person, Amaris."

The task took only twenty minutes. When they finished, she collected her slicker and hat. Outside, the rain had slackened. Trying to ignore his footsteps behind her, she strode to the shed and began saddling Renegade once more. The gelding was certainly putting in duty-time this day. "I know, I know, old boy. I'm as tired as you are."

Sin, having already mounted, rode alongside her. "Thank you for coming, Amaris."

"There's no reason to thank me," she said crossly. "Celeste is my friend. But even if she weren't, I'd come. The loneliness is tough enough on a white woman without even taking into consideration the bearing of children."

Without a moon, the two horses had to pick their way carefully over land riveted with gullies, which slowed the journey. A misstep in one of the profusion of wombat holes would bring a horse to the ground.

Amaris could sense Sin's impatience. His mouth was set in a tense line. Compassion stirred her. Seeking to distract him, she asked, "How do you avoid the trap of boredom while you're working the sheep?" She was specifically thinking of Francis's complaint about station life.

"I play four-handed whist."

She could hear the humor in his voice. "By yourself?"

"Certainly, me girl. I deal four hands facedown. As I play each hand, I am most careful never to expose the cards. It makes for a challenging game, I assure you."

She chuckled. "I can imagine. However, I would think that the game would be disappointing since three of the four aspects of your player-self always lose."

He chuckled this time. From there the conversation drifted into the usual subject of sheep: his new woolshed, the lambing season, her concern about the dingoes that were decimating the flocks, his horse business.

"You are still determined to ride back alone?" he asked in that deep brogue that against her will she found attractive.

She shrugged. "I have a pistol."

"'Tis a particular brand of obstinate courage you have."

She considered what he had said. She didn't mind riding alone in the dark and drizzle. Nevertheless, she discovered a certain solace in Sin's company. He was an articulate man with courage of the toughest fiber. And yet—thinking of his conduct with women and children and animals—he could behave, paradoxically, as a gentle man.

The wind died down and the rain abated. The three-hour ride went quickly for her, with the conversation dominated by the political direction the Australian colonies were taking. Sin totally rejected anything English.

Soon, a speck of light signaled they were drawing near the Tremayne house. Lantern glow spread through a front window to illuminate a portion of the yard. Jimmy was outside on the veranda steps, waiting to take hers and Sin's reins. "The missus, Sin, she h'aint doing so well."

"Wait here," Amaris told the two men and strode inside, her spurred boots clinking a dirge on the puncheon floor.

Yellow candlelight splashed a sallow pool over a woman's small frame. Amaris stared in open-mouthed shock at her friend. Celeste's sweet rounded figure was gone, replaced by a drawn, thin look. The pure alabaster skin was weathered and brown. Miscarrying a child couldn't be totally responsible for the condition Amaris beheld.

Clearly, Celeste was withering in the harsh clime. When she was her usual vibrant, chattering self, one didn't notice the subtle physical changes taking place, not until illness stilled the vivacious woman, although Celeste could hardly be termed *still* at that moment. She was making little mewing sounds. Curled up in a fetal position, she hugged her stomach and trembled with each passing contraction.

Amaris felt her forehead. The fever alarmed her. "Celeste, it's Amaris."

The young woman opened her eyes. They were dulled and reddened from weeping. "Amaris," she whispered. "An angel. Thank God. I hurt, Amaris. You always come to help me."

"You'll be all right." She tried to think of what the old women and Pulykara did for the pregnant women at the home. "I'll need to check your progress with the baby, Celeste."

"I'm going to lose our baby," Celeste said, eyes closed.

"I'll be the judge of that." She pushed back the coverlets and raised the young woman's blood-stained gown. The towel between her thighs was soaked. "When was this last changed?"

"Sin . . . just before he left."

Gingerly, she folded back the towel. She swallowed hard. The fetus was visible on the towel, although its sex was indeterminate to her. "There will be other babies, Celeste."

Tears seeped from the corners of the younger woman's closed eyes. "Then I've already lost the baby."

"Aye," she said softly. What worried her was the absence of the full afterbirth. Celeste's fever signaled the possibility of infection from the retention of a portion of it. It would have to be removed. "Celeste, you must trust me."

"Go ahead . . . I know something must be done . . . if Sin and I hope to have other children."

Celeste ladened Sin's name with such passion that the image of her and Sin in the throes of lovemaking flashed in Amaris's mind. In the next instant, she pursued the natural course of her thought: What would it be like to be made love to by Sin?

The image exploded in an intense burst of sensations. Her hand latched on to the bedpost to keep her from sagging with sudden and intense desire. Never, in all her life, had anything happened like that.

Its repercussion was a clamoring, demanding need to experience its realization with him. Right then!

Why Sin? He wasn't handsome; he was a former convict; an Irishman, a thoroughly irritating man.

Ridiculous! Irrational! Yet now she would never be able to look at him without thinking . . . fantasizing . . . and worse, fearing he would see the speculation of passion in her eyes.

She steadied herself, forcing herself to focus on Celeste and her needs. "Oh, you needn't worry about having more children," she said, keeping a steady stream of chatter to distract Celeste—and perhaps herself from the task at hand. "You will be known as the Old Lady in the Shoe, who had so many children she didn't know what to do."

"Amaris."

At the soft yet insistent tone, she looked up at Celeste's face. Her feverishly bright eyes were fastened on her. "Yes?"

"Have I ever told you, Amaris, what a dear,

wonderful person you are? Sin and I are so lucky to have you living so near."

Guilt flushed her face. She looked down at her bloodied hands. "I think I've been able to remove the remainder of the afterbirth. I'll prepare an herbal for your fever and get a fresh gown for you."

Too exhausted by the ordeal, Celeste only nodded. Her eyes were already closed. Amaris rummaged through a chest and found at last another gown, although it was threadbare.

Her search for cider vinegar and honey took less time, and while the potion was brewing, she had Sin bring her a scraping of gum beads from its tree bark. She wasn't certain that the beads actually helped that much, but it would give Sin something to do.

Meanwhile she carefully removed Celeste's old gown. The young woman protested weakly. "This won't take long, and you'll feel better."

She poured a pitcher of fresh water into the basin and washed the thin young woman, then just as carefully redressed her.

When Amaris attempted to spoon the concoction into Celeste's mouth, she whispered, "You're so good to me, Amaris."

"Ssssh, go to sleep now."

She spent an inordinate amount of time straightening the disarrayed bedroom, emptying the dishpan of bloodied water, securely wrapping the fetus for disposal.

She knew the reason for her delay. She was stalling facing Sin. The light rap at the door told her she could stall no longer.

"Amaris," he said, his voice muffled, "is Celeste all right?"

Amaris went to the door and opened it. Sin's face was in the shadows. With her back to the candle, she knew he couldn't make out her expression either.

She stepped into the shadowed hallway, closing the door behind her. Her voice lowered to a whisper. "Celeste will be all right. But losing the baby has taken its toll on her." Against her will, Amaris blushed. She didn't know how to express delicately the situation.

"Go on," he prompted. "We've discussed birthing before. Don't go maiden-shy on me now."

She realized, with a smarting pain, that he considered her one of the boys. That made what she had to say easier. "You must not try to, ah, lie with Celeste for a while. She's, ah, weak." She could feel the heat suffusing her face. "In a couple of months . . ."

"I have more common sense—and self-restraint— than you credit me with." He braced a hand on the wall, near her head. His voice was deeper, indicating his own fatigue. "Why don't you stay the night and get some rest? I can ride back with you tomorrow morning."

"No. No. I need to start back to Dream Time now. With it being lambing time, I need to be there." She couldn't sleep in the same house with Sin. Not the way she felt about him now.

Even at that moment, standing so close in the dark, she was weakened by her body's betraying demands.

"Now this doesn't make sense. If you ride back tonight, you won't be in any shape to work tomorrow. Get some sleep, and you can start back early."

"No. I'm leaving now." She pushed past his arm that blocked her way and strode into the main room to collect her hat and slicker.

He followed on her heels. "Damn it, Amaris, if you're going to act like a man, you've got to think like one."

She swung around on him. "What the hell does that remark mean?"

He grabbed her by the shoulders. "You bloody damn well know what I mean!"

Defiant, she stared up into his eyes. "No. Tell me."

His fingers gripped her shoulders, then he released her with a push. "Go on with yeself, then. Be an ocker. I'll saddle the horses."

"No! I don't need you escorting me back. I can find my way on my own, thank you."

She stomped outside, slamming the door behind her. Taking the porch lantern from its peg, she crossed to the stalls. Quickly, she began to saddle Renegade. The horse turned its head and eyed her balefully.

"Mrs. Marlborough, you want me to saddle Renegade?"

Startled, she spun around. Jimmy crawled from the next stall over. His sloping eyes had that sleepy look, and hay littered his frizzy orange hair that was thinning at the crown.

"No, I can manage, thank you," she said, giving him a tired smile.

As she was mounting, she noticed he stood at the door watching her, concern evident on his ruddy, sunbaked face. Then the darkness and the emptiness of the outback swallowed her.

Overhead, the Southern Cross glittered. Her lodestar. She loved her aloneness. She was at one with the land and the night. She wasn't afraid.

Unless she listened too closely to the ghostly echo of her horse's hooves.

16

Within three weeks, the injured aborigine was walking with a sprightly step. Each day that passed, Amaris expected him to disappear back into the bush, but she would be riding boundary and come upon him, repairing a pen's rail, cleaning the woolshed, or relaying a damaged spout pipe for washing sheep.

Come lunch or supper time, he would be waiting on the porch. Her expression timorous, Molly would give him a plate of whatever the fare was and watch him take it out to the stables. There he would squat on his hindquarters and shovel the food into his mouth without benefit of utensils.

Obviously, the little man was not going to leave.

Finally Amaris communicated to him her curiosity about his intent. His usually stoic face took on a guarded look. He replied in surprisingly passable English. "Baluway work hard. Fix hard. Herd sheep hard. Eat good."

She tried not to smile. "In return for hard work you want room and board? Is that it?"

He nodded enthusiastically. His grin showed the missing teeth.

"All right, let's give it a trial period then."

The trial period was never necessary. Baluway had the uncanny knack of anticipating potential problems. She had no sooner planted a garden than he erected a rabbit-proof fence. Several times she had lent him Renegade, and it was obvious he could have been born to the saddle. He could track stray sheep better than a mastiff a runway convict.

Moreover, he apparently appointed himself her protector. To Francis, he gave taciturn obedience. To her, adoration. Whenever evening caught her out in the bush, she was sure he would soon find her. In silence, he would trail her on foot until she returned to the station.

She might have identified Baluway as her ghostly companion the night she returned late from Sin's house, except that her aborigine overseer had been laid up, and she would have sworn she had heard the clip-clop of horse hooves.

Soon it became obvious that Baluway could accomplish much more work mounted rather than afoot. She decided to ride over to the Tremaynes' to bargain with Sin for one of his horses. Besides, it would be an opportunity to visit with Celeste, whom she had not seen since the miscarriage.

Early summers were beautiful in the Never-Never. What appeared various shades of brown suddenly caught color from the intense sunlight, like rainbows in a rain. The vegetation ran the gamut of glorious greens, and she saw terra-cotta snakes, chartreuse lizards, tea-colored ground squirrels, red-gray kangaroos. A flock of dark brown emus paced her and Renegade.

A black speck was moving fast across the level plain, too fast for a solitary kangaroo or emu. Soon she made out that it was a lone mounted man. She felt for the reassurance of her pistol in her saddlebag but needn't have worried. The man was moving swiftly in a diagonal away from her.

The rider was one with the wild picturesqueness of the surroundings. The wind filled his loose white shirt, making him seem gigantic. Her interest flared. In the vastness of the Never-Never, she was passing another ship. The silent desolation was vanquished by the unknown purpose and life of the rider.

She hated to see him vanish. He didn't. Suddenly he reined his mount sharply and dismounted. Then she saw his purpose. He was chasing a whirlwind spinning across the heated plain.

Her attention was charged. She was excited. Was the man demented? All at once, he did the unexpected. He extended his arms outward from him and began to spin like the whirlwind. She heard his shout, a shout that came from someone who was living the moment.

Envy filled her. She wanted that childlike abandon. Fascinated, she sat still in her saddle and watched. Too soon, his unconventional behavior ended, and he remounted, wheeling his mount around to canter back. He must have spotted her and realized he had had a witness. His horse slowed its pace, then altered direction again—toward her.

As Sin rode within speaking distance, she said nothing. Neither did he. The bright noonday sun revealed his expression to be a mixture of chagrin, defiance, and a boyish shyness that she had not expected beneath that scarred wall of manhood.

His shirt lay open to the waist, and sweat glistened in the whorl of hair on his chest and the smooth, muscled midriff. Desire unfolded in her, a blossom of sweet, wild wanting.

"You wanted me?" he asked, his tone deep, breathless from his ride.

She almost laughed. Want him? Did sunflowers want sunlight? All these years she had denied her attraction to him. Feared the power his maleness might wield in subjugating her female . . . until she had witnessed his self-abandon. No, he would not dominate her. He would complement her. Except he was not hers to have, nor she his.

"I came to buy a horse. For me. To bargain. A good stock horse. I saw a liver roan you have." What in God's green earth was she rattling on about?

He leaned his forearm on the saddle horn and watched her with a disconcerting steadiness. Oh, my God, he knew. He knew she wanted him. He knew her weakness. The reins trembled in her hand.

"I have a dun that would better fit you. All four feet stockinged."

"How is Celeste?" Celeste, her defense, her wall between her and surrender of the self to this strong-willed man.

"She's doing fine. 'Tis geranium beds she be digging around the house now. She's determined to make the outback bloom out of season. Her father and mother will be paying a visit, and she wants the place to look grand."

In accord, they turned their horses toward Sin's station that he had taken to calling Never-Never. "Jimmy will be disappointed Molly didn't come with you. He's sweet on her."

They rode close enough that their legs brushed in the stirrups. "Molly mopes when she goes too long without seeing him."

Why was she talking about Molly when she wanted to talk about Sin, to know where that little boy she had glimpsed today had come from? "You never told me . . . why you were transported."

His blue-eyed gaze was fastened on the distance. Somewhere she had once heard that blue-eyed people made the best marksmen, but she had never seen Sin carrying a pistol or rifle. "I didn't think you were interested."

"I am," she said softly. "After all, we've known each other more years than I care to count. Yet I know very little about you."

He flicked her a glance. "And I know everything about you. At least, everything since you were the age of twelve, too tall for twelve, and gauche. Since you stared down at an emotionally and physically beaten convict, not with compassion. That would have made me feel even more self-pity, something I didn't need. No, you stared at me with outrage. That outrage filled me soul and overflowed it with the energy and will to survive."

She was astounded by the passion in his voice. "I thought you detested me, Sin."

"I admire your strength. For those you love, you

will be a source of good and caring and giving, a source whose taproots reach far down into Australia's underground tablewater."

She felt breathless. "You are eloquent."

"I should be. I was a law student. I was protesting English repression of me country." He shrugged those broad shoulders. "That's how I lost me heritage, me land and ancestral home . . . and me freedom."

"But you have your freedom again."

"Aye, and I'll not give it up any easier this time."

"This time?"

His eyes narrowed, as if seeing even farther than the horizon. "As Australia's prosperity increases, Great Britain will start taking even more interest— and taking away the autonomy of the people. But Australian colonies, like the American ones, are too far from the mother country. We have that in our favor. We only need men like the American General Washington who will be willing to lead when the time comes."

"That could be you," she said softly.

He glanced at her sharply. "No. I'll fight me own private battles. But lead? No, there are men better suited for that."

By this time, they were riding into the station yard. Still astride Renegade, she watched Sin dismount and talk to Jimmy. There was such purpose in Sin's movements and voice. Such vitality in his being.

He strode back to her and held up his hand. She stared at it, unsure of what he was wanting. He looked from her face to his hand, and she realized he thought she was repulsed by its mutilation. "I was offering to help you dismount," he said and began to turn away.

At once she took his hand. "I didn't know. I've never had anyone offer to help me."

"You always seem so capable," he said, releasing her hand to take her waist and lift her down.

For only a moment, she allowed herself to be held, reveled in the exquisite feeling. Contact with Sin excited her in ways that she didn't know were possible. She took his hand again, her fingers clasping those two callused ridges that were absent of fingers. "I see your hand and am reminded of a time we shared, a crisis."

"A bonding." He squeezed her fingers. "Come on. Celeste will be eager to see you."

Celeste was on the other side of the house. Amaris came around the veranda to find her on her knees with a spade in hand. One cheek was streaked with dirt. Her brown hair fell in damp ringlets at her neck. She looked like a little girl, Amaris thought. A too-thin little girl who enjoyed life and people to the maximum.

Celeste glanced up, and pleasure lit sparklers in her eyes. "Amaris!" She tossed aside her spade and sprang up to hug Amaris. "Now my day is complete. The two people I love most are here."

Amaris realized that Celeste was including Sin, who had followed her around the veranda. Celeste turned to slip her other arm around her husband. "The three of us together," she said softly. "How blessed I am."

That summer, Baluway was a remarkable sight, proudly dressed in a short breechcloth, spurred Hessian boots that had been worn to the sole, and a station owner's bush hat. Amaris had put it on her list when she ordered stores from Melbourne, the closest port.

Flour, sugar, pepper, mustard, fencing wire—each order had to be prepared with great care as anything overlooked had to wait for the next order, which would be another six months away.

Baluway had become so efficient that he had taken over keeping an inventory of what needed to be ordered to maintain the sheep stock. His inventory was a mental one, since he could neither read nor write, but she could depend on it to be as accurate as her own.

Because she relied upon her aborigine overseer, she felt at ease in leaving him in charge while she was away for several days. The major and Elizabeth were hosting a celebration of the January twenty-sixth founding of Australia in 1788. Amaris and Francis planned to travel to the major's station, some twenty kilometers distance, in the company of Celeste and Sin.

When Molly discovered Amaris and Francis were going to Never-Never before journeying on to the major's, she said, "Oh, missus, please let me go with you to Never-Never. With you gone, I don't need to be a'cooking. I want to see me Jimmy."

Amaris stared down at that once world-wearied face. It was radiant. She envied the woman, who felt no guilt in her passion for her middle-aged swain. In the outback, no impropriety was found in a courting couple sleeping together.

"Of course, Molly. There's plenty of room on the dray."

They set out early in the morning. The flat bed of

the open dray was covered with a layer of straw. Boxes were used for seats. The oxen were slow but hardy. By midday, they reached Never-Never.

Molly jumped down from the dray and ran to Jimmy, who swept her off the ground with a shout of "Whahoo!"

"You don't mind if she stays while we are at the major's, do you?" Amaris asked Celeste.

Celeste's eyes twinkled. "It looks as if we will be needing your father to come out here and officiate at a wedding."

At that moment, Amaris decided to write her parents and persuade them to come to Dream Time. After all, Nan and Tom had traveled this far to visit Celeste.

Waving good-bye to the couple, the Tremaynes and the Marlboroughs set out once more. Amaris drove the bullock team so Celeste could ride with her and they could talk, while Francis and Sin rode horseback.

All were in high spirits. None more so than Celeste. Taking off her broad-brimmed hat, she turned her sun-browned face to the sky to soak up the sunshine. Her skin had once been pure alabaster. A heated breeze tickled the wisps of hair at Celeste's nape. "Ahh, Amaris, I love it out here!"

"So do I. Until the sun boils, or the sky pours rain, or the earth puffs up dust storms for days on end. You know what I want on the next stores shipment? A hip bath. My legs are so long I have to stand in the half barrel we use."

"Not I. Not with my short legs. No, I want a set of long-stemmed glasses. I remember Mama's pale pink crystal."

"You miss your old life, Celeste?"

She looked thoughtful. "I miss the rituals. There

was something lovely and reassuring about them. Tea at four. Wine with dinner. But my life has purpose here, with Sin."

Amaris cast her a sidelong glance. For all her contentment, she appeared tired. Her rounded figure was gone, replaced by that drawn, thin look.

"Let's stop there for our afternoon break," Celeste said, pointing at a small pond hole bordered by the ubiquitous gray-green gum trees. "I'd like nothing better than to unbutton my shoes and wade into that water."

Amaris laughed. "Then let's do it." She turned around and signaled to Sin to halt.

The wagons stopped in a spot where the grass was plentiful. Celeste spread a blanket, and Amaris took from her basket wedges of bread and paper-thin slices of mutton.

Sin surprised everyone by producing a bottle of sherry. "From a drover, looking for work. I couldn't afford him. But he was in need of a billy and willing to trade the sherry bottle that another soul had paid him for shearing the day before."

"So even you miss the amenities of civilization," Francis said, opening the bottle.

Though his tone had been a little pompous, it had been amiable enough and the remark well intentioned.

For some reason Sin took umbrage. The dark side of his Irish nature turned his beautiful voice caustic. "Though a former convict, I nevertheless share with mere humans their affinity for simple pleasures such as this."

Celeste put her hand over his. "You deserve more

than simple pleasures, darling, and one day you will have those and more."

There was such tenderness and love in her eyes. In Sin's presence, she was a woman content, while Amaris was still restless and disturbed. Watching the smile of contrition he sent his young wife, Amaris felt that old stab of jealousy. Except now the jealousy was worse because its recipient was the sister she had come to love.

Amaris knew that jealousy could destroy her soul, and she hated herself for it, but she couldn't fight the attraction she felt for Sin. She disguised her discordant feelings with banter. "I don't know about you men, but Celeste and I are going wading."

They reached the major's station just before sunset. The big house the major had built was impressive. Of two stories, there had to be at least eight rooms.

Elizabeth had surrounded it with an aesthetically laid-out, very English garden. With care and maintenance to be considered, due to climate difference, the garden was all the more lovely and unexpected there in the outback.

In the parlor, ornate oil lamps and porcelain objets d'art filled the room. Portraits of family members looked down from gilt-papered walls. French doors opened onto a veranda bordered by a section of Elizabeth's garden.

Predinner drinks were served in the parlor as refreshment for the travel-weary guests. Naturally, the men and women divided into separate groups.

The men discussed the usual: drought, stock disease, wool prices, and aborigine attacks.

The women discussed recipes, children, the lack of supplies for running the household efficiently.

Amaris was in the enviable position of being capable of joining either group. Usually, because of her interest in running sheep, she joined the men. This evening, she joined neither group. Standing a little apart, she observed.

Her gaze quickly passed over Sin. To think about him only invited dissatisfaction with her life. From among the group of men, she sought out her husband's face.

Despite the accumulation of the day's dust on his clothing and in his hair, which was beginning to thin slightly at the crown, he was by far the most handsome man in the room.

Two years before, he wouldn't have mingled with egalitarian ease among the squatters, who were from all ranks of society. The outback was gradually eroding Francis's vanity. Grudgingly, she conceded it wasn't that difficult to love her husband.

He caught her watching him and gave her a roguish grin. She knew that message. The opportunity of sleeping with her in a different setting excited his passions.

She had to admit, also, that over the last two years his values had changed. Still headstrong, he amazed her by occasionally being willing to forsake his own selfish drive for little pleasures that made her happy. Smiling back at him over the rim of her glass, she recalled the afternoon she had been riding the south paddock. Foolishly, she had stepped in a wombat hole and twisted her ankle.

When she had limped into the house later that evening, he had been quite concerned and had knelt to help her remove the boot from her rapidly swelling ankle. He had been wearing his red-and-black hunting attire, once used to ride to the foxes, now used whenever he hunted the ferocious dingoes, another of his grand passions these days. That and drinking. But that afternoon, as he had knelt before her, she thought how princely he looked. She might have been Cinderella.

Well, she was Lady Marlborough, for all she cared.

"Crystal stemware," Celeste said at her side, disturbing her reverie. Smiling, the younger woman held up her wineglass. "My wish today was granted, temporarily, at least. Shall we change for dinner?"

"I don't need any further encouraging."

Excusing themselves, they left the parlor. Before they reached the staircase, just off the entry, they passed the library, and Amaris paused at the open door. Three walls were lined with books. In her mind flashed the scanty collection of her father's—Burns, Browning, and a complete Shakespeare, and a few other works. How she treasured those few bound volumes she had brought from her father's house. She had read and reread them many times.

"Are you coming?" Celeste asked, waiting patiently at the bottom of a staircase of carved cedar.

"Yes," she replied absently. She was feeling the sting of homesickness. She, who had always considered herself independent and rootless. She hoped her parents, she never thought of them as her

adoptive parents, would decide to come and live at
Dream Time.

Her distraction was immediately arrested when
she and Celeste began to change their dusty travel
clothes. Clad only in her chemise, Amaris poured a
pitcher of fresh water in a daisy-painted basin. She
was washing her face, throat, and arms, when Celeste
mumbled something about needing help with her
petticoat ties.

Turning around, Amaris stopped short. Celeste
was silhouetted against the candlelight. Her thin
frame was abruptly distorted by her obviously
mounded stomach. "You're with child again!"
Amaris exclaimed in a tone more accusatory than
questioning.

Celeste looked at Amaris. A flush washed over her
pale cheeks. "Yes. I haven't told anyone because I
wanted to be certain I could carry this one past the
first six months."

"How far along are you?"

Her smile was madonna-soft. "Nearly five
months."

"But you—shouldn't you have waited a year or so,
until you get your full strength back?"

She smiled shyly. "We want children. And . . .
well, I guess I am sort of . . . brazen, Amaris.
Whenever Sin pulls me close to cuddle me in the
night, I, uh, can't help but want to, hmmm, touch
him. His body is so beautiful. I get so . . . excited. I
suppose I shouldn't be talking like this."

"No, that's all right, I understand."

But she didn't. Why didn't she feel that way
about having sex with Francis? It wasn't the repug-
nant act that some women in the home had made it

out to be. Yet neither was it . . . exciting, nor did it make her breathless like Celeste when she thought about it.

"Here," she said to Celeste, "let me help you with the ties. One is knotted."

Later, when she and Celeste joined the other guests, who had also changed, she couldn't help but dart speculative glances at Sin. Already she knew she enjoyed being with him more than any other man she had known. He had her father's erudition and a stockman's rapport with the land. Men from every walk of life respected him.

And the women?

She glanced along the dinner table at the various women who occasionally chatted with Sin and the other men. She couldn't believe it. Why had she never noticed? The women—from old Elizabeth to her young daughter, Eileen, now engaged to Thomas—flirted behind their fans with him. With Sin, the ex-convict, not Francis, the nobleman.

She glanced back to Sin. He was taking their flirting in good-natured stride. Still, there was an undeniably heavy-lidded look in his gaze and a sensual curve in his smile that were all the more appealing because he was unconscious of it.

"A toast," he said, raising his glass. "To Australia. May her star shine as brightly as the Southern Cross."

"Here, here," the others chimed in, and lifted their glasses in unison.

After dinner the major and Elizabeth led the guests back to the parlor, which a servant had cleared of furniture and rugs. Two men, who must have been shearers or drovers for the station, if their weather-beaten faces were any indication of their occupation, stood ready to play a fiddle and a Jew's harp. Elizabeth sat down at the piano and launched into a Beethoven sonata. Candles in their elaborate holders lit the music sheet.

The sonata soon lapsed into a popular quadrille. At once the guests began to clap to the music, and the braver ones sallied out to dance in the room's center. Francis and Amaris joined them. Recalling all those dance lessons at the Livingston mansion, she performed the steps smoothly and easily.

At one point, she and Sin were momentary partners. Looking up into those keen blue eyes, she knew that he, too, was recalling that afternoon he had been forced to serve as her partner.

Lately she wondered if he felt any of the attraction for her that she felt for him.

If he did, God help their souls. The dancing lasted far into the night, for such get-togethers were rare in the bush. Finally, Francis, who had been enjoying the nicotine-spiked brandy, grew sleepy. She wasn't. She couldn't remember smiling so much.

"Shall we go on up to bed, darling?" Francis said with a suggestive smile.

"No, I don't think I'm quite ready."

He looked surprised. For a moment, amidst the trappings of polite society, he had once again reverted to the role of lord and master. Forgotten were all those times she had toiled side by side with him in the bush.

"Go on to bed, Francis. I'll be up shortly."

His mouth curled in a petulant pout, then he inclined his head in that familiar way, nodded, and weaving only slightly, headed for the doorway.

No sooner had he left, than she was besieged by several men, each claiming her for a dance. "One at a time," she said, laughing. She knew she could have looked like Jimmy's prize pig, and she still would have been sought after, since white women were as scarce as black swans in Europe.

She danced with a cook, a bullocky, a forwarding agent, and a shearer. She was whirled around the room so much that it began to spin even after she stopped. "No more," she begged off, trying to catch her breath.

She turned toward the French doors and their promise of fresh air. Several men were outside, smoking their pipes and doubtlessly discussing either sheep or Australian politics.

She was no different from those men. Sheep was the foundation of all their plans, their schemes. Like them, she rarely wasted an opportunity to soak up any kind of information.

Politics, however, touched an emotional spot. She realized now that her rage with the injustice of female transportation had been just one portion of her rage with the whole system of British tyranny. Only now was she beginning to experience that entire spectrum of repression of personal freedoms.

Nevertheless the men felt unaccountably reluctant to discuss politics in her presence. She had demonstrated her competence running a sheep station, which was certainly not a woman's domain. But politics was definitely out of the question in regard to female mentality.

The men all glanced up as she stepped through the double doorway. "Major, Sykes, Jimmy, Thomas . . . Sin," she said acknowledging them.

"Evening," the major said. Over the years, his stern military countenance had mellowed to that of a prophet, framed by white hair and beard. His smile welcomed her as if she were one of their gender. None of the men came to their feet in deference to her sex. By now, they were accustomed to her trading off sheep stories with them and probably would not have been astounded if she had produced a pipe to smoke.

"Harry here," the major said in his clipped voice, "says that a drover who came through last week reported several hundred sheep infected with catarrh up in the Blue Valley."

"My word for it," said the old-timer known as Harry. "Had to be killed and burnt. All of them."

"Could be worse," she said, settling alongside Sin on the bench. His back was to the veranda's cedar post and one leg was drawn up on the bench. "Could be scab."

"Then there's nothing to do but sell the place and stock for what they will fetch," Sykes said.

"No, there's a lot more a man can do," Sin drawled in that seductive brogue. "He can fight to his last breath."

"And face certain ruin," another added in a reproving tone.

She stared through the lantern-lit night at the stocky man called Brantwell. "Nothing is certain."

"The lass is right," the major interjected.

She was particularly conscious of Sin's steady gaze upon her. She grew uncomfortable, and when the conversation turned to tail docking of the lambs, she excused herself and went up to the bedroom she and Francis had been given.

The candle had burned low. Even as she
undressed, it sputtered out. In the dark, she groped
for the nightgown she had laid out on the back of a
rocking chair. How wonderful it would be, she
thought, to go to bed with nothing on. No worry
about the hot muslin sticking to her thighs or the ties
binding her wrists and neck.

But Francis would be shocked. And after that,
aroused. Then later, shocked again. Sighing, she
pulled the gown over her head and climbed into bed
beside him. He turned over, and she lay still, hoping
he wouldn't awaken.

He didn't, and she relaxed, listening to his light
snoring.

Before drifting off to sleep she thought of two
things—about how much cooler it would be if she
could open the shutters, but the bugs would devour
them; and about Sin and Celeste. Even now, were
they making love? Did a man, could a man, make
love to a woman if she were five months with child?
Celeste's ecstatic face when she talked of lying in
Sin's embrace continued into Amaris's restive
dreams.

The following day was reserved for games and
relaxation. One game consisted of throwing an ax at
a small mark on a tree while riding past on a galloping
horse. All the men participated. There was no doubt
in Amaris's mind that Sin was by far the best
horseman and so had the advantage of burying the ax
blade closest to the mark.

Wagering was made all around, even among the
women—a pair of gloves against a parasol and so on.
"A dance tonight with your husband if he shouldn't
win," a heavy-jowled woman called to Celeste.

Celeste, who sat with Amaris on a blanket spread beneath a gum tree, laughed lightly. "I have no fear of forfeiting even one dance with him. Sin shall win handily."

Amaris attempted to appear indifferent to the contest. The contestants were eliminated one by one until only Sin and a scraggly bearded squatter from over Yarrow way remained.

"A tight match," Francis said, dropping down on the blanket between Celeste and his wife. He gave her a sheepish grin. She hadn't seen him all morning, since he was still sleeping when she arose and went down to breakfast. "It's said the overseer can cut the eye out of a flying mosquito with his stock lash."

"I'd wager no one has ever seen him do it," she said with equally dry humor.

Her humor was short-lived. Sin and Johnson made their last pass at the tree. Her lungs suspended action. Dust flurried. Why was it so important to her that Sin win? The dust cleared and applause rippled through the spectators. Johnson's ax had found its mark, besting Sin's aim by the breadth of a centimeter.

Her pent-up breath zephyred from between her lips.

"I get the dance with your husband," the heavy-jowled woman crowed.

"It will be his good fortune," Celeste replied pleasantly and politely.

Sin cantered over, an easy smile on his lips. Perspiration dotted his upper lip and dampened his shirt so that it clung to his torso, emphasizing the breadth of his chest and his stomach's corrugated muscles.

Afraid he would catch her staring, Amaris quickly glanced away. She had thought she was over her gauche days, but now she was finding herself tongue-tied—and over nothing. Nothing had happened between them. She had simply become aware of him in a sexual way.

He leaned from the saddle and presented Celeste with his ax. "In the days of courtly love, the triumphant knight presented his lady with a jeweled crown or something similar. I am the vanquished knight, but would me fair damsel accept me battle weapon along with me humble regrets."

Celeste smiled up at him. Amaris thought the young woman had never looked so beautiful. "You will always be the champion of my heart, Sir Sin."

Amaris rose, brushed off her skirts, and excused herself. "I think I'll take a nap before the festivities tonight, Francis."

She didn't even wait for his reply. She knew she was behaving churlishly. Instead of enjoying the three-day outing, she had become self-conscious and unable to relax. That she would revert to such childish behavior aggravated her.

Feeling restive, she forewent the nap and strolled through the grounds. On the veranda, guests played cards or discoursed. Rather than have to invent excuses, she rambled farther from the big house.

For days she had looked forward to visiting the major's station and mixing with the other squatters and station hands. Now she only yearned for the seclusion and silence of Dream Time.

She wandered down to the bank of Wallabee Creek to inspect the major's new wash pen. She had to lean over the bridge to view better the suspended stage for the washers. The station hands were then lowered into a pen that was waist deep in the rushing water. The creek's current washed the sheep's wool, which, when clean, resulted in cheaper freight than wool made heavy by dirt and grease.

Her lace underskirts, her only petticoat, caught on a nail. Cursing beneath her breath, she bent to unsnag the lace—and lost her balance. She fell against the railing. She felt the rough timber skin her cheekbone, then heard the cracking as the railing gave way.

Her fall was broken by the pen below, which kept her from being swept downstream. Gagging on water she had swallowed, she fought to stand upright. Her heavy skirts, thoroughly wet now, were entangled around her legs and the railings. Her left shoulder felt bruised and both knees stung as if scraped.

"Well, bugger it!" she said. "Of all the bloody—"

Laughter interrupted her cursing.

Her gaze darted toward the bank. Sin stood there, arms akimbo, legs spread in that arrogant stance of his. "Are you going to stand there like a bloody fool," she sputtered, "or are you going to help me?"

"Ahh, so you're the helpless female now."

"You damned insolent paddy."

He turned and began climbing the tree-fringed embankment.

"Wait!"

He peered over his shoulder. Those long-lashed eyes danced. "You wanted me?"

"Damn it, Sin, aye!"

He gave that one-sided grin. Its sheer masculinity sucked the last vestige of breath from her lungs. At that moment, hardly a passionate moment, she realized that it was the force of his masculinity that threatened. Her father had been something of a passive male. She could deal with him. She didn't know how to deal with Sin, or maybe it was that she didn't know how to deal with the feelings he aroused within her.

He waded alongside the chute that funneled the washed sheep back up to the bank. Soon, water poured over his knee-high Hessians.

Waiting, she clung to the railing. She never took her eyes off him. He waded into the water and climbed through the chute. At last he reached her and scaled the pen to drop inside with her.

Neither of them moved. She realized the very thing she had been avoiding during the holiday festivities had happened: coming face to face with him when no one else was around. He was within arm's reach. At that instant, she wanted to be held in his muscular arms. Had he embraced her, she would not have resisted. But he did not.

The realization of how close she was to capitulation panicked her; she wondered what had happened to her self-control.

"Well, are you going to help me?" she demanded. Her breathlessness was the only evidence of how much he unsettled her and hopefully he would attribute that to her present circumstances.

"I am mightily tempted not to."

Still gripping the railing, she glared at him. "My hands are getting tired of holding on."

"The pen won't let you go anywhere."

"Sin!"

He grunted. "All right. Turn your back to me somewhat so that I can unhook your skirt fasteners."

"What?"

"There is no way I could lift you out of the pen, me luv. Not weighted down as you are by those wet skirts."

Me luv? Memory of Rose calling her by that endearment stung tears behind Amaris's eyes. Docilely, she did as he bade.

His fingers were dexterous for being so large, and soon he worked her skirts and petticoats down over her hips and thighs so that they were swirling around her high button shoes.

He straightened. His gaze followed his ascent, taking in her state of semiundress—her damp, revealing pantalettes; her breasts, barely covered by her camisole. Even so, her wet nipples had hardened and were thrusting against the material.

Why, with him, was she always so intensely aware of her womanhood?

"Well? You've seen me in pants and a shirt before. This isn't so much different!"

As if dazed by a punch, he blinked, refocused on her face, and said in a voice as grating as a rusted wagon wheel, "You know better than that, Amaris."

He reached past her shoulder and pulled on the rope that lifted the chute gate. "Grip the railing, and you can work your way to the bank."

Without glancing at her again, he led the way through the narrow chute. Hand over hand, she hauled herself along in his wake. Splinters poked into her palms. After a half-dozen steps, the water level lowered abruptly so that she no longer needed to hold on. She followed in Sin's long striding footsteps until she and he reached dry land.

"Wait," she called.

He stopped but did not turn around. She stalked past and whirled to face him. "You're running away."

"Celeste is your friend."

She took a deep breath. "She's more than that. She's my half sister."

His voice came out in a choked whisper. "What?"

"My half sister. But if she were to ever learn that fact, it would devastate her. I know you love her, so please for her sake—"

"Aye, I do."

Suddenly, she felt deflated. Had she been hoping he would deny his love for Celeste?

"Would you care to tell me how this blood tie came about?"

"No. Yes. Maybe someday. But you're right. This wanting of you can only end up hurting everyone concerned."

There it was—out in the open—the acknowledgment of her desire for him. She felt unworthy.

Pushing back the hair that plastered her forehead and cheeks, she glanced down. Not until that moment did she realize that a veritable pool of water was forming around her and Sin. As his had with her, her gaze traveled up the length of his long legs and halted on his crotch. The wet nankeen material clung to the distinct bulge there. She smiled. "It seems nature has taken its course with both of us."

He looked down, then back at her. A slow smile

started at the end of one corner of his mouth and erupted into a full grin. "Nature has exposed both of us for shams. Shall we start back?"

As she donned her dress and petticoats, her relief spilled out into her laughter. Sin's grin answered hers. Together yet forever separated by a tacit, mutual agreement, they returned to the big house.

17

The gala at the major's was a turning point for Amaris. From that time on, she committed herself to Dream Time and to her husband. Somehow, by acknowledging her attraction, she was freed from it.

Gradually, Dream Time began to prosper to the point where she and Francis were able both to pay Baluway a monthly salary and to hire two shepherds, fellow tribesmen of Baluway's, as well as a new cook.

Molly had gone to live with Jimmy that fall at Never-Never, and Celeste took pity and hired her as cook. The new cook Amaris hired was Ryku, a cousin of Baluway's. The tattooed young woman was comely. Amaris found it difficult to believe she was a relative of the ugly little gnome Baluway.

In her own way, Amaris was content. She now had more time to devote to making the rustic house a home and to becoming more a wife and less a business partner to her husband.

In trying to love Francis more, she discovered that it wasn't that difficult. The outback had taken the vapid, inexperienced young man and forced him to overcome challenges, which gave him confidence.

Sitting across the dinner table from him one evening, she listened as he proudly described his effort to lay a boundary line for the paddock he was fencing.

"When it was dark, I had Baluway light a fire at one end of our paddock, and I lit one at the other. Then we started out with our lanterns and worked toward each other, mounding a cairn of stones as we went. As long as we kept the distant fire and the other's lantern in line, we were pegging a straight boundary."

"What a marvelous idea, Francis." She put down her spoon and leaned forward, her chin in her palm. "How did you come up with that?"

He grinned. "I was forced to cross a creek downstream from where we should have been laying the line. The water made me think about the ocean. From there, I recalled ships at sea and how they signal at night."

She touched his hand, sunburnt to a brown only slightly lighter than that of Ryku. "I am most fortunate to have you for a husband."

And she meant it.

To add to her contentment, she received a letter, written over two months before, from Rose and William. They had decided to join her and Francis. With Dream Time as a base, her adoptive parents wanted to make treks into the wild Never-Never to convert the aborigines.

For several days, she stayed around the house, pacing the veranda, with Rogue dogging her endless steps. She had other duties that demanded her time, but she would stare off into the blinding sunlight for sight of a dust spiral, sometimes a signal of approaching visitors.

Or merely a whirlwind, a haunting memory of Sin.

Just as she began to worry that something might have happened to William and Rose, Baluway rode in with news he had spotted their dray coming up Bitter Creek Valley.

Like a whirling dervish, she began cooking and baking. Suddenly, the house that had seemed adequate for her and Francis looked woefully bleak. Like Celeste, Rose possessed that knack for arranging a vase of wild flowers or embroidering a colorful throw pillow to brighten the austere rectory house.

Rose's cherished proverb "Cleanliness is next to godliness" spurred Amaris to scour the place spotless. The house hadn't been that clean since the first weeks after it was built.

At last the dray rolled into the yard. Amaris was there waiting. Tears streamed down her face at the sight of her parents, looking much older under the duress of the six-week journey.

They climbed down from the dray in movements made stiff by long sitting. Amaris ran down the veranda steps and enveloped the two. "Mother, Father!"

She would always think of them so. They might not have been responsible for her birth, but they had parented her—and done so with hearts full of love.

"Stand back, Amaris," William said. Tears glistened in his rheumy eyes. "Let me get a good look at you."

Smiling, she stepped back.

"H'ain't she looking grand, Willy!" Rose said, staring up adoringly at her daughter. "How strong and healthy you are, me luv."

Her mother, she noted, was plumper, far from the image of William's pet name for her, Elfin. "Come on inside. I've been expecting you for days now. I had begun to worry. Did you have any trouble with the aborigines?"

"No," William said, assisting Rose up the veranda's short flight of steps. "Not with the aborigines but with bushwhackers. Three of them were determined to be thieves and make off with our horses."

"And leave us stranded in the middle of nowhere!" Rose added indignantly.

"But I convinced them that if they repented, they would be forgiven just as surely as Jesus forgave the thief on the cross."

"They left the horses?" she asked, leading them inside. "Who would have believed—"

"Oh, our horses they be leaving alone," Rose said dryly. "But the wicked men made off with the rectory's donations for starting our mission out here."

"The bushwhackers are getting bolder by the day. Sit down, and I'll pour tea. I had our Ryku put a pot on as soon as I saw your dray's dust."

"Ryku?" William asked.

"Our cook. She's aborigine. And as beautiful as any English debutante."

Rose settled her plump body into the rocking chair

she had given Amaris as a wedding present. William lodged his lanky frame on one of the hardwood chairs. He was almost completely bald now with only fringes of graying hair flecked with brown.

"Does one ever become accustomed to the emptiness, to going where no one has ever been?" he asked.

Laughing, Amaris handed each of her parents a cup and saucer. "That's hardly the case. I'll ride after stray sheep, through gullies and ravines as far as my horse Wind Runner will carry me, then climb down sheer cliffs and push through narrow passes over-grown with brush. I'll be thinking I am walking where no human has ever tread. Then I'll come upon a rusted matchbox or a druggist's colored bottle."

"Where is Francis?" he asked, just realizing her husband's absence.

"He's in the south paddock." She took a seat opposite her parents, and Rogue curled up at her feet. "He should ride in by dusk."

Rose took a sip of her tea. "Hmmmm. Your Ryku brews a tasty pot, me luv." One veined hand stroked the scrolled arm of the rocking chair. "I have often imagined you rocking a wee one in this chair."

She could feel herself blushing. It was as if she were a little girl again. "Not so soon, Mama. Francis and I haven't even been married five years yet. There's still so much to do here before I could ably care for a baby. I can cut back when stores become short. An infant couldn't."

William smiled indulgently. "If you wait for the perfect time, I can tell you now it never comes."

She leaned over to scratch Rogue behind the ears.

She felt uncomfortable discussing childbearing. She had often wondered why she hadn't conceived. She supposed she could be much worse off. The week before, Celeste had just lost her second child, a boy she had carried almost full term. Sin had buried it and built a cairn over the grave to keep out the dingoes.

"How are Celeste and Sin doing?" Rose asked, as if reading her daughter's mind. "In one of your letters, you mentioned they were your closest neighbors."

"Almost twenty kilometers separate our homesteads. Celeste isn't doing that well, Mama. She has lost two children now who arrived before they were due. I am more concerned about her hea—"

She broke off as Baluway crashed through the door. Rose screamed and William sprang upright from his chair. "Fire!" the aborigine gasped. "Big fire! Wallabee Plains."

"Oh my God!" Amaris exclaimed.

"Amaris!" William reproached, disappointment clouding his lined face.

She grabbed her hat and headed for the door. "Father, you haven't seen a bush fire. That was a prayer I uttered, believe me."

Baluway and Rogue followed at her heels as she raced for the stable. "Get the water cart!" she yelled over her shoulder to him.

She grabbed a dozen gunnysacks that had been stored for this purpose and rushed to the stables and the horse Sin had insisted on giving her for her help with Celeste.

Scarcely was Wind Runner saddled, than she was astride and riding into the yard. William and Rose stood on the veranda, watching Baluway harness Renegade to the wagon cart.

"Can we help?" her father called.

"Yes! Find all the pans and pots and tubs—anything that will hold water. Fill them from the creek. It's just beyond that line of trees behind the house. Be ready to use them should the fire change directions and race this way. The ewes that are lambing—drive them from the lambing pen."

That was all she could think of in the extremity of the moment. She spurred Wind Runner's flanks. The black cloud layering the sky was clearly her destination, maybe fifteen kilometers distance.

The midafternoon sun was hot, but the very air grew hotter, heating her cheeks as she galloped into what amounted to an open furnace. Baluway's water cart dropped farther behind her.

By the time she was close enough to see orange tongues of flame dancing across the plains, Wind Runner was blowing foam, and her face felt seared.

Sunlight was no longer visible. A score of kangaroos, fleeing the area, bounded past her. The crackling of the fire sounded paradoxically like a heavy downpour of rain. Only the nauseating odor of singed vegetation belied the illusion.

Human silhouettes sprinted across the orange-red backdrop. She kneed Wind Runner in their direction and passed two other water carts driven in from nearby stations.

At the blast of heat, her mount pranced nervously. Behind her, Renegade whinnied with fear. "You're not ready to be put out to pasture yet, old boy," she called to him.

"Over here!" one of the dozen figures shouted.

The identity of the person was unknowable because of the soot blackening his face. Then she identified him as the man called Johnson, the overseer from Brighton cattle station who had competed against Sin at the major's January 26th celebration.

Dismounting, she yanked one of the gunnysacks from the roll strapped to the saddle. Close behind her, she heard Baluway's wagon rolling to a halt. It took only a moment to tie Wind Runner to the wagon and dampen her sack from the water cart. Baluway had climbed down from the wagon seat and was doing the same. Together they raced toward Johnson and the others.

As they drew nearer the wall of flames, she felt as if her skin were raising in blisters. Ahead of her, patches of fire appeared to leap magically from grass clump to grass clump.

At once she started swinging the dampened sack. She worked methodically and mindlessly, beating back an advancing line of flame in one spot, then turning to another. Her eyes stung. Sweat beaded her skin only to evaporate instantly.

Every few minutes, she would return to her cart to redampen her gunnysack or grab for another if the old one was burned beyond use, then go back to the line of flames. They were burning a path that would eventually consume Dream Time.

Occasionally she looked up and glimpsed working alongside her friends, their faces as smudged and tired-looking as hers: Jimmy, Sykes, Thomas, Lemuel, Brantwell.

Then she'd focus once more on swinging the sack. Along with the others, she thrashed the flames until she was blacker than a chimney sweep. Everyone would rush in upon the fire for a few moments and then retreat, choked and breathless.

People were arriving in a continual stream to help fight the fire. Some she did not recognize but were most likely recently hired blokes from the surrounding stations. There was a mateship tie here. Laboring side by side were ex-convicts and native-born Australians. The distinctions between them held little significance in the bush. The people probably knew little and cared little about each other's origins.

When the soles of Amaris's boots began smoking, she retired to the water cart to douse them. Steam hissed up. She began laughing.

Suddenly, the energy that had been galvanized by the crisis fizzled. Weakness sapped her remaining energy, and she braced her hands on the rim of the wagon wheel.

From behind, other hands gripped her upper arms. "You all right, me luv?"

Her head swiveled, and she looked over her shoulder up into Sin's smoke-smudged face. The flames' light danced in his indigo eyes. The exigency of the moment ignited its own exhilaration in his powerful face. That exhilaration leaped like the wildfire to her, rejuvenating her once more. She grinned up into that lively gaze. "I am now."

Smoke swirled around them. He continued to hold her. The moment seemed an eternity. Courage, the capacity to work hard and survive in a hostile and harsh environment, were qualities they could recognize in each other—and this recognition drew them together.

Sin lowered his head. His lips barely brushed hers.

What happened next, she had not anticipated: that total merging of her body and mind into a powerful energy force. The result was disorienting.

Dizzy, she clung to him. Their bodies pressed against each other, seeking to unify completely. At that first kiss he had bestowed on her years before, she had withheld herself.

Not this time. What her torso could not do, her tongue did. The pounding of his heart reverberated against her chest, so that her whole body thudded in symphony to his inner rhythm. Wave after wave of pleasure inundated her. The intensity of their kiss staggered her. She had no idea how much time elapsed.

At long last, she was united with the one man who matched her body, her roving mind, her passionate emotions.

Too soon, Sin somehow found the reserve to draw away. Still holding her upper arms, he stared down at her upturned face. His gaze, vibrant only moments before, was a black cloud, its depths turbulent. "That was hello, Amaris . . . g'day."

Slowly she shook her head, trying to regain her senses. "No, you cannot bury feelings as strong as this."

"We can and we will." His big hands dropped away.

She felt as desolate as the seared landscape around them. She couldn't even cry, so dehydrated was she. Her throat wouldn't work. She took a step behind her, then turned and ran back into the holocaust.

"You didn't see the sky blackened with smoke?" Amaris asked incredulously.

Francis yawned and stretched. "Not until the wind had already changed. By then I knew I wasn't needed."

She turned over on her side in the bed, her back to him. He was right, of course. Still, she wished he had made the effort to assist her and the others. Even after the wind had changed, blowing the flames toward the river, there was the clean-up work to do.

Over five hundred sheep had burnt as well as three fourths of Brighton station's grass. A shepherd was discovered, his charred and lifeless form in a sitting position, reclining against a rock, and by his side his faithful dog, which had shared his master's fate. Two hands from another station had also perished in the flames.

Totally exhausted, Amaris snuffed the bedside candle. She had gone thirty-six hours without sleep.

Francis put his hands on her shoulders and began massaging them. "Tired, darling?"

"I've never been so tired in all my life." Her lids drifted closed only to open a second later as Francis's hand slid around her ribcage and began to fondle her breast. "Francis, please. I'm not up to it tonight."

"I've missed you," he whispered against her ear. "I'm so bloody grateful you weren't hurt. When your parents told me you had gone to fight the fire, I was sick with worry."

"Well, I wasn't hurt, but I really need to sleep. Unless you were there, you can't understand how—"

"Oh, Amaris, don't risk your life like that again." He moved up over her. "I love you so damned much." He began nuzzling her neck.

"Francis, why now?"

"Because you understand me and what I need. You love me for me."

Guilt assaulted her. She stroked the nape of his neck and let his mouth claim hers in a demanding kiss. She could remember when she thought those needy kisses were exciting. But then, Sin had never kissed her as he had today. A kiss of giving, of restoring, of succoring.

Kissing Amaris had been a mistake. A moment of weakness.

Sin wrapped his arms around the sleeping Celeste. She was pathetically thin. The loss of another child, and she might not make it.

He had thought he could sexually satisfy her and still withdraw in time to prevent getting her with child. In spite of his precautions, he had twice done just so.

Since the loss of their last child, a beautiful stillborn son, his practice of abstinence had been a bloody hell of frustration for him.

If it hadn't been for that bush fire. Amaris had appeared amid the swirling smoke. She had been disheveled, her expression animated, her body pulsating with vivacity—all had combined in an overpowering temptation for him. Like a man athirst in the Never-Never, he had crushed her against him and kissed her, drinking deeply of her nurturing womanhood.

At first, he had been struck by how sweet she had tasted, her breath baby fresh. And then, foolishly, he had forgotten everything to experience that filling of himself, that renewal, that completion of himself.

Maybe it was that sixth sense that often warned

him of impending danger, but something whispered of devastation: emotional peril, jeopardy to the soul, the loss of self with the loss of integrity.

And yet, for him, that kiss was an acknowledgment of what he had known all along: that he and Amaris were well matched. The Irish aesthetic in him would proclaim that their souls had been thirsting for the stream of life that ran in the other since the stars in the Southern Cross first made their appearance in Australia's heavens forty-five million years before.

18

"Amaris, you're sure!"

Francis sat up in bed. His face, adorned with a beard now, was alight. Gone were the harsh lines of worry. His once delicate English skin, now sunbaked and porous, glowed with the joyful news.

She nodded. "Sometime this winter, the last of July, the best I can estimate." She was almost twenty-nine, well past the prime time for a woman to become a mother.

"Then we'll have more than one reason to celebrate at the Tremaynes' tonight." Leaning on one forearm beside her, he pushed the tumbled hair from her face. In his face was a boy's mischievous expression. "If it's a son, his given name will be Lord. Lord Marlborough."

She chuckled. "Don't even think about it. A plain name it will be."

They shared the news with her parents on the journey that beautiful fall morning in mid-April to

Never-Never, where Celeste was giving a party in honor of England's new monarch, the nineteen-year-old Queen Victoria. Any excuse for a get-together was reason enough in the outback.

William suggested a name for his future grandson. "I should think Richard or Harry, both fine English kings."

"But, Willy, the name Robert is the best—a grand king of the Scots, he was," Rose lovingly teased from the back of the dray.

Francis took the debate over his future child's name in good stride. What concerned him was the possibility that her parents might attempt to control his son's upbringing. He had murmured as much that morning before they left for the Tremaynes'. "I don't want them trying to implant religious dogma in my son's head."

Francis's spirituality bordered on agnostic. "Dear," Amaris said, "all my parents have ever tried to impart to the congregation is the belief that we are all one and the need to love one another."

His brows had peaked but he had said nothing. Whatever reservations he had about her parents' missionary zeal, he liked and respected them, she knew.

Despite the outback's dry clime, arthritis was twisting the joints of Rose's fingers. But in her face was complete acceptance of humankind. Nonjudgmental, she went out into the bush with her Willy for days at a time, sleeping on the back of their dray and administering love along with the Word to the aborigines.

Amaris yearned to possess Rose's no-nonsense spirituality, but for Amaris each day was a seesaw between selflessness and a desire that came not from her ego but from her very soul.

Since the day of that bush fire at Brighton Station, she had tried to resist giving in to what her soul clamored for: union with Sin. It was a daily battle.

From that day on she and Sin had both avoided all situations of potential intimacy. The result had been a decrease in the times their two families visited.

Now, now that she was with child, she felt as if she had donned an amulet against the attraction she and Sin shared.

So Amaris, sitting on the back of the dray with Rose, felt lighthearted and looked forward to the celebration of Queen Victoria's reign. A woman. A young woman. Anything was possible!

Her hand settled on her stomach. She was well into her fifth month, but because of her height and bone structure her condition did not show.

Not even Celeste could believe the news. No jealousy showed on her gaunt face when Amaris told her. Celeste hugged her. She was astounded by how painfully thin the woman was. Almost all bones, she no longer looked the younger of the two.

"That's wonderful, Amaris! A beautiful blessing for a beautiful friend."

Celeste and she, along with Rose, bustled around the kitchen, dominated by the large fireplace where dishwater boiled. "Since Molly left Jimmy and ran off with that drover, I've had to learn how to cook all over again for the hands," Celeste was saying.

Amaris hefted the steaming caldron over to the iron trivet on the table. "Everyone cleaned the dishes of every last morsel. I think that proves you are the best cook in the outback, Celeste."

"We all know Elizabeth is by far the best," Celeste said without a trace of mock humility. "She swears it's the cast-iron stove the major ordered."

"I'll believe that when I see it."

Rose began stacking the dishes in the cauldron. "An old hand like meself can wash these in no time. You two inexperienced young women join the others on the veranda."

The sun had set, although a vibrant faint pink lingered in the western sky. The veranda was cool, and the scent of honeysuckle Celeste had planted competed with the evocative scent of the men's pipes.

Celeste settled in a leather slung chair beside her husband and slipped her hand into his free one. Their fingers intertwined. Amaris glanced away. She was acutely aware of her big, ungainly hands.

She sought out a wicker chair slightly behind and to one side of Sin. Through her lashes she peered at his strong profile. Watching him as he listened to her father, she felt sexually charged. This disappointed her mightily. All her feelings of being above that sort of thing now that she was carrying Francis's child seemed suddenly pompous.

"Well, Francis," Celeste said, beaming, "did you tell Sin your wonderful news?"

Francis grinned boyishly. "I was getting around to it. I thought maybe William here might make the announcement, considering all the babies he has christened—and that the news concerns his future grandchild."

It seemed all eyes turned on Amaris. She saw only Sin's speculative gaze. "I think you just made the announcement." She felt uncomfortable being the sudden object of attention.

Francis said, "Sin, we need another mount. For Amaris. I want her to learn the sport of fox hunting after the birth of our child."

"Or dingo hunting," Sin said. "As the case is here?"

Amaris kept the subject on horses. "A mount at the right price, of course. Everyone knows how wily you Irish horsetraders are when it comes to filling your pots of gold."

He tapped out his pipe. "Only the leprechauns deal in pots of gold. The rest of us Irish are content just to toil in the soil."

"And raise the best horseflesh anywhere. Well, will you let us see your wares, sir?"

Chuckling, Sin rose. "I think I have a mount you might be interested in."

"Drive a hard bargain, Amaris," Francis urged. "I trust your judgment."

"My daughter will get the best of you, son," William called after her and Sin. "We menfolk must stick together. Don't let her try to talk you down."

She and Sin walked in silence toward the stables. Their bantering had been for the sake of the others. Now she didn't know what to say. It was he who broke the quiet of the early evening. "Congratulations, Amaris."

"Congratulations?" For a moment, she didn't know what he was talking about. "Oh, yes." Automatically, her hand went to her stomach. "My child. Francis's and mine."

His gaze lowered to her stomach. She flushed and quickly dropped her hand. "I have a gift for the wee one," he said, shifting his eyes to the grass-denuded track leading into the stables.

"You do?"

"Aye. Over there. The third stall. A blooded mare out of Wind Runner. She's just foaled. A colt. Come look."

Amaris peered over the stall door. The colt stood on spindly legs, nursing from its mother. "Oh, Sin, it's absolutely beautiful!"

"It's sire is a Morgan. A New England breed noted for their strength, endurance, and speed. They'll do well here in the outback. When it's weaned, I'll bring it over, just about the time you are . . ." His voice trailed away in a loss of appropriate words.

Feeling secure in her maternity, she laughed. "About the time I am ready to foal?"

He slanted her a grin, and all her newfound security was vanquished. He smiled so rarely that when he did it caught the attention. At the moment, his devil-take-it grin was loaded with seductive power. "Knowing you, Amaris, you'll give birth and be up and at it as easily as this mare did."

"Do you?" she asked quietly. "Do you know me? Really know me?"

The soft glow of the lantern enveloped them. In the quiet of the evening, a low whinny, a horse pawing the straw, were the only noises. "I've known you since before either of us were born."

She couldn't force her gaze away from his. Nor could she deny what he said. Her equanimity was in jeopardy. "Don't say such things again."

She brushed past him, but he caught her elbow. She looked from his hand up into his face.

He gazed at her long and intensely, then said, "The mount you wanted—I think I have what you want. The second stall from the end. 'Tis a Rockingham.

Caught the brumby running wild near Teather Creek. Had a hell of a time breaking him."

She followed Sin deeper into the stable where lantern light was faint. His broad back and powerfully muscled hips held her gaze.

He stopped before a stall, and she almost ran into him. To back away would show her unease. She held her ground only inches from him. "Rocky stands sixteen hands and can carry up to seventeen stone all day. I guarantee you the Rockingham can outlast and outpace any camel. He's been doing well in the brush."

She forced her attention to the horse, a black. Its confirmation was excellent—a muscular, crested neck, strong shoulders, and clean lines. Delighted, she said, "It will make a marvelous hunting horse."

"With its stamina, it should."

"What do you want for it?"

He stared down at her. His face, cast in shadows, was difficult to read. "More than you can give."

"Give or have?"

"Give."

It was a challenge. Excitement surged through her. "What is your price?"

He shifted his stance, glanced away as if deliberating, then returned his gaze to her. "Consider the horse a loan."

Just playing the word game with him exhilarated her. "To be repaid . . . when?"

He ended the game. "Repayment isn't necessary between friends. Shall we go back to the house?"

His curt tone made her feel foolish, childish. "No. I don't want to be beholden to you, Sin. Name your price."

Even in shadows, his face seemed to darken. "You are pushing for it, aren't you?"

It was too late to back down. "Aye."

He took hold of her shoulders and backed her against the stall door. His mouth ground down on hers. At the same time, his hand dropped from one shoulder to splay over the slight mound of her stomach. He rubbed it gently. "Mother Earth," he murmured against her lips.

"Aye," she whispered, glorying in the one thing she could give him Celeste could not, a child. At the same time she felt shame and guilt stab like a blade into her conscience.

His leg wedged itself between hers, and his hand moved upward to cup one breast. He began kneading it gently. "Full, suckling breasts. Are their nipples darker?" he rusked. "A dark, rich brown?"

"Aye. Aye." That was all she could murmur. She wanted him to take her, there on the straw floor. Now.

His head dipped to nuzzle her neck. His breath was hot on her skin. Her hand crept up his corded neck into his hair. She pressed his head against her breast.

He shook her hand free and raised his face so that he could see hers. "Me price?" he said, his voice hoarse, his lids heavy with unslaked passion. "Me price is that you deny me the love I would take from you."

Her insurgent desire evaporated with his clipped words and was at once replaced with a deep aching sorrow. "A heavy price," she whispered.

"A heavy price for both of us." He bent his head once more and grazed her forehead with his lips.

"Gads, 'tis been so long since last I held you." With a sigh, he straightened. "Shall we go back now?"

She brushed past him and hurried through the now-dark evening across the yard to the house. Rose had finished the dishes and joined the others on the veranda. Her knitting needles clacked while her husband talked.

Apparently, William was discoursing on the aborigines. " . . . Dangar's property, the aborigine women are living with his overseer, Hobbs."

Francis took a swallow of rum left in the bottom of his glass and said, "That's not unusual in the outback. A man has needs, William."

Embarrassed by the crude statement, Celeste lowered her head.

Realizing his blunder, Francis tried to clarify himself but only made it worse. "I grant you the church looks upon this as a sin, but—"

"The sin is not in loving," William said, "but in hurting. Men like Hobbs are destroying the aborigines' way of life. The aborigines know nothing of ownership. Everything is provided by nature. That a person can own sheep is as preposterous to them as claiming to own the geese."

Rose ceased plying her needles. Her voice echoed her husband's concern. "As the aborigines' wild food decreases with each new white settlement, they are facing certain death by starvation. We must help them."

"While they slaughter us like sheep?" Francis asked. "Two sawyers were speared last week, and just before that several aborigines attacked the workers at a limekiln. The stealth of these . . ."

Amaris only saw her husband's lips moving. His

words made no impact on her brain, because at that moment Sin returned from the stables to rejoin the group. Rather than take a chair, he slouched to the wooden floor beside Celeste's chair, his back against the wall. Celeste's hand drifted down from the arm of her chair to alight on his shoulder. The gesture went unnoticed by everyone but Amaris.

She loved them both . . . her half sister and Sin, her soul mate. Nevertheless, observing their obvious devotion to each other was a pain equal to an unseen hand squeezing her heart.

Like a creek, the months flowed gently by for Amaris. Toward the end of her term, she grew so large she wondered if she might be carrying twins.

In bed at night, Francis would feel her stomach and jest that she had swallowed a melon seed. She wasn't as agile, that was true, and Baluway assumed many of her duties.

"You want I should take the hands to the western paddock and dock the sheep tails?" he asked her.

They stood on the veranda, watching the sun come up. Her parents had driven out in their dray to take food and supplies to Baluway's tribe. Francis had risen early and taken the bullocks to plow the wheat and potato paddocks. With the coming of fatherhood, he was acting more responsible, taking the initiative.

"Aye," she told the little man who still insisted on wearing nothing but a breechcloth and boots. "That would be a good idea. I'll go with you."

His expression never changed. "You will ride?"

She laughed. "With difficulty. Saddle Wind Runner for me, and I'll change into a riding habit."

The habit didn't fit, of course, so Rose had sewn panels into the jacket. Ryku was helping Amaris pull on her boots. "When my husband comes in for lunch, tell him I should be back by late afternoon."

Ryku's sloe eyes regarded her steadily. "You are sure?"

Here it was again, the aborigines' amazement that a woman with child should assume activities normally relegated to the male realm. She smiled. "Aye, 'tis sure I am."

The slender young woman nodded solemnly. "I clean the breakfast dishes now." She retreated from the room on silent, bare feet, her dark skin melding with the corridor's shadows.

Feeling as if she were straining every muscle in her body, Amaris mounted Wind Runner and rode with Baluway and three hands out to the paddock where a flock of new lambs were to be marked.

The men, all ex-convicts, accorded Baluway a respect that few white men did for the aborigine: His skills as a spear thrower and sheep rancher were well known. He was not as brutal as many white overseers, and the grateful ex-convicts worked diligently.

She worked alongside the men, envying their brief attire. Hampered by her clothing, her movements were constrained. As the sun rose higher, she grew hotter.

When lunchtime came, she climbed a grassy slope to sit where she could catch a breeze. She was toying with a dandelion, watching its fluffy seeds take sail on the breeze, when she sighted several figures moving at a steady pace on the distant plains. At first she thought they might be wallabies, the medium-sized kangaroos.

With awkward movements, she pushed to her feet and, shading her eyes with her hand, watched as the figures drew closer. They turned out to be three aborigine runners.

With careful steps she made her way down the hill and joined Baluway and the hands just about the same time the runners arrived. Despite the distance they must have run, they were breathing lightly. Ignoring her, they spoke with Baluway in a rapid, excited patois.

Baluway nodded several times. Beneath his wide nose, his mouth was flattened in a solemn line. He turned to her. "The Gagudju tribe makes war on mine. Much death."

At first, the import of his words didn't sink in. Then she realized. Her parents were in danger—if not already murdered. "How far is your tribe from here?"

"Maybe one—two days to Hollow Hill."

"We're going back to the house." She swung around and started for her hobbled mount, all the while she talked. "We'll need more ammunition, food rations, bandage strips and ointment—"

Her mind raced on, calculating all that would be needed, how long she might be gone. Francis would have to watch the station.

By the time she reached the house, she was in a fervor to make the provisions and ride out. "Francis!" she called out and hurried inside. In contrast to the hot, sun-bright afternoon, the house was cool and dark.

Francis stumbled from their bedroom. "You're back already?" he asked, his hands busy pushing in his shirttail.

Something was amiss in his voice. Even in the dimness of the room, she could tell his hair was mussed. Then she knew, as Ryku coalesced behind him in the doorway. She was adjusting her long skirts. Her eyes met those of Amaris. At once, Amaris guessed what had taken place. The smug expression in Ryku's gaze confirmed what she surmised.

She intertwined her arms and stared hard at Francis. "Well?"

"It's not what you think."

She was trembling inside, but her voice was steady. "What do I think?"

"For the love of God, Amaris, it's been almost two months since I've touched you. A bloke could go crazy with—"

"I never said no to you."

He tunneled his fingers through his sun-gilded hair. "I know, I know. But how can a man get aroused when he fears hurting the—"

Fury, sorrow, guilt all surged through her veins at once, threatening to burst them in an overload. She knew she hadn't been receptive to Francis's advances the last few months. But it had been so hot, and she had been so miserable with her size, and felt so unattractive, even repulsive.

Worse, she felt somehow she was betraying Sin when she submitted to Francis. If that wasn't a sign of someone who belonged in Bedlam, she didn't know what was. That must be it. She was going mad, living virtually alone in the outback as women did.

Behind Francis, Ryku slipped past them to disappear into the darkness of the house. Amaris tried to pull herself together, but darts of nerves were assaulting her stomach. Everything was coming down on her at once.

"Look, Francis, we will discuss this later. Baluway's tribe has been attacked by another. Apparently, he thinks my parents may be in danger. We've got to get there as soon as possible."

"Of course," Francis said, obviously glad to shift the focus from himself. He crossed to the mantel and took down the rifle and leather pouch of balls. "We can—"

"Ohhh!" A dagger-sharp pain ripped through her stomach, and she doubled over, sinking to her knees.

"Our baby?" Consternation contorted Francis's face. "It's time?"

She nodded. "It's early . . . two weeks by my . . . calculations."

He crouched beside her and gingerly lifted her to her feet. Slipping her arm up around his neck, he said, "Let's get you into bed." A contrite grimace stretched his lips. "I've never been a father before. With Rose away, you'll have to tell me what to—"

"Listen to me, Francis. Waiting for a baby to be born can take days. These could be false pains. You must take Baluway and the hands with you and ride to their village to help Mother and Father."

He sat her down on the bed. "I can't leave you here alone to go through—"

"Ryku can help me with the delivery should the baby come before you can get back."

Reluctance showed in his face. His jaw tensed, as if he were preparing to argue with her.

"Francis, if you don't go, I will—if I have to dismount and squat and have our baby alongside the trail. Besides, I haven't had any more pains. It could well be another two weeks. Now do as I ask. Go with Baluway. Do this for me, please."

He drew a deep breath. His lips tightened. Finally, he nodded. "All right, but I don't like leaving you here alone. Ryku has no knowledge about delivering babies."

She managed a wan smile. "Neither do you."

He dropped a good-bye kiss on her cheek, then straightened. "I'll be back as soon as possible, if it means galloping all the way."

"Francis," she called to his departing back.

He stopped at the doorway. "Aye?"

"Take care of yourself."

After he left, she lay there, watching the shafts of sunlight slip down the walls. Tiny pains nagged her stomach—and nagged her baby, apparently, because it kicked its displeasure just often enough to make her keep to her bed.

She placed her hands on her enormous belly and concentrated on the baby. By the time it reached school age, she would have to hire a tutor. Sin could teach it to ride like a true Irishman. She was sure the child was a boy. Not that she cared, just so it was healthy and perfectly formed.

She would not let herself think of her parents' safety or of that of Francis—or, most of all, of his betrayal. Not now. Later, when she had the strength of all her resources. Later, when the baby was born and Francis and her parents were safe back at home, then . . .

Ryku appeared in the doorway. Her expression was uneasy. In a neutral voice, she asked, "You want me make dinner?"

"No. I'm not hungry. Go on to the hut. I'll be all right."

But she wasn't. As the room settled into early evening shadows, her pains began to intensify. Cramping contractions made her gasp in agony. She managed to get out of bed and stagger to the front door. Clutching it to stand erect, she called out, "Ryku!"

Only the cooing of a dove broke the silence.

"Ryku!"

Another pain attacked Amaris. Her hands slipping down the door frame, she sagged to the floor. "Oh, my God," she whimpered. She was going to give birth to her baby alone.

She rolled onto the floor and lay on her side, her legs drawn up in their own fetal position. Her fingernails dug into her palms, and she moaned. Another pain struck her, and she screamed out her anguish. Suffering with each bolt of pain, she rolled from side to side, her arms wrapped around her enlarged stomach.

She didn't even hear the booted spurs clank on the veranda's planking; she only felt the arms gather her, lifting her, cradling her.

"Sssh, me luv, it's going to be fine," Sin whispered against her forehead as he carried her back to her bedroom.

"What . . . are you doing here?" Each word was a monumental effort to get out.

"I brought over the weaned colt I had promised you." He laid her gently on her bed and started unbuttoning her high-top shoes.

She gasped as another pain racked her. She felt as if she were being torn asunder. "The baby is coming. Now!"

A vein ticked at his temple. "Where is your mother? Francis?"

Her breathing seemed rapid in her ears. "He's on his way to . . . Baluway's village. Aborigine attack. My parents . . . oh, God, Sin, I hurt!"

"Ryku?"

"She might . . . be in her hut." Amaris felt so alone, so weak, so vulnerable. She wanted to unburden the pain of her discovery of Francis's treachery. Instead, she compressed her lips, even as smarting tears trickled from the corners of her eyes. "I called . . . she didn't . . . answer."

Sin leaned over her and brushed away a tear streaming along her cheekbone. He stared down at her. "Did something happen before I got here?"

He was so damned perceptive. "No." She tensed as another pain began and bit back her moan.

"Then it's you and me, luv." He began rolling up his sleeves. "I've never helped a wee one into life, but there is always a first time for everything. Me mother did a lot of midwifing. Me sister, too. But they always shooed the men out, which doesn't give me much headstart on midwifing for this one, does it now? Still, this promises to be a grand adventure."

She knew he was talking to keep her mind off her misery, but when he began removing her clothing, she exclaimed, "No! I don't want you to see . . . me . . . like this!"

"Don't be foolish." He stripped her skirts from her legs, so that her stomach protruded like a creamy dome just below her chemise.

All she could think of was how embarrassed she was. Then another pain chased away her embarrassment.

With a tenderness that amazed her, he encircled her swollen belly with his large, callused hands and began massaging its contracting muscles. "The village folk would say that you have an outy, Amaris."

His saturnine face was so grave, so contemplative, that she became alarmed about her condition, which was unusual for her. She had always taken her good health for granted. "A what?"

"An outy." His finger traced concentric circles around her navel. "Your belly button . . . it pops out. But I imagine it shall change to an inny once this one makes its appearance."

She saw the mischievous gleam in his eyes. She smiled, then began laughing.

"You are the most beautiful I have ever seen you, luv."

Her dimpled grin changed to a grimace. "Oh God, Sin, it's coming."

"I recall something about clean linens for the wee one and yourself, but I don't think there's time."

She latched on to his hand and squeezed, as the part of her she had given life to demanded the right to draw breath.

"Push, Amaris. It can't be too much different than foaling, after all."

His attempt at jocularity elicited a weak smile from her; then she gasped as a wave of pain blackened everything around her. When her vision coalesced, mystification, astonishment, disquietude, were all playing across Sin's marvelously mobile face.

"It *is* coming, luv! I can see a small part of its head. Come on now. Push. Let the wee one enter our world. That's it. Shhh, it's decided it's tired of waiting."

"I'm tired of waiting, too," she complained, hurting too much to be excited. Her hands crumpled the sheet as another shattering thrust extended her pelvis.

"One more push. There you go! Why, look what we have here, me luv."

She heard a sputtering little cry, like a kitten's mew, but couldn't muster the curiosity or strength to raise her head and look.

"A fine boy, it is."

At the weight on her chest, her eyes snapped open. A reddened, wizened, wet little human flailed tiny arms and kicked and cried.

Sin proceeded to cleanse the infant with a soft cotton cloth, then he edged up her chemise and cupped her breast. "Give the mite what he wants, and maybe he'll hush that infernal shrieking."

Her gaze shifted from the baby suckling at her nipple to Sin's face. Tears spilled down his beard-shadowed cheeks.

19

Dream Time station had become a village of sorts, a fact which never failed to amaze Amaris. How had so many years passed since she and Francis set up housekeeping in what amounted to little more than a shed?

Gathering spring's wild flowers, she stood on the slope of the ridge and gazed down upon the station: the house, the barns and dairy and all the outbuildings, the men's quarters and the row of married-worker's cottages, their dining room, the kitchens, the store, and now a chapel and a graveyard. More than forty people were on the Dream Time payroll.

No wonder just keeping the books had become a full-time job for her. But she missed the adventure that came with working outdoors.

Picking her way down a footpath, she headed for the graveyard. Her parents had been the first to be interned within the picket-fenced enclosure, located beneath a leafy canopy of gum boughs. The aborigines'

mutilation of their bodies three years before had
made Francis's return from the burned out village a
horrendous affair.

Entering the gate, she stopped between the two
graves, each marked with a large, white wooden
cross. One day she planned to erect something more
substantial with fitting epitaphs. The day her parents
left the world, Robert had entered.

One door closes, another opens.

Sighing, she rose to return to the house. Her gaze
fell on Francis, who plowed behind the plodding
bullocks in the west pasture. Astride his shoulders
perched Robert. She had to acknowledge the boy
made a better man of the father. For Robert's sake,
Francis worked harder. The nobleman had become a
common man, a man of the soil.

He was trying harder to be a good husband, also.
Two days after Robert's birth, Ryku had returned to
the station. Baluway told Amaris that while she was
still abed, Francis had ordered Ryku off the premises.
Apparently, the station hands believed the punishment
was the result of Ryku's desertion when the mistress
was in need of aid.

For Robert's sake, Francis was also involving himself
in the community. He had volunteered to accompany
Sin on a wagon train headed to Sydney with the wool
baled from the various stations. The local station owners
had requested Sin to negotiate with a Sydney agent to
send the wool to the London sales.

Since wool could be sold only once a year, this
presented a cash-flow problem. A broking company
in Sydney paid the sheep rancher an advance on the
wool's value and arranged the shipping and sale—the
benefit to the station owners and squatters being that

they received their money much sooner, almost a year in most cases, than if they sent it to London themselves.

Francis spotted her and stopped his plowing. Grinning, he beckoned her to join him. As she drew nearer, Robert called out, "Mama!" and wiggled this way and that atop his father's shoulders in an attempt to get down.

"Whoa, son," Francis said. Sweat was dripping off of his brow and beard, bleached almost white by the fierce sun.

"Why not take a break?" she suggested. She slipped her hands underneath Robert's arms to transfer him from his father's shoulder to her hip. "One of the workers could be doing this."

Francis wiped the back of his arm across his perspiring forehead. "I like working with my hands. It's something my father would have frowned upon."

Strange, she thought, that the salon-raised Francis enjoyed more working with the earth, and Sin, who had so toiled most of his life, found greater pleasure in people and ideas.

Francis shaded his eyes, fanned with wrinkles, against the harsh sunlight. "Going to be the best crop yet, Amaris."

"If the rains ever come." Robert was getting restless and heavy, and she shifted him to her other hip. "Don't forget Robert's birthday party. The Tremaynes will be here this evening."

She looked forward to seeing Celeste and Sin, who would stay the weekend. Celeste adored Robert. When Amaris watched her hug and talk to the three-year-old, her heart went out in sympathy to her friend. Celeste yearned so for a child but apparently had resigned herself to remaining childless.

How was Sin dealing with a wife who risked her life each time she made love? Amaris's imagination was fertile. She visualized Sin and Celeste in bed, their limbs entangled in the throes of lovemaking.

Did he withdraw before spilling his essence into her? Or perhaps he didn't even take that risk. Perhaps he sought out the arms of another woman for release, taking to bed one of the aborigine women as Francis had done.

Or, worse, maybe he found solace in the arms of a white woman in Sydney on those journeys on behalf of the syndication of local stations.

Jealousy, hot, explosive, and blinding, roared through her. She pivoted away from Francis before she could betray her volatile fury and stalked back to the house. Her anticipation of the Tremaynes' visit was dampened.

As she prepared the birthday dinner, Francis sat playing with Robert. A small replica of Francis, the toddler was blessed with a riot of blond curls and large beautiful brown eyes.

At the moment, Rogue was tugging on one of his stockings, and the toddler was laughing. His chubby cheeks were a cherubic pink. He was so precious to her. She missed that first year and a half that she had nursed him. Sin had been the first to put her son to her breast.

Sensing her deflated mood, Francis tried to engage her in light conversation. She had to admit he had been penitent and sensitive to her needs ever since the incident with Ryku. "There is talk that the major is pushing Sin to run for a territorial seat."

"I doubt Sin wants to get involved in politics. His law student days cured him of battling for the masses."

"A smart Irishman."

She ignored the remark and concentrated on applying a butter glaze to the cake.

"Countryside is beginning to look seared. Do you think the rains are just late this year?"

"Are you asking if this is more than just a dry spell, if we're facing a drought? No one can determine the start of a drought until afterwards."

She felt her words had been testy. Taking a swish of the glaze on one forefinger, she presented the swirl for his taste. "Your approval, sire," she said, smiling.

He wrapped an arm around her waist and, taking her finger between his lips, sucked the sticky substance. "Hmmm, you get sweeter by the year."

"And you get more randy." She grinned and pulled away to glance down at Robert, who had fallen asleep at his father's feet. A protective Rogue rested his grizzled muzzle in the boy's lap.

She bent to collect her son and cradle him in her arms. "Robert's been so excited about seeing his Uncle Sin, he didn't sleep well last night." She pushed back the sweat-damp forelock that had fallen across his forehead.

"I'm not too keen on Sin's teaching him to ride at such an early age."

Her defensive instincts surged to the forefront. "Sin is always very careful."

She wondered if Francis could be jealous of the affection between their son and Sin. Robert loved his father, but he absolutely worshiped his Uncle Sin. With Robert's delivery, a bond had been forged between her son and Sin.

In every way she was tied to Sin, except in the one that was most important to a woman in love.

"Robby!" A flamingo-thin Celeste whispered and bent to kiss the napping boy.

Robert stirred. His lids fluttered and he awoke with a grin.

Celeste picked the toddler up from his bed and planted loving kisses on his baby-fat cheeks. "Oh, Robby, you have a new tooth since I've last seen you. Aren't you growing into a handsome lad. Keep this up and I'll be able to marry you. I'm waiting for you, you know."

Behind her, Sin said, "You'll have to wrestle me for her, Robert."

At the sight of his uncle, Robert's face radiated. Another smile erupted. "Uncle Shin!" he gurgled.

"Alas," Celeste said, passing Robert to Sin, "I must yield to someone held in greater favor by my prince."

Sin grasped Robert around his chubby waist and held him aloft so that his baby face was close to Sin's own. Rubbing noses with Robert, he laughed and so did the toddler.

Amaris loved the sound of their laughter. This was what life was all about.

"A prince are you?" Sin teased. "I'd much prefer to be a toad. They have more fun. They get to play in water. You'd like that, wouldn't you? Or better yet, how about fishing, me lad? Shall we do that?"

His glance strayed over the toddler's head to meet her gaze. His smile altered. It was still a smile but there was a subtle, fine thread of something more.

At her side, Francis said, "Come along, cobber.

Amaris has burned the supper, I fear, and 'tis up to us to provide it."

"Oh, you cad!" Amaris responded in mock indignity. "Don't believe him, Celeste."

Over a dinner of roast mutton, snow peas, cooked greens, and steamed rice, the conversation skipped from dress patterns to the deepening draught. Sipping from their vineyard wine, Sin told of a new hand he had hired, a British migrant who had come to Australia and the outback to make his fortune. Well-connected, he had letters of introduction but had no idea what it took to adapt to station life.

Sin leaned back in his chair, glass stem in his hand. "Mr. Crane was a Yorkshire man who insisted on taking the cattle out to look for water two months ago. He didn't return, and I rode out to follow his tracks but they disappeared from a water hole on a stretch of flat water-worn pebbles. This morning I found his skeleton only forty meters away from the water hole, hidden by brush."

Francis tossed down the remainder of his glass. "Our native-born jackeroos might be as inexperienced as these damned British migrants but at least they know and understand the land."

Amaris chuckled. "It wasn't so long ago, Francis, you were one of those damned British migrants."

He laughed with the others. "I guess I've become a dyed-in-the-wool Australian."

"Wool," Robert chirped. "Wool." He had learned early the most important word to most station owners.

Sin lifted him from his chair. "Now listen, me lad, you need to learn to say horse, too."

"Horshey?" Robert repeated, and they all laughed again.

"So, you're ready to ride, huh?" With Robert tucked into his arm, he strode from the dining room. "We horsemen are going riding before it gets dark."

"He's a sheep man," Francis corrected in a good-natured tone.

Everyone trooped outdoors to watch the two in the riding arena. With a delighted Robert perched in front, Sin trotted Wave Runner, his gift to Robert at his birth. Applause erupted from the spectators, which included not only Francis, Celeste, and herself, but also several station hands. No more than a half dozen were married, and those women also turned out to watch. Tough women, jilleroos who would endure the rigors of outback life, they looked as if they had been ridden hard.

Robert took his turn at the reins and beamed proudly when Amaris applauded a well-executed circle, never suspecting that Sin's knees completely controlled the magnificent animal.

Although many stations hired contract horse breakers, Sin broke his own. Her gaze claimed by the play of his thigh muscles beneath the well-worn denim trousers, she could well remember watching one day as he mastered one of his rogue horses.

It had been obvious after only a few minutes that this was to be a contest of wills between man and beast. When both were speckled by blood, she feared that neither would give until one died. Celeste had not watched. "I cannot hide my worry for Sin. If he were to be hurt . . ."

Despite desperately loving Sin, Amaris had known no fear for him. Rather, watching him tame the animal into submission, she felt an excitement that had been almost sexual.

This was a man whose will would never be mastered. Neither convict punishment nor the hostile environment of the Never-Never had broken his will.

This was a man whose will matched hers.

This was her man . . . a man she could never have.

Of course, after a long and bloody battle, the rogue horse had eventually yielded, its head bowed, its nostrils blowing foam, its chest laboring hard.

When darkness put her son's riding performance at an end, she returned to the veranda with the others to sit and talk and cherish those rare moments when they could relax among friends.

Later, after everyone went to bed, Amaris lay wide awake. Robert slept contentedly between her and Francis. Her urge to shift to another position was repressed simply because there was no room to turn. Despite the open window, heat lay over the room.

Trying not to awaken the other two, she slid from the bed and felt her way through the darkened house to the front door. The coolness of the night breeze wafted along the veranda. Her sigh joined the breeze. It played with the hem of her muslin nightgown, rustled the ends of her loose hair mantling her shoulders, and lured her to the steps where it collected the scents of honeysuckle with which to wreath her.

Above her, the night sky was studded with stars. Arms wrapped around her knees, she sat in contentment. How wealthy she was. Not all of Nan Livingston's riches could equal the blessings she enjoyed: a precious son, good husband, good friends like Sin and Celeste, and her own place that carried her own stamp as valid as any waxed seal.

Over the years, although she had managed to acquiesce to Francis, to let him lead even when she knew his decisions were sometimes in error, the local people nevertheless referred to Dream Time as Amaris's run.

Yielding to Francis was probably one of the hardest things she had ever had to do—to be less of a person, to sublimate herself because she was a woman.

A movement in the shadows caught her peripheral vision. Even as she tensed to spring from the steps, a hand clasped her forearm, detaining her.

"'Tis only me, Amaris."

"Oh, God!" she whispered. "You gave me a fright, Sin."

He lowered his large frame to the step just above hers. She could feel his body heat, smell his scent that she associated only with him. She knew that his hands, dangling between his knees, were dusted with hair. She knew how his hair swirled in one direction at his nape. She knew that his temples were beginning to gray.

She knew so much about him, except how it felt to lie beneath his weight, how his hands felt stroking her inner thigh, how it felt to have him fill her with himself.

"Robert is no longer a baby. He's becoming a little boy you can be proud of, Amaris."

Not "you and Francis" can be proud of but only "you." "Robert adores you, you know."

"He's a special little boy." His voice was husky with his yearning for the child he would never have.

"I know." Her heart went out to Celeste, unfulfilled as a mother. Yet, if Amaris had to forego her love for Sin, she could at least take comfort in the fact that Robert was a bond between them.

"It appears that each time you and I watch the night sky together," he said in a low, very quiet voice, "the Southern Cross is brighter than normal."

"I used to think you didn't like me."

His hands clasped into a single knot. He was silent for a long time. She thought that he wasn't going to answer. Then, at last, he spoke. "That was the problem. I always liked you. I liked your courage, your determination, your spirit. You never gave in and wept and said, 'Poor me.'"

Still staring up at the crystal-speckled heaven, she asked, "Then why did you either ignore or mock me?"

"I didn't approve of your social climbing. But then, who am I to judge? I love not only my wife but another woman I can never have."

Incomprehensible that they could sit never glancing at each other and talk quietly about such intimate feelings. They could just as well have been discussing the drought.

"Could it be the age-old plight of wanting what you can't have?"

She heard the dry, self-mocking humor in his voice. "That's what I tell meself."

"Amaris? . . . Sin?" Celeste chided softly from the doorway. "Are you two children sneaking out at night to play?"

So guileless was she that she was totally unaware of the import of her words. She stepped out onto the veranda. Despite the long nightgown sheathing her from wrist to neck to ankle, she had appropriately wrapped a hand-knitted shawl about her shoulders. Amaris realized she should have put a robe over her long gown.

"My, isn't it beautiful out tonight?" Celeste said. "I can't blame you two for escaping the confines of the house." She settled next to Sin on the step, her shoulder touching his, her knees brushing Amaris's spine. "This is like the old days, isn't it? We three?"

Sin put his arm around her waist. She was so thin, Amaris thought, she was almost a wraith. "You couldn't sleep either?" he asked of Celeste.

She rested her hand on his knee and her head on his shoulder. "I'm not accustomed to having the entire bed to myself."

"As much as you grumble about me sprawling, giving you no room?" he teased.

Whatever guilt Amaris felt was chased away by the sudden question that nudged her mind: Did Celeste know after all of the love between Sin and her and—sinless soul that Celeste was—choose to ignore it? Amaris shivered at the possibility of such a thing.

"You can't be cold." Celeste said.

"Not really. The late hour is just catching up with me. I think I'll try again to get to sleep. Good night, Celeste, Sin."

But, of course, she didn't sleep the rest of the night.

Francis's drinking deepened along with the drought.

Amaris watched the running creek turn into a series of billabongs, pools of water left in dried-up riverbeds. By the end of the following year, the grass had long since disappeared. The face of the countryside was shifting red and gray sand, blowing wherever the wind carried it. Dead sheep and fallen tree trunks became sand hills. Birds were dropping dead out of leafless trees.

She had sent to Sydney with Francis and Sin only

seven hundred bales of wool, whereas the year before she had sent away more than two thousand. Her flock had dropped from one hundred thousand to six thousand.

The gardens yielded no vegetables, and meat was lean to starvation. Butter and milk had long been food only in name. How was she going to feed over fifty-six people for whom she was now responsible?

When she looked into her five-year-old's trusting eyes, she both wept and raged inside. She was helpless against the elements, against the wrath of nature.

"Stop pacing the floor," Francis said one evening from the dining table, where he sat drinking rum. "You're making *me* jittery." He was not a reader like she; and with so little opportunity for socializing with his peers, he found nothing better to do than drink.

"'Tis not my pacing that's making you jittery, 'tis your drinking," she snapped.

"Mama? Are you a bad girl?" Robert peered up at them through his incredibly long lashes. He sat on the hardwood floor and played with a corncob horse Baluway had fashioned for him. Next to Robert, Rogue watched her just as intently.

She had to smile. "No, not bad—or mad. Just . . . just talking aloud."

Later that night, in bed, Francis voiced her own fears. "If rain doesn't come soon, we're going to lose the place."

Hands behind her head, she stared up into the dark. "The place is always mine . . . ours. We won't lose it."

Francis, only a hand length away, didn't even try to touch her tonight. She could smell his rum-laden breath. "The land is worth nothing if we all die of starvation."

"We won't." She was tired of trying to reassure him when she wasn't even certain herself.

"Damn it, look at yourself. He put his hand on her pelvis. "Your hip bones are as prominent as a skeleton's. "You're not eating enough."

"Tomorrow, the major, Sin, Thomas, Sykes, and a few other graziers are coming over to discuss finding a solution. I won't let us starve, so stop worrying, Francis."

"Well, neither will I. If I have to, I'll go to Sydney and request a loan from Nan Livingston. She's always been supportive of me. More than you have. You don't trust me to do anything. Always suggesting a better way. Or following along behind me and doing it over."

The mention of Nan Livingston struck ice in her heart. Wouldn't Nan enjoy taking over Dream Time! What revenge! "You're rambling drunk."

Later, as she lay in bed, she tried to still the welling panic. There had to be a way to keep the run from going under.

The candle sputtered. She reached to pinch it out—and stopped. Tallow! If not mutton, then tallow! She couldn't wait until the next afternoon.

Hands jammed in breeches pockets, she paced before the five men crowded into Dream Time's small office. Its window looked out on the garden, which now consisted of little more than brown withered vines and wilted flower stalks whose blooms had never unfurled.

"I'd say that the Livingston woman would sell her soul in exchange for power," the major was saying.

"She and Randolph are going to duel it out yet, mark my words."

His words brought her steps to a halt. She pretended to be studying the landscape outside. Nan Livingston. A shadow that followed her, even into the Never-Never.

"I disagree," Sin said. "Nan Livingston is ruthlessly ambitious. That's all. A lesson that wouldn't hurt for everyone in this room to learn."

"Well, we don't have to worry about the high cost of shipping the Livingston woman charges, since our sheep are bringing not a farthing."

Hands still in her pockets, Amaris turned back to the men. "Gentlemen, sheep are worth about six pence each for mutton, but only if a buyer can be found. Surely there must be enough in a sheep to make it worth more than that."

She paused, dramatizing the moment. "I suggest there is. Tallow. People need soap, candles. Tallow used for these is running between two and three pounds a hundredweight in London. If we boil down a sheep, we'll render between twelve and twenty-five pounds of tallow. If we boil down eight hundred sheep and send the tallow to London, it will fetch us six shillings per sheep. That, gentlemen, is a good deal better than six pence!"

A silence held sway in the room. Then the major slapped his thigh. "By Jove, Amaris, you may have something there."

"Her simple arithmetic may well save the Australian sheep industry from oblivion," Sin said.

The way he looked at her made her suggestion, made anything, pale in comparison. Just the look that passed between her and him was enough to sustain her, she thought. Now she could live through those emotional droughts when she went weeks without seeing the man who held her heart.

Almost listlessly, her gaze drifted from the brown earth and brown vegetation beyond to the brown fence posts and even farther to the brown horizon. Dull, drab, lifeless. She felt utterly drained.

Then her eye caught sight of color!

On the horizon boiled green-purple-blue clouds. A rainstorm was in the making. A rainstorm of magnitude, judging from the combination of garish colors.

She turned and hurried down the stairs, taking them two at a time, and ran out onto the veranda. "Francis!" she shouted. "Francis!"

She found him in the store. The door's lock had been removed. Inside, the shafts of sunlight were sifted with dust in the air. The store's shelves were bare of supplies, and she had stopped coming here weeks before. Her ledger lay dusty on the counter.

At the sound of her footsteps, he turned. For the first time, she noticed that his tawny hair was streaked with gray at the temples and over the ears. "Oh, Amaris, I was just checking to see if any empty food tins remained."

"Francis, come look! Clouds. Wonderful, boiling rain clouds."

For a moment, he stared at her uncomprehendingly. Then he ran past her, out the store door, and into the wagon yard to observe the clouds. As if they were some miracle sign from heaven.

She caught up with him. "Beautiful, aren't they."

"Aye."

It was all he said. He appeared mesmerized. They

stood and watched the formation rumble across the sky toward them. Maybe thirty minutes passed, and they were still standing. Wives and children came out of their cottages to watch. The hands put aside their work to join the others.

Pinned to the clouds was a tattered blue-black curtain of rain. Robert scampered to the gate, and Amaris opened it and caught him up in her arms. At six, he was tall and awkward as a colt. "Rain," she exulted, pointing toward the phenomenon.

Soon a breeze gently lifted the tendrils of her hair. Following on the fringes of the breeze were droplets of rain. Great, globular droplets that made *plfat* sounds as they smashed against the hard-baked earth.

She spread her palm to feel the sting of the rain and stuck out her tongue to taste it. Its dusty smell filled her nostrils. She began laughing.

Francis wrapped his arms around her and Robert, who was laughing also. All three of them. He pushed the wet hair back from her face. "You didn't give up, Amaris. When all around us station owners were selling out or going under, you found a way to keep us going. You're beautiful, do you know that?"

She could see he really meant what he was saying. He really thought she was beautiful! After all these years, now that time and weather had begun honing her face so that her character showed through, her husband found her beautiful. Sudden tears mixed with the raindrops on her face.

Feeling the abiding love for this man, her husband, she kissed him. He looked astonished. Then he grinned.

"Kiss me, Mama!" Robert said. His eyes were wide as he tried to assimilate the euphoria that had swept across the station. Around them, the hands were hugging one another and shouting in exultation.

She and Francis pecked Robert on both cheeks and he laughed with delight.

At last, she thought. At last, they were coming into a family unit in all ways.

The alternative to having no water at all was often having too much. Droughts were usually followed by higher than usual rainfall that could produce floods.

As the rains continued into weeks, then months, Amaris had taken the precaution of having Baluway bring the lambing flock inside for protection. Some of the lambs were put in the shed and others were yarded nearby.

Everything was saturated. The crops could not be put in because the fields stood in water. Clothes in trunks and armoires were mildewed. The sheep had been standing in mud and water for nearly a month.

At first, during the drought, everything had seemed to be colored brown. Now everything was colored gray: the clouds, the sunlight, the river, even the mold.

She tried not to let the weather depress her, but the mud-mired trails made travel difficult. Those visits between Dream Time and Never-Never had to be curtailed.

Then one night she was roused by a shout from Baluway: "The water, it is rising in the sheep yard!"

She grabbed her robe from the end of the bed and rushed downstairs just ahead of Francis, who was struggling to button on a pair of trousers.

"What the bloody hell now!" he muttered beneath his breath.

Rushing out onto the veranda, she found that the house was on an island, the water separating it from the workers' cottages and other outbuildings. Lanterns in the distance reflected eerily on the water's surface. She could hear exclamations by those who had been aroused by the rising creek water. From the intervening gulf, Baluway called out, "The sheep, they drown!"

She and Francis were closer to the sheds, but even then a rivulet of untried depth divided the house from the sheep pens and sheds. In the dark, there was no gauge as to just how deep the rivulet was. Who knew how much more the water would rise?

Without even looking for Francis, she waded into the water. The rivulet turned out to be a gully rushing with cold water up past her hips.

"Come back!" Francis shouted between cupped hands.

She ignored him and concentrated on finding footholds in the silt. She could tell she had passed the deepest part because the water was receding from her thighs. On the other side, the lambs bleated their terror. Half a dozen or more had ventured too close to the waters. Their carcasses bobbed against the fence, of which only a meter or so showed above the water's crest.

Once on the other side, she let the lambs out and trod through mud with them to high ground farther up. "Rogue," she ordered, "stay with them."

The dog watched her, barked, and wagged his tail, as if assenting.

As she waded back to Francis, she reminded herself that the flood would also benefit the land in resulting feed and full water holes. The creek had risen more than twelve meters, and she could practically row a canoe to the other doorways. Realistically, she estimated that she would probably have five hundred sheep drown.

Francis caught her by the waist and supported her as they returned to the house to wait for daylight. Her robe and nightgown were sopping wet. He helped her strip away her clothing, cold and clammy against her skin. His fingers chafed her flesh. "You're trembling. Just get out of this and get into bed."

His hands lingered at her shoulders, then slid to her waist. By the gleam in his eye, she knew he was aroused. "Your nipples are erect," he murmured.

"From the cold." She was too exhausted to be excited by the way he massaged the small of her back, then her ribs. She turned from his embrace and took another gown from the chest. "Francis, I am exhausted beyond belief."

"Of course," he said and climbed into bed with her, but she could hear the disappointment in his voice.

The warmth of his body next to hers was welcome. Tomorrow she would worry about how many sheep she had lost. Right now, she wanted only to count the kind of sheep that came with sleep.

Yet as she drifted deeper asleep, something niggled the back of her mind. Her nape prickled. She sprang upright.

"What is it now?" he demanded, struggling to sit up beside her.

"The house—'tis too quiet."

"What?"

Then she knew. A sixth sense triggered something too horrible to bear thinking about. "Robert! All this commotion should have awakened him!"

Throwing back the covers, she rushed from the bedroom to the one across the hall. Fear's talons clutched at her heart. Robert's bed was empty!

Francis took one look, glanced at her, then stricken, he dashed from the room and down the stairs. She followed in his footsteps. He ran out into the dark night, but she paused long enough to grab a lantern and light it. Her chest was pounding painfully hard. She could not breathe.

Ahead of her, Francis began circling the house's perimeter. "The lantern," he yelled. "Bring the lantern!"

The horror in his voice communicated to her. *Oh God, don't let it be so.* No! She wouldn't let herself think that far ahead.

When they reached the point at which they had set out, he whirled on her. Frustration and panic contorted his features. "Maybe Robert is in the house somewhere."

"Of course. Aye, that's it! I'll go look." Lifting her gown, she ran back toward the house. She could hear the workers once again stirring, and the lights of other lanterns glinted across the temporary lake like fireflies.

"Robert!" she called, running through the house. "Robert!"

She searched in the parlor, behind his bedroom door, under his bed, then hers and Francis's. She called Robert's name again and again in a frenzied voice. She peered under the couch and searched through armoires. Passing a mirror, she caught sight of her face and only then realized she was crying.

"Missus!" It was Baluway. His breechcloth waterlogged, he appeared in the library doorway. "Mr. Marlborough—he's gone!"

"Baluway!" She grabbed his arm. "We can't find Robert!" Suddenly she felt hope. The solid little man represented strength. Baluway could track anything. "You must help us!"

"You don't understand." There was such a sadness in his face that she knew she didn't want to hear what he was saying. "Mr. Marlborough . . . he found . . . he found Robert."

"He did? Is . . ." She saw the almost imperceptible shake of the aborigine's head.

She pushed past him, but he grabbed at her. "Let me go!" she ordered.

"You must listen to me first, missus. Mr. Marlborough, he went into the water after Robert. He was trying to carry the boy ashore. There was a drop off. The Englishman don't swim too well. I tried to get there, missus. I was too late."

"Francis . . . too?"

He nodded. Water drops dripped from his woolly hair.

All life drained from her. "'Tis raining again," she commented.

"The angels, they are crying, missus."

20

The Dark Night of the Soul. That was what Sin had called her grieving. Sin and his dark Irish view of life.

"Every soul goes through the experience. It can last a day or years, but eventually light returns. When it does, one has been tested. One is stronger."

"And those who aren't?" she challenged, angry. Angry with life and everyone who had someone to love and love them in return.

"They exist, they survive, but they don't thrive. You see them everyday, with the emptiness behind their eyes."

It had been Sin who, in searching the creek banks along with the others, had found Francis's bloated and blackened body lodged in the fork of a tree two days after the flood. Robert's body had been found the following day, entangled in underbrush where the water had receded.

It had been Sin who had taken her in his arms in

the privacy of her office and simply held her, not saying anything.

She had been hollow-eyed, cold, rigid. His hand had stroked her back slowly, as if they had all day and there weren't fifty people waiting outside to hear some kind of an announcement from her. Celeste had kept the people at bay.

Gradually, Amaris's blood had started flowing, and she had been able to take control once more—at least outwardly.

The tragic aftermath of the flood was a turning point in her life. She tried to focus not on her loss but on what was left for her.

No more did she have to defer to Francis. No more did she spend time rectifying mistakes made out of his hardheaded judgments. No more did she have to maintain her silence. Over that next year, she worked harder than ever. Hard enough to make Dream Time one of the most successful sheep stations in the area despite the hardships plaguing Australia.

If she was making a name for herself as a shrewd and formidable woman of the Never-Never, Nan Livingston had far outdistanced her, going on to become Australia's wealthiest woman. That was the gist of the occasional gossip that reached the bush from Sydney.

Amaris knew the woman was astute enough to maintain the illusion of Tom as New South Wales Trader's figurehead. However, a faded seven-month-old copy of the *Australian Herald* that Amaris had received in one of her stores' packages indicated not everyone bought that charade. One being the *Herald*'s owner, Miles Randolph. Randolph, also premier of New South Wales, attacked Nan, rather than her husband, in print for New South Wales Trader's supposedly unpatriotic policies.

Sometimes, mostly in the deep of night, when Amaris couldn't sleep, when the loneliness threatened to burn a hole through her heart and the ache choke off her breath, she would wonder wildly whether Nan Livingston had indeed sold her soul in exchange for the power to rule Australia and the power to deal death blows to those who stood in her way.

Losing Francis and Robert had been a death blow to Amaris's soul.

Occasionally, she and Sin and Celeste met for dinner or some celebration or maybe just to discuss business trends. Sin had certainly done well by diversifying his investments and was easily the most respected man in the outback.

Amaris looked forward to these times when the three of them got together. These were the times she could relax with friends—and that was all she let herself consider Sin: a friend.

Finally, she thought, she had made herself immune to the powerful attraction he held over her, had always held over her.

She never let herself think for one moment about the needs of her woman's body clamoring to be met, the yearnings that tortured her soul.

She never let herself think about Sin's own intimate needs. If his soul hungered, she never knew. Whether in the presence of others or dangerously alone, she and Sin treated one another with respect for the other's business acumen and with the deep affection that might exist between brother and sister.

The years seemed to fly by. Then, at the age of

thirty-two, Celeste announced that she was with child once more.

There was no doubt as to the veracity of her statement. She had regained all of her beauty, that look of a Durer Madonna and that soft roundness that made any man in the outback look twice with appreciation.

The serpent Jealousy coiled around Amaris's heart again. Celeste had Sin. Celeste knew the thrill of being fulfilled as a woman. Celeste knew Sin's passion—all of which Amaris would never know.

As Celeste drew near the last month of her term, Amaris made arrangements to leave the station in Baluway's capable hands. After packing some clothes, she went to stay at Never-Never. By now there was a score of women living on the station, including Mrs. Delaney, their Scottish housekeeper. Any of them could have acted as midwives and assisted Celeste in birthing her baby, but Celeste wanted only Amaris.

As a precaution, Celeste had taken to bed that last fortnight. The afternoon of Amaris's arrival, Celeste held her hand. The most beautiful smile Amaris had ever seen gently curved Celeste's mouth. "We're all three together again, Amaris. All these years and all the tragedies we've suffered, and we're still together. What a blessing the Lord has given us."

"You sound like my father now," Amaris teased tenderly.

"I want you to know that if I have a daughter, she will be named after you." Celeste's eyes were full of loving compassion. "If I bear a son, his name will be Robert."

Amaris swallowed. "You know, Celeste, you are

right. I am extremely blessed. I have you and Sin as friends. One can ask no more."

Except for the release of the ache rending her heart whenever Sin was near.

Later that evening, she observed him from Celeste's bedroom window as he rode into the yard. A true Irishman, he rode magnificently, seeming a part of the horse.

She watched him approach in that arrogant wholly male stride. She tried to remind herself that she was thirty-seven. Too old to be thinking suggestive thoughts.

She heard him climb the steps, his spurs clinking. When he entered the bedroom, his presence filled it. His glance took her in, her lavender-sprigged morning gown in contrast to her usual masculine attire. He removed his bush hat and dropped a kiss on Celeste's cheek. In a protective gesture, his big fingers grazed her mounded stomach. "'Tis feeling all right you are?"

Celeste's smile was like dawn's soft light. "Wonderful. I've never felt so wonderful in all my life."

Detachment. Amaris strove for total detachment. She watched two people she didn't know. She felt nothing. She was merely an observer.

Sin turned to her. His face was sun-browned and dusty. His expression was as detached as hers. "Thank you for coming, Amaris. Your presence means a lot to us."

Us. The word was full of significance and substance. Of belonging. Oh, to be cherished like that. To be loved like that.

Reverting to the most mundane subject of which she could think, she asked, "Have you heard about the camel train? The stores should be due to arrive any day now."

"The bush drum hasn't brought any word," he said, just as matter-of-factly. "Has Baluway heard anything?"

"Not a thing."

"I hope the supplier provides something close to the baby crib I described," Celeste said. "Last time I ordered crockery, white dinner plates with blue edging, we received plates painted with pink roses."

The talk turned quite naturally to the stations with Sin recommending that she consider establishing a string of stations in areas of high rainfall as guard against a drought like the last tragic one years before. "The rainfall has been even for so long that we're due for a change."

At last, shadows deepened, and Sin lit a lamp. Mrs. Delaney brought up dinner for the three of them. "Why, Mrs. Delaney," Sin teased, "you've outdone yeself. A cobbler, no less."

Her apple-dumpling cheeks were flushed with pleasure. "For a special occasion." She liked Amaris's no-nonsense approach to work, the same as hers.

The casual, relaxing conversation continued through dinner and the brandy afterward. Watching and listening to Sin, Amaris wondered how long she could remain at Never-Never in such close proximity to him.

Of course, the nights would be the worst . Knowing he was so close. Only a room away . . . but holding Celeste.

"It's here, it's here!" The aborigines came running from the creek. Everyone stopped work. The rail-thin bespectacled old governess dismissed the station schoolroom. The house staff hurried out to watch with the station workers as the supply train approached.

Slowly, silently, the great packing cases creaking as they swayed, the long string of camels came padding into the station compound. They looked haughty and slightly disdainful. Their great packs, weighing slightly more than five hundred pounds, were unlashed.

At once, all the hands began opening cases and carrying goods to storerooms. Even such things as foodstuffs were a thrill when they came only twice a year. Amaris helped Sin inventory the arriving cases: three tons of flour, twenty bags of sugar, fifteen saddles, and, among the other packing cases—a baby crib.

When Sin carried it upstairs to Celeste, her face lit with joy. "The supplier couldn't have picked a more perfect crib."

Amaris watched her hands, the soft color of porcelain, stroke the smooth wood, painted white with light blue morning glories stenciled around the scrolled edges. In admiration of the touching scene, Amaris forgot her envy.

Later that evening, just before dinner, when she wandered out onto the veranda to watch the children playing in the lingering sunlight, Sin joined her. Handing her a glass of brandy, he sat down opposite her. "Sometimes, when I watch the children, I find meself silently praying that they will never know hunger or harm. I tell meself that their lives don't have to be the way their parents' lives were as children."

"Like yours?" she asked softly. There was an

intimacy to the evening's quiet, to their solitude.

"Me life wasn't that bad. Aye, we went hungry sometimes. And there were the British to fear. But I was loved. And I was educated. As you were loved and educated. Despite having been given away as an infant. That left its scar, didn't it?"

The compassion in his eyes was nearly her undoing. Her fingers curled around the chair's arms. Her voice was low, strangled. "I always wondered what was wrong with me. Was I such an unlovable, unlovely baby? Other convict women kept their babies. Why was I not worth keeping?"

"You *are* beautiful—and worth keeping. You deserve love. Speaking of which, 'tis been too long for you to stay in mourning."

She felt the heat of her blush coloring her cheeks. "How do I know a man courting me is not just after Dream Time? Regardless, the men are not standing in line at my door. I think I intimidate them."

"You be needing someone to complement your strength of will."

"That sounds like condemnation. Am I not woman enough, Sin? Feminine enough?"

From out of the dark came his deep and smooth brogue. "That and more." He tapped out his pipe. "Mrs. Delaney should be taking dinner up to Celeste. Shall we go on up?"

"Ohh, God!" Celeste gasped. "Oh, God, Amaris, I hurt."

"Take a deep breath. It can't be much longer."

Celeste's lips stretched in a ghastly parody of a smile. "That's . . . what you said three hours ago."

"I know, I know." She pushed Celeste's damp hair back from her forehead. Dipping the washcloth in the basin of water once more, she sponged Celeste's temples and cracked lips. Who would have thought it could take so long to birth a child, more than twenty hours. Something was wrong.

She dropped the washcloth in the basin. "I'm going for fresh water. I'll be back in only a moment."

Celeste's hand gripped hers. "Hurry, please."

Amaris watched her friend fight back a scream. "I'll wait. Breathe deeply. Push, Celeste. Breathe deeply and push."

Pain racked Celeste's body so that she shuddered. Eyes closed, one hand knotted into a fist, the other digging into Amaris's, she bit her bottom lip until it bled.

When the contraction passed, Amaris relinquished Celeste's hand and hurried from the bedroom. She found Sin sitting in the parlor. A glass was in his hand, the whiskey untouched. His eyes were red. He looked from her back to his glass. "I'm going to lose her, aren't I?" he asked in a monotone voice.

"Sin, we're going to have to take the baby."

He shot up from the settee and hurled the glass against the wall. The sound of the shards tinkling against the floor was evocative of a crystal chandelier chiming in a breeze-filled room. "The only good thing in me life and I am going to lose it! I'm going to lose her!"

"You don't know that." She grabbed his arm. "I need your help. You've taken a colt before when the mare couldn't birth it normally. Help me now."

He whirled on her. "God, do you know what you're asking of me?"

Her stance was unyielding, her voice harsh. "I'm asking you to save the one good thing in your life."

With a groan, he tunneled his hands through his hair. "Aye, I'll do it."

She went to the sideboard, where Celeste kept the station's medicine chest. In it was an assortment of bandages, splints, pins, and other necessities, together with a selection of drugs: quinine, castor oil, chlorodyne, and laudanum.

The administration of the laudanum was of a highly experimental nature. How much was safe to give to Celeste?

When she returned to the bedroom, Sin was drying his freshly washed hands. He glanced at her, then turned back to Celeste. "If we're to save the wee one, me luv, this is necessary. With the laudanum," he added, stroking her perspiration-drenched hair back from her neck, "you won't feel any pain."

Celeste's hand clasped the back of his. "I'm not afraid. Never, when you're with me."

He swallowed hard. "I'm with you always."

Then he nodded at Amaris, and she moved to the bedside. Smiling with a reassuring falsity, she took Celeste's fingers and squeezed tenderly. Her friend was far braver than she could ever be.

"You're here, too," Celeste murmured. "I'm with the ones I love."

Those were her last words before Amaris gave her a couple of tablespoons of laudanum until a drugged stupor claimed her conscious thoughts and her lids drifted closed.

Amaris listened for her soft breathing and watched her chest, praying that the imperceptible rise and fall of sleep continued for a while longer. "I think we've done everything we can do to prepare her," she told Sin.

Sweat glistened on his forehead. He stared at her across the span of the bed and his drugged wife. "You know few women survive something like this, not in the outback, not under conditions like this!" It was a cry from the pit of his stomach, a cry of fear.

"No woman survives when the baby is lodged within her belly."

He closed his eyes and nodded. "So be it." He reached for the knife he had stropped to a razor-sharp edge and sterilized. In the candlelight, the blade glinted like thirty pieces of silver.

She steadied herself. She did not let herself think about what she was watching. She merely followed Sin's instructions, placing her hands at either side of the thin red line and gently separating the tissues after each incision of the razor-sharp blade.

At some point during the arduous process, something went wrong. Amaris didn't know what, only that hemorrhaging had started.

"No!" Sin cried. His eyes flared. He glanced up at her. She saw the wild animal cornered in their depths. "No!" he screamed.

It was useless. All his frenzied, frantic efforts could not stop the outpouring of blood.

In Amaris's mind ran Celeste's last words: "I'm with the ones I love."

Within the month, the bush drum told of all sorts of rumors. That Sin was gradually going wild with grief, condemning himself for succumbing to lust; that he had turned to drink and had burned down the house; that he wouldn't leave his wife's graveside, that he had gone tropo, sitting there day after day in the hot sun.

Once more leaving her sheep station in Baluway's care, Amaris set out for Never-Never. Even as she approached, she could see signs of deterioration in the one-month lapse in supervision of his sheep station: railings were down, an outbuilding door was off its hinge, the corralled horses looked ungroomed.

She stopped at the cemetery. The flowers bedecking Celeste and the baby's grave were wilted. Anger spread through Amaris. The graves should have been as lovingly tended as Celeste had lovingly tended to Never-Never. Only sunflowers bloomed at that time of year, but Amaris took long enough to gather a posey and spread the flowers like a yellow blanket over her sleeping sister.

Spurs clinking, she stalked through the house, which was as dark and stuffy as a tomb, until she came upon the housekeeper. "Where is Mr. Tremayne, Mrs. Delaney?"

The triple-chin lost a fold as the old woman nodded her head upward. "Been closeted in the bedroom for three days now. 'Fore that he rode all day, from sunup to long after midnight."

Amaris climbed the steps. With something akin to dread, she opened the bedroom door. Sin sat in Celeste's rocking chair. He looked unkempt, his hair rumpled, the beginnings of a beard on his face. He raised his gaze from the remade bed to her. "You're back." It was a statement, not a question.

She folded her arms. "And none too soon, it appears. Come on, we're getting you to bed. And not this one, either."

She expected a hassle. He pushed himself erect, but she could tell he was extremely tired. Taking his arms, she said, "You'll feel better after a deep sleep. I'll prepare an herbal."

Like a child, he let her lead him to the bedroom he had been using during the last months Celeste carried their child. Once Amaris had pulled off his boots and tugged off his shirt, she tucked him into the four-poster bed and went below to prepare the potion.

When she returned, it frightened her the way those piercing blue eyes stared unseeingly at the ceiling. It was unnatural. She gave him three spoonfuls of the medicine, talking all the while to ease the volcano of tension within him. "The medicine tastes like sheep dip, but it'll make you rest easier. I'll sit here until you go to sleep."

He closed his eyes, but it wasn't until maybe an hour later she sensed he was truly asleep. She would have stayed longer, just so she could observe her beloved's face undisturbed, but things needed to be taken in hand. Leaving Sin, she went down to the yard. With a tyrannical hand, she took over management from Jimmy, who actually seemed grateful for direction. He reminded her of a lost puppy. His eyes had that soulful look.

"I want the gates and fences repaired and painted. What supplies you don't have, send to Dream Time for. Fire the stable help. The horses haven't been groomed."

Next she tackled Mrs. Delaney. "I want fresh vegetables at every meal. Lots of them. A savory roast or a leg o'mutton will do for the main entrée this evening. Have someone pick flowers and put vases of them throughout the house. I want the banisters and furniture all polished with beeswax, and get rid of all the gutted candles. Replace them with fresh, scented ones."

She herself went through the house pulling open the curtains to flood each room with sunlight. While she was upstairs, there came from below a commotion. Going to the window, she peered out. In the late afternoon sun could be seen a buggy approaching. The people of Never-Never were turning out to see this latest mode of transportation. The rockaway was a light four-wheel carriage with open sides.

Curious as to the visitor's identity, she went downstairs and out onto the veranda. In shock, she observed Nan Livingston dismount. Despite the distance the old woman had traveled, she was dressed impeccably with nary a wrinkle or speck of dust to spoil her black crepe dress.

Amaris's first reaction was chagrin that, in comparison to Nan, her own clothing was dirty—and quite masculine. Her next reaction was more a physical one. The hair at her nape rose. Nan Livingston was here to make good her threat.

Foolish, she thought. What could the woman take from her? Dream Time? Dream Time was solvent. That achievement had been a hard one for Amaris. Many times, she had been tempted to take up Sin's offer of a loan, but her pride would never consider it.

With the dignity of visiting royalty, Nan approached the veranda. In one hand she held a black parasol; in the other she carried the hem of her skirt, lifted out of the dust. Behind her, her bowlegged driver toted her bags.

At the bottom of the steps, she stared up at Amaris. "Taking Francis from Celeste wasn't enough, was it? Is it Sin you want now?"

Amaris reeled from the scathing, loathing tone of Nan's voice. Nan always suspicioned the worst in people. She stared down at the rouged, wizened little woman. Did Nan Livingston find it as difficult to accept her as her daughter as she found accepting Nan as her mother? "Sin and Never-Never need me right now."

Nan brushed past her. "Where's Sin?"

She caught up with the old woman at the door and barred her way. "Let him sleep. He's on the brink of collapse."

Nan's lips pressed flat. "I need a respite myself. I'll see him at dinner." She sailed past Amaris and on into the house. Her driver dutifully followed her inside.

"Oh, Mrs. Marlborough?" Jimmy called out from the sheep shed. "Do you want us to go ahead and schedule the branding? We have been, er, waiting for Mr. Tremayne to give us the go ahead."

"Schedule it for first thing tomorrow."

By the time Amaris returned to the house, all the curtains had been drawn once more. Amaris stalked to the pantry, where Mrs. Delaney was inventorying the tinned foods. "Why did you draw the curtains again?"

The hefty woman looked offended. "Mrs. Livingston did that, ma'am. Said she was taking charge."

The sun floated on waves of steam just above the western horizon. Even though evening was nigh, February's heat was unbearable. Nan couldn't understand why anyone, much less Celeste, who had led such a sheltered life, would want to move to the Never-Never.

With quivering lips she could not still, she knelt beside Celeste's grave. Fresh sunflowers were strewn atop. By whom? Sin certainly wasn't in any condition to consider doing anything appropriate at this point.

She picked up one of the sunflowers. Reluctantly, she acknowledged that Amaris had most likely made the thoughtful gesture. Amaris appalled her. Her daughter wanted to assume her half sister's place! Amaris knew nothing about propriety!

Nan ignored the niggling reminder that she used to yearn for just such an outward show of strength and had only been able to act from the principle that a proper woman stayed in the background, operating from behind the scene. She had been a victim of her times.

Well, she thought, the time would come to deal with her wayward daughter. Nan's veined and palsied hand crushed the sunflower's petals.

Sin was a different man, though Amaris couldn't quite put her finger on it. He had shaven, of course, and his clothes were immaculate as ever, his stock an ivory white beneath his swarthy and brooding face. One of Sin's assets had been his vital and forceful personality. Strong-willed and purposeful, he could climb from rock bottom to rocky heights.

Surreptiously observing him from across the dining table, Amaris decided that it wasn't so much that with Celeste's death he had lost his will to live, but that his will no longer blazed in those blue eyes; it was an ember that only needed fanning.

Amaris did know that in death Celeste stood between her and Sin more than she ever had in life.

Celeste would always be young and beautiful. The harsh Australian outback would never wither or age her. Further, Celeste had never fought for her station, never had been bitchy or masculinely domineering. Sin had fought for her.

At the other side of the table sat Nan. The candelabra cast eerie shadows beneath her gaunt cheeks and deepened every wrinkle that all the rouge and powder in Australia could not conceal. She had become a caricature of herself—but still a formidable woman and opponent. Amaris would not let herself underestimate this woman, her mother.

She thought of the ivory-and-pearl brooch Nan had given her as a wedding gift. All these years it had lain untouched in a small box of gewgaws that Amaris found too feminine.

With the elegance of an aristocrat, Nan cut a bite from her serving of lamb. "I would advise getting rid of your supervisor, Sin. Jimmy was a good employee at the company, but he grew lax and I had to let him go. You need someone more competent than Jimmy to oversee in your absence."

"Jimmy has been a loyal employee for years," Amaris countered.

"Not loyal enough to see that affairs at Never-Never continued to run smoothly while the master was . . . indisposed."

Amaris laid down her fork. "Jimmy, like every other hand on the run and every woman and every child worshiped Celeste. Her death affected all of them. Apparently, everyone suffered but you, Nan Livingston. You charge in here to try and dominate everyone, just as you have always done."

"And you," Nan said with ice weighing her words,

"charge in here to try and take Celeste's place in the marriage bed."

Sin set down his wineglass with a thud. His eyes blazed. "That is enough!"

Nan's eyes burned with their own wrath. Majestically, she rose from her chair. Her fingertips were planted at either side of her dinner plate. "Both of you conspired to take Celeste away—each for your own selfish ends. Bad begets bad. You two will yet rue the day you entered my domain."

By the next morning, Nan Livingston was packed and gone. Watching the dust her buggy kicked up, Amaris had to acknowledge that in a way, the dowager was right. Despite their being mother and daughter, Nan Livingston felt nothing for her. No, that wasn't true. Nan Livingston loathed her only surviving daughter and planned to bring about her downfall.

Tired and utterly weary, Amaris returned to Dream Time without telling Sin farewell. Work awaited her at Dream Time, and she needed to attend to it.

She was thirty-seven and not quite so sure why she still struggled. Because of Robert, she thought. Because of Francis. Their memories were all she had, for Sin belonged to himself.

Months slid into a year. A year without seeing Sin. Occasionally she would talk to the major or Sykes or Thomas and learn that Sin was immersed in a new project of some sort. Anything to keep himself from feeling, she thought. She understood this. They both were plowing their energies into keeping their stations running.

She imagined that Sin, as she did, felt that there had been too much between them ever to make for a peaceful relationship. Combustion was spontaneous when they came together, and after all these years they both wanted only peace in their lives.

Peace appeared to be a quality that was not imminent in her life or those of the other station owners. Then word reached them of the discovery of gold in California.

In an exodus for the golden land, thousands of laborers, sheep tenders and shearers and their families, set sail. It was all she and Baluway could do to keep her station running, because it was much larger and there were many more responsibilities than in the earlier days when only she and Francis and Baluway had had to contend.

Often, too tired at night to change out of her clothing, she would wonder how Sin was coping with the loss of labor. Or, for that matter, with the loss of money. All the station owners were in dire straits financially.

And she would wonder if he ever went to nearby Ballarat to appease his sexual hunger. Or maybe of the workers left at Nver-Never, one of the wives or daughters attracted his interest.

She could stand that, she thought. Just as long as she knew he was close by. Somehow beneath the Southern Cross, they might have been star-crossed as lovers and soul mates, but at least she could occasionally see him or hear word of him.

Then, one afternoon he rode into Dream Time to change even that.

*   *   *

"My heart is no longer in the station. I'm assigning Never-Never to you."

She stood facing him, her office desk between them. He removed his bush hat and tossed it on the rocking chair. The thick hair was much grayer now and mussed where the sweat band had been.

Slowly she rose and came around to stand only inches from him. Those intense blue eyes gave her no quarter. They challenged her to emotional honesty.

"Get to the point. You're leaving. Why? Where are you going?"

He took her hand—she didn't realize she had made a fist—and smoothed out her fingers, one by one. Her hand stiffened with that old urge to hide, and he said, "No."

"Don't do this." Her voice was a raw whisper.

Still cradling her hand, palm up in his bigger one, he said, "I've always admired your hands, Amaris. Capable. Capable of work. Capable of giving love. They're caring hands."

Tears welled in her eyes. With her free hand, she pushed back the thick mahogany lock that had fallen across his brow. "Why do you have to go? I love you, Sin."

His smile was sad. "You love your autonomy. Think of it. With Never-Never and Dream Time as one, you'll be a powerful woman, a worthy opponent of your mother. That is something that ye must come to terms with, Amaris. I have my own past to come to terms with."

She jerked her hand from his. "Damn it, Sin. The past is dead!"

His finger stole out to touch the scar on her cheek. The scar was faint after all these years, but nevertheless it was his brand, a result of that day long ago when he had smashed the rum bottle against a tree. Sighing inwardly for what might have been and would never be, he reached down and collected his hat. "I'm going to prospect for gold."

The breath went from her. "You, too? You're selling out for gold? You're sailing for California?"

"Mayhap, I'm prospecting for meself. The adventurer in me is calling, I suppose. But not to California. Gold has been discovered here, in the Never-Never, if you haven't heard. You once said that whatever any other place had, Australia would have it twice as big, twice as much."

He wasn't asking her to go with him. She braced her hands on the desk edge behind her to sustain her weight. She was so damn tired. But he mustn't know this. He thought she was strong. Capable. "You don't have to assign Never-Never to me. I'll hold it in trust for you until you return."

"I'll not be returning, Amaris." There was an adamant glint in his eye.

"I see. Then God go with you, Sin. I hope you find more than gold—I hope you find whatever it is you are looking for."

He took her face between his large hands. His eyes searched hers. "You are looking too, me luv. And I am not what you are looking for. I can't be to you or anyone the answer."

He lowered his head over hers and kissed her very softly. She stood still, eyes closed, savoring the exquisite feeling that would have to last forever.

Helplessly responding, she wrapped her arms around his neck. She would make him respond to her as well. Her lips parted. Her tongue grazed his lips, seeking entry.

He put her from him. "Don't make the parting any worse than need be." His tone was unyielding, his mouth set in a determined line.

Dry-eyed, too anguished to permit herself the luxury of tears, she whispered, "Then good-bye it is, my darling."

Amaris now divided her time between the two stations. The pleasure she had once thought would be hers at owning what amounted to an empire was nonexistent. Most of the time, she was exhausted at the end of the day—which was good, because then she was too tired to ache for Sin.

But she was a woman, with a woman's needs. How many years had gone by since she had felt a man's hands on her. At night, her body cried out for a man's touch to assuage her rampaging desires.

It was Baluway who forced her to look at the truth of her life. She was working on the station's books when he knocked at her office door. Even after all these years, his appearance still elicited amusement from her. His hair and beard were not completely gray.

"You smile," he said, then added, "but not much anymore."

"Too much work and too little time." She was wondering just why he had come up to the office. Usually any request or anything he needed to tell her he saved until she came down to the yard.

"Your time is going."

She tilted her head. "What?"

"One day, no more time. No more hope. No more nothing."

Her eyes narrowed. "No more nothing, eh?"

His head bobbed. "Bloody right."

She laughed. She laughed until tears streamed down her cheeks. "*You're* bloody right, Baluway."

21

One might have thought a plug had been pulled and the male population of the outback had emptied like a cistern in a rush toward the diggings at Ballarat, a mere seventy-five miles west of Melbourne. In Eureka Valley, where Ballarat was nestled, the earth's seams and surfaces contained gold almost as a man's flesh and veins contained blood.

Melbourne itself was said to be both a ghost-port and a continuous saturnalia. Almost two-thousand people were arriving weekly, lured by the fabulous reports of gold finds in northern Victoria. Melbourne's Port Phillip Bay had become a Sargasso sea of dead ships. With the desertion of the captains and the crews for the gold fields, the ships rocked empty at anchor, bilges unpumped, their masts a barren forest.

By the time Amaris arrived in Ballarat in May the driving rains of the Australian autumn had turned the newly created town into a mudbath.

Reins in hand and with Wind Runner trailing

behind her, she joined a sluggishly winding column of men: grocers and sailors, lawyers and army deserters, oyster sellers and ex-convict shepherds. Italians, Americans, Maltese, Greeks, Chinese—all nationalities were to be seen trudging beneath the weight of tents, blankets, crowbars, picks, shovels, pans, and billycans, hastily bought at gougers' prices.

Along with them, she stumbled toward a dream: theirs was incredible wealth; hers, incredible love.

Was it possible, or only a dream, this love for this one man who had been in her mind and her heart since she was twelve years old?

She meant to find out.

As she slogged through the mud toward the shanty towns and bark huts in the valley below, she committed herself to giving unreservedly. At thirty-eight, she was too old to settle for less. Sin was everything to her. A reflection of herself. Without him, her complement, she was incomplete.

If he was not willing to surrender himself to a love that could move beyond the common, then she was unwilling to settle for less. She would return to Dream Time and Never-Never, supervised in her absence by her loyal Baluway, and would live out the rest of her years alone. Not lonely, maybe, but unfulfilled.

This was her resolve, but her feelings churned in her like Sin's untamed horses, stampeding, restive, wild. Her heart wanted and waited to be conquered. Only Sin could do so.

After stabling her horse in a livery that had no stalls left, only the corralled yard behind, she set off in quest of Sin. In the grog shops and hotels that lined the filthy, traffic-jammed streets of Ballarat, she almost sank to her knees in mud when she inadvertently stepped off the boardwalk. Rather than watching where she was going, she was looking for Sin's face in every clay-colored man.

Around her, diggers, a name they wore with pride, were lurching down the rain-sluiced street, drinking their gold away. She watched a gray-whiskered miner who stood beneath a storefront awning lighting his pipe with a five-pound note. Another man, accompanied by his floozy, poured gold dust into the cupped hands of a hackney driver. When she observed a drunken septuagenarian digger pouring bottle after bottle of champagne into a horse trough and inviting passersby to drink up, she wondered if she could stay in Ballarat, even to be with Sin.

Of course, the ultimate decision as to whether she stayed or not would be up to Sin. At that thought— and the realization that he had to be somewhere nearby—her heart started to beat double-time.

Every so often, she would stop and inquire of the whereabouts of a Sin Tremayne, but there were so many new people deluging the town that no one knew anyone else. No one bothered her because most mistook her for one of them—a filthy, wet, and hungry stranger.

As the afternoon waned, she knew she was going to have to find a place to stay and belatedly realized that it was going to be difficult.

Time and again she entered the hastily, and shabbily, erected hotels only to be turned away. Strangers were sharing beds, and the floors were covered with blankets. The only beds left were those in the government camp's military barracks, and that was only because a troop of its soldiers were policing the gold fields.

Pausing in front of a red-painted Chinese joss

house, she took off her bush hat and stared dejectedly at its sodden mass. She wanted simply to lie down and sleep in a dry place.

A big man with a strong accent took her under his wing. "You look mighty dragged out, miss."

She stared back at the robust man through the drizzle. Grizzle-bearded, he was much older than she had first thought, maybe sixty-five or even seventy. There was something about him . . . "I know you?"

"Yes."

"You worked at Dream Time?"

"No."

"Never-Never?"

"No. You need a place to stay?"

She should have been cautious, but she was tired and dirty and wet. And, for some reason, she trusted him. "Aye. Who are you?"

He took her arm and started walking away from the government camp. "Josiah Wellesley. I occasionally had some dealing with Nan Livingston."

She stiffened. For all his years, he held her arm with a firm grip. "I won't harm you, gal. Come along. My place is up on the ridge. Me and Dick been here four months now. Got us enough bags of gold dust to live comfortably. But it's not the gold I'm after. It's the adventure. Life's getting short on me."

He was talking, she knew, to put her at ease. "Dick?"

"Me partner. Dick Cooper. Any gear with you?"

"All I have is tied to my saddle. Over at the livery stable with my mount."

"Let's get it and head for home." He grinned broadly. "If you can call a tent home. It ain't much smaller than me ship cabin was, and that was home for lo many years. 'Course home, I always contended, was made by a woman's touch."

"You never married?"

"The right woman didn't want me."

"Nan?" she asked incredulously.

"Sin?" he said. "You're wanting him?"

A sad smile touched her lips. "Always."

Tents of every color flowered the ridge. They, and a few bark huts, were of primitive construction. Only a few yards of calico stretched between a few poles provided all the protection most diggers needed against sun, wind, or rain.

She ducked her head and entered a blue calico tent Josiah pointed out as his. His partner wasn't inside. He sat her down on one of the cots while he poured a cup of tea from the billy and explained to her that most of the diggers worked in teams of two to six men.

"One man picks and shovels the earth, while the other wheelbarrows it from the hole to the water. Then we take turns cradling it until any gold is parted from the earth." He passed her some damper bread. "Problem is the government limits us to claims no more than eight feet square. Then twice weekly they descend on us for permit searches. No permits and we're hauled off to jail. The permits are damnably expensive to boot."

"How many men do you think are camped here?"

His grin split his gray beard. "Half of Australia's entire population I hear. Maybe 350,000."

She sat stunned. How would she ever find Sin? She had been foolish to abandon all to come here. Suddenly, she felt very tired—and very old.

"Look, why don't you stretch out and rest a mite.

Dick would be coming in and we'll fix up a bit of stew. That should bring you 'round."

Dare she trust him? On the other hand, she had so little to lose. If she weren't to awaken, would it be so bad? "Thank you, Josiah. I think I shall rest awhile."

Her sleep was deep and dreamless. She awoke to the tempting smell of food cooking. For a second she didn't know where she was. Without moving, she glanced quickly around. She spied a strange man at the foot of her cot. He was removing one of her muddied boots.

Maybe ten years younger than she, he had a boxer's battered face and glorious hair like the gold everyone in Ballarat was seeking. He appeared thoroughly mean until she glimpsed in the depths of his brown eyes that eager puppy-dog-with-a-wagging-tail look. He wore a digger's coarse dungarees.

He smiled sheepishly. "I thought you'd sleep better."

Having a man do something so intimate, something a woman usually did for a man, shook her composure. "I was awakening anyway." She swung her feet over the side of the cot. "What do I smell?"

"Digger's stew." He stood quickly and bumped his head against the low ridge pole. "Yowl!"

She sprang up to console him and banged her own head. Gingerly, her fingers probed the swelling knot. "Ooohhh!"

They both began to laugh. Their initial embarrassment was over.

The tent flaps were pushed aside, and Josiah's rusty-hinged voice preceded him. "I see you're showing her how to do the Virginia Reel. Amaris, my partner, Dick Cooper."

Dick surveyed her like an assayer and determined

she was genuine and not fool's gold. "Pleasure, ma'am."

"Dick's from Georgia. Swears he's gonna return to the United States and live like a gentleman the rest of his life. Wagered with him that after he's seen the Never-Never, he'll never, never want to go back to Georgia."

Abashed, Dick rolled his eyes. "For a salty dog, Josiah, you sure can blather."

"Just being friendly. Stew's ready."

When Amaris went outside, night had completely settled on Ridge Creek Camp. The rain had stopped, and stars twinkled. Camp fires flickered like fallen stars. Josiah hunkered over his stew. At his feet sat a half pint of gin with which he liberally seasoned his concoction and taste buds.

She helped herself to the stew and observed the approval in Dick's expression. Josiah noted it, also. "She's looking for a man, Dick."

He looked crestfallen. "Enough of us around."

"One man in particular," she said between bites. The flavor wasn't bad at all. "Sin Tremayne. He's tall, as tall as Josiah, with brown hair going gray, blue eyes, a broken nose, and an Irish brogue that is as thick as this stew."

Dick chewed thoughtfully. And loudly. The way he sat, a lackadaisical slump, told her nothing really bothered him.

"'Fore we teamed up, Josiah, there was one of those micks that fit that description. He was raising a ruckus about rights. Diggers' rights."

She swallowed acrid tea from a can Josiah passed her. "No, that's not like Sin to get invol—" she broke off, recalling what he had told her about himself as a young law student. "What kind of ruckus?"

"Challenging the mayor and the council, while they were visiting the camps. He's hot—like all of us—about the latest miner's tax. We Yanks call it taxation without representation."

"That might be him." Excitement rushed through her. "Tomorrow I will start searching the other camps around Ballarat."

"A digger camp ain't safe for a woman alone," Josiah said.

"I'll be all right. I have survived in the bush, I can survive in a miners' camp."

Over the fire, Josiah's eyes sought out Dick's. "Well, what do you say, mate?"

"Sounds like an adventure. Count me in."

Josiah set down his tin plate and slapped his hands on his knees. "Well then, Amaris, there are three of us to hunt for Sin. Three musketeers. Three wise men. Three—"

"Three blind mice." Dick laughed.

She stared at the two men, seeing the reflection of the firelight in their eyes. "Why? Why are you two doing this?"

"I for one," Josiah said, "believe in everything coming full circle. I try to do my part to keep my beliefs intact. It reassures me that I'm not crazy."

"And you?" she asked Dick.

He took a swallow of his tea, as if fortifying himself. "Me? I've decided that I like you and want you for mine. You won't be as long as you are hankering after him, this Sin fellow. Find him, and then make up your mind."

She peered at him with new respect. "One day spent with someone and you know something like that?"

The mouth crimped. "We Yanks are more open."

"Dick, I'm at least ten years older than you."

"Doesn't matter a whit. I still want you."

Sin proved to be elusive. Wherever she asked of him, she was told he had been there but had just moved on. Sandhurst, Bunninyong, Bathurst, Warrandyte. All mining towns. All looked the same. Canvas towns of intense suffering and unbridled wickedness and sensational wealth.

In every camp she visited, he had been exhorting crowds, stumping for changes in the territorial government. Apparently he had become a grass-roots politician. The very thing he had railed against, she thought.

Josiah and Dick accompanied her as if they were her personal bodyguards. They were. In their company, no man made more than one off-color remark. The glare in the eyes of her protectors made the unwise man back off.

The days grew colder. Freezing drizzle sometimes made travel out of the question, and the three of them would be sequestered in a camp for a week or more. With Josiah and Dick, she would take her turn cooking, an event that invariably lured additional guests, hungry for home cooking. Soon, diggers sought her out to bind injuries and treat wounds.

Word preceded her. When her quest led her and her two male companions back to Eureka Valley and Ballarat, she had two callers. Both known to her.

The first was female—Molly Finn. The freckled, flighty Molly Finn no longer existed. A tired, wasted woman who looked more fifty than forty sat forlornly on the cot next to Amaris and talked.

"Me man up and left me within a year after I moved away from Never-Never." She hung her head and twisted her reddened hands. "I was too ashamed to get Jimmy to take me back. So I—I became a . . . gray dove."

Amaris said nothing.

Encouraged by Amaris's nonjudgmental expression, she continued. "Now the men no longer want me. With the gold rush, too many pretty faces . . ."

Amaris took her shabby coat and tawdry feathered hat from her. "Why don't you lie down. Once you've rested and eaten, we can better chat."

Those chats over the following days became more open: "I felt a man in me life would be the answer," Molly said while she was helping wash the pans and tin plates one evening. "But no man had the answer."

Amaris passed her a plate. "The answer is in yourself."

"Aye. I'm a little late in finding that out."

Amaris smiled wistfully. "I'm still discovering that. My strengths grow in number each day. Yet I also feel there is a mate for me. A soul mate."

"Ye looking for Sin, h'aint you? That what is said around the camps."

"Aye." The word was almost a sigh. Her gaze flickered back to Molly. "You've seen him?"

"No. Nor has any of my sisters serviced him, if that's any relief for ye. Let me help. Let me be a part of ye search group. If ye remember, I can cook a mean meal."

In astonishment, she stared at Molly. Such a yearning colored the woman's voice. "I would welcome that. But my friends—Dick and Josiah—have their own say."

Of course, Dick and Josiah would never turn a woman away. Dick, in particular, took it upon himself to be Molly's protector. Absurd, when Molly could handle herself quite well in the boomtowns. Yet, wondrously, she softened and acquired an innocence in his circle of light.

Amaris's second caller was the least expected, especially considering the weather conditions. It was an August evening so bitterly cold that trees snapping sounded like pistol fire. Dick was mumbling about it being the worst winter he had ever spent. "Up in North Dakota, being the exception. Got so cold that my horse's breath froze in a steam from its muzzle to the ground. Swear to God, you could thump the vapor and it would shatter like crystal. Damnedest thing I ever—"

Suddenly, the tent flap was thrown back. A man stepped through. He was big enough for his presence to fill the tent. He wore a fur cap and greatcoat. His beard and mustache were white with frozen moisture. Above the red, chapped cheekbones, the chilly blue eyes burned like steam off ice. "You were looking for me?"

Uncomprehendingly, she stared at the man. Then the timbre of the voice reached her, that rich, deep Irish resonance. "Sin!" she cried and rushed to throw her arms around his neck.

He caught them and held her away from him. "Why are you looking for me?"

She met his hard stare. "Because I want to be a part of your life, to share it."

His gaze flicked to Josiah, who understood the question in it. "You be a fool, Tremayne. Apparently, you don't remember me. Josiah Wellesley. I did business with New South Wales Traders."

Sin said nothing. His eyes moved to Dick and Molly. If he recognized her, he didn't acknowledge it. Then his gaze returned to Amaris.

She started talking. Rapidly. She didn't know how long he would listen to her. "It matters not how many women you take to ease your pain of losing Celeste. I'm still here, loving you. And I'll eat humble pie the rest of my life, even if it means being second to a ghost in your affections."

A vein ticked in his temple. If only she knew what he was thinking. He slung a glance at Dick, who smiled cheerfully. "Dick Cooper. I'll kill for Amaris. She has only to order."

Sin's gaze settled on her upturned face. "Well, are you going to have me slain?"

She pretended to give the idea consideration. "No," she said at last. "I want you alive. So that I can take pleasure in tormenting you the rest of your natural life. By the way, did you know you look like hell?"

He laughed. "I've missed you, Amaris, me own."

It was a dance of love.

Josiah, Dick, and Molly had tactfully retreated to a neighboring tent for the night. Shed of his greatcoat, Sin took both her hands and stood facing her. "Do you know that I am at last doing something I really wanted?"

Her eyes intertwined with his. "And that is?"

"Working for a new order, a better system for people to live within." He smiled. "Even doing what I wanted, a part of me was still empty, an aching need filling the void."

She leaned toward him and lightly kissed his cheek. "Why?"

"Because you weren't there." He pulled her close, her hands still clasped in his. His head lowered, and his lips claimed hers in a butterfly-gentle kiss. His mustache softly tickled the edges of her lips in a disturbingly exciting fashion.

Against her mouth, he whispered. "From the day I set foot on Australian soil, you've been there, ever in me thoughts. So that you and the country are one, intermeshed in me heart."

"Like marriage. Freedom yet commitment and responsibility."

"Aye." His tongue parted her lips.

Her mouth sheathed that lovely sword, and she swayed against him. A wondrous knotting feeling began in her stomach, then burst to radiate through her chest and throat and her thighs. All the while, his hand stroked her neck. Her fingers crept into his thick, raggedly cut hair.

"So," he said, releasing her from the aching sweet kiss, "I believe a marriage is in order."

She leaned into him and kissed his ear, taking delight in the tremble her touch elicited from him. "Do I have any say in this?"

He turned his head and gave her a worried look. "This isn't a forever thing for you?"

She chuckled and pulled his shirt from his trousers. "You are a forever thing for me. Marriage, I'm not so certain of." Her hands slid around his waist, her fingers taking delight in feeling the ridges his muscles made.

He smiled slyly. Tugging her plaid shirt one arm at a time from her, he began talking, as if he were undressing a child for bed. "Well, 'tis an independent lass you've become." He ducked his head to trace the line of her chemise with light kisses. "I see I shall have to convince you of the benefits that come with the bonds of marriage."

She laughed outright. "*Bonds* is an accurate term." Then her laughter died away as he lightly kissed her nipple through the chemise's flimsy material. Shudder after shudder rippled through her.

Slowly, he lowered her chemise, kissing as he went. All the while holding tightly and stroking her back. "Then I shall have to convince you of the benefits that come with me loving you. Ahh, so wildly, so wantonly, Amaris!"

And that it was. Wildly, passionately manifesting what she had only dreamed and imagined all those years. Clothes shed and with a cot their bridal bower, he kissed her breasts with a vibrating tongue, then rained kisses all over her upper body. With deliberate, prolonged love play, his kisses descended downward past her breast toward her navel.

Whatever chill lingered with the removal of her clothes was quickly chased by the flush of heat radiating from a place low in her stomach. His fingers stroked the paths of his kisses, past her navel, along the indentation of her hip bone. Her breath sucked in.

"Do ye give, Amaris?" he asked in a passion-filled voice. "Will ye surrender your independence?"

"Aye, for an interdependence." His body was so beautiful, features so powerfully carved, his mouth so gentle. It touched inside her thigh and she gasped.

"Interdependence? You already have that from me. Lo, all these years." His head lowered again between her legs, and his tongue began a love play that sent pleasurable shock waves rolling through her. Her body arched, and his hands captured her hips to hold her quiescent.

Something happened then. Something she had not expected or believed in: that total letting go of self-will. In doing so she left her body in a flight of exquisite freedom. Soared. Experienced a sensation of colors and sounds and feelings so intense, so beautiful that she wanted to weep when her body ceased its spasmodic response.

She didn't realize she was crying until Sin moved up over her and began kissing away her tears. "We're beginning late, me luv, but we're only just beginning," he whispered. "Loving ye as I do, as I always have, the best is yet to come."

22

The harshest of winters make for the most glorious springtimes, in life as well as nature.

Brilliant daisies dazzled the eye by laying thousand-acre carpets of gold over Dream Time and Never-Never. Workers from both stations turned out for the wedding, held outdoors on the banks of Yagga Yagga Creek.

Amaris had never looked more beautiful, more softly, eternally feminine. She wore a cream-colored gown of lace and silk with leg-of-mutton sleeves. Her hair was unbound and clasped at her nape with a large ecru sateen bow. She smiled rapturously.

Gazing down at his bride as he took his vows, Sin had never appeared more gentle, more tender. Time had tempered his features. A distinguished, handsome man had emerged from the rough-and-bitter looking convict.

After the vows were exchanged, Amaris and Sin greeted the guests and thanked them for coming. As they moved among their friends, the couple continually touched each other. During all those years when they each belonged to another, it was enough to know that the other was there in the Never-Never. To have wanted or dreamed of anything more would have been to invite disaster, to destroy all that was good and fine in themselves and others.

Now that they could turn their dreams to reality, there would never be enough time in all the years left to them to touch and love and look into each other's eyes and read the intimate thoughts finally and fully revealed.

At one point in the evening, Amaris singled out Baluway and hugged his wiry body. "You've taken care of Dream Time and Never-Never well during my absences. This land once belonged to your people. So be it again. For your continued care, one half of Dream Time is yours."

Those surrounding the newlyweds—the major and Elizabeth; Eileen and Thomas; Sykes and his new bride, the schoolmarm Mary; Josiah; Dick and Molly; old Jimmy, who had his own sweetheart, Brighton Station's wizened widow; the workers and their family members—all stared with incredulity. Surely they hadn't heard correctly.

She wanted to know what Sin thought of her gesture, but she knew his expression would tell her nothing. Later that evening, he did tell her, or rather he questioned her in the privacy of their bedroom. He had backed her against the door, his strong, weathered hands at either side of her head. His lips nuzzled her neck. The house was filled with sleeping guests, but sleep these two could not.

"A good portion of your life has been invested in

Dream Time," he murmured. "Giving up half of it . . .
you are sure about this?"

"I'm not giving it up," she whispered against his
cheek. "I've become a part of it. My breath is the
wind that rustles the eucalypts and wattles, my flesh
is the soil that nourishes the crops, and my blood the
water that assuages the animals' thirst. You and I are
the land, Sin."

He lifted his head and looked down at her
upturned face. "I know that now. Australia can never
be taken from us." His fingers played with a swath of
her ebony hair. A curious smile crossed his marvelous
mouth. "Our wedding night. I would like for tonight
to be spent out in the Never-Never, beneath the
Southern Cross."

"Sin." It was all she could say. What other man
would appreciate and share that same love and longing
for something so intangible, something that no deed
or title could ever validate?

They rode out from Never-Never in the deep of
night. The wind stroked their cheeks and tousled
their hair. From sheer delight, they laughed. He
stretched his arm across the intervening space of
their two mounts to take her hand and squeeze it.
"You are beautiful," he said. "And I love you. So
bloody much!"

They found their trysting place. Instinctively,
intuitively, they returned to that stretch of prairie
where she had watched him, arms outstretched,
chase the whirlwind—and where, chagrined, he had
later joined her.

With a tenderness and adoration that brought
tears from the outer corners of her eyes, he removed
her riding boots, jacket and skirt, then her blouse and

chemise. She stripped him of his silk shirt and his tight breeches. The warm sand was their bridal sheet, the orange flowers of the wattles their bridal bouquet, the cool, yellow moonlight their protective bedcurtains. In that vast land, there were only the two of them, coming together, making love, joining in a wondrous union.

"Pulykara was wrong," she said, lazing in his arms.

"How so, me love?" His fingers traced lazy concentric circles around her gradually hardening nipple.

"She said that the sex act was only that—like the mating of the dogs or horses."

His laugh was low and husky. "Oh, no. What took place between us tonight was so much more. When the mind and heart are involved, there is nothing in all the world to equal this."

The night air was cooling her feverish skin, and she snuggled closer to Sin's bare body, honed to muscle and bone by years of competing against the elements of the outback. "I remember the journey out to the Never-Never. I remember sitting beneath our wagon that first night and changing into a stuffy nightgown and thinking how glorious it would be to sleep naked on the prairie."

"Then sleep, me Amaris." His fingers touched her eyelid. "Sleep and let me hold you and let me love shelter you. For now and ever."

What the Lord had taken from Amaris, He restored in the birth of hers and Sin's babies. Twins: a daughter whom Amaris named Celeste Anne and a son Sin named Daniel for one of the great Irish leaders.

During the year since their marriage, she and Sin

had divided their time between their stations and the mining camps of Victoria. She had followed Sin and taken up his cause for a free Australia. If ever there was hope of that happening, it was symbolized in the stouthearted men who had had the courage to follow their dreams of gold and glory to the Never-Never.

Once more, Sin delivered her of her babies—in a tent in the mining camp of Gresham, while Molly delivered minute-by-minute reports of her progress to Dick, Josiah, and the rest of the male populace gathered outside.

"The gold fever must be rotting me brain," Sin said, sitting beside her and stroking her damp hair, "but I feel the mighty urge just to hold ye and cry."

She stared lovingly up at him, cradling a squalling infant in each arm. Tears glistened in his dark eyes. Could anything ever ruin the happiness she was feeling at this precious moment?

23

In the afternoon, a crowd gathered on Bakery Hill under the Southern Cross flag, the first one to fly without the Union Jack on it. It was only October and already one of the hottest days of the year.

For days, the diggers had been fomenting and fuming, but with no direction. This Thursday, a leader was thrust forth before them: the Irish rebel, Sin Tremayne.

The diggers went wild with cheering, but he held up his hands for quiet. "Think seriously about the consequences of what we must do. Would a thousand of you, no four thousand, volunteer to liberate any man dragged to the lockup for not having a license? Are you ready to die?"

Watching from the crowd's perimeter, Amaris shuddered. Had she waited all these years, wandered the outback, only to lose Sin at the last, when she finally found him, when he finally loved her so completely that she often cried secret tears of joy as they made love?

A roar of "Aye!" exploded from the mass of diggers. While a sort of military organization took shape over the next few minutes, with the election of captain and divisions of men, she kept her eye focused on Sin.

A council was appointed and Sin was elected commander in chief. She wanted to fix this moment in her memory forever, every detail about him. A warm breeze ruffled his silver-winged locks. His eyes glowed with an inner fire, with that purpose for which he had hunted—and been haunted by—all of his adult life.

He was truly alive now.

With more than five hundred armed men, he knelt to take an oath. With his right hand held up, he intoned in that beautifully rich Irish resonance, "We swear by the Southern Cross to stand truly by each other and fight to defend our rights and liberties."

Years before, she might have been jealous of Sin's passion for Australia and the rights of its inhabitants. Now she could understand his intense nature and deep emotions, because now her own were allowed to run as deep and intensely as his.

As commander in chief, Sin was required to be away from her for days at a time. She would hear word of him exhorting the diggers up on Mount Alexander, arguing with the territorial parliament in Melbourne, or issuing ultimatums to the colonial governor, Miles Randolph.

If she had expected to be lonely in his absence, she found instead she had no privacy. In Sin's absence, and as the commander in chief's wife, she was sought out by men and women alike for an audience to which they could present their problems.

Josiah and Dick acted as sergeants at arms. She could only promise supplicants who came to her tent that she would discuss their appeals with her husband, but more often than not the petitioners wanted and needed advice immediately, and she would give her best counsel.

With Dick and Josiah, she ran the operations for reform through disbursing information: newspaper editorials, flyers, placards.

In her own right, she was making a name for herself again. She was becoming a crusader again, but writing more passionately from the perspective of experience than she ever had from idealistic youth. She was no longer looking through the window from the outside. At forty-two, she had become the beautiful woman the child never was. Sin, the twins, her writing, fulfilled her to such a point that serenity graced her sculpted face.

"A madonna," people remarked of her and she had to smile wistfully, thinking how paradoxically she had so often envied that same quality in her half sister.

Sin went among the people of the territory of Victoria—down on Melbourne's wharves to talk with the sailors, in the wool sheds, through mining camps scattered in the hills.

One day as she sat nursing the twins and wondering if the rest of her life were to be spent longing for her beloved, he pushed back the tent flap to enter unexpectedly. "Sin!" she cried out in happiness.

Careful of the infant she held, he nevertheless bent and pressed an impassioned kiss on her cheek. "I've missed you like hell, me luv."

"Don't go away, ever again."

He pushed back a lock of hair. His mouth tightened. "I'm only here for a little while. I have to go to Sydney. Parliament's meeting, and I mean to be there for Miles Randolph's speech. Now that he's been elected governor, he believes he can make his own policies. 'Tis time his policies were challenged."

She swallowed her protest and turned away to lay a sleeping Anne in her crib before cradling Daniel to her other breast. "How long is a little while?"

"Twenty-four hours." He sighed. "While I am gone, I have arranged for Josiah and Dick to have a cabin erected. You and the twins need something more substantial than this."

She knew she should be pleased that he had thought of her and Anne and Daniel when there were so many other things to occupy his mind, but she felt perverse. She should have been jubilant with motherhood, but that same creative force was demanding expression in other ways.

"We need *you*, Sin," she said softly and nudged her breast against Daniel's rosy little cheek.

Sin leaned close to stroke his son's downy hair. Such a look of tenderness passed over Sin's countenance that she was surprised his next words were not of their son but of her. "You are more beautiful than I have ever seen you."

She felt her face suffuse with pleasure. How could such simple words elicit such overflowing joy in her? "Hurry back," she whispered.

"Save some for me," he said, smiling. His finger tucked her nipple into the little mouth frantically searching for sustenance. "I'll come back to take me turn as soon as possible."

Sin came back—but not to her.

Irishmen tended to rebel regardless of the odds. For them, the tradition of glorious failure ran deep. It was as if they were preparing less for a fight than for an act of communion. The love of freedom and the wrongs of Ireland brought a hundred and fifty men to lie down and sleep beside guns, pistols, and pikes in the Eureka stockade. It had been made from slabs of timber they used to line their mine shafts on the night of December 2, 1854. No longer would they submit to brutal police searches and the license tax on gold mining—a revolt against taxation without representation.

From her cabin window, Amaris watched Sin stride up the hill to meet with the miners. He had come straight from Sydney to be met by Josiah and Dick and ushered to the stockade. Only Sin had been allowed inside.

For the past several days, Dick and Josiah had insisted neither she nor Molly leave the cabin for fear the situation would turn violent. It appeared their fears bordered on manifestation.

Sin hoped to dissuade the diggers from their folly. His point was that until they had enough political and military clout it would be suicidal to bait the queen's soldiers.

Fires still burned late on the night of the third in the stockade when soldiers of the Twelfth Regiment, mounted police, and troopers charged it. Amaris heard the shots and sat upright in her bed. Fear prickled the hair at her nape. In the other room, the year-old babies started crying.

She sprang from her bed and ran past the awakened and crying babies to fling open the front door. Mounted soldiers flashed by as they charged up the hill. Cold moonlight and colder firelight gleamed on bayonets they wielded.

On bare feet, Molly descended from the loft where she slept and came up behind her. "H'it's come, h'ain't it?"

"Aye. As Sin expected, only too soon."

She ran back to her babies and picked up Daniel, balancing him on her hip. Her free hand caressed Anne's cheek. "Sssh," she cooed to the tots. "Oh, please don't cry. Not now."

At the doorway, Molly said, "If Dick should be—"

A rapid rapping at the front door interrupted her. Dick burst in. "It's over! Ten minutes and the police have won!"

"Sin?"

Behind him, a bleeding Josiah said, "Alive but chained. Those who lived through the massacre—a score or so—are being marched to the lockup at the government camp."

She forced her words past the cork of fear in her throat. "What will happen to him?"

Josiah shrugged and wiped the trickle of blood from his cheek. The small gash welled with blood again. "Just what you think. A hasty trial before the miners across the country can band together in outright defiance. Governor Randolph and the colonial office don't want another American rebellion on their hands."

She didn't have to ask what would be the outcome of a hasty trial.

Thirteen leaders were arrested and tried for high treason. Because of the volatile feelings of the citizens of the territory of Victoria, Sin, as commander in chief, was transferred to Sydney.

"He's to be incarcerated at Fort Dennison," Dick told Amaris two days after the rebellion. He and Josiah had spent money and precious time trying to ascertain Sin's fate. Both men had returned to the cabin exhausted and sat at the table trying to hold their heads up and their eyes open.

Like them, she had not eaten or slept. At the mention of Fort Dennison, she shuddered. The island just off Sydney's shore had been known to the early settlers as Old Pinchgut.

Molly returned from the kitchen lean-to with hot hoecakes, cheese, and ale. "H'if you don't eat, you three won't be any good to Sin."

Listlessly, Amaris poked at the food while plans were arranged for travel to Sydney. "We can't do anything here," Josiah was saying and chased a large mouthful of hoecake with a swig of ale.

"The quicker the better," Dick said. "The guards and Sin have a twenty-four-hour start from what I can tell."

"Could we intercept them?" she asked, pushing her filled plate away.

"Too many guards," Josiah said. "Sin's valuable as a scapegoat. Punish him and let the rest go free. The lesson is made without inflaming the entire countryside."

"I'm leaving now," she said, rising from the bench.

"Whoa," Dick said. "You can't get to Sydney any

quicker than if you wait and catch a paddle steamer out of Echuca tomorrow morning."

He was right, of course. With Molly and the twins, she boarded the steamer that next day. Travel by river would have been lovely, but impatience, frustration, and paralyzing fear kept her from doing little more than standing at the gingerbread-ornamental railing with her gaze focused on the eastern horizon.

When at last they docked at the semicircular quay in Sydney, she stared in wonder at the improvements that had taken place in her years of absence: a sparkling museum and a university instigated under the auspices of the grand dame Nan Livingston now made Sydney respectable. Woolclippers bearing New South Wales Traders registry bobbed like cork-studded nets in the cove.

Compared to the self-satisfied mediocrity of the model British colony of New Zealand, Sydney, settled by its brash, tough convicts, was a bustling, expanding nerve center.

For Amaris, it was more than returning home. A strange combination of exhilaration and terrible dread seesawed her emotions: exhilaration at being a part of a battle waged against Great Britain for Australians' self-rule; dread that she would not win Sin's release.

Governor Randolph would not see her. He let her cool her heels in the Government House's anteroom four hours before his secretary came out. The peanut of a man fiddled with his spectacles, before saying, "Ahh, Governor Randolph has declined to see you."

Hands braced primly on her parasol knob, she

glared at the little man. "I'll be back again tomorrow. And every day until he will see me."

But time was running out. She summoned Josiah and Dick to a counsel in the tiny room they were renting above a butcher shop. "No amount of appeal is going to sway Randolph. Not with my notoriety as a reformer. Is there any possibility we can break Sin out of Fort Dennison?"

Dick rubbed his chin. "With enough men behind us, a good plan laid out, aye. But we'd have to have an element of surprise."

Josiah shook his shaggy head. "You don't know your husband very well, Amaris, if you think he'd trade off the lives of any of his supporters for his own. That's what he's fighting for, isn't it? Equality?"

Her head bowed. "Yes," she said so softly they almost didn't hear her. If Sin were executed, a vital part of herself would be destroyed.

"There is one possible source of help," Josiah said, his voice heavy. "New South Wales Traders."

Dick shifted his wad of tobacco to the other cheek. "Why would Tom Livingston help him? Sin has actively campaigned against some of the Livingstons' business dealings."

"Tom Livingston is noted for being a fair businessman."

"Fair is one thing," Dick said. "Foolish is another. Tom Livingston wouldn't be that foolish."

"He's Sin's former father-in-law."

Dick gaped.

Tom Livingston's office was elegant with dark mahogany furniture imported in New South Wales

Traders ships from Africa. A gold clipper served as an inkwell, its sails a concealed pen. The enormous desk was practically bare of paperwork.

Tom had put on a great deal of weight and wore spectacles, but altogether he appeared a man whom life had treated well—Amaris supposed because he had treated life well. From all that she knew of him and heard about him, he had done his best, hurting no one in the process. Nan would have undoubtedly pronounced her husband a man of mediocrity, but staring into those mild eyes, Amaris would have to say he was a success. Undoubtedly, he went to bed at night and slept easily.

More than she could do these days. She was so damned tired. Tired of hoping. Tired of losing at every turn. If she lost Sin . . . well, only the twins were left her. In a way, they were everything to her because they were the best of her and Sin combined.

"I need your help, Mr. Livingston. I was your daughter's best friend. Sin loved Celeste and she loved him. I know that you thought highly of Sin. Even though your wife was against their marriage, for Celeste's memory, will you help him?"

Tom's head drooped. "Randolph is after a sacrificial lamb. New South Wales Traders doesn't have that much influence."

Heart beating like a death knell, Amaris knocked on the same door she had knocked on at the age of twelve. Not that much had changed about the Georgian mansion. A patina of charm had come with its age. The rural surroundings were gone, and shops and businesses jostled for room along the cobble-stoned street that now fronted it.

Another Irish maid, as homely as Molly had been, greeted her. She closed her parasol. "Would you tell Mrs. Livingston that Amaris Tremayne is calling on her."

Once again Amaris waited in the parlor, her gaze traveling over different paintings, different statues and objets d'art.

And Amaris was different. She was a grown woman now, fighting for the man she loved. Her fingers rose to touch the brooch on her morning coat. She was converting the brooch to a talisman against her most formidable opponent.

The maid returned and led her down the hallway to Nan's office.

Behind a desk littered with papers sat the command-ing old woman. Her mouth was seamed and heavily rouged, as were her cheeks. Yet the power of a young person emanated from her eyes. She nodded toward the wing chair opposite her desk. For a moment, the women stared at each other.

Nan and Amaris dominated their respective elements of society: the commercial and the pastoral. Mother and daughter—each unable to forgive the other. Nan peered over her tented fingertips. "So, at last you come begging."

Amaris's stomach was a twisting, wreathing knot. "For someone who dislikes me so, you appear pleased by my presence."

"I've waited a long time for this." Her smile grew wider, thinning even more her thin mouth. "I know, of course, why you're here."

Amaris leaned forward. Her throat was full to choking. "In all of Australia, only you have the power to get Sin released."

Nan settled back in her chair, her veined hands resting on its padded arms. "You know what I want in exchange?"

"I can guess. You want us to leave Australia. Sin would never agree to being exiled. Not as long as there is a breath left in him."

"He won't have that choice. He's to be transported to Norfolk Island."

"Norfolk Island?" She knew she sounded like a parrot, but her heart froze like a heavy block of ice. Norfolk Island was a thousand miles away and infamous for cruelty. Two thousand prisoners were crowded onto the island in despicable conditions. The administering regime promoted torture that filled the mind with horror.

Nan's eyes were crystal orbs of satisfaction. "I see you understand the grave situation facing Sin. 'Tis my opinion he'd rather swing from the gallows than endure a life sentence on Norfolk Island."

Her words were a bare whisper. "What is your price?"

"Think of the ultimate price." She paused. "That you give up what was your sister's: Sin."

Her breath turned to stone. Tears stung her eyes. She should have known it would come to this. Nan Livingston never lost. Nan Livingston was as strong and indomitable as legend made her out to be.

"Well?"

She bowed her head. "Aye." The choked sob escaped her.

"That brooch," Nan whispered. "It was my mother's, you know."

Amaris steeled herself. "It was my mother's, also."

For a long moment, the silence filled the office

like a heartbeat does the ear. Then Nan sighed and rubbed her temple. "I find no pleasure in my victory. There must be an end to this bitterness between us. I can promise nothing. But I shall see what I can do."

Amaris stared at Nan Livingston. She refused to let the joy of relief fill her heart. After all these years, she did not know if she could trust the old woman, could trust her mother.

The two faced each other across the dining table. The two most powerful and influential people in Australia. The man, Miles Randolph, openly acknowledged for his political power; the woman, Nan Livingston, heralded for the clout she wielded behind the scenes.

"Release Sin Tremayne from Fort Dennison?" A silver brow climbed the wrinkles laddering Miles Randolph's forehead. He found it difficult to believe that he had ever been the lover of the old woman across from him, spry and well preserved though she was. "Why should I?"

"I won't insult your intelligence by saying 'for old times' sake.' I meant nothing to you, did I?"

He took a pinch of snuff from the back of his hand and inhaled it up one nostril. "You revolted me with those eyes that were always begging, 'Love me, love me, love me.'"

She appeared not in the least affected by his cruel words. "Did I? Well, life is a trade-off. Send your butler away. What I have to say requires the utmost privacy, as you will soon agree, I am sure."

He snapped his fingers, nodded toward the door, and the hovering butler vanished as if by magic. Then

Miles turned back to her. "Your statement is highly intriguing. Do proceed."

"I want Sin Tremayne freed. I could ask you to do it out of fatherly interest."

"Fatherly interest? I find it hardly plausible that the Irish blackguard could be an offspring of mine."

"Amaris Tremayne is our daughter, Miles."

Mild curiosity rippled through him. "So that's what is behind this appeal."

"Not exactly. She and I have been at cross-purposes since the moment of her birth. Nevertheless, I want her husband freed of all charges."

"What you want is vastly different from what I may choose to—"

"What I want is what I get . . . sooner or later. Free him. Or else I shall use this with relish." She fished a piece of time-yellowed parchment from her reticule and tossed it on the table.

He unfolded the scrap and read the scribble. He could feel the color draining from his face. His heart muscles squeezed painfully. "No one will believe this piece of fodder. A man who claims I raped him nearly forty years ago when he was only a boy—a man who can barely sign his name."

The old woman shrugged. "You are doubtless correct. Most people will not only disbelieve the evidence but most likely not even care, to judge by Sydney's morals. But your wife will certainly be influenced by my witness. He's still alive, you know. Living safely in England at my expense. I knew one day I would have need of his testimony. Tell me, Miles, do you think your wife would continue to support you as I have Morton Freely all these years?"

*   *   *

From her view from the office window, Nan Livingston watched the scene being enacted below. A small boat was rowed by a red-jacketed sailor from a brig toward the wharf.

The prisoner, his hands manacled, sat at the boat's far end beneath the muzzle point of a lax guard. A tall, lithe woman, her ebony hair burnished with moon-silver streaks, waited on the quay. When the prisoner's cuffs were removed and he was ushered ashore, the woman flung herself at him. The couple kissed in a passionate embrace that Nan had never known and had forever and ever yearned for.

She had dreamed the scene before her into a reality. Ah, well, one may get one's wishes in this Dream Time land, but not always in the way one anticipates.

As she watched the performance, she thought that her daughter was very grateful for her intercession on Sin's behalf. Grateful enough to allow her to see her grandchildren. Nan patted Anne's head indulgently as the tot played with the doll Nan had bought for her.

Nan turned her attention to Daniel, who sat on her knee. She jogged her knee and recited in a raspy voice, "Horsey, horsey go to town. Horsey, horsey don't fall down."

The boy gurgled in delight.

Here was a strong spirit that with the right guidance could take the boy to the top of Australian politics, Nan thought. Sin was too selfless. But with her backing and her connections, well, who knew. Perhaps her grandson would become Australia's answer to the British prime minister.

Nan smiled.

AVAILABLE NOW

DREAM TIME by Parris Afton Bonds

A passionate tale of a determined young woman who, because of a scandal, wound up in the untamed Australia of the early 1800s.

ALWAYS . . . by Jeane Renick

Marielle McCleary wants a baby, but her prospects look slim—until she meets handsome actor Tom Saxon. Too late, however, she finds out that Thomas isn't as perfect as he seems. Will she ever have the life she's always wanted?

THE BRIDEGROOM by Carol Jerina

A compelling historical romance set in Texas. Payne Trefarrow's family abandoned him, and he held his identical twin brother Prescott responsible. To exact revenge, Payne planned to take the things his brother loved most—his money and his fiancée.

THE WOMEN OF LIBERTY CREEK
by Marilyn Cunningham

From the author of *Seasons of the Heart.* A sweeping tale of three women's lives and loves and how they are bound together, over the generations, by a small town in Idaho.

LOST TREASURE by Catriona Flynt

A zany romantic adventure set in Northern California at the turn of the century. When her dramatic production went up in smoke, actress Moll Kennedy was forced to take a job to pay her debts—as a schoolteacher doubling as a spy. Then she fell in love with the ruggedly handsome Winslow Fortune, the very man she was spying on.

SAPPHIRE by Venita Helton

An intriguing historical tale of love divided by loyalty. When her clipper ship sank, New Orleans beauty Arienne Lloyd was rescued by handsome Yankee Joshua Langdon. At the very sight of him she was filled with longing, despite her own allegiances to the South. Would Arienne fight to win the heart of her beloved enemy—even if it meant risking everything in which she believed?

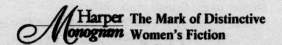 **Harper Monogram** The Mark of Distinctive Women's Fiction

COMING NEXT MONTH

RAIN LILY by Candace Camp

Maggie Whitcomb's life changed when her shell-shocked husband returned from the Civil War. She nursed him back to physical health, but his mind was shattered. Maggie's marriage vows were forever, but then she met Reid Prescott, a drifter who took refuge on her farm and captured her heart. A heartwarming story of impossible love from bestselling author Candace Camp.

CASTLES IN THE AIR by Christina Dodd

The long-awaited, powerful sequel to the award-winning *Candle in the Window*. Lady Juliana of Moncestus swore that she would never again be forced under a man's power. So when the king promised her in marriage to Raymond of Avrache, Juliana was determined to resist. But had she met her match?

RAVEN IN AMBER by Patricia Simpson

A haunting contemporary love story by the author of *Whisper of Midnight*. Camille Avery arrives at the Nakalt Indian Reservation to visit a friend, only to find her missing. With the aid of handsome Kit Makinna, Camille becomes immersed in Nakalt life and discovers the shocking secret behind her friend's disappearance.

RETURNING by Susan Bowden

A provocative story of love and lies. From the Bohemian '60s to the staid '90s, *Returning* is an emotional roller-coaster ride of a story about a woman whose past comes back to haunt her when she must confront the daughter she gave up for adoption.

JOURNEY HOME by Susan Kay Law

Winner of the 1992 Golden Heart Award. Feisty Jessamyn Johnston was the only woman on the 1853 California wagon train who didn't respond to the charms of Tony Winchester. But as they battled the dangers of their journey, they learned how to trust each other and how to love.

KENTUCKY THUNDER by Clara Wimberly

Amidst the tumult of the Civil War and the rigid confines of a Shaker village, a Southern belle fought her own battle against a dashing Yankee—and against herself as she fell in love with him.

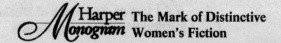

Harper Monogram The Mark of Distinctive Women's Fiction

SEVEN IRRESISTIBLE HISTORICAL ROMANCES BY BESTSELLING AUTHOR
CANDACE CAMP

HEIRLOOM
Juliet Drake, a golden-haired beauty who yearned for a true home, went to the Morgan farm to help Amos Morgan care for his ailing sister. There she found the home she sought, but still she wanted more—the ruggedly handsome Amos.

BITTERLEAF
Purchased on the auction block, betrayed British nobleman, Jeremy Devlin, vowed to seduce his new owner, Meredith Whitney, the beautiful mistress of the Bitterleaf plantation. But his scheme of revenge ignited a passion that threatened to consume them both.